PRAISE FOR RANDY SINGER

"A book that will entertain readers and make them
think—what more can one ask?"

PUBLISHERS WEEKLY
ON *THE JUSTICE GAME*

"Singer artfully crafts a novel that is the perfect mix of
faith and suspense. . . . [*The Justice Game* is] fast-paced
from the start to the surprising conclusion."

ROMANTIC TIMES

"At the center of the heart-pounding action are the moral dilemmas
that have become Singer's stock-in-trade. . . .an exciting thriller."

BOOKLIST
ON *BY REASON OF INSANITY*

"Readers will be left on the edge of their seats by
Singer's latest suspense-filled thriller."

CHRISTIAN RETAILING
ON *BY REASON OF INSANITY*

"Writers of courtroom dramas and thrillers can often fool
a non-lawyer but rarely a lawyer. Randy has painted an
accurate picture of what an insanity defense entails."

DON GUTTERIDGE
ATTORNEY, ON *BY REASON OF INSANITY*

"In this gripping, obsessively readable legal thriller, Singer
proves himself to be the Christian John Grisham. . . ."

PUBLISHERS WEEKLY
ON *FALSE WITNESS*

FATAL
CONVICTIONS

TYNDALE HOUSE PUBLISHERS, INC., CAROL STREAM, ILLINOIS

RANDY
SINGER

Visit Tyndale's exciting Web site at www.tyndale.com.

Visit Randy Singer's Web site at www.randysinger.net.

TYNDALE and Tyndale's quill logo are registered trademarks of Tyndale House Publishers, Inc.

Fatal Convictions

Designed by Dean H. Renninger

Published in association with the literary agency of Alive Communications, Inc., 7680 Goddard Street, Suite 200, Colorado Springs, CO 80920, www.alivecommunications.com.

Scripture taken from the Holy Bible, *New International Version,*® NIV.® Copyright © 1973, 1978, 1984 by Biblica, Inc.™ Used by permission of Zondervan. All rights reserved worldwide. www.zondervan.com.

This novel is a work of fiction. Names, characters, places, and incidents either are the product of the author's imagination or are used fictitiously. Any resemblance to actual events, locales, organizations, or persons living or dead is entirely coincidental and beyond the intent of either the author or the publisher.

Library of Congress Cataloging-in-Publication Data

Singer, Randy (Randy D.)
   Fatal convictions / Randy Singer.
     p. cm.
   ISBN 978-1-4143-3320-5 (pbk.)
   I. Title.
   PS3619.I5725F38 2010
   813'.6—dc22   2010020829

Printed in the United States of America

16 15 14 13 12 11 10
 7   6   5   4   3   2   1

*"If you've been called to be a lawyer,
don't stoop to be a king."*

JOHN PATRICK MADISON

1

ALEX MADISON PULLED his black Ford F-150 into the designated clergy parking area, loosened his tie, rolled up his sleeves, and walked briskly across the parking lot toward the emergency room door. He clutched a Bible in his right hand and checked his shirt pocket for his pen and business cards with his left. The business cards were double-sided. On one side, *Alexander Madison, Pastor of South Norfolk Community Church*; on the other, *Alexander Madison, Attorney-At-Law*.

Alex's grandmother had called four hours ago to let him know that Evangeline Buford was in the hospital, suffering from an obstructed bowel. Doctors had stabilized her and were trying to treat it without surgery, but they were monitoring her closely. She was in the ICU—a place Alex could find in his sleep.

When the automatic doors slid open, Alex greeted the skinny gentleman sitting behind the intake desk. His name tag said *Foster*, but Alex had never heard anyone call him that. "What's up, Bones?"

"The Right Reverend Alexander Madison," Bones said, looking up from his magazine. "You're running late tonight. The ambulance got here fifteen minutes ago."

"That's because you didn't call," Alex said. He opened his Bible, retrieved a church bulletin, and tossed it in front of Bones. "Five bucks off at Shoney's," Alex said.

"Your generosity knows no bounds."

"You got something against Shoney's?" Alex reached into his back pocket and withdrew two tickets for a Norfolk Tides game.

"Now you're talkin'," Bones said, eyeing the tickets. The man could tell stories for hours—*had* told stories for hours—about every major league star who had spent time in Norfolk on the way to the big leagues.

"You doing anything next Friday night?" Alex asked.

"Callin' in sick. The Orioles got two players rehabbing from the majors."

Alex handed Bones the tickets. "You got a room number for Evangeline Buford?"

The information desk was in a different part of the hospital from the ER entrance, and Alex knew that if it were anyone else asking, Bones would say as much. But for Alex, he punched in a few keys. "Four-three-one-two."

"Thanks." Alex stood there for a moment, shifting his weight. A mom carrying an infant in one arm and pulling a toddler with the other came through the door and lined up behind Alex.

For some reason, Bones always made him ask. Alex lowered his voice. "Anything serious tonight?"

Bones smiled—the big toothy grin of a man who had something his buddy wanted. "Nothin' tonight. But there's a closed head injury in 4103 that transferred in from Chesapeake General last night. She's still in ICU. Unfortunately for you, she might make a full recovery."

"Whose fault?"

"Don't know. Definitely an auto accident."

Tides tickets were a small price to pay for this type of intel. "I owe you," Alex said.

"Just say a prayer for me Sunday."

Alex left the ER and navigated his way through the hospital, breathing in the sterile smell of antiseptics mixed with meat-loaf leftovers from the nearby cafeteria. He said a quick prayer for Bones and tossed in a word of thanks for the new client he was hopefully about to land. His practice needed a closed head injury about now. With any luck, she'd been hit by a truck driver running a red light—a couple of independent witnesses would be nice—and the trucking company would have lots of insurance coverage. The pastor in him hoped the woman would be all right. But the fatalist in him, as well as the lawyer, knew that accidents were bound to happen. And if they did, they might as well happen here in Hampton Roads, to people who would get dragged in to Norfolk General, and they might as well have a long and expensive recovery before being released.

Alex arrived at the elevators about the same time as two older women. When the elevator arrived, Alex turned on the charm and stepped aside, then followed them in. He smiled, and they tried to return the gesture, but their eyes betrayed an unshakable sadness. They thanked him, punched a number, and rode in silence.

The women exited on the third floor, the cancer ward, a place Alex knew all too well. Two years ago he had practically lived there, watching his grandfather waste away. Even now, when Alex got off on the third floor to visit other senior saints from his small congregation, the sadness still washed over him.

His grandfather's passing had rocked Alex for a number of reasons. It was tough to watch a man who had once been so vibrant—a civil rights lawyer who taught Alex everything he knew about how to practice law—reduced to an emaciated shadow of his former self. Spiritually, Alex had never prayed harder—and never felt more betrayed when his prayers weren't answered. And emotionally, Alex had lost the man who helped raise him after an automobile accident killed Alex's parents when he was just twelve.

For Alex, the cancer ward wasn't hell, but you could smell it from there. He was thankful that Evangeline was on the fourth floor—one story above the scent of Dante's Inferno.

When Alex entered her room, Evangeline's face lit up to see him. He told her how good she looked, which was a stretch, even for Alex.

She had multiple machines attached to her body and looked like she had been shrink-wrapped. She wore none of the makeup that she normally layered on for church. Her gray hair was matted against the pillow, and her skin sagged on the exposed portions of her arms and around her neck. Her right arm was blue where the nurse had inserted the IV, and it made Alex feel a little queasy. He would have made a terrible doctor.

Evangeline gave Alex a detailed rundown of her condition, including the precise time and place of her last bowel movement, pausing occasionally to catch her breath. Alex chatted for a few minutes but could tell that the excitement was taking a toll on his parishioner. He held her hands and said a quick prayer.

"You're going to be all right," he told Evangeline. She braved a small smile at his words. "The whole church is praying for you," he added quickly. He didn't want Evangeline to think her healing would be hanging on his prayers alone.

"You're the best pastor we've ever had," Evangeline said, her voice hoarse. "Pastor Bob didn't get to the hospital for two days when I had my kidney stones. I'd passed 'em by then. You practically followed me here."

"I'm good at tailgating ambulances," Alex said, but Evangeline didn't smile. He squeezed her hands. "We're going to get you through this."

2

A FEW MINUTES after leaving Evangeline's room, Alex found himself outside 4103, where he hesitated in the hallway, arguing with his conscience. The woman in the room probably needed legal representation. She could either get it from some shyster who advertised on television, or she could get it from Madison and Associates, a firm that would treat her with a little respect. They would work her case hard and take the insurance company to the brink of trial before cashing in. Most importantly, she would be more than just a case file to Alex and his partner, Shannon Reese. Alex would minister to her spiritually. Shannon would befriend her. She'd get Christmas cards from the firm for the rest of her life.

The nameplate on the door said *Ghaniyah Mobassar*. Alex decided to call her ma'am.

He stepped inside and flashed a friendly smile—nothing over the top, the professional kind of smile your attending physician might give you.

Ghaniyah was in rough shape. Her right eye was black and blue, and she had a sizable lump on her forehead. Machines cluttered the area around the head of her bed, buzzing and beeping and pumping life-giving fluids into her body.

Her eyes were closed, which presented a problem. *The family members must be in the waiting room.* Alex pulled a chair up next to her bed, took a seat, and began praying. He prayed softly, just loud enough to be heard from the doorway if somebody entered but not loud enough to sound like a lunatic. He peeked a couple of times. Ghaniyah kept her eyes closed. She was breathing but hadn't moved.

After a few minutes, Alex ran out of things to pray. He took out a card and decided to leave a note, pastor side up, saying he had stopped by and she should call if she needed anything. He thought he heard footsteps outside the door and quickly bowed his head again, mumbling another quick sentence or two.

"What are you doing?" a deep voice said.

Alex turned and looked toward the doorway, where an older gentleman scowled at him. He was about Alex's height—six-one or so—with the long limbs and the square shoulders of a scarecrow. He had dark hair, a long black beard, and brown eyes that were filled with a mixture of sadness and surprise.

"I'm a pastor," Alex quickly explained. He stood and took a few steps toward the man, extending his hand. "I heard your wife was in a bad car accident, and I came to pray for her."

The man shook Alex's hand—a strong grip—but didn't relax. Alex clutched his Bible with his left hand.

"Are you with the hospital?" the man asked.

"No, sir. I'm just a local pastor."

"We're Muslim." The man's tone was matter-of-fact, not harsh. "I'm the imam for the Norfolk Islamic Learning Center. I appreciate you coming by, but lots of our people are already praying."

"I'm sorry," Alex said, kicking himself for not picking up on the name. He had been intoxicated by the thought of a profitable case, and his brain had shifted into neutral. He quickly switched back into lawyer mode. "Do you mind me asking what happened?"

The man looked past Alex at his wife. He lowered his voice, perhaps not wishing to disturb her with memories of the event. "Ghaniyah ran off the road and hit a tree. We don't really know how it happened."

Alex resisted the urge to pester the man with questions. Were there skid marks? witnesses? Could she have been run off the road by a driver who didn't even bother stopping? What are the limits on your liability policy? Do you understand how uninsured motorist coverage works?

"The doctors say she suffered closed head injuries," the imam continued. "Now, if you'll excuse me . . ." He stepped around Alex and moved to the side of the bed.

Lesser lawyers might have succumbed.

But not Alex. He stepped back toward the bed and delicately placed a card on the nightstand next to the gentleman. "I'm also a lawyer," Alex admitted. The man glanced at Alex as if the words hadn't registered. He returned a concerned gaze to his wife and took her hand, checking on the machine readouts.

"I'm not like most personal-injury lawyers—only worried about the money," Alex spoke quickly, as if a trapdoor might open beneath him at any moment. "I care about my clients' spiritual health as well as their physical health. I take cases on a contingency fee and normally charge 10 percent less than most lawyers so my clients can give that money to their church or mosque or whatever."

The man turned to Alex, contempt beginning to fill the dark eyes. "This is not the time or the place," he said simply. "I am not concerned about American lawyers or American lawsuits or, as you say, a cheap deal on a contingency fee. My prayer is that Allah will restore Ghaniyah to full health." He paused, pinning Alex with his gaze. "And now, if you don't mind, I would appreciate some privacy. Certainly there are others in this hospital in need of your prayers."

"You're right," Alex replied. "This is no time to worry about a lawyer." He nodded and started backing toward the door. "But when she starts to feel better, give me a call if she wants to talk."

The man turned back to his wife, taking a seat.

I'll never see them again, Alex thought. *Why not go for broke?*

"I may seem a little over the top," he admitted, "but trust me, when you need someone to take on the insurance companies, you're going to want someone brash and obnoxious."

The man didn't move.

"I'm actually handling another case for a Muslim client," Alex added, though he suddenly felt a little stupid for bringing it up. "A store is trying to make her ditch her head scarf."

The imam did not look impressed. Or even remotely interested.

"Blessings on you," Alex said softly, standing in the doorway. "I've handled closed-head-injury cases before. I know that the first few days are critical. May God be merciful to your wife."

The man turned and looked at Alex, his eyes sad and subdued. "Thank you. Now, if you don't mind . . ." He returned his attention to Ghaniyah, and Alex finally took the hint.

On the way out, Alex made a point of circling back around through the ER. Maybe somebody had been admitted in the last few minutes.

"How'd it go?" Bones asked.

"It's not quite a lock," Alex admitted. "But then again, her husband didn't take a swing at me."

"That's progress," Bones said.

3

BY NOW, the nurses knew the routine. Ghaniyah had been in the private ICU room for nearly twenty-four hours, and Khalid had performed the salat four times. This would be his fifth.

He glanced at the monitors, kissed Ghaniyah on the forehead, and shut the door to her room. It still seemed strange going through the salat without her. Though the couple had their differences, Khalid had never questioned his wife's loyalty to Allah. At each salat, she would place her prayer mat behind Khalid and repeat the prayers with him. Her voice was passionate and unwavering. She never seemed to harbor the questions and doubts that sometimes tarnished her husband's faith. But yesterday and today, Ghaniyah had remained silent during the prayer times, her eyes vacant, her lips unmoving. Khalid had tried to muster the faith for two.

Purity was half the faith, a concept that had been drilled into Khalid since childhood. He used the bathroom sink for his purification ritual, taking off his shirt and washing his hands and forearms up to each elbow. He washed his mouth and nose, snorting the water back into the sink. He washed his face from forehead to chin and ear to ear, including his entire beard. He wet his right hand and passed it over his thick black hair. Then he washed his feet, up to the ankles. He put on clean clothes, a loose-fitting long black shirt and clean slacks. He washed his hands again and left the bathroom, rolling out his floor mat at the foot of Ghaniyah's bed.

He told her that he was getting ready to say his prayers.

She stared into space, giving him no reaction.

"Do you want to join me?"

She nodded. But he could tell from the faraway look in her eyes that he would be going through the ritual alone. The doctors said he needed to be patient. Give her time. She would remember a little more every day; her personality would return little by little.

"Will she fully recover?" he had asked.

"I wish we could be more definitive, Mr. Mobassar. But truthfully . . . it's impossible to say."

Khalid stood now at the edge of his mat, hands together, chest facing toward Mecca. He silently recited his intention to pray, focusing his thoughts on Allah.

He took a deep breath and began his chants. *"Allahu akbar,"* he said, cupping his hands behind his ears. Allah is the greatest. In rhythmic motion, he moved his hands to his side. *"Subhana rabbiya al azeem. . . ."* Khalid's words were strong and confident. He resisted the urge to tone down his prayers so that he didn't disturb others in adjoining rooms. Allah would not honor those who were ashamed.

He faithfully performed each *raka'ah*, the supplications to Allah and recitations from the Qur'an, some in a standing position, others sitting, some prostrate, his forehead and both palms touching the prayer mat. It felt lonely without the strong voice of Ghaniyah behind him.

He was in a prostrate position, his first *sujud*, when he thought he heard her repeat the words he had just spoken. *"Subhaana rabbiyal Allah"*—to God be the glory. He feared it was a psychosomatic reaction on his part, the way victims report pain in their hands even after an amputation. She had been there for so long, affirming and repeating his prayers, that his mind was playing tricks.

He rose to a kneeling position, hands on his thighs. *"Allahu akbar."* This time he heard it more clearly—a hoarse voice from the bed. He resisted the strong urge to go to her and instead began the second *sujud. "Subhaana rabbiyal Allah,"* Khalid chanted. His wife had definitely joined him again, her voice feeble but determined.

Khalid tried to finish his prayers without rushing, a deliberate focus on a merciful God. He said the last *Allahu akbar* with an intensity that had been missing earlier in the day. Tonight, Allah was a miracle worker.

He stood and moved next to his wife's bed. He took her hand, and she squeezed his, as if she knew that something significant had just happened. He bent down and kissed her on the forehead.

"*Allahu akbar,*" she said.

Khalid stood and gazed at his wife of thirty-two years. Though she had tubes in her nose and her face was swollen and purple, her eyes showed signs of life and recognition.

"Welcome back," Khalid said, though Ghaniyah didn't respond. "Praise be to Allah."

4

THE FOLLOWING WEEK, Alex Madison walked into the Virginia Beach Circuit Court building carrying his grandfather's worn leather briefcase. For the first time in months, he felt like John Patrick Madison might actually be smiling down on him. His grandfather had been a crusty old civil rights lawyer, a veteran of the school desegregation struggles in Virginia and a legend around the courthouse. When he died, the phone had pretty much stopped ringing at Madison and Associates. To make a living, Alex had transformed the practice into a personal-injury shop. On good days, the firm's waiting room looked like a hospital ward.

And his grandfather was probably rolling over in his grave.

But today, Alex walked a little straighter. He took his seat next to sixteen-year-old Aisha Hajjar at the counsel table. His client, a teenager of strong convictions, believed it was her duty to keep her head covered with a *hijab*, or head scarf. That conviction didn't sit well with the owners of the Atlantic Surf Shop in Virginia Beach, a competitor to Alex's favorite surf shop. When Aisha applied for a summer job, they told her that she didn't fit with the outlet's "Look Policy."

Twenty-four hours after receiving the call, Alex had filed a discrimination suit.

They were in court today under a Virginia statute that allowed for a summary jury trial. Each side had already taken depositions and would now have an hour to present its case to a panel of seven jurors. Alex had agreed to be bound by the result because he wanted to get a quick resolution before the summer employment season ended, and he would have to wait months for a normal jury trial. It also played to his strength. Alex was, in his own humble opinion, a gifted communicator. It was the detail work that always tripped him up.

He wasn't sure why the lawyer on the other side, a young Harvard graduate named Kendall Spears, had agreed.

After Judge Thomas, a friend of Alex's grandfather, explained the process, he invited Alex to present his case. Alex stood facing the jury with a single piece of paper in his hand. "I hope some of you don't apply for a job at the Atlantic Surf Shop," he said, "because some of you don't quite have 'the look.'"

"Objection!" Kendall Spears said, standing to face the judge. "He's asking the jurors to put themselves in the plaintiff's shoes. He can't do that."

Technically, Kendall was right. Lawyers weren't allowed to argue the Golden Rule. But Kendall's objection illustrated the difference between his Harvard education and Alex's apprenticeship with his grandfather. Raising the objection only served to highlight Alex's point.

"I think he's right," Judge Thomas said. "Why don't you avoid that line of argument."

Alex shrugged. "Sorry, Your Honor." He turned back to the jury and eyeballed the young man in the second row. He was wearing an earring, and tattoos covered his arms. Alex certainly had his attention.

Alex held up the paper in his right hand. "Atlantic Surf's Look Policy says that the store wants to project an 'All-American image' with a level of dress and grooming that represents what people expect from the brand. Okay. Nothing wrong with that.

"But that's just the first sentence. The rest of this page dictates every aspect of how you need to look. The first sentence: 'Employees are expected to have a natural and classic hairstyle that enhances natural features and creates a fresh, natural appearance.'"

A few days earlier, Alex had gone to a Hair Cuttery and asked them to use a number three blade, shortening his blond hair to little more than a buzz cut. He ran a hand over his head. "This is certainly natural and fresh," he said, "but is it 'classic'? And that's the problem: Who defines these things? Should a bad haircut keep you from a good job?"

He returned to the document. "Colored fingernail polish is

prohibited, and toenail polish must be worn in appropriate colors, to be determined by the store management.

"No facial hair, of course. Eyebrow pencil, eyeliner, lipstick, and eye shadow are allowed only in natural shades."

Alex again surveyed the jury. A few of the women wore dark eye shadow; one raised an eyebrow at him.

"And here's my favorite." Alex pointed to the fourth regulation on the page. "'Inconspicuous tattoos are acceptable only if they represent the Atlantic Surf Shop look.'"

He smiled. "I'm not sure who gets to inspect those inconspicuous tattoos, but I'll bet that's a fun job."

"Objection!"

"Sustained."

"You know what's not on here?" Alex asked, unfazed by the objection. "A BMI number. A requirement that you work out every day at Bally's and have a six-pack. But it should be."

Using a remote, Alex flicked on a PowerPoint presentation. "These are pictures of me with all the employees that were working on the day I visited the store."

Kendall rose to object but apparently thought better of it. This was, after all, a summary jury trial. The lawyers were supposed to present the evidence they would use at trial.

"Notice how they could all be straight from an Abercrombie and Fitch catalog," Alex said. "'All-American image' is apparently a synonym for *ripped*."

Alex looked at his motley little group of jurors. Nobody would accuse these folks of being even remotely in shape, much less ripped. "Atlantic Surf pays almost double what other retail outlets pay," Alex continued. "Think they might be paying a premium for good looks?"

"Objection! That's not the issue here," Kendall said.

Judge Thomas twisted up the corner of his mouth, a look of indecision. "I'll let it go," he said.

"Oh . . . one thing I forgot to mention," Alex continued. "No hats. And that's where my client, one of those rare people who could probably comply with every other aspect of this draconian policy, didn't make the cut. She's a member of the Islamic faith. And she believes that, for the sake of modesty, women should have their heads covered with the type of scarf she's wearing today."

For the next several minutes, Alex switched into lecture mode and explained the impact of Title VII of the Civil Rights Act. Employers have a duty to reasonably accommodate employees' sincerely held religious beliefs unless doing so would impose an undue hardship on the company. Aisha's scarf, Alex argued, would certainly not create an undue hardship.

"Atlantic Surf says the purpose of its Look Policy is to enhance its brand by reflecting the type of look acceptable to its customers. But I would submit to you that its customers look very different from these store employees. Here are pictures of the first twenty customers that went into the store on the day I visited."

The people were a typical slice of beach life—tattooed, underweight, overweight, dyed hair, skimpy bathing suits . . . and lots of painted fingernails.

"And for your review, here are the store employees." Alex returned to his pictures of Atlantic Surf's staffers—beautiful and buff, all dressed in tight T-shirts that showed off hard bodies.

"In this sea of skin-deep beauty, is there not room for one teenager who believes in honoring God with modest dress and hair covering? Even though I disagree with the store's implicit requirement that you have to be beautiful to work there, Aisha fits that criteria. Where she fails is in her desire not to flaunt it.

"We don't live in the Aryan Nation," Alex continued. "We live in America. We allow people to be themselves. Diversity is a way of life. Religious. Political. And yes, even in the way we dress.

"In America, you should not be forced to turn yourself into a sex object just to get a job selling surfboards."

5

KENDALL SPEARS could have landed a job at the Atlantic Surf Shop with no problem. He was tall with thick black hair, deep-set eyes, and a chiseled jaw. He wore a Brooks Brothers suit. He was a rising star in a large downtown Norfolk firm. He spoke in a rich, bass voice.

If Kendall Spears was anything, he was smooth.

"Airline pilots wear uniforms. So do gymnasts, basketball players, Olympic swimmers, and Supreme Court justices.

"Every hospital and fast-food restaurant in America has hygiene standards, or at least they ought to. And who wants to go to Radio City Music Hall and see Rockettes who weigh two hundred pounds? This case isn't about whether companies can have dress codes or body-weight standards or other policies about how their employees present themselves. This case is *supposed* to be about whether Atlantic Surf Shop can reasonably accommodate Ms. Hajjar's sincerely held religious beliefs without undue hardship."

Kendall took a sideways step and fired up his own PowerPoint. "To answer that question, we need to understand the plaintiff's sincerely held religious beliefs. So I asked her some questions about those beliefs during her deposition."

For the next few minutes, the jury watched a video of Aisha's deposition, in which she explained the reasons she wore a hijab. She talked about modesty and honoring her parents and her religious traditions. She talked about not wanting to attract the wrong kind of men. She talked about being willing to stand up for her faith even when others ridiculed her.

It was, Alex thought, very compelling testimony. He had been proud of Aisha three weeks ago when he had defended her deposition. But as he watched her now, he had a sick feeling bubbling up in his stomach. Opposing lawyers didn't show your client's best answers unless they had something up their sleeve.

Alex slid to the edge of his seat, ready to object.

"Frankly, it all sounded pretty compelling," Kendall said, "until I went to her Facebook page."

Alex felt his heart skip a beat. Her Facebook page! Why hadn't he checked that?

"This is a picture that one of her high school friends tagged," Kendall explained. It showed Aisha and two of her friends at the beach in bikinis. Aisha's was orange and skimpy and looked like it might be a size too small. A small tattoo peeked out on her left hip. The next picture was a close-up of her head. "You'll notice that she's not wearing a head scarf," Kendall said, suppressing a grin. "And not much else either, for that matter."

A few of the jurors snickered, and Alex knew he was toast. He would have a few minutes to try to rescue this case during rebuttal. But right now, he couldn't think of a thing to say.

"I ask you," Kendall continued as the camera zoomed back out, "does this look like someone who has a sincerely held religious belief that she must be covered from head to toe? Or does this look like someone who has a sincerely held belief that she might be able to cash in on the Atlantic Surf Shop Look Policy?"

6

BEFORE ALEX STOOD, Aisha leaned over and whispered in his ear. "It was spring break with my friends," she said, her voice tentative and shaky. "I borrowed one of their bikinis. The tattoo's not even real."

Alex looked at his client and saw the tears beginning to form in her eyes. She was certainly embarrassed, maybe even humiliated. "It's okay," he said. He put a hand on her shoulder and stood to face the jury.

He walked to the jury box, carrying no notes. He stood there for a moment without saying a word. He definitely had their attention.

"Have you ever done something you regretted later?" Alex asked. "Even something against your religious beliefs?"

He looked down, thinking of examples. "Maybe you went out and tied one on with the boys. Or you cursed and took the Lord's name in vain. Or in a worst case, you had an affair. Does that mean you should be forced to drink or swear or have sex with someone just to get a job?"

The questions at least had them thinking—he could see it in their eyes. "Doing something against your beliefs doesn't make those beliefs go away. It doesn't make you a pagan; it just means you're human. In my religious tradition, the apostle Paul said that he had the desire to do what was good but he couldn't carry it out. Instead, he kept doing what he knew he shouldn't do. Did this make him an atheist? No, it made him normal. A believer beset by his own human nature.

"C'mon, folks. These were three girls on spring break. Aisha didn't post that picture on her Facebook page; one of her friends did. A sixteen-year-old girl borrowed a bikini because she wanted to be like her friends for a week and not stand out. She rubs on a fake tattoo. And now Mr. Spears wants you to believe that this whole lawsuit is just a scam."

Alex shook his head, as if he couldn't believe his opponent could stoop so low. "During the week, I'm a lawyer. But on Sundays, I serve as the pastor of South Norfolk Community Church. And I'll tell you one thing—if pictures from my college spring break trips were the litmus test, I wouldn't be preaching very long.

"We all stumble sometimes. That's why we all need a little grace. If you've ever been shown grace, maybe you could extend some yourself. I know that Aisha would really appreciate it."

Alex thanked them and returned to his seat.

"My dad is going to kill me," Aisha whispered.

7

WHILE THE JURY DELIBERATED, Alex tried to do what he did best—cut a deal. He proposed to Kendall Spears that Atlantic Surf Shop hire Aisha part-time. "She's even willing to spend most of her time in the stockroom," Alex offered.

But Horse-Trading 101 was apparently no longer offered at Harvard. "I'll take my chances with the jury," Kendall said, his arrogance on full display. "Win or lose, we've gotten some great publicity out of this case."

That's when it hit Alex. There were four camera crews waiting on the courthouse steps. Judge Thomas had allowed one camera into the courtroom as the pool camera, and the newspaper had also sent a reporter. Alex had played right into the defendant's hands. Atlantic Surf didn't care whether the politically correct crowd liked their policies or not. They sold merchandise to surfers. And Alex's little slide show had put the employees on beefcake parade, generating free publicity from all four local networks.

"Good point," Alex conceded. "If you don't really care about justice, this could be a win-win for you guys."

He left the courtroom and pulled out his cell phone. Two could play this game.

◁▷

One hour later, the jury returned with its verdict. Judge Thomas looked at the verdict sheet and frowned. "Is this your verdict?" he asked the forewoman.

"It is, Your Honor."

"So say you all?"

The jurors nodded their heads.

Thomas studied the paper for another moment and looked at Alex and Aisha. Though *Hajjar v. Atlantic Surf Shop, Inc.* didn't exactly have the high stakes of a capital murder trial, Alex still felt his heart in his throat. *It's a summer job,* he reminded himself. But he knew it meant a whole lot more.

"'We the jury, in the case of *Hajjar v. Atlantic Surf Shop, Inc.*, find our verdict in favor of the defendant,'" Judge Thomas read.

Alex felt the gut punch and heard Aisha exhale next to him. "It's all right," he whispered. "You did the right thing by filing this case."

It was hard not to stare at the jury with contempt while Judge Thomas thanked them for their service. Alex found himself hoping that they would someday be victims of discrimination. After the jury left, it was even harder to shake Kendall Spears's hand and congratulate him.

The blow was softened somewhat when Judge Thomas asked Alex to approach the bench before he left the courtroom. "You did a great job," the judge said softly. "You've got your granddad's style."

Except my grandfather would have won, Alex thought. But he was a good enough lawyer to keep that sentiment to himself.

"Thank you, Your Honor."

8

UNLIKE MOST ATTORNEYS, Alex had no law school diploma hanging on the vanity wall of his office. Virginia was one of the few states where a lawyer could still "read the law," pass the bar, and receive a law license. Under Virginia's law reader program, an aspiring attorney could study under an approved lawyer and qualify for the bar exam once he had completed certain prescribed courses. Thomas Jefferson had become a lawyer that way. As had Patrick Henry. Several generations later, Alex's grandfather had followed in their steps.

Alex became a law reader more out of frustration than tradition. He had attended Richmond Law School for a year, but he hated the endless debates on esoteric legal theories and the word parsing that seemed to dominate his law school curriculum. Alex wanted to be a trial lawyer, quick on his feet like his grandfather. But his classes seemed to emphasize intellectual mind games. Some of his professors had never seen the inside of a courtroom.

Having worked in his grandfather's law firm during the summer after that first year, Alex felt like he learned more about the practice of law in three months than he had in his first full year of formal education. His grandfather, no fan of law schools himself, said he was not surprised. He suggested that Alex consider reading the law while he made some money working at the firm.

Two years later, Alex became one of the handful of Virginia lawyers who passed the bar without graduating from law school. He framed his law license with no small amount of pride, though the phrase "law reader" also came with a little baggage and a huge chip for the shoulder.

Like his grandfather, Alex would have to go through his career proving that he belonged.

Taking the place of a law school diploma on Alex's vanity wall was a framed piece of yellow legal paper with his grandfather's sloppy handwriting on it. The page was labeled:

Madison and Associates—Competitive Edge

His grandfather had written the list the day he told Alex that he was dying from cancer. "I guess you'll take over this firm a little sooner than we planned," John Patrick Madison had said. "Here's a few things you need to keep in mind."

He wrote down ten items, talked to Alex about them for thirty minutes, and then told Alex they needed to get back to work. Not one tear was shed. It was like every other teaching session Alex ever had with his grandfather. No nonsense. Keep it real. Can the drama. His grandfather had faced death with the same level of fear he exhibited before a big case. In other words . . . none.

Alex kept the list and had it framed after his grandfather passed away.

The first sentence was characteristically blunt:

Good lawyers don't advertise.

Alex thought about that advice as he stopped to chat with the news crews in front of the Virginia Beach courthouse. His grandfather never paid for advertising, but he also never turned down a free interview. He told Alex that only legal dinosaurs turned up their noses at the media. "I'm an advocate for my client," he explained. "And sometimes I want to send a message to the jury *before* we get into the courtroom."

Alex handled a few questions while Aisha stood next to him. He waited until somebody asked whether they were going to appeal before he made his announcement.

"We've decided not to appeal," Alex said, "because if we win, Aisha would end up working at Atlantic Surf Shop, and it's pretty obvious they don't want her there. But fortunately for her, not all surf shops have a Look Policy that forces you to check your religious beliefs at the door. In fact, the owners of Burke's Surf on Laskin Road believe strongly that the surf culture wants people just to be who they are. They've therefore offered Aisha a job for the summer, hijab and all."

A few reporters congratulated Aisha, and she gave them a beautiful white smile. She told them how excited she was to start at Burke's. Alex even added that most locals preferred Burke's to the Atlantic Surf Shop anyway. By the time the interview ended, it was hard to tell who had won and who had lost the court battle just a few minutes earlier.

Alex smiled for the cameras as well but would be kicking himself all the way back to the office. He should have checked Aisha's Facebook page. He had been complacent. His grandfather would have never missed that important detail.

Alex had not just lost the case. He had violated principle number five on his grandfather's competitive edge list, a sentence he knew by heart, just like every other sentence on that yellow sheet of paper:

Never get outworked by an Ivy League lawyer.

9

FOR KHALID MOBASSAR, sleep had become a luxury. He spent each night in the reclining chair next to Ghaniyah's bed, waking when she stirred, checking on her while she slept, exulting in each small step on the road to recovery. When Ghaniyah was moved from ICU to the brain trauma rehab center, Khalid followed her, hauling his small duffel bag of clothes and toiletries, his briefcase full of books and papers, his computer, his prayer rug, and his Qur'an. He left her side for only a few hours each day to go home and shower and to stop by the mosque.

The medical side of things was confusing at best. Khalid became familiar with the vocabulary of treatment for traumatic brain injury, or TBI, both from listening to the doctors and from scouring the Internet. Ghaniyah had been admitted to the hospital with a 12 on the Glasgow Coma Scale, indicating moderate brain damage. She had briefly lost consciousness before rescuers arrived at the scene. Fortunately, a CT scan and MRI showed no swelling of the brain or the type of cranial bleeding that would require surgical intervention.

But according to the doctors, many closed head injuries produced microscopic changes not easily detectable on the radiological tests. Ghaniyah's official diagnosis was moderate traumatic brain injury with diffuse axonal injury and ischemia. Her prognosis for a full recovery was "guarded."

Five days after the accident, a neuropsychologist had performed a basic neurological assessment designed to reveal the extent of the damage. A full battery of neuropsych testing would come later, but the preliminary results were sobering. Though no longer in a coma, Ghaniyah had suffered memory loss, personality change, and moderate impairment to her executive functioning skills. She had a hard time trying to focus and couldn't handle more than one task at a time. She experienced mood swings and depression. These were all symptoms of right frontoparietal injury, the neuropsychologist explained. For Khalid, it felt like someone had taken the woman he married and placed another person in her body, someone more sluggish and with unpredictable emotions.

But Khalid was determined to love her back to a full recovery. What else could he do?

He read to her for hours each day from the Qur'an, an activity that soothed her and moderated her mood swings. She joined him in the salats as well—from her hospital bed the first few days but on her prayer mat after that. Still, she seemed to lack the religious fervor of the woman Khalid had been married to for thirty-two years. It was this aspect of her personality change that gave him the most heartache.

The doctors said he could take Ghaniyah home in a few days, a prospect that terrified Khalid. His wife wasn't ready to be left alone— you could tell that by looking in her vacant eyes. But the insurance company was insisting that she could recover at home with outpatient therapy just as well as she could at the hospital. For Khalid, it felt like she would be out of sight and out of mind, the neuropsychologists and brain-injury specialists moving on to the next patient.

These thoughts preoccupied him as he watched the news on Thursday evening while shuffling through some papers. Lying on the bed, Ghaniyah dozed in and out.

The subject matter of a local news story caught his attention—a teenage Muslim girl being discriminated against because she wanted to wear a hijab to work. The young lady was not a member of Khalid's mosque, but he admired her boldness. It seemed a little strange that she was so insistent on working in a surf shop, but then again, who could understand the mind of a teenage girl? At least she had the courage to stand up for her convictions, even if it made her feel like an outcast.

When the story segued to the courthouse steps, Khalid almost dropped his papers on the floor.

"Him?" Khalid said out loud when Alex's face first appeared on the screen. Khalid reached for the remote and turned up the volume.

The same lawyer he had met in Ghaniyah's room last week was explaining how he had landed his client a job at a competing surf shop. He talked about the importance of a pluralistic society and accommodating one another's religious beliefs. He talked about accepting people for who they were instead of turning them all into Madison Avenue clones. His client stood beside him, beaming at the prospect of working at Burke's Surf Shop.

When the news moved on to the next story, Khalid turned down the volume and thought about what he had just seen. Maybe he had misjudged the Reverend Alexander Madison. The man hadn't seemed like a crusader when he came into Ghaniyah's hospital room; he had seemed like a sleazy, opportunistic lawyer. Maybe he was. But Khalid had to give the man credit—Mr. Madison was resourceful. And they certainly needed that type of lawyer for Ghaniyah's case . . . if she had a case at all.

Ghaniyah couldn't remember the impact or the events that immediately followed, but she remembered what led up to the accident. A tractor trailer had pulled out to pass her on North Landing Road—a narrow, two-lane road that wound through the southern part of Virginia Beach. When an oncoming vehicle appeared around the corner, the driver of the tractor trailer swerved back into Ghaniyah's lane even though his rig was not all the way past her. Ghaniyah had no choice but to swerve to the right. The last thing she remembered was her tires leaving the pavement as she careened toward a pine tree.

Now Khalid faced piles of medical bills and perhaps long-term care for Ghaniyah. If the driver of the tractor trailer had caused the accident, why shouldn't he pay for the consequences?

They just had to locate him first. The driver hadn't stopped, and the police had no leads. But one of the men in Khalid's mosque had worked as an insurance adjuster. He explained to Khalid that such events might be compensable under the uninsured motorist provisions of his automobile policy.

Khalid quietly searched Ghaniyah's room for Mr. Madison's card. When he couldn't find it, he pulled up the firm's Web site and wrote down the office number. He would call Mr. Madison as soon as Ghaniyah was released from the hospital and things settled down a bit. What could it hurt?

A Muslim imam and a Christian pastor. This could make for some interesting dynamics.

10

HASSAN IBN TALIB, like every assassin, was once a child.

At five years old, he and his siblings had gathered on the living room rug each night for lessons in Islam taught by his mother. She began by placing the Qur'an on the coffee table with great reverence. The book was frail, its pages yellow and worn. When his mother opened it, a mustiness filled the air, transporting the children in time and place to the mighty battles between Muslim warriors and Jewish infidels. To be sure, there were pages of long and confusing teachings and sayings that a young boy did not understand. But there was also lots of action, and nobody could bring the old stories to life better than Hassan's mother.

She was ordinarily a quiet woman, stern with her children, respectful of her husband in public. But when it came time for the lessons, her demeanor changed, and the almond eyes intensified with the spark of a true believer. Hassan had learned the hard way that horseplay, whispering, and poking at his siblings would earn him the switch.

On some nights, like tonight, his mother would read a few verses from the Qur'an and then launch into a story that Hassan had never heard before. Like all the best stories, this one was about a true hero.

"Our third imam, Imam Hussein, was a man of faith and action. He worshiped Allah and would carry sacks of food to the houses of the poor at night, cheering them up. He would always tell his followers, 'Be in touch with the needy, for Allah does not love the arrogant.'"

Hassan didn't understand the word *arrogant*, but he already liked Imam Hussein. Hassan's simple view of the world, fostered by his mother's stories, was black and white. Good guys and bad guys. Muslims and Jews. Imam Hussein would be a good guy. Strong in battle. A slayer of Jews.

"But during the time of Imam Hussein, an evil ruler named Yazid Ibn Muawiya rose to power and made everybody accept his leadership. Everybody except Imam Hussein and a few brave followers, that is. Imam Hussein was the true successor to the Holy Prophet Mohammed, and he would not bow to the leadership of somebody as evil as Yazid."

Hassan's little hand shot up in the air. His brother gave him a look of disdain.

"Yes, my son."

"What does *successor* mean?"

His mother smiled. "Imam Hussein was the grandson of the Great Prophet Mohammed. He was supposed to take over for Mohammed when Mohammed died."

"Oh."

"That's a stupid question," Hassan's brother whispered, drawing an evil eye from their mom.

"So the people of Kufa, who were followers of Imam Hussein, invited him to come to their city and lead them in revolt against Yazid and his army. But on the way to Kufa, Imam Hussein and his family were met by a large army of men. The men surrounded the camp of Imam Hussein and would not allow his people to get food or drinking water. For days, Imam Hussein, his family, and his followers were not allowed to leave their encampment while the army gathered reinforcements and grew. Eventually, there were *30,000* warriors." Hassan's mother emphasized the number and then, as the expert storyteller, paused for effect.

"How many did Imam Hussein have?" Hassan asked. This time, he forgot to raise his hand.

"Seventy-two."

Huh? Even for a young boy, the odds seemed overwhelming.

"For eight days, the blistering hot sun scorched the desert sands as Imam Hussein waited for the people of Karbala, a nearby city, to rally to his support."

Hassan's mother lowered her voice. "To their great shame, the people of Karbala never came. And so, after more than a week of no food or water, many of Imam Hussein's followers became so dry that they could not swallow, their tongues sticking to the roofs of their mouths. That's when the imam took his six-month-old son in his arms and walked toward Yazid's army, holding his baby up so the leaders could see that the boy was dying. He asked them to take the baby and give the child water even if they intended to kill Hussein."

Hassan's mom held her arms out with the imaginary baby resting in her hands. Hassan scooted forward, holding his breath, his eyes wide.

"One of Yazid's men shot a poisoned arrow through the neck of the baby, killing the child and pinning his neck to his father's arm."

Hassan gasped. A baby killed! And not by Jews or infidels! By other Muslim warriors!

"They demanded that Imam Hussein surrender, but he would not. 'Death is superior to disgrace, and I am ready to die defending Islam and the Muslims,' he said. And then the battle began."

Hassan listened breathlessly as his mother described the conflict— the imam mounting a black stallion and wielding a sarif, cutting down dozens of Yazid's soldiers. But eventually, the brave man was overwhelmed by his enemies. "The evildoers cut off his head and left his body to rot for three days without burial," Hassan's mother reported with great sadness.

Hassan was crestfallen. The good guys seldom lost in his mother's stories. And when they did, it was never like *this*. Killed. Left to rot. His baby dead in his arms.

Hassan looked toward his older brother, checking for a reaction. As usual, his brother was stone-faced. Just as he had been the day that Hassan's mother taught Sura 99, the lesson about the earthquake and the Day of Judgment. Hassan had shivered in fear as she described the tormenting flames of hell. "If your bad works outweigh your good works, you will go to hell," Hassan's mother had explained. And Hassan had known immediately that hell would be his lot. His conscience had tormented him for days, and nightmares had haunted his sleep.

But his brother had seemed unfazed. What did he know that Hassan did not?

His mother's voice brought him back to the story. "But it didn't matter what Yazid's men did to Imam Hussein's body because he was no longer there," Hassan's mother explained, her tone reflecting the excitement of a big secret she was about to share. "He was sitting on the shore of a crystal river, surrounded by many women who were feeding him and taking care of him."

Hassan recognized the description immediately. It was *Jannah*! Paradise!

His mother closed the Qur'an and looked solemnly from Hassan to his brother. "We call Imam Hussein 'Sayyid al-Shuhada,'—the Lord of the Martyrs. When you die a martyr—a shahid—you do not feel death. It is more like the minor pain of a mosquito sting. You wake up in Jannah, and Allah smiles at you, placing a crown of virtue on your head."

Hassan's mother held two of her fingers and her thumb together now, opening them slightly, as if letting go of a tiny precious thing. "No matter what you have done wrong in this life, you will be forgiven with the first drop of your blood that is spilt. With the second drop, you may redeem seventy family members who would have gone to hell.

"To die a martyr is to never die at all."

◁▷

THE PRESENT
WASHINGTON, D.C.

Hassan received the text message on Wednesday night. The young wife of a prominent leader in a Norfolk mosque had left the faith. She had been seen in the company of a married American man, a devout Christian. She was making a mockery of her marriage and, more importantly, of Allah.

The Norfolk mosque to which she belonged had been started as part of the Islamic Brotherhood's Strategic City Initiative, a plan to plant prominent mosques in all of America's most important cities.

Norfolk had made the list because of its strategic military bases as well as its proximity to Washington, D.C. The mosque was one of the few Islamic success stories in the South, exceeding all projections for growth. Its imam, Khalid Mobassar, was a highly respected, charismatic leader, though he pushed reformist ideas that were sometimes detrimental to the faith. Others in the mosque, outspoken defenders of the orthodox faith, served as a counterbalance. Fatih Mahdi was one such man.

But now, Mahdi's young wife had become an infidel.

The first text message Hassan received was terse and unequivocal:

> *Ja'dah Fatima Mahdi has converted to the Christian faith. She has defiled herself by consorting with an American man, disgraced her family, and dishonored Allah. She must be given only one opportunity to repent and return to the faith. If she refuses, the honor of her family must be restored.*

The second text message had a picture attached—a photo of a young Lebanese woman and a middle-aged American man. The second message was shorter than the first:

> *If you attend Beach Bible Church on Saturday night, you will find her there. May Allah guide you.*

11

IN HASSAN'S VIEW, Beach Bible Church epitomized everything wrong with American Christianity. It seemed like a godless blend of amusement park, social club, and rock concert. The parking lot spanned acres, the "sanctuary" would have dwarfed most concert halls, and the music was so loud that Hassan had a headache before the third song ended. The women dressed in provocative clothes while the men pretended not to notice. There was no community prayer, no reverential silence, no dignified reading from a holy book. It was all flash and glitter and noise.

A worship service, Hassan thought, *without worship.*

He sat on one of the padded folding chairs three rows from the back, trying to remain inconspicuous in a church that was surprisingly full for a Saturday night service. The people were friendly, though he tried hard to ignore them.

There were no cameras in the church. No security guards. There didn't appear to be anyone surveying the crowd, looking for suspicious strangers with Middle Eastern complexions and hard eyes. This was America, not Beirut. The members of Beach Bible Church were blissfully ignorant.

The pastor talked about sacrifice, about taking up a cross daily and following Christ. But the examples he used were trivial. What if somebody insults you? What if you lose your job? What if your classmates start rumors about you because you're too radical in your faith?

What did Americans really know about sacrifice?

What if Allah asks you to lay down your life? Hassan wanted to ask.

What if he asks you to strap a bomb to your body and blow up as many infidels and Jews as possible? To the American Christians, sacrifice was a theoretical concept. For Hassan, it was a way of life.

Ja'dah Fatima Mahdi was indeed in the service. Hassan had followed her from her home in downtown Norfolk to this church in the Kempsville area of Virginia Beach. She had made one stop along the way, pulling into a deserted parking lot, where she sat in the car as it idled for several minutes. Hassan had parked too far away to see what she was doing. But when she pulled out of the parking lot, he drove close enough to get a better look and realized that Ja'dah Mahdi had changed her clothes.

When Ja'dah had left her home, she'd been dressed conservatively, wearing a hijab to cover her head, though she did not veil her face. When she arrived at church, she was wearing too-tight jeans and a white blouse with a neckline much lower than would ever be allowed in any mosque, and her hair was pulled into a tight braid. She was a beautiful woman, maybe fifteen years younger than her husband, but she was no longer modest. Hassan believed that beauty was like a jewel—if something was precious, you kept it hidden until the treasure was meant to be uncovered. Only Western women advertised their wares for the entire world to see, leaving little to the imagination. For Hassan, a place of worship—even godless worship like this—seemed a strange venue to promote lust.

During the service, he positioned himself on the opposite side of the sanctuary from Ja'dah. Occasionally, he would steal a glance at her. During the singing, he noticed that Ja'dah sometimes closed her eyes and raised her hands. At one point, he thought he saw a hint of moisture in her eyes.

After the service, Ja'dah went to an out-of-the-way restaurant with a group of church members. They were all relaxed and smiling. Hassan recognized one of them as the man from the text message. An hour and a half later, Ja'dah came out of the restaurant with the middle-aged man. The man climbed into the front seat of Ja'dah's car, and the two of them talked for another thirty minutes. The man had his Bible open, and before he left, they bowed their heads and prayed.

As the man walked across the parking lot, Hassan started his car and drove past the line of parked cars that had separated them. When the man looked up, Hassan slowed and allowed him to walk right in front of the car. He was midforties and getting a little soft around the middle. Blond hair, soft blue eyes, pudgy nose, and smooth skin. The man gave a quick wave of thanks to Hassan for allowing him to cross.

Earlier, when the group was eating dinner, Hassan had found the man's name in the church directory Hassan had grabbed earlier that evening. Martin Burns. He had two older children with him in the directory picture—a daughter who appeared to be in high school and a son who looked to be in middle school. There was no mother in the picture. Most likely Burns was separated from her. And now Burns was putting the moves on another man's wife. Men like Martin Burns didn't deserve to live another day. Hassan would be doing everyone a favor.

Sacrifice. Martin Burns had undoubtedly nodded along when the preacher told him how much he should be willing to sacrifice for the cause of Christ.

Hassan would help him understand what sacrifice really meant.

12

"**ACCORDING TO C. S. LEWIS,** there is danger in the belief that 'all will be well' when in fact all is *not* well." As Alex looked out on the faces of his congregants at the start of his sermon on Sunday morning, it was clear the words were falling on deaf ears. Literally as well as figuratively.

The average age at South Norfolk Community Church was somewhere north of mandatory retirement. Attendance was holding steady at about seventy on most Sundays, and the women outnumbered the men by about two to one. Pastors weren't supposed to play favorites, but Alex was especially fond of a group of six or seven silver-haired widows who sat toward the front on his right side, snuggled firmly into the padded mauve pews, who couldn't resist an *amen* or two even during Alex's weakest sermons. When it came time in the service to greet one another, Alex went straight to the little pack of senior saints, gave each a hug, and came away smelling strongly of old perfume.

"We have an amazing ability to deceive ourselves," Alex said. "Christ knew this. He told his followers that many would think they were going to heaven, saying 'Lord, Lord, didn't we do many wonderful works in your name?' But he would tell them that he never really knew them."

Deacon Harry Dent stifled a yawn. Somebody's cell phone rang. A visiting single mom, sitting two-thirds of the way back on the left, turned red when everybody stared.

Alex didn't let it bother him but kept preaching as if he had a stadium full of rapt listeners. Just before the closing prayer, he walked out from behind the podium, down the front steps of the platform, and into the aisle. Like most churches, there was some unwritten rule that nobody could sit in the first two pews, so Alex positioned himself at the beginning of row three and made sure he had their attention.

He looked around and realized that he really did care about these folks. Working class. Old school. Salt of the earth.

"We come to church all dressed up in our best outfits," Alex said, though he knew it wasn't entirely true. A few of the younger members of South Norfolk Community Church subscribed to the Sunday casual dress code, sporting polo shirts or shorts or even jeans. Alex left his own board shorts, flip-flops, and T-shirts in Virginia Beach. On Sunday mornings, he donned a white shirt with cuff links, a bold-print tie, a freshly pressed suit, and—before his recent buzz cut—an extra dab of hair gel. The women in the senior saints club always told him how handsome he looked.

Alex brushed both arms of his suit coat. "Nice suit, huh, Fred?"

Fred's head jerked up from his bulletin. "Hm. Not bad for a lawyer."

There was a smattering of chuckles. Alex smiled along. "On the outside, we look like we've got our act together. 'How are you?' 'I'm great, thanks.' But inside, we're dying."

As he talked, Alex removed his suit coat and elicited a few gasps from the congregation. Some of the younger families snickered. He had mutilated his white shirt—ripping it, spattering red paint on it to look like blood, rubbing it in the dirt. The only part that wasn't messed up was the part everyone could see when he had his suit coat on—the cuffs, the center buttons, and the collar.

He tossed the suit coat on a pew. "God wants us to get honest with him," Alex said. "He knows what's under that spiffed-up exterior. The only way to get things right is to admit that you're hurting underneath that nice new suit. To admit your failures and fears and addictions."

And inadequacies, he wanted to say. But he left that out. It felt too personal. Who was he to be preaching to these good folks?

"The greatest danger is the belief that all is well when all may not be well."

Alex paused and looked from one member to the next. Maybe he wasn't the kind of spiritual giant that pastors were supposed to be, but he did have a gift for public speaking, for motivating people by talking to their hearts. It's why he always wanted to be a lawyer, though he found that the practice of law was more about grinding it out in the office than wooing a jury.

But today, even a few of the deacons were slowly nodding their heads. This message, thought Alex, would at least be hard to forget.

"Let's pray."

13

ON THE WAY TO WORK Monday morning, Alex's own words kept echoing in his head. *The greatest danger is the belief that all is well when all may not be well.* He could apply that principle to so many areas of his life right now. His carefree and relaxed exterior covered deep fissures about to be exposed. One was his church and the fact that his congregation was slowly dwindling. He attributed the malaise to a stubborn refusal to change with the surrounding community, but he knew that some, including a few deacons, thought it had more to do with the inadequacies of Alex as a part-time pastor.

Another involved Alex's own feelings that he didn't really belong in the role of pastor. He had stepped into this position two years ago as an interim solution when the church was without a pastor. He had never intended to stay this long and couldn't help feeling like the good folks at South Norfolk Community Church deserved more than he could offer. Maybe he should step away. But could he really leave the church without a pastor again so soon?

Then there was the law practice. Financially, the firm was taking on water. Most months they had negative cash flow, bumping their line of credit a little higher. They needed a big personal-injury case to set things right. Alex had already cut non-personnel expenses to the bone.

Madison and Associates was located less than a mile from Alex's condo and less than two miles from the oceanfront. The firm occupied half of a gray vinyl-sided building in a small office park on Laskin Road. The building had a seventies look, as did the office furniture.

The view from Alex's office, the one previously used by his grandfather, overlooked the parking lot. John Patrick Madison had not been a big fan of expensive office space in the Town Center area of Virginia Beach. As a result, he could offer lower hourly rates than most of his contemporaries.

He posted those rates for all to see in the firm's waiting area. In the seven years that Alex worked there, he could never remember the rate changing. And Alex still had the same sign up, two years after his grandfather's death.

> We charge $200 per hour.
> $250 if you call more than once a week.
> $300 if you want to advise us on how to do our job.

By the time Alex pulled into the small office lot on Monday morning, the firm's other two employees' cars were already there. Inside, Sylvia Brunswick, the firm's receptionist/legal assistant/den mother, sat hunched over her computer and didn't bother looking up. She was only forty-five or so, but her spine had permanently curved, and she had periodic attacks of various ailments that routinely kept her out of the office, mostly on Fridays and Mondays. She was rail thin, with a grating voice that reminded Alex of Olive Oyl's.

Alex's grandfather had hired Sylvia about five years before he died and never had the heart to fire her. So far, Alex hadn't mustered the nerve to do so either, though he had promised himself more than once that she wouldn't make it to the end of the week. Every payday, Alex swallowed hard while signing Sylvia's check and thinking about her health insurance, payroll taxes, and sick leave benefits.

"What's up?" Alex asked, walking quickly past Sylvia and heading down the hall toward his office. Sylvia immediately started reciting a list of things Alex needed to get done. Fingernails on a chalkboard, but he managed to block it out.

If Sylvia was excess baggage, Alex's partner was the little engine that could. Not surprisingly, she was already in her office, talking on the phone. She had probably billed at least two solid hours already.

Alex first met the legal dynamo that was Shannon Reese nearly seven years before, during their first semester of law school when they ended up in the same study group for Torts. The group was an unwieldy alliance of hard-charging 1Ls, each trying to outsmart the others while harboring secret fears about failing.

The self-appointed leaders of the group didn't take Alex seriously because he dressed like a surfer and failed to complete his outlines on time. Shannon couldn't get a word in edgewise because she looked even less like a lawyer than Alex. She was short, athletic, and cute, a former gymnast who pulled her hair back into a tight ponytail, spoke with a voice that seemed like it was stuck in puberty, and radiated a high-energy enthusiasm for the law that was decidedly uncool. She had that fresh gymnast's look—complete with a perky and innocent face—that masked an iron will and an ultracompetitive drive. Her success in gymnastics had been built on athleticism and power, not graceful elegance, and she brought that same intensity to her legal studies.

Three weeks before finals, Alex and Shannon peeled off and formed their own two-person study group. Shannon ultimately received the book award for the best grade in Torts and a smattering of other As and B-pluses. Alex was entirely happy to have earned straight Bs. The next semester, the pair declined a number of invitations to join other groups.

Even after Alex dropped out of school that summer, he and Shannon stayed in touch. Alex talked his grandfather into hiring Shannon as a clerk for the summer following her second year, and she eventually signed on to work full-time after graduation. Alex and Shannon studied for the bar together, and when the results were announced, the number of licensed lawyers at Madison and Associates tripled.

Alex's grandfather had loved Shannon's work ethic, and Alex's grandmother was hardly subtle in her attempts to get the two young lawyers to become more than friends. But Shannon had other plans. She bounced around between boyfriends before landing with a gymnastics coach at the University of Georgia who was intense, possessive, and controlling. After three years of dating, and while they were engaged, Shannon caught him fooling around with a coed.

Alex helped her pick up the pieces. But just when he was ready to ask her out, Shannon swore off relationships and said she wanted to concentrate on her law career. With the pressure off, their friendship had blossomed during the past two years to the point where Alex couldn't imagine practicing law without her.

He poured a cup of coffee and checked his voice messages. When he heard the voice of Khalid Mobassar calling about his wife's case, Alex perked up. He called the imam back and set up a meeting. Then he pumped his fist and strutted down to his partner's office. He plopped down in one of Shannon's client chairs, holding two yellow stickies in his right hand with information about his cherished new case.

He watched Shannon edit a document on her computer, her face knit in concentration, as she refused to acknowledge his presence.

"Got a minute?" he asked.

"Not really, Alex; I've got to finish this brief."

"Fine." Alex shrugged, making no effort to rise. "Then you're probably not interested in this huge new personal-injury case I just landed."

Shannon paused and looked up, her face a cross between annoyance and curiosity. She'd heard it all before. "That's correct," she said. "Your huge, can't-lose, once-in-a-lifetime, pay-all-the-bills case is just going to have to wait until I get this brief done on a garden-variety motion to compel in a case where the client is paying us real money."

Pronouncement over, Shannon returned to her screen and resumed typing.

"Brain injury," Alex said.

Shannon checked a document next to her computer, turned the page.

"Clear liability."

She typed a few more sentences.

"Insurance coverage of $100,000. Unless we can find the truck that caused the accident; then maybe half a million."

When even this didn't slow Shannon down, Alex reached over and picked up the calculator from her desk. "Let's just say the jury goes crazy and gives us two million. . . . We divide that by three. . . . Oh, not good—$666,666. Mm. Too many sixes."

Though Alex wasn't superstitious, there was no sense playing around with the mark of the beast. He punched in a few more numbers. "That's better. If we go for 35 percent, we net $700,000. And seven's the perfect number."

Shannon sighed loudly, a big show, then stopped typing and looked at Alex. She was cute when she tried to act perturbed. "Three minutes," she said.

Alex took ten to tell her about the case. He recounted how Ghaniyah Mobassar had been minding her own business when a tractor trailer essentially ran her off North Landing Road and into a tree.

"We can sue John Doe and probably recover a hundred grand under uninsured motorist coverage," Alex said. "So right there, that's $33,000. But if we can find that truck driver, he's probably covered for a couple million."

"Do you have an accident report?" Shannon asked.

"Not yet. I'm getting that this afternoon."

"Is the brain damage showing up on an MRI or CT scan?"

How did Shannon always manage to drill right into the weak spots? "No. But there's no question she suffered traumatic brain injury. She was knocked unconscious and suffered short-term memory loss. Lots of damage to the passenger side of the car. She hit the tree almost head-on."

Shannon remained visibly skeptical, but she was no longer stealing glances at her brief. "How'd we get the call?"

"Apparently Mr. Mobassar saw my press conference after Aisha Hajjar's case," Alex said.

Shannon's facial expression changed from skepticism to mild surprise. "That's cool," she said. And then, just to be sure that Alex didn't get a big head, added, "And he doesn't mind that his prospective new lawyer lost that case?"

Alex reached over and put the stickies on her desk. "Not when he meets the real brains behind the operation. Can you meet with us at three?"

"Today?"

"It could be a great case," Alex said, his tone changing. He would beg if he had to. Whine a little, if that's what it took. Alex could bring the work in the door, but Shannon was the one who knew how to get it done.

She sighed and frowned, checking Outlook. Alex suspected she was just trying to torture him a little.

"I might be able to sneak it in. What time will we be back?"

"Five at the latest," Alex promised. "It sounds pretty straight-forward."

"Right."

14

ALEX GOT DELAYED at an afternoon appointment and called Shannon to let her know he was running late. She was, of course, already there. "No problem," she said in a cheery voice. But Alex and Shannon had been partners long enough that he could sense a sliver of ice in the tone.

He pulled into the driveway fifteen minutes late, blocking a few other vehicles, and grabbed his suit coat from the passenger seat. The Mobassars lived in a modest duplex a few blocks off Shore Drive, one of several identical duplexes squished together like soldiers lining the streets. Cars jammed every square inch of curb and driveway space. The places looked like they had been built in the eighties, with brick facades, overgrown shrubs, and a few small shade trees in the front yards.

Frankly, Alex had expected a more ornate home for the imam of a mosque that had cost thirteen million to build.

Shannon answered the door next to Khalid, and Ghaniyah stood just behind them. Alex shook hands with his new clients and felt Shannon discreetly step on his toes. Looking down, he noticed her bare feet and the shoe trees next to the door. After introductions, he slid off his loafers and placed them on one of the trees. *Maybe I should have worn socks.*

"Khalid was just showing me around his study," Shannon said. "Ghaniyah is fixing a few things to snack on."

Though he wasn't one for small talk, Alex dutifully followed Khalid and Shannon back into Khalid's office. It surprised him a little that

Khalid seemed so comfortable around Shannon, given what Alex thought he knew about the way Muslims treated women.

The study featured oak paneling on one wall and floor-to-ceiling bookshelves covering the others. The space was cramped, but the bookshelves were neatly arranged. Arabic artifacts were sprinkled among the hard-covered texts. There was a lone book on the top shelf.

"The Qur'an," Shannon said, following Alex's eyes. "They keep it up there as a sign of respect."

Alex thought about the various places he typically left his Bible around the condo. Right now, it was probably lying on the floor next to his bed.

"I was just asking Mr. Mobassar about this shelf," Shannon said, pointing to an eye-level space that contained, among other books, an English version of the Qur'an. Each of the books on the shelf had an ancient look, a soft leather cover, and gold embroidering on the spine.

"These are all versions of the Qur'an," Khalid explained. "But they are not in Arabic; therefore they are considered merely commentary on the text and not the holy text itself." He looked from Alex to Shannon and slipped briefly into lecture mode. "We believe that the Qur'an was spoken directly from the angel Gabriel to the Prophet Mohammed, peace be upon him, in the Arabic language. For this reason, Muslims believe that the language of heaven is Arabic and our holy text should only be read in that language."

Alex nodded.

"What are the other languages?" Shannon asked.

Khalid went to the shelf and put his finger on the spine of each book in turn. "French. English. Turkish. German. Spanish. Mandarin. Russian."

"And you speak all those languages?" Shannon asked.

Khalid flushed a little. "Yes, but it is not so impressive. Most Lebanese grow up speaking Arabic, French, and English. Many European languages have the same origins." He paused. "Mandarin was hard. But not as hard as our native tongue. Some say that Arabic is the language of heaven because it takes an eternity to learn it."

"Your English is excellent," Shannon said.

"As I said, I have spoken English from my youth."

Alex knew what Shannon was doing, and he studied the shelves a little more intently. Client assessment was the key in deciding whether or not to take a case. You could learn a lot about a person by spending some time around their favorite books.

And for a Muslim cleric, Khalid's choice of books surprised Alex.

"You seem to be a fan of Thomas Jefferson and Martin Luther," Alex said.

"I am somewhat of a disciple of both," Khalid responded. "They believed in the common man. They were reformers, as am I. Jefferson's ideas regarding equality and the virtue of the common man would make him popular among my people. But Luther . . . not so much."

"Why is that?" Shannon asked.

"My home country has always been the world's greatest laboratory for democracy," Khalid began, then cut himself short. "Are you sure you want to hear all this? Some people are bored by my lectures in civics."

"Absolutely," Shannon answered with her gymnast's enthusiasm.

"Sure," Alex said, though he was starting to worry about whether they were being rude to Ghaniyah.

"Most Americans would be surprised to know that a majority of Muslims—including in the Middle East—believe democracy, not theocracy, is the best way to govern their country," Khalid said. "A study done by the Pew Global Attitudes Project found this to be true in Muslim countries like Pakistan, Kuwait, Indonesia, and of course, Lebanon. In my country, there are many different religious sects and nationalities—we are the melting pot of the Middle East. But the big division is between Christians and Muslims. By law, our parliament is divided fifty-fifty between Christians and Muslims. Our president must be a Maronite Christian, the prime minister a Sunni Muslim, and the speaker of the parliament a Shi'a Muslim. While this sounds nice in theory, the effect is to blunt the voice of the growing number of Shi'a Muslims. I would like to see more of the one-man-one-vote style of democracy that Thomas Jefferson helped champion in this country."

Alex processed this for a second. "But wouldn't that disrupt a fragile political alliance?"

"That is, of course, the argument. But every country with ethnic or religious minorities has wrestled with the same problem. The strongest solve it by protecting minorities through a legal system, not through a quota system in the representative branch."

"Makes sense," Shannon said, though Alex wasn't so sure. The Lebanese had a nasty habit of killing each other for political advantage. Some countries weren't ready for representative democracy.

"Where does Martin Luther fit in?" Alex asked.

Khalid's tone turned reverential. "I identify with Luther more than any other historical figure. Reformers live in turmoil. They become marginalized by those they love. Their ideas terrorize the powers that be."

Khalid's hands started gesturing more as he warmed to his topic. "Before Luther, the Christian Mass was in Latin, the Holy Book inaccessible to the average person. The Christian faith became whatever the pope and priests wanted it to become because only they could understand the Scriptures and the ceremonies, and they told the people what to believe.

"Luther and the reformers changed that, both inside and outside the Catholic church. The Scriptures were translated into the language of the common person. This made it possible for the Christian God to communicate directly with every person of faith. Soon, Christians started believing that they could speak directly to God without the priests as intermediaries. This is very simplified, I know. But the point is, the masses were empowered, and the stranglehold of religious leaders was broken."

Khalid lowered his voice, as if he wasn't quite ready to announce to the world where his thinking was taking him. "The Muslim faith has yet to experience such a reformation. In the more fundamental Islamic countries, the mullahs and imams control *everything*. Sharia law becomes whatever the clerics want it to be.

"I am working on my own modest little proposal to challenge that thinking. I am certainly no Martin Luther. But still, his life is an inspiration."

Khalid looked past Alex's shoulder, checking the doorway. "Sorry," Khalid offered. "You discovered my weaknesses—politics and religion." He lowered his voice. "Ghaniyah has a hard time performing tasks in sequence right now. Perhaps if you could move into the living room, I could help her in the kitchen and join you momentarily. Then we can discuss what really brings you here."

When Khalid walked past him, Alex caught Shannon's eye. Her little nod confirmed what Alex was thinking.

The jury's going to like this guy.

15

THE LIVING ROOM was neat and stark, with no pictures or trinkets. A low ceiling, dim lights, and narrow windows made it feel a little claustrophobic. Alex and Shannon quietly discussed the case while they waited for their hosts to join them.

When Khalid appeared, he placed a tray with a brass coffeepot and demitasse cups on the small table. Ghaniyah placed a second tray next to the first, one that contained a pastry covered with syrup and nuts, along with bread and olive oil, plates and forks.

"How do you like your coffee?" Khalid asked. Shannon, who normally didn't drink more than one cup a day, surprised Alex by saying she liked lots of cream. *She must want this case bad.* Alex requested extra cream as well, particularly after he saw the thickness of the jet black syrup that Khalid poured into the tiny cups.

"This is baklava," Khalid said, pointing to the pastry. "It's a little rich, but nobody makes better baklava than Ghaniyah. We also have hummus if you prefer."

To be polite, Alex and Shannon each took a piece of baklava along with their coffee. They settled into the two chairs in the room, and the Mobassars sat together on the couch.

After a few minutes of small talk and nibbling at their food, Shannon put her plate on the floor, took out a yellow legal pad, and smoothly took control of the meeting. She asked Khalid to retrieve a copy of his automobile insurance policy and explained to the Mobassars that their coverage would be limited to $100,000 of uninsured motorist coverage unless somebody could find the truck driver who caused the accident. She politely began asking Ghaniyah questions about what happened.

Alex studied the vacant look in Ghaniyah's eyes as her husband volunteered most of the answers. The imam's wife wore a traditional Muslim robe and a colorful scarf but no head covering. She used no makeup, and her thin face looked gaunt and extremely pale. Her most prominent feature was a long and slender nose, slightly hooked at the end. Khalid, sitting next to her, showed none of the hard edge Alex remembered from the hospital.

As Shannon gently prodded for details, Ghaniyah did her best to provide answers. She had been driving south on North Landing Road in Chesapeake, going to meet with some women who attended the mosque. She met with them most every Thursday.

Alex pretended to take a sip of the coffee and slid forward a little in his seat.

"I remember a large truck coming up behind me," Ghaniyah said. Her words were flat, as if she could barely summon enough energy to talk. "I saw the front grill in my rearview mirror, and I knew he was going to pass. When he started to go around me, I saw another car coming."

Ghaniyah shrugged and looked past Shannon, as if trying to see the accident happen. "I tried to slow down, but the truck couldn't get by fast enough and came back into my lane, so I swerved to the right. . . ."

Her voice trailed off, and Khalid touched her shoulder gently. "She remembers heading toward a tree, and that's basically the last thing she remembers," he explained. He talked as if Ghaniyah wasn't in the room. "The doctors say she's lucky the injuries weren't worse. In fact, she's fortunate to be alive."

For the next few minutes, Shannon peppered both of the Mobassars with more questions. Was the car totaled? Did Ghaniyah remember anything about the license plate number of the truck? the color? any writing on the side?

Ghaniyah apologized but couldn't remember much in the way of details. The cab was red, she remembered. And the trailer was white. There was writing on the side of the truck, but she couldn't remember what it said. Everything had happened so quickly. And there was a picture on the side as well—fruits, maybe vegetables. It was some kind of produce truck, maybe. Ghaniyah had no idea about the license plate number. She wasn't sure that she ever saw the back of the truck.

Her melancholy demeanor and pained expression were a stark contrast to Shannon's bubbly enthusiasm. "It's okay," Shannon told her. "You're doing great just remembering this much. Your main job is to get better."

When Shannon finished her questions, Alex pulled the contract from his file. Alex and Shannon had decided beforehand that he should be the one to present it, given the inclination toward male authority in the Muslim world.

As usual, he had actually brought two contracts along—he would first present the one that gave the firm one-third if they settled and 40 percent if they had to file suit. If the Mobassars balked, Alex would whip out a second contract with identical terms except the percentages were lower—25 percent if the case settled and one-third if they filed suit.

But as he watched Ghaniyah's lifeless demeanor and her husband's tender manner, Alex suddenly felt a little guilty for conspiring to take so much of his client's money. Unless they could find the truck driver, the Mobassars would recover a maximum of $67,000 after attorney's fees, an amount that probably wouldn't even cover the medical bills. And it looked like Ghaniyah might need some kind of long-term care unless she improved.

Alex put the contract with the smaller percentages on top. "I think we've got enough information to move forward," he said. "We need to let Mrs. Mobassar get some rest."

"Thank you," she said.

He nodded and gave her a smile.

He explained how contingency fee contracts worked—"We don't get paid unless we win"—and told Khalid that it was important that the firm get started on the investigation right away. "You can read it if you want—" Alex shrugged, eyeing the two-page contract as if it were a copy of *War and Peace*—"but most people just sign."

"I'm sorry," Khalid said as Alex handed him the contract. "But I've learned to read everything. Is it okay?"

"Of course."

"Would you like another piece of baklava?" Ghaniyah asked.

"No, I'm good. But it was great."

Alex and Shannon waited in awkward silence as Khalid reviewed each provision of the contract. To make it worse, Khalid's cell phone rang; he answered it, asked Alex and Shannon to excuse him for a second, and took the phone into a different room. They could hear him speaking rapidly in Arabic.

After Khalid left, Ghaniyah just stared straight ahead, and Alex started talking to Shannon about the case just to ease the awkwardness. Alex thought about how natural it was to talk as if the person with brain damage wasn't even in the room.

When Khalid returned, he apologized and seemed distracted. "Where do we sign?" he asked, without reading another word.

Alex showed him and soon had the signatures of both Khalid and Ghaniyah. "Is her signature in this condition valid?" Khalid asked.

"I'm not sure," Alex admitted. "But that's why we had you sign it too."

Khalid seemed ready to wrap up the meeting. He thanked Alex and Shannon, told Ghaniyah that he would see the guests to the door, and stepped outside with the two lawyers.

"She says she's fine," Khalid explained. "And I think that one of Allah's blessings in all of this is that Ghaniyah doesn't know how badly injured she is." Khalid paused and appeared uncertain about how much of his private life he should reveal. "Sometimes, when she gets dressed, she puts her blouse on backward." He looked down, as if he was a little ashamed of talking about his wife behind her back. "She can't remember the simple things in the morning. One thing she can remember, but not two things in sequence. I have to tell her—brush your teeth . . . brush your hair . . . take a shower.

"Her personality . . . she used to be so . . ." He struggled to find the word. "So forceful . . . in a good way. Opinionated. Outgoing. It's like somebody took that woman and replaced her with someone I don't know."

Khalid looked from Alex to Shannon and back to Alex. "I know you can't fix all that . . . but I just wanted you to understand that . . . well, I don't know what to do."

"We understand," Shannon said. "And I can promise you that we're going to do everything in our power to get her as much help as possible from this case."

"Thank you," Khalid said.

It struck Alex that the man might know how to speak multiple languages and how to cope with the political chaos of a country like Lebanon. But when it came to living with a spouse who had a brain injury, Khalid was in uncharted waters.

"And, Mr. Madison," Khalid said to Alex, looking his new lawyer directly in the eye, "I might appreciate a few of those prayers after all."

16

ALEX HEADED STRAIGHT HOME after his meeting with the Mobassars and didn't feel the least bit guilty about it. Shannon would undoubtedly head back to the office, but Alex had long ago stopped trying to keep up with her. He wanted to get in an hour or two of surfing before it got too late. He assuaged his conscience by reminding himself that he had landed a big new case today and could always bill a few hours at his home computer later if he got inspired.

Right after he changed into a pair of board shorts and a ratty T-shirt, his BlackBerry started vibrating. He was ready to hit ignore but checked the caller ID first. *Shannon.*

"Please tell me you're not back at the office," Alex said.

"I like this guy," Shannon answered, ignoring Alex's statement. She had perfected that part of her job. "Have you Googled Khalid?"

He hadn't, of course. But why would he need to with the obsessive Shannon Reese for a partner? "What'd you find?" Alex asked.

"Interesting stuff. He lost a son who was working in a refugee camp when the Israelis bombed Lebanon in 1996 as part of Operation Grapes of Wrath. For a while he became an outspoken supporter of Hezbollah. But eighteen months later, he lost his second son during a suicide bombing mission in southern Israel.

"And here's the really intriguing thing: instead of fueling Khalid's hate for the Israelis, this somehow mellowed him. He became a leading voice for an Islamic reformation and an outspoken opponent of those who preached violence and jihad. He came to the U.S. on a teaching visa about five years ago and started the mosque in Norfolk."

Alex was delighted to see Shannon's growing enthusiasm for the case. But most of this information seemed irrelevant. "And this helps us how?" Alex asked, slipping into his Chacos.

"Credibility. I mean, the only evidence we have that there's a John Doe vehicle is the testimony of Ghaniyah Mobassar. The defense will never say it, but they're going to play the Muslim card, painting the Mobassars as radicals who can't be trusted. I'm just saying—they're not that way."

"Good," Alex said. "I'm glad you like these guys. Now, why don't you go home and get a life."

"This *is* my life. Somebody around here's got to work for a living."

◁▷

Two hundred fifty miles to the north, on the outskirts of Washington, D.C., Hassan Ibn Talib was also thinking about Khalid Mobassar. It had been nearly a week since Hassan had received the text message from Mobassar's phone. This weekend, he would complete the assignment and send a one-word message in response: *Finished*.

Afterward, he would toss his phone into the river, get a new phone, and wait for further instructions. These honor killings, he knew, were just the beginning.

17

HASSAN WAS in the fourth grade when he first had the dream. It came the night after he betrayed his best friend, Mukhtar.

The two skinny Muslim boys had been walking home from school together, trying to pretend they weren't nervous as they crossed through a neighborhood where a gang of Sunni Muslims hung out. Hassan had grown up hearing about the Lebanese civil war between the Christians and Muslims, but to a nine-year-old, those conflicts were ancient history. In real life, Hassan was less afraid of the Christians than of the Sunni Muslims, especially the gang of older boys who sometimes surrounded Hassan on his way home from school, demanding money and threatening him with his life if he ever told his parents.

Once, they had stopped Hassan when he had no money. They made him turn his pockets inside out and pushed him back and forth between them, shouting curses at him. They waived a knife in front of his face. "Don't ever come here again empty-handed, *lout*!" One kid stepped forward and kicked Hassan between the legs, causing the most intense pain Hassan had ever experienced. He yelped and collapsed in a ball on the sidewalk.

The boys laughed. "Maybe he will talk like a girl now," one of the boys teased. As they walked away, one of the boys spit on him.

Since then, Hassan had learned to save up portions of his lunch money, even though it meant going hungry a few days a week. It was the price of peace on the streets of Beirut.

On this day, wearing a white shirt and his hand-me-down black pants, he felt relatively safe. He was walking with Mukhtar, and he had a few Lebanese lirat in his pocket, enough to keep the bullies at bay. Hassan hated himself when he paid them, and he always dreamed the rest of the way home that one day he would stand up to them and fight. But he knew the next time they met, he would pay them again.

When Mukhtar saw the Sunni boys hanging out on a street corner several blocks away, he nudged Hassan, and they quickly crossed the street. They both fell silent and walked a little faster, eyes fixed on the sidewalk in front of them.

One of the bullies called out to them, but Hassan and Mukhtar refused to acknowledge him. Walking faster, Hassan watched the boys out of the corner of his eye. They started strolling toward him and Mukhtar, a pack of four or five of them. There were no adults around—no help on the horizon.

When the Sunnis shouted again for Hassan and Mukhtar to stop, Hassan bolted. He had good speed for a fourth grader, and in a few steps, he had left Mukhtar behind. Adrenaline fueled his body, causing Hassan's heart to pump wildly, his shoes barely touched the pavement as he sprinted for his life. He could hear the Sunnis chasing him, shouting curses as they ran. Apartments and shops flashed past, and Hassan glanced over his shoulder. The boys were gaining!

He cut across a side street, dodging between cars and forcing a taxi driver to slam on the brakes. Horns blared. The older boys gained ground. Hassan took a sharp left turn, but one of the boys anticipated the move and had the angle on him.

Hassan stopped, circling back to the right. He saw a small convenience store half a block away—close enough that he might be able to get there first. He sprinted toward the store, bounding up the steps just before the fastest of the Sunnis arrived.

Hassan burst into the store, panting, one of the boys right behind him. Before Hassan could say a thing, the shopkeeper barked at both of them. "Don't bring your roughhousing in here." The man was heavyset with small dark eyes, curly hair, and a two-day growth. "You knock over something, and you've just bought it!"

"We're just getting something to drink," the Sunni boy said, catching his breath. He slung his arm around Hassan's shoulders, and Hassan felt the sharp point of a knife in his ribs. Fear paralyzed him for a moment, and the older boy pushed him toward the back corner of the store.

"How much you got?" the kid whispered. He had cold eyes and dark, curly hair. He was wearing braces, and the metal gleamed when he smiled. It gave Hassan the chills.

Hassan reached into his pocket and retrieved the lirat. His attacker looked at them and frowned. Another Sunni entered the store.

The braces kid snatched the lirat from Hassan's hand, his knife still pressing against Hassan's ribs. The kid stuffed the money in his pocket and put his arm around Hassan, pulling him close. "We're goin' now," he said under his breath. "Give me any trouble and I'll start slicing off body parts."

Terrified, Hassan left the store in step with his captor. The other kid joined them outside. A block away, Hassan saw other Sunnis pushing Mukhtar into an alley.

Once the kid with braces had pulled Hassan a half block away from the entrance to the store, he waved the knife in front of Hassan's face. "You ever seen a dog neutered?" he asked.

Hassan shook his head quickly.

"If you ever run from me again, or if you tell anybody about today, you won't have to see it, 'cause you'll know what it *feels* like."

Hassan nodded, his eyes wide with fright. He could hear Mukhtar begging for mercy in the alley. Then he heard the thump of fist on bone and Mukhtar begging for them to stop.

"Get out of my sight, you Shiite dog," the older boy hissed at Hassan. He pushed Hassan backward, and Hassan tumbled to the pavement. Both boys kicked Hassan and made barking noises as he scrambled to his feet.

Hassan turned and stumbled away from his assailants. He glanced over his shoulder when he heard wails of pain from the alley. He stopped—torn between fear and his loyalty to Mukhtar.

"Get out of here!" the kid with braces yelled. He took a step toward Hassan, who tripped backward, turned, and started running. The tears stung his eyes and rolled down his cheeks as he sprinted away, too terrified to stop, too intimidated to try to get help for Mukhtar. His friend's screams faded in the distance as Hassan made his way to the safety of the Shiite neighborhoods.

Mukhtar would not return to school for two days. He told his parents he had been mugged by two grown men looking for money. When Mukhtar did come back, he and Hassan started taking the long way home, avoiding the Sunni neighborhood altogether. Though Mukhtar said he didn't blame Hassan for running away, their friendship was never the same.

Whether or not Mukhtar blamed him, Hassan blamed himself. The night of the assault, he lay awake in his bed, thinking back to his mother's description of hell. Her face had been stern and somber, her eyes so intense that Hassan had to look away. "In hell, there are flames so hot that the skin will melt from your bones. You will wail and gnash your teeth, but there will be no relief from the fire and the unquenchable pain. Once your skin is burned from your body, another layer will appear, and the process starts over again." His mother paused, and it seemed she was on the verge of tears. Hassan wanted to hug her, tell her it would be all right. "I don't want any of you to ever be in such a horrible place," she said.

At the time, Hassan had wished he could assure his mother that he would live in such a way that hell would never be an option. But now, after turning his back on Mukhtar, Hassan realized for sure that he had been destined for hell all along.

His works would never save him; Hassan knew that much. His only glimmer of hope came from another lesson—the story of Imam Hussein and those who followed in his footsteps as shahids—martyrs for the faith. "No matter what you have done wrong in this life, you will be forgiven with the first drop of your blood that is spilt. To die a martyr is to never die at all."

And shahids, Hassan knew, were not just saved from the great horror of the Day of Judgment; they were given the crown of virtue and a place in Jannah along with seventy-two black-eyed women.

It was, Hassan had thought when he first heard the concept, quite an impressive list of benefits, though he couldn't understand why any shahid would want to be bothered with seventy-two women. But by the fourth grade, Hassan's thinking on the seventy-two women had begun to change as well.

The night of the assault, he tossed and turned, as if roasting over the flames of hell already. He wanted to tell his parents what had happened, but he knew they would confront the other boys and their families. The Sunnis would bide their time, but sooner or later they would exact their revenge. Visions of the knife flashed through Hassan's head.

The house had been quiet for hours before Hassan finally fell asleep.

◁ ▷

Hassan sat on a powerful black horse, the tents of his family and friends scattered around him in the intense heat of the desert. He held a sarif—a heavy, two-sided Muslim sword—in his right hand. His chest glistened with sweat and rippled with muscles. The heat shimmered over sandy dunes, engulfing the armies that surrounded the camp in a mind-warping haze. There were thousands of them— Jews, Americans, infidels of all nationalities. But mostly, there were Sunni Muslims, hordes of them on foot, some with knives and spears, others with bows and arrows, all with bloodshot eyes. A handful of other warriors came out of their tents and mounted horses, joining Hassan as the opposing armies closed in.

Hassan looked to his left and right, nodded, then reared his stallion back and led the charge. The eyes of his enemies grew large with fear, some throwing down their weapons and turning to run.

Hassan rode through them all, swinging the sarif left and right, each deadly arc severing the head of another infidel soldier. The warriors following him started chanting, *"Allahu akbar! Allahu akbar!"*

The battlefield turned chaotic. Swords and spears and arrows flew all around Hassan as his Shiite brothers dropped from their horses, soaking the ground with their blood. He felt a stab of pain as an arrow pierced his own chest, dropping him from his horse, and he looked down to see his own blood flowing. The hordes surrounded him, raising their spears to finish him off, their eyes demonic in victory. And then . . . a blinding light, just before everything became calm. He looked ahead and saw the golden carpet and the magnificent throne of Allah.

Paradise!

Heavenly power coursed through his veins, healing every wound, his heart beating with joy. He had done it! A martyr! He had become al-shahid!

He stood now as Allah held the scales, Hassan's bad deeds weighing down the left side, his heart sinking within him. But then Allah reached his right hand above the other side of the scales and gently opened his fingers, releasing drops of precious blood, followed by a broad smile. He set the scales down and, as Hassan knelt before the throne, placed the crown of virtue on Hassan's head.

A chant began from all sides, first as a low rumble and then as a booming echo, filling all of paradise. *"Islam zindabad! Allahu akbar!"*

The crescendo only stopped when Allah raised his hand. "Al-shahid!" he bellowed, his voice filling the air like thunder. "Welcome to your reward!"

18

HASSAN JERKED AWAKE and was half out of bed before he could gather his thoughts. Feet on the floor, he looked at the clock: 3:30 a.m. He felt his heart pounding, the images still vivid in his mind. His childhood dream had returned, as it often did the night before a gruesome assignment. But it had been different tonight, distorted by what lay ahead.

He had again been riding through the armies of infidels, wielding his sarif, severing heads. But this time, in the midst of the conflict, he had been surrounded by women and children, even infants. Nevertheless, he kept fighting until he felt the piercing arrows enter his body.

When he appeared before the throne of Allah, there was no chanting. Hassan bowed his head, mindful of the women and children he had killed.

Once again, Allah had dropped Hassan's blood on the scales and placed the crown of virtue on his head. But rather than thundering his approval, Allah's voice was soothing, his sad eyes registering his approval. "Only my loyal Hassan would complete such a difficult task," he said tenderly. "Welcome to your reward."

Hassan shook away the lingering images and turned on his light. He put on a pair of shorts and walked out onto the second-floor balcony. The parking lot was quiet at this hour, the night air muggy and thick. He took a deep breath and looked up to the heavens, asking Allah for courage and discernment.

The task ahead was more difficult than combat against armed

adversaries. When the enemy took the form of a pleading woman or when collateral damage included small children, Hassan's nerves and devotion were tested to the limits. He forced himself to look past the innocence in their eyes and into the darkness of their souls. Allah made no mistakes. Some were destined to die.

He went inside and got out a flint stone and his long, double-edged sword. He removed the sword from its brown leather scabbard. The blade glistened as it reflected the glare from the overhead light. He began stroking the edge of the sword with the flint, first one side and then the other. The sword was already razor sharp, but the task calmed his nerves and strengthened his resolve.

Perhaps Ja'dah Fatima Mahdi would repent and renounce her Christian faith. Perhaps Hassan could spare her life and deal only with Martin Burns, the infidel who led her astray. But if not, he could at least make her execution as painless and quick as possible.

He made a few more strokes with the flint.

The handle was made of steel covered with well-worn leather. The crosspiece was brass, polished so it reflected Hassan's face like a mirror. Hassan's name and a verse from the Qur'an were engraved on the upper end of the blade.

> Verily the promise of Allah is true: nor let those
> shake thy firmness who have no certainty of faith.
> Al Qur'an 30:60.

19

ALEX STRUGGLED to get out of bed Saturday morning and didn't make it to the Belvedere Coffee Shop until 8:15, fifteen minutes late for his weekly breakfast. He chained his beach cruiser to a bike rack in the parking lot and squeezed his way past the line of tourists that snaked out the door of the restaurant.

Inside, the coffee shop was cramped and narrow, about half the size of a typical Waffle House. Booths lined one wall, and about ten barstools faced a Formica-topped counter on the opposite side. The saving grace of the place was the wall of windows that surrounded the booths, giving nearly every diner a view of the beach. Alex had tried to talk his grandmother into other restaurants, but she was a creature of habit—greasy eggs, strong coffee, a big glass of orange juice, and a two-mile walk on the boardwalk. Rain or shine, unless Alex was out of town, he and Ramona met here on Saturday mornings.

His grandmother usually commandeered a booth, but today she was sitting at the counter. Her purse marked the stool next to hers as *taken*. She had on knee-length shorts, a T-shirt, and white sneakers. Her sunglasses hung around her neck on a sky blue Croakie.

"Sorry I'm late," Alex said, giving his grandmother a quick peck on the cheek.

She told him not to worry about it, then let the cook know they were ready for breakfast. Alex almost always ordered French toast, and his grandmother had already placed the order. The place smelled like grease, and Alex tried not to watch the cooks manning the grill in front of him.

"You look tired," Ramona said.

"I'm fine."

"How much sleep are you getting?"

Alex dumped three creamers into his coffee and took a gulp. He didn't like lying to his grandmother, so he decided to dodge the question. "I don't need much."

His grandmother shook her head. "Too little sleep makes you irritable, intellectually sluggish, and overweight."

"Overweight?" Alex asked, his voice still husky. He had never had a problem with weight in his life, and he typically slept only about five hours a night. After a good day of surfing, you could count his ribs.

"That's what they say." Ramona neglected to mention who "they" were. "Of course in your case, metabolism overrides the normal rules of nature."

Ramona pulled a folded copy of a page from the *Tidewater Times* out of her purse and placed it on the counter next to Alex. "I know you don't get the paper, so I brought this for you."

Alex glanced at the story on the local news page about Aisha's case. He had already read it online, but he thanked his grandmother anyway. They talked about the case for a few minutes, and then Ramona gave him updates on various church members—who needed what kind of surgery, financial hardships for several others, compliments she had heard about Alex's sermons.

But hearing the second-hand compliments also brought to mind the murmuring Alex knew was out there. In the months following Alex's unexpected call to ministry, the church had grown at a somewhat dizzying rate, climbing from sixty to nearly ninety. But recently things had plateaued, then slowly declined, and the church members had started taking sides. The older women all loved Alex, as did the handful of teenagers. But a few of the deacons blamed the lethargic attendance on the absence of a full-time pastor. Alex wanted to get his grandmother's take on the situation but decided he should wait until they got outside, where they could talk without sitting elbow to elbow with complete strangers.

After they finished eating and Ramona paid the bill, they left the restaurant for their Saturday morning power walk. They headed down the boardwalk toward the south end of Virginia Beach.

There were bikers and skaters sailing by on the bike path, runners grinding it out on the boardwalk, and lots of tourists lining the various hotel and restaurant patios and verandas. The heat was stifling, but there was a mild ocean breeze. Despite the conditions, his grandmother never messed around on these walks, keeping up a pace that might qualify as a slow run for some. She pumped her arms to complete her full-body workout.

For a few minutes, they walked in silence, and Alex considered whether to even broach his concerns about the church. He hated to worry his grandmother, and he knew his preaching was a great source of pride to her. But he also wondered if it wasn't time for South Norfolk Community Church to hire somebody who actually knew what he was doing.

Though he had the bloodline for the ministry, Alex would be the first to admit that he became the pastor of South Norfolk Community more by accident than by calling.

His dad had been a pastor, a church planter who spent two or three years getting a church off the ground so he could pass the reins to a less-restive man. His last church had been in the suburbs of Las Vegas, the ministry cut short when a drunk driver had killed Alex's mother and father on a rainy Friday night. Alex, an only child, was in sixth grade.

After the funerals, Alex had moved in with his grandparents in Virginia Beach, where his free spirit met its match in the strict discipline of Ramona Madison. Alex's grandfather had little time for church in the midst of his busy law practice, but Ramona was there every Sunday with Alex in tow, even during his rebellious teenage years. As soon as church ended, Alex would grab his surfboard and head to the beach.

He never once dreamed of being a pastor.

But two years ago, at his grandfather's funeral, Alex climbed the steps of the platform, stood behind the podium, and quietly eulogized one of the most galvanizing men that had ever graced the doors of the church. He used his grandfather's Bible, particularly the margin notes his grandfather had written, as a road map to his grandfather's life. Later, Ramona would tell Alex that some of the church members didn't even know his grandfather had owned a Bible.

Alex told the rapt audience about the conversation he'd had with his grandfather the night before his death. Though Alex had not been ready to lose him, John Patrick Madison was ready to go. With no regrets. "The test of faith is not just whether it helps you live well," Alex said as he concluded the eulogy. "The real test of faith is whether it allows you to die well."

South Norfolk Community was without a pastor at the time, and Alex's stirring eulogy was followed by a mediocre message from a retired pastor who now lived out of town. Not one person thought that Alex had been outpreached.

The next week, a fill-in preacher called at the last minute to cancel. One of the deacons asked Ramona if Alex could take his place for just that week. One week led to two, which led to a month. Six months later, after three candidates had turned the church down, the pastoral search committee disbanded. The board of deacons ordained Alex to preach.

A second job for which he lacked a diploma.

"Can I ask you a question?" Alex said, matching his grandmother stride for stride.

"Of course."

"Do you think it might be time for me to step aside at the church?"

Alex half-expected the question to draw some kind of dramatic response. Maybe his grandmother would quit walking altogether and look at him like he'd lost his mind. Maybe she would launch into a big think-of-the-lost-souls pep talk. Maybe she would wax philosophical about God's will and the building of Christ's church.

She did none of those things. She took the question in stride, as if Alex had merely asked about her favorite restaurant. "Why do you ask?"

"I don't know. It just seems like maybe we're stuck as a church. I know some folks would rather have a full-time pastor. Maybe we need someone with a little more experience and I should stick to the law."

"Is that what you want to do?"

Alex looked at his grandmother and frowned. "What is this, a counseling session? You're answering every question with one of your own."

"Am I?"

Alex chuckled. "Seriously, Grandma. What do you think?"

They were coming up on a spot behind the Hilton Hotel now, just under the shadow of the giant statue of King Neptune rising up out of the boardwalk. The tourists were thick here, and the two of them had to weave in and out.

"First of all, the people who are complaining have always complained. They complained when we changed the color of the pews. They've complained about every full-time pastor we've ever had. You can't listen to them, Alex. You've got a gift. Your dad had it too. You're every bit as good of a preacher as he ever was. You inspire people, make them think. . . ."

She paused, and Alex sensed there was more. They'd been together so long, he felt like he could read her mind.

"But . . . ?" Alex prompted.

"What makes you think there's a *but*?"

"I'm a Madison, Grandma. I've got thick skin. Tell me the rest."

She glanced at him, then returned her focus straight ahead. "Okay." She hesitated for a moment, gathering her thoughts. "You're young, Alex. And sometimes people get the feeling that maybe you haven't figured out whether you're totally committed to this. People want to follow someone with convictions, not questions. Smooth eloquence can never take the place of unwavering belief."

They walked in silence for a few minutes as Alex digested that assessment. If anyone else had said those things, Alex would have been defensive. But his grandmother was such an encourager. She always had his best interest at heart. There was a Bible verse someplace that said the wounds of a friend are better than the kisses of an enemy.

She was speaking the truth. Alex just didn't know what to do with it.

"It's a matter of calling," his grandmother said, as if reading his mind. "You know that list your grandfather made—the one with some things to keep in mind at the firm."

"Sure."

"What was the last item on the list?"

Alex didn't hesitate; he looked at the list every day. "'If you've been called to be a lawyer, don't stoop to be a king.'"

"The same thing applies to pastors, you know," Ramona said. She was getting a little winded now. They usually didn't talk much when they walked. "You've just got to figure out what you're called to do."

The way she said it signaled that the conversation was over. She picked up the pace and pumped her arms a little faster. Alex hoped that the tourists would be nimble enough to stay out of the way of Ramona Madison.

20

COMPARED TO THE COMPLEXITY of Hassan's missions in the Middle East, capturing Ja'dah Fatima Mahdi was almost too easy. On Saturday night, he followed her from her home to the out-of-the-way parking lot of an abandoned Home Depot store. Ja'dah parked in the far corner of the lot, well away from any other vehicles, and left the car idling. After watching her routine the week before, Hassan knew she would be changing clothes.

He stayed on a side street out of her line of sight for about two minutes, just enough time for her to be in the middle of changing, and then crossed the parking lot and drove straight toward her. As he approached, he watched her scramble to put on a blouse and button a few buttons. He pulled in next to her, his SUV heading in the opposite direction from her vehicle.

Hassan smiled and rolled down his window. "Can you tell me how to get to the Marriott Hotel at the oceanfront?" he asked, using a heavy Lebanese accent. He raised his hands to show his confusion, a bewildered expression on his face. This was the risky part. If she drove away now, Hassan would let her go and resort to plan B—kidnapping her on the way home from church. But he was counting on her desire to be nice to confused strangers.

She initially seemed surprised and a little confused by the request. Hassan asked again, a little louder. He turned off his SUV's engine.

Ja'dah's window was halfway down, a polite smile on her lips. Her eyes showed apprehension, but she did not bolt. "I'm sorry," she said.

"I'm not all that familiar with this area. But if you get back on the inter-
state . . ." She motioned behind her.

"How do I do that?" Hassan asked. He checked his mirrors just to
be safe. There was nobody in the vicinity, nobody watching them.

"Get back on this road and make a left—"

Before she could finish, Hassan threw open his door and jumped
out, pointing a gun through Ja'dah's window. "Don't move."

His actions were so sudden, the gun so unexpected, that it froze
Ja'dah for a second, enough time for Hassan to reach inside her door
and open it. He slammed his own car door shut with his foot. "Don't
say a word," he growled.

She stared at him, wide-eyed, shaking her head, the tears starting.

"Move over," he ordered, already cramming himself into the
driver's seat.

Clumsily, Ja'dah climbed over the console and into the passenger
seat, on top of the folded Muslim clothes she had placed there. Hassan
grabbed her left bicep and pointed the gun at the back of her head.
"Bend over," he said.

"Don't hurt me," she begged.

"Do as I say."

He pushed her head down, and she let out a whimper of pain. He
placed the gun on the console and wrenched her arms behind her,
binding her wrists with a thick plastic tie, which he pulled tight. She
winced as it bit into the skin. He pushed her back in the seat and
strapped the seat belt around her. Then he took a pair of sunglasses
out of his pocket and put them on her.

"Don't take these off," he said. He pulled a baseball cap out of his
waistband and put it on Ja'dah's head so that the bill came down low
over her eyes. "This either."

He picked up the gun and kept the barrel lodged in Ja'dah's ribs as
he drove out of the parking lot and took back roads toward Sandbridge,
a small beach community about ten miles south of the main Virginia
Beach strip. He drove in silence, ignoring Ja'dah's trembling questions
about where they were headed and why he was doing this.

Halfway to Sandbridge, Ja'dah began to sob, then tried to fight back the tears. To Hassan, it sounded as if she was praying under her breath, whether to Jesus or Allah, he did not know.

Once they arrived in Sandbridge, he would find out.

21

IT WAS DUSK when Hassan arrived at the Sandbridge beach house. The sun painted pastels over the small bay that bordered the two-mile-wide strip of land covered with vacation homes. He parked in the car-port, checked in all directions, and duct-taped Ja'dah's mouth before he moved her into the ground floor of the house. He dragged her into a corner of the rec room and shoved her to the floor, then pulled out another thick plastic tie and cinched it around her ankles. He left the duct tape over her mouth for the time being and avoided looking into her eyes.

Hassan had already moved all of the furniture to one side of the room, stacking the barstools next to the pool table and wicker furniture, and had covered the floor and the bottom half of the wall with heavy plastic. He had pulled the blinds and turned on an overhead light. The room was now quiet except for Ja'dah's ragged breathing.

He squatted in front of her. "I am about to perform the evening salat," he said softly. "Will you join me?"

Ja'dah's eyes were rimmed with tears and wide with fright. She shook her head quickly. Decisively.

Hassan rose without speaking and headed to the wet bar at the far end of the room. He washed quickly. First his hands—right, then left. Then his face three times. His mouth. His nose. A dash of water to his hair and beard. Next his arms, wrists to elbows. Last, he washed his feet.

He pulled a prayer mat from a nearby bedroom and unrolled it on the plastic in the middle of the floor, facing east, toward the ocean.

His melodic chants echoed off the walls, and soon he lost himself in the rhythmic worship of Allah. The prayers calmed his nerves. Strengthened his resolve. Deepened his convictions. At first, he was cognizant of Ja'dah watching his every move, trembling in fear. But soon enough, he became oblivious to her and lost himself in reverence.

He concluded his prayers, prostrate before Allah, and rose to his feet. Without speaking, he returned the prayer mat to the bedroom and knelt to face Ja'dah again. She had stopped sobbing and trembling. She regarded him with a mixture of curiosity and terror, her eyes locked on his.

"You have dishonored Allah," he said, his voice low but firm. "You have dishonored your family."

She shook her head again, and rage welled up in him. He grabbed her chin and squeezed, holding her head still. Her eyes popped open with a new wave of fear.

"You have become a prostitute," he sneered. "A whore of the West."

She didn't move, frozen by fear.

He let go of her chin, took a breath, and relaxed. "You must renounce the Christian faith and return to your family." His voice was again soft, a plea of reason. "Perhaps Allah will have mercy on your soul." Slowly, he reached out and stripped the duct tape from Ja'dah's mouth.

To her credit, she didn't try to scream or curse or otherwise lash out. Her lips shook, and when she spoke, her voice was barely audible. "I cannot," she stammered. "I am no longer a Muslim."

As she said these words, Ja'dah looked past Hassan, but then she gathered the strength to again look him in the eye. "Nor are you. The Holy Qur'an teaches submission, not the sword."

Enraged, Hassan slapped her. "'I will cast dread into the hearts of the unbelievers,'" he said, his voice staccato. "'Strike off their heads, and strike off all of their fingertips.'" He was quoting Sura 8:12, the words of the Prophet.

"That is not what that Sura means," Ja'dah responded, her voice soft but certain. "I can quote Suras on mercy and forgiveness. Islam is submission to Allah. I have submitted to the God I hear."

Hassan did not react emotionally to the blasphemy. He would

not avenge the name of Allah in a fit of rage. His convictions were grounded in the certainty of the Prophet's words and the faithfulness of a warrior's heart. He was an instrument for Allah, nothing more.

"Renounce," he said simply.

"I cannot."

He shook his head in pity. She was a beautiful woman, full of courage and conviction. He could understand why Fatih Mahdi had chosen her. He had to protect his own heart from desiring her even now.

"Then you must pay."

Ja'dah Fatima Mahdi did not respond.

Hassan rose and went into the adjacent bedroom to retrieve his sword. Returning to the rec room, in plain sight of Ja'dah, he removed the weapon from its sheath and placed it on the floor. Light reflected from the polished metal. Hassan studied his captive. Staring at the sword, her eyes glistened with tears.

He dragged her to the middle of the room and raised her into a kneeling position. He picked up the sword.

He had expected her to collapse in fear. She had been shaking almost uncontrollably as he pulled her to the middle of the room. But now, she seemed to find a new resolve. She looked straight ahead and closed her eyes. The trembling stopped. She held her head high, her hands still tied behind her back, her neck an easy target.

Somehow, in these last few moments, she had found the courage to accept her fate with dignity. She was still wrong. Still an infidel. Still destined for Allah's wrath. But in that moment, Hassan couldn't help but admire her.

He took a breath, whispered a quick prayer, then swung the sword in a giant arc, its swoosh filling the room as it sliced through the air. Ja'dah kept her eyes closed, her head held high, and let out a muffled shriek of terror.

He stopped the sword—inches from her neck.

She froze for a second in a state of shock, then collapsed to the floor. She curled into the fetal position, her knees tight to her chest.

Hassan knelt next to her.

"Renounce," he whispered into her ear.

Ja'dah lay trembling for a moment, as if enduring a seizure that his words could not penetrate. After a few seconds, she grew still.

"Renounce," he insisted.

She opened her eyes and tilted her head slightly to face him. Her eyes hardened, and she gave him a small shake of the head.

Hassan shook his own head in sadness and disappeared once more into the ground-floor bedroom. This time, he returned with a black hood and placed it over Ja'dah's head. He pulled her back to her knees, held her there with one hand, and said a final prayer. *Was this truly what Allah required?*

Hearing nothing, he stepped back to swing the sword again. Just as he did in his dreams, this time he would swing with all his might. There could be no mercy. The sword would complete its deadly arc, and Mahdi's honor would be restored.

"Allahu akbar," he said as the sword sliced through the air.

22

FOLLOWING THE EXECUTION, Hassan did not allow himself the luxury of emotion. There was nothing to celebrate, nothing to mourn. He was only following Allah's will. There was still much to be done.

The marriage between Ja'dah and Fatih Mahdi could now be expunged. It would be as if she had never existed. The gruesome manner of her death would strike fear into the hearts of other Muslim women who were considering dishonoring their families. At the same time, it would repulse and terrorize Americans, reminding them that there were jihadists among them, here on American soil.

Beheadings were commonplace in parts of the Middle East, an accepted form of capital punishment. But in America, they were regarded as a grotesque novelty, one that would have the media chattering for months. Muslim scholars and moderate imams would condemn the brutality and claim Islam was a religion of peace.

But radicals like Hassan would be energized by it. A personal attack deep in the heart of the enemy's territory. A clinical strike. One that would frustrate millions because the agents of the Great Satan would never find the responsible party. On the other hand, Hassan would make sure the bodies were found, even though they would never be traced back to him.

Though Ja'dah's death would be repulsive to Americans, in truth she did not suffer. Hassan hadn't wanted her to. She was courageous, though misguided. He understood her resolve and commitment, a reflection of his own. She was in many ways a victim. The one who shouldered the greater part of the blame was this man named

Martin Burns, an infidel who had lusted after a Muslim woman and led her astray.

For him, death would not come so easily. Ja'dah's beheading would deter other Muslim women, but Hassan needed something just as strong to deter American men. Martin Burns had to suffer. He needed to die in a way that would play on the fears of Americans, something that would command the attention of even those who gorged themselves on Hollywood horror movies. And Hassan wanted to create some religious symbolism as well. It would be a shame that the irony would be lost on most.

Using Ja'dah's cell phone, Hassan sent a text message at about 8:30 p.m., timed to coincide with the ending of the Beach Bible worship service. Ja'dah had not programmed Martin Burns's cell number into her contact list, but Hassan had done his homework. Burns was a real estate broker, and Hassan had called his place of business earlier that week, pretending to be a new client anxious to talk. It had not been hard to get Burns's cell number. Greed was a handy tool in dealing with Americans.

The text message was simple.

We need 2 talk privately. It's important. Can we meet?

He didn't sign Ja'dah's name. The call history on her phone showed several calls to Burns's number. Burns would recognize the source.

A few seconds later, Ja'dah's phone rang. Hassan let the call from Burns kick into voice mail. He waited a few seconds and then sent another text.

Can't talk on my cell. Can u meet with me? Please?

This time, Burns sent an immediate reply.

Sure. Where are you?

Hassan responded.

*I needed to get away. Very confused. Can u meet at the
parking lot at the far end of Sandbridge—by the Pavilion?*

Hassan assumed this might throw Burns a little. He was prepared
to meet the man anyplace private, but Sandbridge would make things
easier. Hassan also knew that every word of these text messages would
eventually be discovered by the authorities and would, in turn, help
them narrow their search for the bodies. It would be better if they
found the bodies before a great deal of decomposition.

Sandbridge?

It's a long story. I'll tell u when u get here.

Hassan waited. The phone vibrated.

On my way.

Hassan smiled. One more text message. This one, the most important of all.

Don't tell anyone, ok? I need this to be just u and me.

The response was exactly what Hassan had expected.

Of course.

23

AFTER A WEEKEND of preparing and delivering a sermon, Alex found it hard to get out of bed on Monday mornings. This week it didn't help that he was facing a mountain of paperwork to review, pleadings to draft, and phone calls to return. He arrived at the office at 9:30, only to find the doors still locked. It could only mean that Sylvia Brunswick had called in sick.

Again.

Alex unlocked the office, turned on the lights, and started a pot of coffee. As he expected, Sylvia had left a message on his voice mail, groaning as she told him about her incredibly painful migraine. She promised to try and come in tomorrow but said there was nothing she could do about it today.

She couldn't have picked a worse day to stay home. Alex had pleadings to file, including some answers to requests for admissions that absolutely had to be served that day. He would normally dictate the answers and let Sylvia worry about the details of typing them up and hand-delivering them to the other side. Now, that wasn't an option.

For the next hour and a half, Alex ignored his phone calls, resisted the urge to look at his e-mails, and typed away on his computer. When he finished and tried to print out the pleading, he discovered that the printer was low on toner. Just like Sylvia not to change the cartridge before she left Friday.

Alex replaced the toner, printed out the document, made some corrections, printed it again, and tried to run off duplicate copies. The copy machine jammed, and Alex spent ten minutes trying to get it back online. Eventually, he conceded defeat and resorted to copying each page on a small copier without an automatic feeder. A five-page pleading. Four copies. Twelve minutes.

He called Shannon's cell phone as he ran the copies one at a time, placing each page facedown on the glass.

"Sylvia called in sick," he told Shannon.

"I know. Migraine."

"Where are you?"

"Our branch office."

"Which is?"

"In my car on North Landing Road, near the site of the accident. I'm coming out here every morning I can this week, just to see if a truck fitting the description Ghaniyah gave us makes routine deliveries on this route."

Alex was stacking and stapling documents. The idea of a stakeout sounded like a long shot to him, a needle in a haystack. Even for Shannon, who sweated over every detail of a case, this was a little obsessive.

"So let me get this straight," Alex said. "You're sitting out there on North Landing Road, waiting for a white produce truck with a red cab to come along so you can follow it to wherever and question the driver about a hit-and-run accident?"

"I'm not really going to question anyone," Shannon said without sounding the least bit defensive. "I'm just going to take a few pictures and copy down the license plate."

Alex's BlackBerry buzzed with a different call. He didn't recognize the number and ignored it.

"I'll show the pictures to Ghaniyah," Shannon continued. "If that doesn't trigger anything, I'll subpoena the manifests from the truck company after we file our John Doe lawsuit. Maybe we'll get lucky and find some deliveries that would place the truck on North Landing Road at the time of Ghaniyah's accident."

"To be honest, it seems like a waste of time to me," said Alex, though he actually hoped she would prove him wrong. "Can't we hire somebody to do that?"

"One, we don't have the money. And two, I'm working on other files and making phone calls while I'm out here. I'll probably bill more than you today."

On that point, Alex couldn't argue. He talked to Shannon for a few more minutes while he assembled the pleadings. After ending the call, he tried to find labels that would work on manila envelopes. He searched his desk drawers, then Sylvia's. There were labels for file folders but no labels for large manila envelopes. He wanted to punch something. He had been working for nearly two hours on a simple task that should have taken thirty minutes. Sylvia's migraine was spreading.

Alex's BlackBerry buzzed again—the same unknown number as before. It had to be some kind of crisis. Reluctantly, he picked it up.

"Alex Madison."

"Mr. Madison, this is Khalid Mobassar. Thank you for answering my call."

"No problem," Alex said, still searching for the labels. The imam sounded a little tense. Maybe something had happened to Ghaniyah.

"There are two detectives from the Virginia Beach Police Department at my front door," Khalid said, his voice nearly a whisper. "They want to question me about a woman in our mosque who disappeared over the weekend. I told them I needed to call my lawyer first."

Alex stopped searching and focused on the phone call. It always made him nervous when the police wanted to question a client. "What do you know about this woman?"

"Her name is Ja'dah Fatima Mahdi. She is the wife of one of our leaders at the Islamic Learning Center. She has been missing since Saturday night."

"Are you a suspect or a person of interest?"

"I do not know."

Alex looked at his envelopes and second-guessed his decision to pick up the phone. It would probably be fine for Khalid to talk with the detectives. They probably just wanted information about the victim's family. But what if there was more to it? What if Khalid *was* a person of interest?

"Do you know anything about why she's missing?" Alex asked.

Khalid hesitated for a moment. "Not really." His voice became softer. "Nothing other than what I might have learned in confidence from Ja'dah or her husband."

"Which is what?"

"As their spiritual advisor, should I not keep that confidential?" Khalid asked.

Now it was getting complicated. "Maybe," Alex said. "Would it help them locate the woman?"

Khalid hesitated again. "I don't think so. But I don't actually know."

Alex sighed into the phone. This was not what he needed. Khalid might have information that would help the police. But there were issues of priest-penitent privilege involved, or whatever you call that privilege when it's a Muslim imam. And those issues tended to get messy. "Tell them you can't speak to them without your attorney present. Ask them to wait outside until I get there."

The next call, which came less than three minutes later, was not from Khalid but from a man who identified himself as Detective Sanderson. "Is this Mr. Madison?"

"Yes."

"Do you represent Mr. Mobassar?"

Not really, Alex thought. But this was no time for technicalities. "Yes."

"Good," Sanderson said, as if that would solve everything. "We're in the critical first forty-eight hours of a missing person investigation. We have reason to believe that the potential victim was taken against her will. And we think your client might have valuable information to help us find her kidnapper, but he says he can't talk to us—"

"Is he a person of interest?" Alex interrupted.

"At this stage, Mr. Madison, most everyone who knows the victim is a person of interest. But we'd like the opportunity to clear your client. And more importantly, we think he can help us find her before it's too late."

Alex thought about this for a moment. The line about clearing Khalid was something the cops said every time . . . just before they finagled a confession and slapped on the cuffs. But the part about helping them find this woman might be legit. Could he really sit by and tell his client to withhold information that would help the police find a kidnapped woman?

"I'll be there in half an hour," Alex said. "I'll want to talk with my client first. And I'll stop the questioning if I sense that you're trying to set him up."

"Time is of the essence, Mr. Madison. We really need to talk with him right away."

"What do you want to ask him?"

"I'd rather not say over the phone."

"Half an hour, then," Alex said. "It's the best I can do. And wait outside. I don't want you talking to him until I get there."

"We'll be in our squad car."

Alex pulled a pen out of his desk drawer and addressed the manila envelopes by hand. He would leave the documents on Sylvia's desk and call a courier service on his way to Khalid's house. He had a bad feeling about Khalid's "interview." In a kidnapping, the cops didn't usually question a family's spiritual advisor. They had something. And there was only one way to find out what it was.

24

ALEX SAT DOWN next to his client on a soft leather couch with old cushions that sagged under his weight. Alex felt like he was sitting on the floor, knees in the air. Unlike the detectives, Alex had removed his shoes out of respect. The officers took the two chairs in the room, the same ones Alex and Shannon had occupied last week.

The seating arrangement put Alex and Khalid at a definite psychological disadvantage. The officers were erect in their chairs, looking down at Alex and Khalid, who slouched into the couch like two schoolboys in the principal's office.

The female officer sat across from Khalid and leaned forward, a clear posture of aggression. She was thin and intense, midforties, with curly blonde hair, small blue eyes that seemed too close together, and a narrow face that looked like somebody had placed it in a vise and squeezed. Age wrinkles spread from the corners of her eyes and mouth, and her left eye was bloodshot. When Alex first shook her hand outside, she had introduced herself as Detective Brown.

"I'm Alex." He flashed a disarming smile. "Do you have a first name?"

"Yes."

Alex waited. . . . "O-kay . . . then," Alex said. *Guess I've discovered which one's the bad cop.*

Detective Sanderson sat directly across from Alex. He was a pleasant guy with clipped brown hair and a linebacker's build. He had a pug nose that made Alex think he might have been a boxer in his younger days. He placed a recorder on the table. "Mind if we record this?"

Alex put his own digital recorder next to it and turned it on. "I was going to ask the same thing."

Sanderson gave his partner a look that wasn't hard to read—*this guy's going to be a jerk*—and shrugged. "Suit yourself."

Detective Sanderson stated the names of everyone in attendance and the time and place of the interview, then assured Khalid that he could terminate the interview whenever he wanted.

"Is my client a suspect or a person of interest?" Alex asked. It was the same question he had asked over the phone, but he wanted a response on the record.

Brown gave him a sharp look, but Sanderson responded with a calm tone. "Right now, this is still a missing-person investigation. But to the extent we determine a crime has been committed, everyone who knows Ja'dah Fatima Mahdi will be a person of interest. So yes, that would include your client."

"Fair enough," Alex said.

The questions began innocently, mostly background questions about Khalid's relationship with Ja'dah and Fatih Mahdi. The two families had been part of the same mosque in Beirut and had resettled in the United States within six months of each other. The husband of the missing woman was a friend of Khalid's and a respected leader in the Islamic Learning Center. Ja'dah, a second wife, was fifteen years younger than her husband.

"When was the last time you spoke with either Fatih or Ja'dah?"

"I spoke with Fatih yesterday."

"Did he mention that his wife was missing?"

"Of course. He was distraught beyond words. He does not show emotion easily, but he was nearly beyond . . ." Khalid searched for the right word . . . "beyond being reassured. Beyond comforting. He was worried that something had happened to Ja'dah. That maybe she had been kidnapped. Maybe she ran away with someone else, never to return."

"Do you have any idea where Ja'dah might go if she was trying to get away from her husband? Does she have friends or family in other parts of the U.S.?"

Khalid thought for a moment, the kind of hesitation that Alex coached his witnesses to avoid. "I don't know," he said. "And honestly, I cannot imagine her leaving Fatih. Not on her own."

"Really?" Brown asked sarcastically. "You can't think of any reason she might want to leave him?"

Khalid looked puzzled, shaking his head.

"What happened to Fatih's first wife?"

Khalid hesitated again, and Alex made a mental note; they would have to work on this. "She was unfaithful to Fatih. He put her away."

"What does that mean?" Brown asked. "'Put her away'?" She emphasized the words, as if Khalid had been talking about putting an animal to sleep.

Khalid kept his voice pleasant, though Alex could see his neck muscles tighten. "Under Lebanese law, he obtained a divorce," Khalid said evenly. "Under Sharia law, it is as if he was never married."

"And you're saying the grounds for this . . . 'putting away' . . . was infidelity?" Brown asked.

"Yes, I believe it was."

Brown checked some notes and gave Khalid a cold stare. "And is it true that under Sharia law, if a woman claims she is raped, she must provide four witnesses or she is presumed to be unfaithful?"

Khalid mulled this over as if it were a trick question. Alex was glad the interview wasn't being videotaped.

"First, I should point out that Lebanon does not operate under Sharia law," Khalid explained. "In Lebanon, Sharia law is more like a moral code that some Muslims follow. So in Lebanon, what you say would not be true. In some countries, such as Pakistan, this could well be the case." Khalid paused, looking unsure of exactly how much he should say. "However, in the case of which we speak, there is little doubt that Fatih's wife was unfaithful."

This response triggered a number of follow-up questions by Brown, insinuating that Fatih had something to do with Ja'dah's disappearance. Khalid steadfastly defended his friend. No, Fatih was not known for a violent temper. Yes, Fatih truly loved his wife. Fatih was a man of truth, Khalid said. His words could be trusted.

"Is Fatih Mahdi a suspect?" Alex asked. It was an obvious question, but he was looking for a chance to inject himself into the conversation.

"Should he be?" Brown looked at Khalid.

"No." Khalid insisted. He sat up straighter and leaned forward but then stopped as if catching himself. "It is not possible that Fatih would do anything to harm her." He looked first at Detective Brown, then at Sanderson, seemingly searching for someone who believed him.

"To the best of your knowledge, is Ja'dah Mahdi a loyal follower of Mohammed?" Brown asked.

The question seemed to throw Khalid off stride. The imam looked at Alex. "I cannot answer that question without revealing my conversations with Ja'dah and Fatih," he said tentatively.

Though Khalid's comment had been directed at Alex, it was Sanderson who jumped on it. "You didn't seem to be concerned about that a few minutes ago when you told us how distraught Fatih was when he talked to you."

Khalid's eyes widened, a deer in the headlights.

"That's different," Alex said. "That wasn't a counseling situation. These other conversations apparently were."

"Are you kidding?" Brown asked sharply. "That wasn't counseling? Fatih Mahdi comes to the imam here and says my wife is missing and I don't know what to do, and that's not counseling?"

Alex tried to slide forward a little to match Brown's aggressive posture, but the sagging couch made it difficult. "Regardless," he said, "I'm instructing my client not to divulge any private conversations between himself and either Ja'dah Mahdi or Fatih Mahdi."

"Let me be clear," Brown retorted, slicing off her words. "We're trying to find a woman who could be in grave danger, and the next twenty-four hours are critical. We believe your client has information that can help us. And now you're saying that your client's conversations with the very woman who is missing are somehow privileged? Don't you think that maybe she'd be willing to waive that privilege if it might help us find her?"

"We don't know," Alex said. "And spiritual advisors can't ignore the privilege based on assumptions."

Brown shook her head and grunted her disapproval. Khalid, who had been following the argument like he would a tennis match, now looked at Alex.

"We're invoking the privilege," Alex said, staring down the officers. "Ask your next question."

This time, Detective Brown measured her words. "Do you know whether Ja'dah Mahdi converted from Islam to Christianity?"

Khalid looked at Alex, waiting for permission.

"I'm not asking what anybody said to him," Brown prompted. "I'm just asking what he knows."

Nice try. "Would you have any reason to know this apart from your conversations with Ja'dah Mahdi or Fatih Mahdi?" Alex asked.

Khalid shook his head.

"Then he's not answering."

"Did you have a conversation with Fatih Mahdi about his wife converting to Christianity?" Brown asked.

"He's not answering."

"Did you talk to Ja'dah Mahdi about her conversion?"

"Next question."

"Have you ever heard of Beach Bible Church?"

At this, Khalid flushed. He again turned to Alex.

"If you've heard about the church outside of your conversations with either Ja'dah or Fatih, you can tell them," Alex said.

"I haven't."

"You're sure?" Like Alex, Brown seemed to suspect there was more to the answer.

"Positive."

"Do you know a man named Martin Burns?"

Before Alex could tell Khalid to restrict his answer to nonprivileged information, the imam responded. "No."

"You're sure?"

"Yes."

"Do you know what an honor killing is, Mr. Mobassar?"

He blanched. "Yes, of course."

"Does the Qur'an support honor killings?"

At that moment, Ghaniyah Mobassar appeared around the corner, carrying a tray loaded with coffee, cups, plates, silverware, and baklava.

She stood in the doorway staring vacantly around the room, some bruises still evident on her face.

Khalid stood and went to her. "This is my wife, Ghaniyah." He motioned toward the detectives. "Detectives Brown and Sanderson are asking me a few questions about Ja'dah Mahdi."

"I see," Ghaniyah said softly. "I wanted to know if I could get anyone something to eat or drink."

"No, thank you," Sanderson said immediately. "But if you wouldn't mind, we'd like to ask you a few questions when we finish talking to your husband."

Ghaniyah looked confused.

"That won't be possible," Alex said.

"You represent her, too?" Brown asked. "Isn't that a bit of a conflict?"

"I think we're fine here," Khalid said softly to Ghaniyah, then turned to the detectives. "I'll be right back."

Ghaniyah muttered a "nice to meet you" and left with Khalid.

Alex quickly explained about the automobile accident and the residual problems that Ghaniyah was having.

"I'm sorry to hear that," Sanderson offered. When Khalid returned, Sanderson told him that he hoped Ghaniyah would make a full recovery.

"Thank you," Khalid said.

"I think I had just asked about the Qur'an," Brown reminded him, "and whether it supports honor killings."

Khalid gathered his thoughts. "Murderers and terrorists use the Qur'an to justify all sorts of conduct, but honor killings are not sanctioned by the Qur'an or any of the hadiths. The prophet Mohammed, peace be upon him, said that we should treat our women with respect and kindness."

Brown checked her notes. "Didn't the prophet Mohammed, in the hadiths, say to women, 'I have not seen anyone more deficient in intelligence and religion than you'? Didn't he say that the majority of hell's inhabitants were women?"

Khalid inched forward on the couch. The questions plainly agitated him. "Those quotes are taken out of context. Before Islam, Arabic women had no right to own property, get an education, divorce, or even be protected from the brutality of their husbands. Islam changed all of that. Mohammed himself affirmed that men and women have equal duties and responsibilities in serving Allah. 'I will not suffer to be lost the work of any of you whether male or female. You proceed one from another.' Those are the words of Mohammed in Sura 3 of the Qur'an."

Detective Brown paused a moment before continuing. "Did you ever talk to Fatih about the concept of an honor killing?"

"Never," Khalid said before Alex could tell him not to answer.

"Do you think Fatih is capable of such a thing?"

"No. Absolutely not."

Brown gave him a skeptical look and changed gears. "Have you ever been to Sandbridge?"

"No," Khalid said, his voice tentative.

"Have you ever rented a house in Sandbridge or considered renting a house in Sandbridge?"

"No."

"Did you have anything to do with the disappearance of Ja'dah Mahdi?"

"No. Of course not."

"Do you have any idea where she might be?"

To this question, Alex detected the slightest bit of hesitation. "No."

"Are you willing to take a polygraph exam if we think it might be helpful?"

Alex didn't give his client a chance to answer that one. "No, he's not."

25

THE MEDIA SOON CAUGHT WIND of the story, and Alex followed the developments on the local news channels. At 4:00, Alex watched Virginia Beach Police Chief Moses Stargell appear before a bank of microphones for a hastily called press conference. The chief was a big bear of a man, universally admired for his quick wit and street savvy. Today, he looked uncharacteristically glum.

The chief reported the following facts: Ja'dah Mahdi had not been heard from or seen since she left her home at approximately 7 p.m. Saturday. Using phone records and cell tower information, the police had determined that Ja'dah had sent text messages from the Sandbridge area late Saturday evening. Ja'dah had no apparent connections with Sandbridge—no friends or acquaintances who lived there.

The police were combing the area for signs of Mrs. Mahdi. The chief described her car, gave her license-plate number, and displayed a recent photograph along with information about whom to contact with any leads.

The reporters started firing questions, but the chief spoke over them. A white male named Martin Burns was also missing. His absence had first been noticed when he failed to show up for work on Monday morning. The chief displayed his picture and said there was no information about his last known whereabouts.

By early evening, the local stations had begun piecing it together. Unnamed members of a Virginia Beach church said that Ja'dah Mahdi and Martin Burns were part of a group of friends who attended

Saturday night church services together. There were rumors that Ja'dah had converted to Christianity. Channel 13 ran an interview with her husband, Fatih Mahdi, who pleaded with Ja'dah, if she was listening, to come home. Various reports implied that Ja'dah had run away, perhaps because she feared reprisals from the Muslim community. Some speculated about the nature of a possible relationship between Ja'dah Mahdi and Martin Burns, but fellow church members dismissed such claims, saying the two were merely friends, part of a larger circle who met together following the church services.

By eleven o'clock, the story was picking up steam on national cable channels. There was video footage of search teams at Sandbridge and snippets of an interview with a square-jawed Fatih Mahdi, his lips trembling as he looked into the camera and asked Ja'dah to at least call and let him know if she was okay.

Alex flipped from one channel to the next, until one newscast nearly jolted him out of his chair. The CNN host was teasing a segment that would air after the break, promising exclusive interviews with the two men who found themselves at the center of the storm—the young pastor of the church attended by Martin Burns and "a prominent imam who leads the Norfolk mosque attended by Ja'dah Mahdi." The host paused momentarily for effect. "I think you'll find their perspectives very interesting."

Alex couldn't believe what he had just seen. Khalid wouldn't talk to the press without calling Alex. Would he?

The interview with the pastor added nothing new. Khalid was a different story. It looked like they had placed a backdrop in Khalid's living room and filmed him there. The cameraperson had used an unflattering angle that somehow accentuated the coarseness of Khalid's skin, his black beard, and the dark circles under his eyes.

The reporter started with some questions about Ja'dah's rumored conversion to Christianity. Had Khalid heard about this? Could he confirm or deny it?

Khalid looked stiff and nervous. "Ja'dah was faithful at the mosque and a good Muslim," he said.

"Did she ever express any doubts about the Islamic faith?"

Khalid shook his head. "I am not at liberty to talk about counseling situations with a member of my mosque."

"There has been some speculation that perhaps Ms. Mahdi converted to Christianity and thought she was in danger. Would you care to comment on that?"

"In our mosque, she would have nothing to fear," Khalid said. "Whatever faith she chose to follow, she would always be treated with kindness and respect."

The reporter looked unconvinced. "There are those who say the Islamic Learning Center has ties with Hezbollah. I think it's only fair to give you a chance to address those allegations."

Fair? Alex wanted to shout. *Ambushing the imam on the air with a question like that is* fair?

Khalid bristled at the question. "We have no ties with Hezbollah," he insisted. "We are just people of faith, trying to coexist in this country."

"Khalid Mobassar," the reporter said, "lead imam at the Islamic Learning Center in Norfolk, Virginia. Thank you for being with us."

"You are welcome," Khalid responded, his face still tight with anxiety.

When the show segued back to the studios, Alex dialed his client.

There would be no more interviews.

26

IF ALEX THOUGHT the furor would die down on Tuesday, he was badly mistaken. Commentators speculated endlessly about honor killings and whether women who converted from Islam faced danger. That question focused the attention on Ja'dah's husband—Fatih Mahdi—and the mosque that he attended.

By early afternoon, cable shows were reporting links between the Islamic Learning Center and Hezbollah. Unnamed sources confirmed that the mosque, which cost an estimated $13 million to build, had been indirectly funded with Hezbollah money.

One show aired an old clip of Khalid Mobassar from 2006, during the heat of the conflict between Hezbollah and Israel, showing Khalid arguing that Israel had overreacted. He bemoaned the destruction of Beirut and the loss of innocent lives and then asked a series of rhetorical questions. "Where will the Lebanese go for medical assistance? Who will help them rebuild? Who will feed the refugees who have lost their homes? Hezbollah. The Lebanese will go to Hezbollah hospitals. Eat Hezbollah food. Rebuild with Hezbollah funds. Israel's bombs have forced the Lebanese into the arms of Hezbollah."

The clip spread like wildfire from one show to the next. By three o'clock, a desperate Khalid was on the phone with Alex. "They're taking it out of context," he said. "I was lamenting the fact that this conflict would only strengthen Hezbollah. Let me talk to them. How can it be any worse?"

But Alex held his ground. If Khalid wanted Alex to be his lawyer, then Khalid needed to heed Alex's advice. No interviews. Period.

"We look like a terrorist cell," Khalid protested. "I can set the record straight."

"Will they be able to trace any Hezbollah funds to the mosque?" Alex asked.

A moment's hesitation told Alex all he needed to know. "It is impossible to say," Khalid stated. "Hezbollah is like the vines in a jungle. It is a political party. It funds charities. It recruits soldiers and trains doctors. Hezbollah is your neighbor. Most of the Shiite mosques in Beirut take two separate offerings. One for the mosque. Another for Hezbollah. Who can say whether *none* of the money that helped us build has ties to Hezbollah?"

"No interviews," Alex said. He had heard enough to keep a gag order on his client until this whole thing blew over. "This is a lose-lose situation."

"This is why Americans think all Muslims are terrorists," Khalid responded. "Because the media wouldn't have it any other way."

"Granted. So let's not feed the beast."

"Unfortunately, the beast has already been fed."

◁▷

By late afternoon, Alex had stopped watching television and tried to get some work done. So far, his own name had been kept out of the coverage. Khalid Mobassar wasn't a suspect, so Alex rationalized that there was no need to inject himself into the story and make it look like Khalid had "lawyered up." Instead, Alex hoped to lie low for a few days until the story went away. Hopefully, Ja'dah Mahdi and Martin Burns would show up in some other corner of the country and do a round of interviews about how unsafe Ja'dah felt after converting to Christianity, and the whole story would soon disappear.

At which point, Alex and Shannon could go back to representing the Mobassars on the case that really mattered—Ghaniyah's closed head injury. If—and it was a big *if*—Shannon ever located the trucking company that started the whole thing, the firm could be looking at a big payday.

The thought prompted Alex to call his partner. "See anything?" he asked when she answered her phone.

"No . . . well . . . maybe." Shannon sounded pretty exasperated. "I don't know, Alex. This whole thing is probably stupid. There are trucks that come by with red cabs and white trailers, but nothing that has pictures of produce on the side. But then again, Ghaniyah didn't even sound very sure about the produce part."

"How long do you plan on staying out there?"

"Every day but Friday. I've got hearings on Friday."

Alex knew what he was supposed to say next. She was waiting for him to volunteer. He checked his Outlook calendar. It was open Friday. He started typing an appointment.

"Can you cover for me Friday?" Shannon asked.

Alex finished making the entry. "I'm booked all day," he said.

"Doing what?"

He should have known she wouldn't give up so easily. "Sermon preparation."

"Good," Shannon said. "You can do it out here."

◁▷

Chief Stargell scheduled the press conference for 5 p.m. so the local networks could run it live. Alex and Sylvia watched on a television in the firm's small conference room.

A woman at the anchor desk said they would be switching to Sandbridge for the press conference, and Alex felt his stomach drop. An announcement from the site of the search could mean only one thing— they had found a body.

Stargell stepped to the microphones with Assistant Common-wealth's Attorney Taj Deegan behind him, just over his left shoulder. Ms. Deegan looked as somber as Stargell. "I will be giving a brief status report about some developments in the case of Ja'dah Mahdi and Martin Burns," the chief said. "I will *not* be taking questions."

He drew a deep breath and faced the reporters. No notes. Weary eyes.

"Approximately an hour and a half ago, at 1535, with the help of state police canine units, we were able to locate the bodies of Ja'dah Mahdi and Martin Burns. The two bodies were buried on a sandy beach on a federal preserve approximately 1.2 miles south of Sandbridge. The site was accessible only by boat."

The chief paused to survey his audience, seemingly apprehensive about the firestorm his next line would unleash. He set his jaw and continued.

"The head of Mrs. Mahdi was severed from her body in an execution-style killing. . . ." Alex could hear a collective gasp from those in attendance. "Mr. Burns was buried next to her. We have not yet been able to confirm an official cause of death for Mr. Burns, but indications are that Mr. Burns may have been buried alive next to the headless body of Ms. Mahdi. We have requested an expedited autopsy and will fill you in as soon as we have the final results."

Cameras clicked and Stargell remained stoic. He informed them that he had no hard leads on a suspect. He gave a phone number for people to call with any information. He thanked the reporters and walked away, their shouted questions following him off-camera.

Coverage switched back to the live news desk, where the anchors struggled to put the developments in perspective.

Alex was no longer listening.

A beheading. A live burial.

He dialed Khalid's cell number. Alex had no long-term plan for his client, but the short-term plan was painfully obvious.

"Lock the doors," Alex said, "and don't answer the doorbell. Shut the blinds. Don't go outside under any circumstances."

Alex rubbed his temple, a headache spreading like fire over his eyes. *Double murder. An honor killing.*

And all roads were leading to his client's mosque.

27

ON THE THIRD DAY of Shannon's stakeout, she hit gold. It was late Wednesday afternoon when the truck went sailing by—a red cab, white trailer, and a colorful array of fruits and vegetables painted on the right side, just as Ghaniyah had remembered. It took Shannon a moment to react, as if a figure from a dream had unexpectedly materialized in front of her. But she snapped out of it, pulled a quick U-turn, and gave chase.

Within a few minutes, she caught the lumbering truck and pulled out her cell phone. While driving—in fact, while tailgating—she put the device in camera mode and took a few shots of the license number. She glanced at the images as she drove. A little blurry and a glare from the front windshield. She definitely couldn't read the license plate in the photos. She had an answer for that, too, dialing her own number and reciting the numbers into her voice mail.

Then she called Alex, got his voice mail, and remembered his saying something about a court hearing on another case. Her adrenaline was surging—*This could be big!*—but she felt a little silly at the same time. *What am I going to do, make a citizen's arrest?*

She stayed glued behind the truck for about four miles, turning from North Landing onto Centerville Turnpike and eventually onto Kempsville Road. When the truck proceeded through a yellow light, Shannon followed through on red. She checked her rearview mirror.

No cops.

Eventually, the truck pulled into the parking lot of a Farm Fresh grocery store, drove down a side alley, and disappeared somewhere out back. Shannon assumed the driver was making a delivery. She also assumed that it might look a little conspicuous if she followed him.

She parked in front of the store, grabbed her cell phone, and hustled down the alley where the truck had disappeared. She rounded the corner and saw that the driver had backed the truck up to a loading ramp and was in the process of opening the doors.

Shannon whistled. "Dooley! C'mere, boy!" She glanced around, trying to look a little frantic but not too out of control.

"Have you seen a yellow Lab?" she asked the truck driver.

"No, but I just got here."

The guy was young, maybe midthirties. He had blond curly hair, a good-size paunch, and a couple of days' growth on his round face. He was wearing a brown uniform.

"He wanders around on me a lot," Shannon said. "We live right over there." She pointed to a residential neighborhood that backed up to the shopping center.

"Like I said, I just pulled in." The guy went back to work, propping the doors open and getting out a hand truck. "If you want to leave me your name and number, I'll give you a call if I see him."

Shannon felt in her pockets. "Um, I don't have a pen." The driver pulled one out of his pocket, but Shannon had a different idea. "Why don't you just give me your cell number; I'll call your phone, and then you'll have my number."

The guy paused for a second and looked like he might dismiss the idea. But Shannon gave him her best cute and innocent smile and checked his finger to make sure there was no ring. "I mean, if you don't want my number in your phone, that's fine."

"No. No," the driver said quickly. "That's a good way to do it."

He recited his number for Shannon, who immediately dialed his phone. She walked next to the truck and stuck out her hand. "My name's Shannon."

"Jim," the driver said. Shannon's call went into voice mail, and she hung up.

Things turned a little awkward. "Well, guess I better keep looking," Shannon said.

"Yeah. Nice to meet you."

"Thanks for keeping your eyes open, Jim. Maybe we'll meet again sometime."

Just for good measure, Shannon pretended that her phone rang, and she brought it to her ear. "This is Shannon," she said, turning sideways to Jim. She took a couple of pictures and talked into her phone, waving as she walked away.

"Hold on a second," she said into the phone. "Thanks again," she called to Jim, over her shoulder. He smiled and waved.

No wonder people hate lawyers, she thought.

◁ ▷

Twenty minutes later, just before Shannon pulled into the parking lot at the office, she received a call from the Mobassars' number.

"I left a message with Mr. Madison," Ghaniyah Mobassar said. Shannon recognized the accent, but there was more emotion in her voice today. "But he has not called back. I am sorry to bother you, but I don't know what to do."

"It's fine," Shannon said. "In fact, I was just getting ready to call you."

"They've arrested Khalid," Ghaniyah said, the words rushing out. "And the police are searching my house, tearing everything apart." Her voice was trembling. "I didn't know what to do."

28

SHANNON HAD TO PARK a block away from the Mobassars' duplex and argue her way through the police working crowd control. Somebody had probably tipped off the media about Khalid's perp walk. All the local satellite trucks were in place and had no doubt recorded the event. The crews were now busy doing the obligatory neighbor interviews.

Shannon spotted Khalid in the back of a police cruiser and approached the uniformed officer who appeared to be in charge—a tall man in his midforties with gray hair and a thin gray mustache. His name badge identified him as Lt. Shaw. Shannon introduced herself, and Shaw asked for identification. He studied her bar card for a long moment and did a double take.

"You're his lawyer?" Shaw asked.

"Is that a problem?"

Shaw studied her, perhaps deciding whether to put up a fight. Shannon had seen it all before. When she showed up in court with Alex, most people assumed she was his paralegal. When she told a new acquaintance that she was a lawyer, the most common response was a one word question: "Really?" But every time somebody underestimated her because of her size or Mary Lou Retton looks, it only made her more determined.

"No problem," Shaw groused.

"Good." Shannon motioned toward the car. "I'd like to speak with my client now."

"We need to finish processing him first. As soon as we finish executing the search warrant, we're taking him down to the station for processing."

"Let me see your warrant," Shannon demanded.

Shaw frowned and produced the paper. Shannon examined the document, returned it to Shaw, and thanked him. She turned and headed toward the cruiser.

"What are you doing?" Shaw asked, following behind her.

She ignored him.

"What are you doing?"

Shannon stopped just outside the tinted glass of the cruiser's back-seat window. Khalid was alone in the seat, hands cuffed, looking up at her with fearful eyes. Another officer came over and stood beside Shannon, placing a hand against the door as if Shannon might try to open the door and spring her client.

Shannon ignored the officer and focused on Khalid. "Don't talk to the cops," she said loudly. "As soon as they ask you a question, demand your lawyer. Don't talk to anybody at the jail—especially your cellmate. . . ."

"Ms. Reese, you can talk to him downtown," Lt. Shaw said sharply, stepping between Shannon and the cruiser.

Shannon looked past Shaw and locked eyes with Khalid. "Got it?" she asked loudly. When he nodded, Shannon turned back to Shaw.

"Try to keep the waterboarding to a minimum," she said.

◁ ▷

The inside of the duplex was trashed. Shannon complained loudly to Detectives Sanderson and Brown, following them from room to room, commenting sarcastically on their handling of the Mobassars' stuff. The officers ignored her as they methodically emptied every dresser drawer, pulled all the clothes from the shelves, shook open every book in the library, and confiscated legal pads, journals, credit card receipts, and Khalid's computer.

After they left, Shannon found Ghaniyah sitting on her bed in the middle of the shambles that had been her bedroom. She was staring at the mess, stunned beyond words at what had just transpired.

Shannon knew she couldn't leave Ghaniyah alone. The poor woman, still trying to recover from her brain injury, would be overwhelmed by the simplest of tasks. She would never be able to cope with *this*.

"Why don't you pack up a few things and spend the night at my place?" Shannon offered. "We can start cleaning up first thing tomorrow."

Ghaniyah looked at Shannon as if she was surprised to discover that Shannon had entered the room. "What did he do?" Ghaniyah asked. "When will they let him go?"

"I don't know," Shannon admitted. She looked at a small pile of Ghaniyah's bras and panties. Shannon thought about how humiliating it must have been for this conservative Muslim woman to have a man pawing through her stuff.

Then another thought hit Shannon. Ghaniyah would be equally distraught at the notion of Shannon helping reorganize Khalid's clothes.

"Why don't you work on the bedroom, and I'll start downstairs on the study," Shannon suggested. "After we get things picked up a little, we can talk."

"Okay," Ghaniyah mumbled.

Shannon glanced over her shoulder as she left the room. Ghaniyah had not moved an inch from her spot on the bed.

29

ALEX FINISHED HIS HEARING in Virginia Beach Circuit Court, packed his briefcase, and headed toward the exit. To his surprise, Taj Deegan was waiting in the back row. With all the events surrounding the honor killings, the sight of the chief deputy for the commonwealth's attorney made his stomach clench.

She stood. "Got a minute?"

Alex checked his watch, as if the president might be waiting in the hallway. "I don't have long," he said.

The two found an empty conference room adjacent to the courtroom. Neither lawyer spoke as they took their seats. Alex noted that Taj didn't have her briefcase or even a legal pad with her.

Taj had the look of someone you could trust. She wasn't a flashy dresser—black suit, white blouse, a pair of black flats—and she had a quick smile, showing lots of perfect white teeth. She was slightly overweight with a rounded chin, intense almond eyes, and a pair of small black reading glasses that seemed more like a prop. She looked to be in her late thirties, and Alex knew she was the single mom of a son and daughter who were both in elementary school. He also knew that Taj was always being touted for this judgeship or that one. Politicians were enamored with the story of a young African American woman who had earned her GED, worked her way through college while her mom helped with the kids, and attended law school at night while working for a private security company.

"Alex, I want you to know that we've just arrested Khalid Mobassar," she said, watching him for a reaction.

Alex took the news stoically, though his mind started churning with questions.

"As Mobassar's attorney, sooner or later you'd be entitled to the disclosures I'm about to make. I thought if I told you about the evidence now, it might help you evaluate whether or not to stay on the case."

Alex's suspicions were on high alert. Deegan played fair, but she was known for her take-no-prisoners approach to high-profile cases. To Alex's knowledge, she had never lost a murder case.

"I've checked you out," Deegan continued, "and I knew your grandfather pretty well. I don't want to see you get sucked into a case like this without knowing what you're getting into. There are plenty of lawyers out there who can represent this guy."

She seemed sincere, but Alex didn't respond immediately. The possibility that this was some kind of trick crossed his mind, but he dismissed it; he wasn't exactly known as the top criminal defense attorney in the area. If this was a tactical move, it wasn't a very smart one.

Deegan shifted in her seat and leaned forward. "What I'm going to tell you is off the record. This conference never happened. If you stay on the case, you'll get all this information through formal channels. Until then, it's entirely confidential."

"Okay."

"For starters, your man is on the DOJ's list for foreign nationals with terrorist connections. As a result, his phone and text messages have been tapped and his e-mails monitored under the Patriot Act since he came into the country. It took us forty-eight hours to work through the Feds' red tape, but we eventually got the messages from your client's allegedly missing cell phone."

Khalid's cell phone was missing? Alex swallowed hard, but he didn't break eye contact with the prosecutor.

"On June 2, your client sent two text messages to a cell phone purchased a week earlier by a man in northern Virginia using an alias. We used GPS positioning data from the cell phone signals and traced the location of that anonymous cell phone on the night of the murders. It's the killer's cell phone, Alex. We traced the man using it from Petersburg to Virginia Beach and then to Sandbridge. Later that night, the cell phone was near the federal preserve where the bodies were buried."

Alex felt his mouth go dry. He liked Khalid and found it hard to imagine that his client had been part of this gruesome killing. "What did the messages say?"

"The first message explained that Ja'dah Fatima Mahdi had converted to Christianity and was attending Christian services with a man whom Khalid did not identify, that Ja'dah had defiled herself with this man, disgraced her family, and dishonored Allah. The message told the killer that if Ja'dah was unwilling to repent and return to the Muslim faith, the honor of her family must be restored. That's pretty much an exact quote, Alex—that the honor of her family had to be restored."

Taj looked at Alex, and he saw her measuring his reaction. "The second message told the killer that he would find Ja'dah at the Beach Bible Church on Saturday night. It contained a picture of Ja'dah and Martin Burns."

The information stunned Alex. It sounded like an airtight case. "So you've got two text messages from my client's phone to a phone whose owner is unknown." He tried to sound unimpressed. "And that's your case?"

"There's more," Taj said matter-of-factly.

Alex dropped the pretenses. "I'm listening."

"Fatih Mahdi, Ja'dah Mahdi's husband, will testify that the *only* person he told about his wife's conversion to Christianity was your client. After Fatih found out about the text messages, he said he would be willing to waive the priest-penitent privilege and testify about what was said in his conversation with your client."

Alex was beginning to feel like a boxer, doubled over in a corner, taking one body blow after another. He couldn't think of a single counterpunch.

And still Deegan wasn't done. "Using a search warrant, we gained access to your client's and the mosque's banking accounts between the time of the text messages ordering the killings and the date of the murders. During that time, the mosque's weekly deposits were down by about 50 percent. About $20,000 was diverted from the mosque's operating account into the mosque's building fund, and a few days before the killings, there was a $20,000 wire from that fund to a bank account in Lebanon. The wire was authorized online by Mr. Mobassar using his account password."

This is what Alex hated about criminal law—the reason he had virtually abandoned the field. The prosecutors held all the cards. The best ones, like Taj Deegan, didn't file charges unless they knew the case was a slam dunk. From day one he would be fighting a losing battle, looking for loopholes, trying to keep his client out of a life sentence.

Which would be bad enough in a normal case. But in this one, the bad publicity alone would threaten what was left of his personal-injury practice.

"Why are you telling me this now?" Alex asked.

Taj leaned forward, her intense stare conveying the moral authority of someone who believed in her position—*truly* believed. A crusader. "This guy is an animal," Taj said. "He had an innocent woman *beheaded*, Alex. And he had Martin Burns buried alive." She narrowed her eyes. "Buried alive. Tied up and thrown into a grave with his beheaded girlfriend, where he was buried one shovelful at a time."

Alex had no comeback for this. The facts were indisputably gruesome.

"This is going to be ugly, Alex, and the press is going to be all over it. Our worst fears about fundamentalist Muslims are personified by Mr. Mobassar. To an unscrupulous criminal defense lawyer, a boondoggle like this case could be a way to get his name in lights so other thugs will hire him. But you don't really strike me as that sort of guy."

Taj took a breath and seemed to relax a little. "I'm not trying to tell you what to do—and someone's got to represent this guy. But out of respect for your grandfather, I thought I should let you know what you're up against before you get in too deep."

Alex sincerely thanked Taj and told her he'd take the information into consideration. They shook hands, and he decided to get in at least one little jab before he left. "Does that mean you won't be offering me a plea bargain?"

Taj Deegan did not smile. "Whether you stay in this case or not, I'm going after Mobassar with everything I have," she promised.

"I'm kidding," Alex said. "I really do appreciate the heads-up."

30

ALEX HAD MISSED nearly a dozen calls while he had his BlackBerry on silent in the courtroom: two from Khalid's home number, three from Shannon, one from his office. A few local numbers he didn't recognize—probably the press.

He ignored them all as he walked to his car in the scorching heat. He put on his shades and took off his suit coat, focused on what Taj Deegan had just told him.

He kicked around various scenarios on his way back to the office. As a lawyer, he was trained to reserve judgment until he had heard both sides. But as a human being, he had to admit that the case against his client seemed pretty damning.

Alex retraced his interactions with Khalid over the last few days and reconsidered those events in light of what he had just learned. Khalid had seemed equivocal on the issue of whether funding for his mosque could be tied to Hezbollah. Khalid had refused to divulge even to his own lawyer the substance of his conversations with Fatih Mahdi. Khalid had lost two sons fighting against Israel. He had condemned Israel's aggressive response to the 2006 Hezbollah provocation.

Perhaps Khalid *was* part of an Islamic Trojan horse strategy. Perhaps he had positioned himself as a voice of reason among Muslim clerics so he could gain a visa to America and fight from within the bowels of the American beast.

What did Alex really know about Khalid Mobassar? And did it even matter? Whatever the true facts, Khalid would soon come to symbolize the oppression of women carried out in the name of Allah. Khalid's case would sear the issue of honor killing into the national consciousness in the same way that Bernie Madoff personified investment greed or Charles Manson personified cult killings.

In the life of a trial lawyer, there were certain cases that defined your career. Johnnie Cochran was O.J.'s lawyer. Ken Starr prosecuted Bill Clinton. David Boies was Al Gore's mouthpiece in the recount litigation.

Khalid Mobassar's case was that kind of case. If Alex didn't withdraw now, he would always be known as the guy who defended honor killings. Even if, God forbid, he won and Khalid really *was* guilty, Alex would symbolize what Americans hated most about lawyers. Lawyers find loopholes to spring criminals. They trample the rights of innocent victims.

And in this case, innocent *Christian* victims.

Alex wanted no part of it. He picked up the phone to call Shannon. The firm shouldn't even make an appearance at the bond hearing. Taj Deegan was right. There were plenty of lawyers champing at the bit to represent even the most despicable defendants if the price was right.

Alexander Madison was not one of them.

◁ ▷

In their five years of practicing law together, Alex could not remember the last time he had been this frustrated with Shannon. They would constantly pick at one another and give each other a hard time, but they didn't have *real* arguments. At least . . . not until today.

He had been on the phone with her for nearly thirty minutes. She was talking in hushed tones from one of the rooms in Ghaniyah's home. Several ladies from the mosque had come by to help Ghaniyah clean up, and Shannon was doing her part.

Alex had already explained the evidence aligned against Khalid, but his partner wasn't listening.

"Since when did we start putting our clients on trial before we take their cases?" Shannon asked. "I can't imagine that Khalid would have ordered something like this."

"And I can't believe we're having this conversation," Alex said.

"I had to twist your arm to represent the Mobassars in the first place. You didn't even want to take Ghaniyah's case, and now you want to represent her husband for an honor killing?"

"I'm not one to cut and run just because the commonwealth's attorney is trying to bring a little heat." Shannon's voice was insistent, though she kept the volume low.

"This isn't about cutting and running." Alex felt his blood pressure rising. "We can't put our whole practice at risk for the sake of one client."

"This is exactly what our practice is supposed to be about," Shannon responded. "It's number nine on the list."

She was referring, Alex knew, to his grandfather's list. The things that made Madison and Associates unique. The ninth item read *A lawyer's highest duty is to defend an innocent client.*

"That's exactly my point," Alex said. "He's not innocent, Shannon. How can he be innocent?"

"You don't even know him, Alex. I've researched this guy. Spent the afternoon at his house with his wife." Shannon was talking faster now, her voice still hushed. Alex had heard this tone before and knew she wasn't going to change her mind.

"I'm going to be at the arraignment tomorrow standing right next to Mr. Mobassar," Shannon continued. "I would really like to have you there with me. But whether or not you show up, somebody's got to argue for this man's bail." She let the words hang for a moment before she put the knife in. "Some of us still believe in the presumption of innocence."

"So now you're the big crusader," Alex said sarcastically. "If it wasn't sad, I might enjoy the irony."

Shannon sighed and apparently decided she had better things to do than go on like this all afternoon. "Right now, the big crusader is just one woman helping another woman clean up her place. If you've got some time, we could use your help."

Alex blew out a deep breath and tried to match her level of composure. "All right. Stay with him through the bond hearing, and then he can get new counsel."

"You aren't listening to a word I'm saying," Shannon insisted. Alex had never heard her quite so dogmatic about taking a case. "Ghaniyah needs our help. And I, for one, believe in her husband. Plus, her civil case could be worth a million dollars or more based on her positive recognition of the truck I photographed earlier. I plan to be at Khalid's arraignment tomorrow morning. You can do whatever you want."

He hated it when his partner became so unreasonable. But there was no use discussing it further right now. "Unfortunately, I'll be busy," Alex said. "Somebody's got to stay in the office and talk the other clients out of leaving."

31

KHALID MOBASSAR'S arraignment was scheduled for 9:00 a.m. in Virginia Beach General District Court. Despite his promise to stay away, Alex pulled into the parking lot at 8:45 and had to walk nearly half a mile in the muggy heat and drizzling rain to the courthouse. By the time he navigated his way through the metal detectors and rode the escalators to General District Courtroom No. 3, it was 8:59.

The bailiff was turning people away at the door, but he let Alex through because he was part of Khalid's legal team. Attorneys, spectators, and reporters filled the benches and lined the walls. Alex pushed his way to the front and found an empty spot against the side wall. Shannon was seated in the second row, waiting her turn and studying some documents. Alex managed to get the attention of the older gentleman sitting next to her. When Shannon saw Alex, her face lit up and she slid past others in the row to come talk with him.

"Thanks for coming," she said.

"How's Ghaniyah?"

"This whole thing has really set her back. She went into a shell. Several women from the mosque came to her place and helped clean up. Her daughter is trying to get a visa home from Lebanon, but that's hit some red tape."

Shannon stepped a little closer to Alex and lowered her voice. "Khalid is despondent and worried sick about Ghaniyah. If the judge denies bail or sets it too high, I'm worried our client might do something drastic."

Our client. The words weren't lost on Alex, but now was not the time for an argument. "Like what?"

"I don't know. I'm just saying that we've got to win this hearing."

There was no need for Alex to remind Shannon of the obvious—if they were hoping for a lenient judge, they had come to the wrong courtroom. By arbitrary assignment, Judge Henry McElroy would be handling the arraignment and bail hearing. A former prosecutor, McElroy wasn't quite the hanging judge, but he was close. In General District Courtroom No. 3, there was a lot of talk about the presumption of innocence. But in practice, the prosecutors and cops were presumed correct until defense attorneys proved them unequivocally wrong.

"What kind of bond could Khalid even post?" Alex asked.

Shannon motioned for him to keep his voice down. "He says there are others in the mosque who could help."

Alex wrinkled his brow at the thought. "If he does that, everyone will assume it's Hezbollah money."

"I know," Shannon whispered. "I've told him that."

A few minutes later the bailiff announced the entrance of Judge McElroy, and the entire courtroom stood.

"Be seated," the judge intoned. McElroy was a large man with a round face, slumped shoulders, thinning hair, and reading glasses that looked about two sizes too small. He seemed to be sitting up straighter than normal today, undoubtedly mindful that the cameras were rolling. It occurred to Alex that this would be McElroy's big opportunity to show what kind of law-and-order judge he was.

He took a few minutes to explain the process, talking more slowly and pronouncing his words more clearly than he typically did. At about nine fifteen, he started the "shuffle of shame." One by one the defendants paraded into the courtroom in handcuffs and leg shackles, sat next to their lawyers, were informed of the charges against them, and were asked how they were going to plead. The defendants had a right to be dressed up and presentable on the day of their trial so that the orange prison jumpsuits wouldn't scream "Guilty!" to the jury. But there was no such right for an arraignment or bond hearing.

To nobody's surprise, McElroy had intentionally saved Khalid's case for last. "Defendant 10-3417, Khalid Mobassar, arraignment and bond hearing," the clerk announced. There was a rustling in the courtroom as all eyes turned toward the side door.

"Let's take a ten-minute break," Judge McElroy said.

During the recess, Alex and Shannon settled in at the defense counsel table. Taj Deegan, wearing a gray suit, came over and shook their hands. She was smiling and looked perfectly at ease. "Is there something special about this next defendant?" she asked.

"You mean other than the fact that he's innocent?" Alex asked.

"They're all innocent," Taj retorted. "It was probably self-defense."

Shannon ignored the banter and leafed through some documents. Taking the hint, Taj wished Alex luck and returned to her table.

32

AFTER AN APPROPRIATE amount of time so the anticipation could reach a fevered level, Judge McElroy reconvened court and asked the bailiffs to bring in the defendant. Alex noticed Shannon wipe her sweaty palms against her skirt.

Khalid came in the side door looking like he'd just been captured from a Taliban assault camp. His hair was unkempt, his beard uncombed. He had dark circles under his eyes, and he put his head down as he did the inmate shuffle toward the defense counsel's table, the chains around his ankles jangling. The orange jumpsuit hung on his thin body, and the pants were partway up his shins, exposing a few inches of bare leg between the bottom of his pants and his flip-flops. Shannon and Alex shook the man's hand and gave him the seat between them.

In a few moments, he would be arraigned on the charge of conspiracy to commit murder. If convicted, Khalid was looking at life in prison. In many other states, it could have been worse. Virginia still adhered to the "triggerman rule," meaning that the only person who faced the death penalty for a murder would be the killer himself, not an accomplice or even someone who ordered the killing. Twice, the state legislature had passed bills trying to change that rule, but a Democratic governor had vetoed them both. Alex suspected that after Khalid's case, the new Republican governor would sign a similar bill into law as soon as he could.

The arraignment itself was mercifully short. Judge McElroy had

Khalid stand and informed him that he was charged with conspiracy to commit murder. He noted that Khalid had retained counsel and asked if Khalid understood the charges against him.

Khalid kept his posture ramrod straight, his chin up. "Yes, sir."

"How does the defendant plead?" This question was directed to Shannon and Alex, who stood next to their client.

"Not guilty," Shannon said. Though she tried to sound authoritative, her voice was more of a squeak than a battle cry.

"I'll entertain argument on the request for bond," McElroy said.

Taj Deegan went first, and the defense lawyers took a seat. "This man has been on the DOJ's terrorist watch list since he came into the country. That's how we obtained the text messages ordering the murders of Ja'dah Fatima Mahdi and Martin Burns."

At this, there was a murmur of excitement in the courtroom and the clacking of computer keyboards. These were fresh details, Alex knew. It would be fodder for the news broadcasts that night.

"We are also investigating whether the mosque led by Mr. Mobassar is partially funded by organizations connected to Hezbollah," Taj continued. "If Hezbollah is involved, no matter how high this court sets bond, Mr. Mobassar will be out of jail in a matter of hours."

The rumors of Hezbollah connections had been swirling in the media for the past several days, but mentioning the terrorist organization in court had a sobering effect. Alex could see it in McElroy's face. How could a judge consider releasing a man accused of honor killings who had ties to a terrorist group like Hezbollah?

"Mr. Mobassar is a foreign national. The risk of flight to a country that would deny extradition is great. If ever there was a case where it would be inappropriate for *any* bond to be set, this is that case."

When Taj took her seat, Shannon moved quickly to the space between the two counsel tables where her adversary had been standing. Judge McElroy was jotting down a few notes, and Shannon waited for him to finish, standing at attention with no notes. She looked as if she might be preparing to make the first run on a tumbling routine.

McElroy looked up. "You may begin."

"At a bond hearing, it's the burden of the *commonwealth* to prove that the release of the defendant would be a danger to society *and* that he constitutes a flight risk. Tossing around loaded buzz words and engaging in fearmongering does not constitute such proof."

Alex knew his partner well enough to read the intensity on the tight lines of her face and neck muscles. This was no act; Shannon believed every word she was saying.

"Khalid Mobassar came to this country at the invitation of a prestigious university because he is an Islamic *reformer*," she continued. "He lost both sons in the endless stream of Middle Eastern violence. He knows better than anyone that the violence must stop. For him, this is not just an intellectual theory. He has been victimized by the same jihadist mind-set that he now opposes with every fiber of his body. Don't let him be victimized by *American* prejudice and stereotypes too."

Shannon paused. Alex could sense an extra layer of tension in the air as a result of her stridency. Even the defiant way she stood there with her jaw thrust forward sent an unmistakable signal that she was ready to take on the world.

"Americans always wonder why moderate Muslim leaders don't speak out more forcefully against terrorism. Well," Shannon said, "here is somebody who did—and look at the treatment he gets. The commonwealth's attorney talks about 'suspected' ties to terrorist organizations. But where's the proof? Where are the funds traced from Hezbollah's accounts to the Islamic Learning Center in Norfolk? Where are the e-mails or phone calls or messages from Hezbollah leaders?" Shannon fired a glance at Taj Deegan as if she actually expected an answer. Taj stared back.

"If the federal government suspected ties to a terrorist organization, why did they let Khalid enter the country in the first place? We all know that the government's activities under the Patriot Act have cast a wide net—at times based on unfounded suspicions. Mr. Mobassar is apparently on the government's list because he is Lebanese and a leader in the Islamic faith. How is that not racial and religious profiling?"

The question elicited a scowl of disapproval from Judge McElroy. The race card. Alex was hoping his partner wouldn't trot it out quite so early.

Shannon took a breath, softened her tone, and talked about the commendable things the Islamic Learning Center did for the community. She ended by noting that Ghaniyah Mobassar had been in a serious automobile accident and needed her husband at home. He would never leave the country when his wife needed him so badly. In fact, Khalid would be willing to surrender his passport until the trial was over if the government was truly concerned about his fleeing to Lebanon.

Shannon sat down, and Alex leaned across Khalid to tell his partner that she'd done a fabulous job. McElroy gave Taj Deegan a chance for rebuttal, but Deegan brushed it off. "We believe the evidence speaks for itself," she said.

At that, the judge announced another recess so he could prepare his ruling.

◁▷

When court reconvened, a somber-looking McElroy had the deputies bring Khalid back into the courtroom. McElroy folded back a few pages on his legal pad and began reading his ruling without looking at the cameras. "Although Ms. Reese has done an excellent job arguing for the defendant's release on a minimal bond, the court is nonetheless convinced that Mr. Mobassar constitutes a risk to women in the Muslim community who might be inclined to switch to another religion. The court also believes that Mr. Mobassar presents a substantial flight risk given his connection to countries that may or may not honor an extradition request from the United States."

McElroy looked up from his notes and focused on Taj Deegan. "The court agrees with Ms. Reese that the commonwealth has presented no tangible evidence of Mr. Mobassar's alleged connections with terrorist organizations like Hezbollah. Therefore, this court cannot and does not consider that type of speculation as part of its ruling."

For the first time, Alex felt a small glimmer of hope. Would McElroy actually cut through all the inflammatory rhetoric and grant Khalid bail? He didn't have to wait long for the answer.

"I'm therefore granting the defendant bail in the amount of 1.5

million dollars. Conditions of bail will be as follows: First, Mr. Mobassar will surrender his passport and may not leave the commonwealth of Virginia. Second, Mr. Mobassar will wear an electronic ankle restraint so that his movements may be tracked at all times. Third, Mr. Mobassar will be able to attend to his duties as imam at the Islamic Learning Center and care for his wife. As part of those duties, he may go to the store and run necessary errands, but other than that he is to be confined to his home and to events at the Islamic Learning Center."

Shannon was on her feet. "May he also go to his attorneys' offices to help prepare for the case?"

"Of course," Judge McElroy answered. He looked at Taj Deegan and Shannon Reese one last time. "Anything else?"

Deegan shook her head and Shannon gave the judge an enthusiastic "No, sir."

"Then court is adjourned." McElroy banged the gavel and left the bench. He had probably angered more than a few conservatives today, but Alex had a newfound respect for the man.

It took guts to ignore public opinion and do what you thought was right.

33

ON HIS DRIVE to the office, Alex thought about the potential backlash from the bond hearing. In his conspiratorial mind, he even considered the possibility that Judge McElroy may have ruled in favor of Khalid for just such a purpose. By allowing Khalid out on bond, he would generate strong reactions against the Muslim community. Conservatives would be especially irate. How could a judge free someone with terrorist ties?

And by setting the bond at a high amount, there would inevitably be questions about where the money came from. But he and Shannon didn't have to play this game. He picked up the phone and called his partner while the thought was fresh in his mind.

He got voice mail and remembered that she was planning on visiting Khalid in the jail. He decided to leave a message.

"We need to tell Khalid *not* to post bond. If he does, there could be such a public outcry that he'll *never* get a fair trial. There'll be all sorts of questions about where he obtained the money. Call me when you get a chance."

When Alex arrived at his office building, he was surprised to find a few reporters camped in front of the building. The attention this case generated was growing by the minute. He hoped his firm could still extract itself from representing Khalid before the firm name became forever synonymous with the representation of suspected terrorists.

Alex took a deep breath and walked past them, ignoring their questions. "Does your client deny he sent text messages from his phone ordering the killings?" "Does the Islamic Learning Center receive funding from Hezbollah?"

Undeterred, a few of them followed Alex into the building. When he reached the firm's reception area, the reporters were still on his tail. Sylvia Brunswick was looking as bad as Alex had ever seen her.

"Migraine?"

She nodded. Alex could almost see the invisible jackhammer pounding away at her temples. She handed him a number of phone slips and ignored the ringing phone, rubbing her eyebrows with her left hand. "These are the messages I took before it got really ugly."

Alex turned and faced the reporters. There was a TV crew, a photographer, and one or two others. Alex had only three seats in his waiting area.

"Make yourselves at home," he said. "But please try to keep it down. My assistant has a migraine."

"Will you be taking any questions?"

"—issuing any statements?"

"Let's at least get a picture of you behind your desk." The man who said this had been snapping pictures since Alex arrived at the building.

"Unlike a lot of lawyers, we do our talking in the courtroom," Alex said. "Mr. Mobassar's not guilty, and we look forward to vindicating him in a court of law. Have a great day."

Alex turned and headed for his office, leaving Sylvia and the reporters to keep each other company.

When he reached his office, he forwarded his calls to Sylvia and started running through his messages. His e-mail address was listed on the firm's Web page, and as a result, his in-box was filled with vitriolic notes related to the bond hearing.

He deleted them and started surfing the Internet for news coverage. He knew he was in trouble when the bond hearing was the lead story on both CNN and Fox News. So far, his firm's name was buried deep in the story, but he knew it wouldn't remain that way for long.

Many criminal cases, Alex knew, were won or lost at a motion to suppress hearing. The commonwealth's case against Khalid hinged on a text message recorded under the authority of the Patriot Act. If

Alex and Shannon stayed with the case, they would have to challenge the Patriot Act and, in particular, whether Khalid's alleged connections to Hezbollah provided sufficient grounds for tapping his text messages. If they lost that challenge, the court would be saying it believed the Department of Justice had sufficient grounds for thinking Khalid posed a terrorist threat. If they won, the public would say that Alex and Shannon had sprung their client on a technicality.

The more Alex analyzed the case, the more he knew the firm needed out.

◁▷

Before Shannon made it to the firm that afternoon, Sylvia poked her head in Alex's office, flinching in pain so that he would not forget how terribly she was suffering, and announced that two members of Alex's church were there to see him.

"From my *church*?"

Sylvia checked a note. "They said their names were Bill Fitzsimmons and Harry Dent."

Fitzsimmons and Dent were the Mutt and Jeff of the deacon board. Fitzsimmons was tall and lanky with a long, hooked nose and black bifocals. Dent was a short, bald man with an Adolf Hitler mustache and a boulder-sized chip on his shoulder. Alex had long ago quit trying to win Dent's affection.

"Send them in," Alex sighed. He hesitated to reward his assistant for her contorted facial expressions designed to highlight her pain, but he decided she was no use to him in this state. "And why don't you take the rest of the day off?"

"Thank you," Sylvia said, as if wondering why it had taken Alex so long to figure out that she was entitled to go home.

Alex spent the next twenty-five minutes listening to Harry Dent share his concerns about Alex's involvement in Khalid Mobassar's case while Bill Fitzsimmons nodded along. Harry understood that Alex was a lawyer and sometimes had to take cases he didn't like. But weren't there other lawyers who could handle *this* case? Couldn't Alex tell the judge that he had a conscientious objection to working on *this* case?

Their little church was already struggling. They couldn't afford this kind of publicity. Harry even threw out the name Jeremiah Wright, which Alex thought was entirely unfair.

Alex considered digging in his heels and staying on the case just to spite Harry Dent. Some of Harry's concerns were legitimate, but he sure had a way of making Alex want to argue with him on every point. Instead, Alex kept his composure and expressed his thanks to Harry and Bill for coming by. "I'll give it some thought," Alex promised.

"Will you know something by Sunday?" Harry Dent asked.

"It's not that simple," Alex responded. Perhaps he needed to remind Harry about the time he had helped Harry's nephew with a DUI. Had Bill forgotten how Alex helped him and his wife through some marital challenges? But Alex decided not to bring any of that up. Why use political chips if he was going to withdraw from the case anyway?

"I need to talk to my partner. But I promise you this: when we make a decision about whether or not to stay in the case, you'll be the first to know."

Alex could tell that Harry Dent was not satisfied with the answer, but there was little left to discuss. "Well, you know our concerns," Harry said. The man always had to have the last word.

"We'll be praying for you," Bill added.

34

SHANNON AND ALEX agreed to meet at a restaurant on Thursday night so they could avoid the reporters staking out their office. They chose a place called Chick's, an oyster bar and seafood restaurant on the north side of Virginia Beach along the Lynnhaven River. It was a favorite watering hole for the locals. Many would arrive by boat, tying up at the pier along the backside of the restaurant for hours while they hung out at the bar.

The night was hot and muggy, so Alex and Shannon asked to be seated inside the air-conditioned plastic canopy. They waited about fifteen minutes until a picnic table cleared. Even in the air-conditioning, it must have been at least eighty degrees, and Alex was sticky with sweat.

As soon as they were seated and had ordered something cold to drink, Shannon launched into an update. The Mobassars' home was nearly back to normal, thanks to help from several of Ghaniyah's friends. Nara Mobassar, Khalid's thirty-year-old daughter, had obtained a visa and would be in town by Saturday. And even though Shannon had passed along Alex's concerns to Khalid about posting a large bond, the imam was determined to get out of jail. Shannon expected his bond would be posted on Friday or Saturday at the latest.

In contrast to Shannon's rather upbeat report, Alex was all gloom and doom. He told Shannon about the visit from Bill Fitzsimmons and Harry Dent. He had also responded to several e-mails from personal-injury clients who were nervous about the firm's continuing to handle their cases. "They think a jury might take it out on them if we're their lawyers," Alex explained.

"I can't believe the entire world has tried and convicted Khalid Mobassar before the first witness has even taken the stand," Shannon said. "How can we get an unbiased jury after this?"

We? Alex thought. He had intended to wait until after they had ordered their food, but he couldn't let that pass. "Look, Shannon, I know you like this family, but I think we need to withdraw from this case." He hesitated while she absorbed the statement. "I mean, we should stay on Ghaniyah's case and help her. But we're in over our heads on this criminal stuff."

After an uncomfortable silence, Shannon's voice was measured and calm. "I like this guy, Alex. I can't imagine cutting and running on him. You know as well as I do that they'll end up with some criminal lawyer who is just in it for the publicity. And besides, I really believe he's innocent."

Alex stared at Shannon in disbelief. There were powerboats motoring by on the Lynnhaven, young singles on the prowl lining the bar, ESPN blaring away on the television—but Alex ignored it all. "They've got text messages from his phone, Shannon. Somebody in the mosque was siphoning the offerings and wired $20,000 to a Lebanese bank account using Khalid's password. The cell phone that received the text messages was at the parking lot where Ja'dah Mahdi was abducted and then was traced to Sandbridge that night. How do you explain all that?"

"Maybe Khalid's phone was stolen," Shannon countered. "Maybe somebody's trying to set him up."

"You don't think Taj Deegan has thought about that? You don't think they've got pictures of Khalid with his cell phone in the days following the text messages? You don't think they can reconstruct the movement of his cell phone using GPS coordinates and show how his cell phone happened to be in precisely the same places that Khalid was in the days after he sent the text messages? Deegan's no amateur. She doesn't file a case like this until she's covered every angle."

"You might be right. But I'm just saying that it's too early to tell. And it's not our job to assume scenarios that would convict our client."

When the waitress came to take their order, Alex asked if she could give them a few more minutes.

He leaned forward and lowered his voice. "Shannon, you did an awesome job this morning for Khalid. I want to believe in his innocence as much as you do. But at the end of the day, we've got a responsibility to our firm, and I've got a responsibility to the people in my church."

Alex decided not to finish the thought. He could tell by the look on Shannon's face that she knew his position was nonnegotiable. But what worried him was that look of flint in her eyes—a look that said she was digging in too.

"I know we both wish that your grandfather was here right now to help us through this," Shannon said softly. "But he's not. And I know that, as much as I loved and admired him, you were a lot closer to him than I was. So I'm not going to sit here and tell you that he would have taken this case." She hesitated and took a sip of iced tea, though Alex could tell she wasn't finished. "But I *can* tell you what seems right to me. And I can't walk away from this man, Alex."

Alex started to respond, but Shannon put a hand on his forearm. "Please let me finish."

Alex nodded. He hated being at odds with Shannon like this.

"I've been thinking about this a lot," she continued. "On the way over here, I decided that the best way to resolve this matter is for me to leave the firm and take Khalid with me. You can continue to represent Ghaniyah and the personal-injury clients who are getting nervous. Your deacons will get off your back, and we won't be abandoning Khalid. And I'm not suggesting this out of frustration or because I'm angry or anything like that. You and I just have different ideas about what it means to be a lawyer. We'll still be friends," Shannon promised. "But maybe it's best if I strike out and start handling criminal cases, and you can focus on personal-injury clients."

The whole thing caught Alex so off guard that he didn't know how to respond. He wrinkled his brow and frowned at the idea. "I . . . I don't know. . . . Shannon, I definitely don't want this case to split our firm."

"It's too late, Alex. It already has."

35

HASSAN IBN TALIB watched the news coverage of Khalid Mobassar's bond hearing with more than passing curiosity. He noticed how haggard the imam looked when he stepped out into the bright sunshine after posting the $1.5 million bond on Friday morning. Reporters shouted questions, but Khalid ignored them all as he climbed into the backseat of a waiting Town Car. After the vehicle pulled away, a field reporter talked about the issue on everyone's mind. Where did a man like Khalid come up with the security to post a bond worth $1.5 million?

Hassan smiled at the television and the idiocy of the American press. Now that Khalid was out of jail, Hassan knew that the next assignment would not be far behind.

◁▷

It was, Khalid Mobassar thought, *Allah's will that I was released in time for the Friday noon salat.*

Prayer was a cardinal tenet of the Islamic faith, the foremost duty after the Shahadah. Like all devout Muslims, Khalid prayed publicly five times each day, allowing the salats to dictate the rhythm of his life. Man existed to worship Allah—*"I have created the jinn and humankind only that they might worship me."* The salats were an outward expression of worship, a spiritual lifeline by which worshipers submitted themselves to the will of Allah.

Khalid had, of course, been faithful to each salat during his time in jail. For a devout Muslim, when it is time to pray, all the world becomes a mosque.

On Friday, Khalid arrived at the Norfolk mosque in time to hear the adhan blare over the loudspeakers: *"Allah is most great. I bear witness that there is no God but the One God. I bear witness that Mohammed is the messenger of God. Hasten to pray! Hasten to success! God is most great! There is no God but the One True God."*

In response to the call, the faithful streamed into the Islamic Learning Center and went about their purification rites. Each worshiper removed his or her shoes prior to the ritualistic washing. The carpet, trampled on by so many wet feet, smelled musty—the stench of sin being washed away.

Khalid delighted in the sight and the smells. The mosque had never been so full!

He led the salat, as always, with the worshipers stationed behind him in straight rows, shoulder to shoulder, all facing the quiblah. As the congregation proceeded through each part of the ritual, Khalid was overwhelmed with the majesty and greatness of Allah. He could see Allah's timing in his release, Allah working out every detail of Khalid's humble life.

Allah is most great.

He prostrated himself before Allah and thought about the opportunity he would have in a few moments to speak not just to his mosque but to a worldwide audience. Khalid's voice of reform, so stifled and insignificant only a month ago, would now be broadcast to the entire planet.

Khalid begged Allah for favor and ended the salat with the invocation of peace called the salaam. Following Khalid's lead, the worshipers turned first to the right and then to the left, uttering the greeting, "May the peace, mercy, and blessings of Allah be upon you."

As they finished and sat down, Khalid turned to face the worshipers. Next came the khutbah, a ten-minute message of solemn importance. Khalid placed his left hand on the front of his right hip and his dominant right hand on the top of his left as he began.

"When the great Prophet Mohammed, may peace be upon him, returned from battle, he said, 'We are finished with the lesser jihad; now we are starting the greater jihad.' For too many years, too many

Muslims have been fighting the lesser jihad and ignoring the greater jihad, the internal battle for purity, a battle with our own evil nature." Khalid's voice echoed with authority in the stillness of the mosque. The worshipers were unusually still and solemn today, anxious to hear a word from someone who had suffered for the sake of Allah, a prophet in their own midst whom they had too long taken for granted.

"This greater jihad will not be won by honor killings and suicide bombers. It will only be won when we peacefully submit to Allah's will. It is time to lay down the swords of the lesser jihad and pick up the plowshares of the greater jihad."

Khalid paused and searched the eyes of the faithful. In some, he saw resistance. They wanted a leader full of threats and bravado. But in others, he saw hope. He realized that his words this day would unleash powerful forces for and against him. He had studied the great reformers, and this was always their lot. Violence. Passion. Hatred. Admiration. Love.

But ultimately—perhaps in his case—there would be one other by-product—the salvation of the world's greatest religion.

36

LIKE MILLIONS OF OTHER Muslim Americans, Hassan watched Khalid Mobassar's khutbah on cable television. Afterward, the talking heads sliced and diced each word and debated Mobassar's guilt or innocence. Most were cynical, postulating that he had used the national spotlight to influence future jurors. They pointed out that he would probably not take the stand in his own defense and that the media coverage of today's events gave him the chance to "testify" without being cross-examined.

Representatives of various Muslim groups took the other side, chastising the media for its rush to judgment. It was a classic case of racial and religious stereotyping, they said.

To Hassan, it was *all* empty rhetoric. Americans believed in talk, like some collective national therapy. It was another weakness of the Great Satan, and Hassan turned off his television before *he* was drawn into its mindless addiction. They wanted to talk? He would give them something to talk about.

His orders came, as he expected they might, nearly four hours later. This time, they came via e-mail from a temporary address that could never be traced. There was a young woman in California, the daughter of a prominent leader in an LA mosque, who had strayed from the faith. She'd had the audacity to get baptized in front of a large congregation in a suburban Christian church.

Hassan was instructed to show no mercy. There would be no opportunity for the woman to renounce her newfound faith. She must die in a way that would send terror into the hearts of the weak-kneed American public.

Hassan was also told to begin surveillance on Taj Deegan, the single mother who would lead the prosecution team against Khalid Mobassar, and to investigate the jury selection process for the city of Virginia Beach. He should be prepared to act as soon as the jurors were selected for Khalid's trial. The Americans celebrated the transparency and openness of their judicial system. What the Americans saw as a great strength, Hassan Ibn Talib would be prepared to exploit as a great weakness.

◁▷

It had been a long time since Alex had stayed home on a Friday night. But that's exactly what he was doing tonight. He flicked from one TV channel to the next, watching the endless loop of coverage on what the media called "the Sandbridge Honor Killings." He sat with his legs extended in front of him resting on a stool, his computer in his lap. Against his better judgment, he scrolled through the comments to the story about Khalid in the *Tidewater Times*. They were overwhelmingly negative and, for the most part, emotional rants by anonymous commenters. *"Muslims like beheadings. Once he's found guilty, this man should be beheaded on the Virginia Beach boardwalk."* Other commenters used symbols to replace certain letters so that the foul language wouldn't get flagged by the automatic filter. A few took shots at Alex and Shannon. *"Typical lawyer scumbags. They'll say anything this guy wants them to so they can make money from his wife's car accident."*

One of the comments took specific aim at Alex's church. *"And this guy calls himself a pastor?"* The same comment gave the phone number for the church and a list of deacons for people to call so they could urge the church to fire Alex.

There was a thread of race-baiting in the comments as well. *"This country is being overrun by radical Arabs. We need to cut out this cancer NOW!!"*

Reading the comments, Alex felt like somebody had tied him to a runaway train and was dragging him down the tracks. He had done nothing to bring this on. But every word printed about him or his firm would stay on the Internet forever. Khalid's story would eventually give way to other stories, and the American public would move on. But when someone Googled the name Alexander Madison, the first page to pop up would show his representation of an accused Muslim murderer.

He normally didn't care that much about what people thought. In fact, he had a way of intentionally antagonizing people just to get a reaction. But the magnitude and lopsidedness of this criticism were overwhelming even for him. Alex was a young professional with his entire career in front of him. Now he would be forever defined as an attorney who had represented a client accused of beheading an innocent young woman.

He hated to leave Shannon alone on the case. He had tried everything possible to talk her out of it. But the more he pressed her, the more she dug in her heels. His partner was determined to drive off a cliff. Alex's only choice was whether or not he would be riding in the passenger seat.

In a way, they had been down this road before. Shannon had stayed with her emotionally abusive boyfriend long after Alex begged her to break it off. He knew that eventually the relationship would crash and burn or escalate into real physical abuse. His role would be to help pick up the pieces.

He admired her spunk, but this time she was in way over her head. This time, the pieces might be damaged beyond repair.

37

ON SATURDAY MORNING, Alex threw on a pair of board shorts, a T-shirt, and Chacos and headed to the Belvedere for breakfast. The entire world may have turned against him in the past few days, but breakfast with his grandmother would be a respite from the storm. He needed someone to help him think clearly and navigate his way out of the case in an ethically appropriate manner. His grandmother wasn't a lawyer, but she had more common sense in her little finger than most people did in their entire bodies.

This morning, Ramona had commandeered one of the coveted booths near the windows. Alex arrived ten minutes late, and she waved him over. Her curly gray hair stuck out from under a visor, and she wore a long, droopy T-shirt with the sleeves rolled up to the elbows. The tourists were out in force, and the small coffee shop was overcrowded to the point that the air-conditioning couldn't keep up. Nothing like sweating a little during breakfast. Alex sat down, and the waitress came over and filled his coffee cup. Just the smell of Saturday morning coffee and sausage on the grill started to relax him.

"I've been trying to call the last few days," Ramona said. "You're harder to reach than the pope."

Alex didn't try to defend himself. He had wanted to talk with his grandmother but hadn't had the energy to go into it over the phone. He knew they'd have some time to hash things out this morning. "I've been a little busy."

"Well, don't forget to brush your teeth, get plenty of sleep, and have your devotions." Ramona smiled, but her matronly humor was lost on Alex. "Oh . . . they *have* gotten under your skin," she said.

For the next twenty minutes, Alex only picked at his food as he unburdened himself with a detailed version of what had transpired over the last few days. He hated to worry his grandmother, but he needed a sounding board. She was generally aware of the developments in the case but was surprised by Alex's meeting with Taj Deegan and all the evidence against Khalid Mobassar. When Alex told her about the visit from Bill Fitzsimmons and Harry Dent, she about came out of her seat.

"Well," Ramona huffed, "they're not paying you a dime anyway. Those two men better be careful what they ask for, or we'll make *them* start preaching so we can criticize *their* sermons."

"I can't really blame them," Alex said. "They're just trying to protect the church."

"I *do* blame them. And Harry Dent has never thought of anyone or anything other than himself."

The more Alex talked, the less appetite he had. There were a number of people in line staring at them, waiting for the booth to clear. With the other diners sitting so close by, Alex suggested that they finish their conversation on the boardwalk.

"You hardly touched breakfast," Ramona said. "Going on a hunger strike isn't going to make this go away."

Alex forced a smiled and pushed away the plate of half-eaten scrambled eggs. "They didn't use enough grease," he said.

They left the Belvedere and walked the half block to the boardwalk. Ramona was seventy-seven, but she moved at a brisk pace. She wore aviator shades under her visor and sported a cute pair of white sneakers with thick soles. As he walked beside her, Alex thought that he just might have the coolest grandmother in Virginia Beach.

"I saw your client yesterday on FOXNews," Ramona said, pumping her arms as she walked. "I thought he came across pretty well in that little sermon thing or whatever the Muslims call it."

"You are in a distinct minority."

"Well, he doesn't have to be Martin Luther King Jr. You've just got to show that he didn't order the honor killings."

Alex sensed his grandmother had already emotionally invested in the case and hesitated to tell her what he was really thinking. "Actually, Grandma, I think it might be my job to find Mr. Mobassar a more experienced criminal defense lawyer."

Ramona gave him a surprised glance but didn't slow down. "Why's that?"

As they walked past other, more leisurely strollers and made their way down the concrete "boardwalk," Alex explained the situation in more detail. His firm couldn't survive the negative publicity. His heart wasn't in criminal defense. When he got to the part about Shannon possibly peeling off and forming her own law practice, his grandmother was audibly grunting her disapproval. "I don't like it either, Grandma. But it was Shannon's idea, and I don't know what else to do if I can't talk her out of representing this guy."

"Alex Madison, you know precisely what you can do. You can stay with the case and give this Muslim fellow the best defense he could ever have."

Alex was a little taken aback by the comment. Since the day he graduated from high school, his grandmother had operated on the philosophy that Alex should live his own life, and she would support him in whatever he decided to do. But this conversation, like the one they'd had about his quitting at the church, was headed in an entirely different direction.

"It's not that I don't think I could do a good job with the case," Alex explained. "It's just that I've got other things to worry about. I've got to consider how this will impact the church. I've got an entire law practice and a duty to my other clients. I don't want them to suffer because their firm represents an unpopular defendant. I just don't think it's in my best interest or Khalid's best interest for me to stay on the case. Shannon's either, for that matter."

They walked along in silence, his grandmother apparently chewing on those thoughts. "Do you want my opinion or my blessing?" she eventually asked.

He really wanted her blessing, but of course he couldn't say that. "Your opinion, of course."

"I think you're making this too complicated. Your job isn't to worry about how people might react or the domino effect on other cases. Your job is to do the right thing. If people can't handle that, it's their problem, not yours."

"So, what's the right thing?"

"You're a Madison; you'll figure it out."

"What's that supposed to mean?"

Ramona stopped walking and sighed. This was serious. The woman never let anything break her stride. "Let's ... um ... let's take a break for a minute."

She walked to the rail at the edge of the boardwalk and worked on catching her breath. Alex joined her and looked out over the sand at the shimmering ocean. He braced for the lecture he knew was coming.

"Your grandfather was one of the most hated men around when he brought those cases for court-ordered integration of the public schools," Ramona said. "They kicked us out of social clubs, sent us death threats, and called us the vilest names you can imagine. People who had been our friends for life wouldn't even speak to us." Ramona frowned, and Alex could tell the memories still brought a stab of pain.

"Your grandfather wasn't perfect; I don't mean that. But the more people turned against him, the more determined he became. Our friends would ask him how he could sleep at night with all of the violence he was causing among schoolchildren, and he would say that he slept like a baby.

"Your dad had that same stubborn streak. John always wanted your dad to follow him into law practice, but your dad had his own ideas." When Alex glanced at his grandmother, he couldn't tell what was going on behind the big sunglasses, but the corners of her mouth seemed tight with emotion. "I think your dad went into the ministry in part to spread the gospel and in part to show your granddad that he wasn't going to let anyone tell him what to do."

Ramona breathed a big sigh and patted one of Alex's hands on the railing. "You remember when you first wanted to be a lawyer?" his grandmother asked.

Alex shook his head. "Not really."

"It was after you read the book *To Kill a Mockingbird*. I don't think you completely understood the story at the time; you were only twelve or thirteen. But the story really resonated with you.

"I think part of it was the relationship that Scout had with her dad. But I think you also really admired Atticus Finch. He was willing to stand in the gap and represent someone the rest of the world wanted to lynch. Even at a young age, you somehow understood the nobility in that." Alex's grandmother glanced at him. "It doesn't surprise me that Shannon's willing to represent Khalid Mobassar. What *you've* got to decide is whether you're ready to help her."

38

BY SATURDAY NIGHT, the positive clips from Khalid Mobassar's Friday khutbah had been replaced by a series of interviews he had done on the Hezbollah television station in Lebanon in 1995. Alex didn't know which cable network had first discovered the footage, but soon the video was playing on all the news channels.

In the video, a younger Khalid described the pain of losing his son in a retaliatory strike by the Israeli armed forces. The interview was in Arabic, but the words were translated by closed-captioning into English. Khalid said that his son Omar had been working on a humanitarian project but that this distinction apparently meant nothing to the Israelis. He criticized the tactics of the Israeli military that had resulted in the loss of civilian lives. He called on the United States to end its hypocrisy and condemn such actions. Where was the international outrage, he asked.

If the Lebanese government was unwilling to defend the innocent civilians in his country, then the people must turn to Hezbollah, Khalid had said. He promised that his mosque would henceforth have two donation boxes at the front entrance. One would be for the operations and ministry of the mosque; the other would support the humanitarian efforts of Hezbollah.

Alex felt sick to his stomach as he watched the clips and listened to the commentary afterward. The experts pointed out that Hezbollah had started the conflict and then stationed its headquarters and weapons among the neighborhoods and refugee camps in Lebanon. The Israeli military had made every effort to avoid collateral damage. Alex knew that in the years following the interview, Khalid had disavowed his earlier support of Hezbollah and had become an outspoken critic of radical Islam. But these fifteen-year-old clips, taken out of context, could seal Khalid's doom before the jury was ever impaneled. There was no longer any doubt as to whether Khalid had ties to Hezbollah. And with the discovery of the clips following so closely on the heels of Khalid's impassioned speech against the violence of radical Islamacists, it made Khalid look like a hypocrite willing to say anything to bolster his case.

Or maybe, in truth, that's exactly who he was.

What did Alex really know about the motives of Khalid Mobassar? What did Alex really know about his relationships with terrorist organizations?

◁▷

That night, Alex waited with Shannon and the Mobassars for Nara to arrive from Lebanon. With Khalid trying to avoid public appearances and Ghaniyah in no shape to drive, some friends of the Mobassars had gone to the airport to pick up their daughter. When Nara arrived, Alex noted the enthusiastic hug she gave her father and her lukewarm embrace of her mother.

"Nara, these are the lawyers I told you about," Khalid said.

Both Alex and Shannon shook Nara's hand. *How does anyone look this good after a transatlantic flight?* Alex wondered. He hadn't expected an imam's daughter to look like a Lebanese cover girl.

Nara was tall and athletic, just an inch or two shorter than Alex. She had thick, dark hair that was pulled back in a clip, accentuating a high forehead, sharp cheekbones, and alluring brown eyes. She moved with an air of confidence, her posture perfectly erect. Alex noticed a faint whiff of perfume blended with the smell of someone who had been sitting in a cramped airplane for fourteen hours.

Khalid's bright curiosity reflected in Nara's eyes, and the imam's daughter mirrored his lithe build and broad, straight shoulders. But Alex saw none of Ghaniyah's facial features in her daughter. Perhaps that was one reason he had been so surprised by her appearance.

"Nice to meet you," Nara said, her diction perfect. "I'm grateful for the help you've given my father. He speaks highly of you both."

After a few minutes of pleasantries, Khalid suggested that Alex and Shannon join him and Nara in the living room. Ghaniyah offered to prepare some coffee and finger foods, but Alex politely declined. After Ghaniyah disappeared, Alex and Shannon spent about thirty minutes bringing Nara up to speed on the legal situation. From the probing nature of her questions, it became immediately obvious that Khalid's daughter was more than just a pretty face.

When Shannon explained that the next step would be a preliminary hearing the following Friday, Nara was anxious to hear details about the strategy. Whom did they plan on calling as witnesses? What was their theory about how Khalid's phone was accessed? Did Alex and Shannon have any other suspects?

Because Shannon had been doing most of the talking, Alex chimed in. "We don't normally ask a lot of questions at a preliminary hearing. The judge only has to find reasonable suspicion that a crime was committed. There's no sense giving the prosecutors a preview of our case if we're going to lose the hearing anyway."

Instead of giving Alex an appreciative look of understanding, Nara frowned. "Do you really think that's true in this case?"

Alex had seen this mind-set a few times before. Clients held out false hopes of early and miraculous dismissals. His job was to disabuse them of these phantom hopes and prepare them for a long ordeal.

"This case is no different than any other on that count," Alex said. "The commonwealth doesn't bring charges unless they think they've got enough to make them stick. Both you and your father need to adopt a mind-set that this is going to be a long and frustrating process and that things will get a lot worse before they get better. Eventually, the truth will come out."

"I'm not a lawyer," Nara responded, "but I know that my father's innocent. And even if we don't win at the preliminary hearing, it seems to me that if we don't start getting our side of the case out there, my father will never be able to find an unbiased jury pool."

"I see your point," Shannon said, though her tone of voice indicated that she wasn't appreciative of a layperson questioning their legal strategy. "But Alex is still right. There are better ways to get your side out there than to preview your case at the preliminary hearing."

"Then how do we do that?" Khalid asked. "Because so far it seems that the cable shows only want to run my interview from many years ago from the Hezbollah channel."

Before Alex could answer, Nara jumped in again. "Actually, I've been thinking about this during my flight. My father's lost two sons in the conflict with the Israelis. Yet he still speaks as a voice of reform and reason for the Muslim faith, opposing the violence of the jihadists. I've lost two brothers and have become a spokesperson for women's rights in the Muslim community." She spoke with serious intensity now, her eyes lighting up. "Our family's story needs to be told."

Nara looked at her father, and Alex could tell that the two had a deep admiration and respect for each other. "I understand why *you* can't tell that story," Nara said. "Your words will be twisted and used against you. But *I* can tell our story. And somebody must, because right now the press is painting my father as nothing more than a tool of Hezbollah."

Shannon made a face. "I'm not a big fan of media interviews that we don't control. The courtroom has rules and processes designed for fairness. I'd rather try my cases there."

"By the time we get to court, it may be too late," Nara quickly responded. To Alex she seemed a little testy from the long flight.

Maybe we should start charging $300 an hour, Alex thought, *since our client's daughter is so intent on giving us advice.*

Shannon allowed Nara's statement to go unchallenged, and the tension dissipated a little. "Why don't you let Alex and me talk about your concerns and see if we can put together a media strategy that doesn't have an unacceptable layer of risk? We could call you tomorrow with our recommendation."

Nara didn't wait for her dad to respond. "We'll look forward to your recommendation. And then my father and I will decide what's in his best interest, because he will be the one spending time in jail if we lose."

Alex watched Shannon bristle at the response, but his partner kept it professional. "Okay," she said. "What other questions do you have about the process?"

The rest of the meeting went better, although there was enough distrust in the air that Alex didn't feel right about announcing his plan to withdraw. The relationship between Shannon and Nara had started off pretty rocky. Alex was afraid that if he indicated anything less than full commitment to the case right now, Nara would talk her father into finding other lawyers.

After the meeting, the two law partners huddled up in the driveway of the Mobassar duplex. "We sure didn't need *her* to ride in here and save the day," Shannon said.

"I agree," Alex replied. "But you've got to admit, she is smart and camera-friendly."

"Okay, you think she's hot," Shannon said, her voice snide. "But that doesn't mean she wouldn't get ambushed and end up making a fool of herself on TV. She comes across as a little too arrogant for me."

Alex didn't argue. He had enough problems right now without getting in the middle of a power struggle between his law partner and the imam's strong-willed daughter.

39

FIFTEEN-YEAR-OLD NARA MOBASSAR was helping her mother in the kitchen of their small Lebanese house when the knock on the door came. As usual, Nara had been going about her chores in virtual silence, her sulking manner a teenager's protest against the stifling rules that applied to Muslim girls. Beirut was straddling two worlds—the secularized culture of the West and the traditional Islamic way of life. For Nara, who had discovered her flirtatious power over the boys at her Muslim school, the standards of the Mobassar household were suffocating.

Her older brother, Omar, whom she idolized, was already helping Hezbollah with their humanitarian efforts in the Palestinian refugee camps. Her younger brother, and Nara's full-time nemesis, was fourteen-year-old Ahmed. Ahmed was determined to be a warrior and spoke with a stridency that pleased his mother but worried Nara's more conciliatory father.

Nara was the rebellious one. Ahmed could fight for Islam, but Nara wanted to fight for her own independence and the ability to think freely. As a token of that quest, she waged a silent protest each night, working beside her mother in absolute silence as they prepared the food for the all-important men of the house.

When the knock came, her mother turned from the stove and told Nara to watch the chickpeas as they boiled, while keeping one eye on the fried pita bread and lamb.

Standing over the chickpeas and absorbing the steaming odor, Nara heard hushed conversation at the front door. Curious, she walked quietly across the kitchen and stood next to the doorway. Her mother's voice grew husky, as if she couldn't accept what was being said. The visitor spoke softly for a few more seconds, until she was interrupted by the insistent voice of Nara's mother.

"No! Not Omar!" Nara's mother was backing away from the visitor, holding out her hand as if pushing the bad news away, shaking her head. "Not my Omar. Not my son."

Nara was drawn into the hallway, her own heart in her throat as she watched her mother edge backward. Without warning, her mother's knees buckled and she collapsed to the floor. Nara rushed to her aid and, along with the visitor from the mosque, helped her mother into a sitting position.

The three women sat on the floor, Ghaniyah looking at Nara in stunned silence. Her next words were a whisper. "The Jews killed him, Nara. Rocket strikes in the Palestinian camps. Omar was collateral damage."

The scene was so surreal, the news so shocking, that Nara couldn't process the words. She stared at her mother and felt waves of grief sweep over her, like somebody had ripped her heart from her chest.

But within seconds, her mother seemed to find some hidden strength. She composed herself, sat up straight, and looked past her daughter. "Allah's will be done," Ghaniyah said. She shook off the help of her friend and rose to her feet. She began a chant. Loud. Insistent. Praising Allah for taking her son to paradise. Over and over and over. The high-pitched chanting of praise that Nara had heard so many times as a call to prayer.

Soon, her mother's friend had joined in, praising Allah, oblivious to Nara, who sat on the floor in utter shock and disbelief. *How can they praise Allah when he has allowed such pain?*

As the chant continued, Nara's shock turned to anger, and she rushed from the hallway. She ran outside and down the sidewalk, sprinting without looking back until she thought she might collapse. She slowed to a walk, sobbing and out of breath, dizzy with sorrow. She thought about the sweet spirit of Omar, the way he had always been her protector. She cried uncontrollably, fighting to catch her breath, her grief not allayed one second by the thought of Omar in paradise. She wanted him here! He was too young to die! What kind of God would allow such a thing?

Later that night, after the purification and shrouding of Omar's body, her father taught about paradise from the holy Qur'an. It was just the four immediate family members gathered in the kitchen.

Nara chose that moment to voice her pain. "Why would Allah let this happen?" Her lips trembled from both sadness and anger. "If Allah is so great, how can he allow the Israelis to kill someone as pure-hearted as Omar?"

The words had barely escaped her lips when the slap came—Ghaniyah's open hand hard across Nara's face. "How dare you insult Allah!" Ghaniyah demanded. "No child of mine speaks that way!"

The slap stunned Nara into a seething silence. Her mother had *never* hit Nara before. It made her want to scream curses at Allah. She wanted to spit at her mother and tell her how stupid she was. But her father's reassuring voice broke in before Nara had time to do any of those things.

"We all feel pain and anger," he said. He placed a hand on Ghaniyah's arm to calm her down. He looked compassionately at Nara, who clenched her teeth in rage. "But Allah should not be the target of our anger. Allah has prepared paradise for your brother. Allah did not send the bombs that killed Omar—that is the work of the Jews and the Christians. Allah, praise his name, will bring justice in his time. At this moment our family must come together."

Nara's father had always understood her, and she knew he could read her eyes right now. She was not buying *any* of this. Later, she and her father would talk—heart to heart, without her mother's disapproving presence. Nara's father welcomed her tough questions about the faith. Nara's mother was afraid of those same questions.

Standing silently in the corner, Ahmed's face proclaimed his own anger that night. His narrow eyes filled with rage against the Jews who had killed his only brother. His look reflected Nara's own raw pain. And for the first time in her life, she was proud to have a brother who believed in conquering evil by force.

40

ON SUNDAY MORNING, Alex was still conflicted over whether he should stay in the case. Something about the meeting with Khalid's daughter was making him reconsider his tentative decision to withdraw. He tried to tell himself that it had nothing to do with her looks. It was already obvious, from the short meeting the night before, that Shannon and Nara would be like oil and water. If Alex didn't stay, those two would end up at each other's throats.

Another reason for staying surfaced after Alex preached a lackluster sermon. Bill Fitzsimmons met Alex in the foyer of the church and asked Alex if he would join the deacons for a brief meeting. During the meeting, Harry Dent asked Alex whether he was going to withdraw from the case.

"To be honest," Harry said with an air of moral superiority, "I've heard from a lot of people in our church who believe it would be pretty selfish for you to continue."

That statement, and the smugness with which it was delivered, turned out to be the tipping point.

Alex's grandmother had made him think hard about what it meant to be a Madison. Could he live with himself if he abandoned Shannon and Khalid? On the plus side, if he took the case, he might get to know the imam's daughter a little better. But what pushed Alex Madison absolutely over the edge was the sanctimonious Harry Dent sitting in a deacon's meeting, his bald head gleaming in the sunlight from a nearby window, trying to tell Alex what cases he should and should not handle.

"I've been praying a lot about this," Alex said, knowing it was a small lie. "And I've been asking myself two questions: What's best for the church? And what would Jesus have me do?"

Alex paused for a moment, actually enjoying this little drama. Truthfully, his decision would have minimal impact on the church. They would have sixty people there next Sunday whether Alex stayed in the case or not.

"I'm staying on the case," Alex announced, and he enjoyed the shocked looks on their faces. "I believe Mr. Mobassar is innocent."

◁▷

That afternoon, Alex called Khalid and explained that it was in his best interest for his daughter *not* to subject herself to a round of media interviews. Nevertheless, by Sunday evening, Alex was watching the imam's daughter do the rounds on the cable news shows. She appeared via satellite from Norfolk, which made the interviews a little cumbersome, but her sincerity and charm could not be denied.

She told how, as a young girl, she had questioned her father about many aspects of Islam, especially the subjugation of women. Her father, according to Nara, had explained that Mohammed, peace be upon him, had actually advanced the cause of women in his society. Mohammed's first convert was a woman. He treated his wives with kindness and respect—unusual in his culture. Nara's father had encouraged her to speak out against the abuse of women by fundamentalist Muslims and to point out that those practices were wholly inconsistent with the teachings of the Prophet.

It was incomprehensible, Nara argued, that this man had ordered an honor killing.

Nara also talked about losing her brothers—one to an Israeli rocket while he worked for a humanitarian mission, the other when he sought to retaliate. Her father's interview on Hezbollah television after Omar's death was not the end of the matter. When his second son, Ahmed, had died, Khalid had gone into the kind of deep mourning that could cause someone to reevaluate his deeply held convictions. He emerged with a firm belief that jihad was not the way. He became a reformer, speaking out against the radicals. That was why Old Dominion University had asked him to come teach. After a few years of teaching, her father had decided to dedicate himself full-time to the growing mosque where he now served as the lead imam.

The interviews came off far better than Alex expected. For the first time, he felt a small shift in momentum. He picked up his BlackBerry to call Shannon. He made a note to feature Nara at the trial.

Even Shannon admitted that Nara had handled herself with great poise. But Shannon also had a sense of foreboding. She had just gotten off the phone with Khalid. "Nara is flying to New York in the morning for some in-studio interviews," Shannon said. "I strongly cautioned against it, but in Khalid's words, his daughter is 'somewhat strong-willed.'"

"You worry too much," Alex said. "She'll be fine."

◁▷

When Hassan Ibn Talib awoke from the nightmare, his skin was clammy with sweat. The dream had never ended like this before. There were the usual scenes of fighting—Hassan riding headlong into throngs of enemy soldiers. But this time, he had killed only a few when the arrow struck him and a spear knocked him from his horse. The ground was not yet red with blood. He felt no pain, but neither did he feel the exhilaration of a raging battle. Once again, he appeared humbly before the throne of Allah.

His bad deeds, as usual, were weighing down the left-hand side of the scales. But this time, as Allah squeezed out a few drops of blood on the right side, the scales didn't move. Allah looked angrily at Hassan, shaking his head.

"Is this it?" he bellowed. "I spared your life all those years for *this*?"

Allah's rage stunned Hassan into silence. He trembled before the throne, ashamed to the core of his soul that he had not done more.

Before Allah could pronounce judgment, Hassan awoke. The nightmare vaporized, but the feeling in the pit of his stomach remained.

"Is this it?" Allah had demanded.

I must work harder, Hassan decided.

I must do more.

41

ALEX WATCHED NARA RUN the gauntlet of morning shows while he got ready for work. He felt a little guilty about not being there with her, but he doubted he could have added much to the conversation. Nara's story was a family story, told through the eyes of an adoring daughter. A lawyer on the set would only emphasize that Nara's father was not just a wonderful Islamic reformer but had also been charged with ordering the beheading of a young woman. And the prosecutors had the text message to prove it.

Nara appeared to grow more comfortable with each interview, though Alex could see the weariness in her eyes. He needed to get to the office, but CBS was teasing its interview "right after the break," so Alex fixed a bowl of Frosted Mini-Wheats and waited. He gave himself ten more minutes before he absolutely *had* to get going. There was plenty of work waiting for him, including preparation for the preliminary hearing.

The CBS interview began by following the same script as the others—a few tough questions about Khalid's ties to Hezbollah followed by a chance for Nara to tell her story. But just before the interview concluded, the host headed in a different direction.

"Tell me about the doctrine of al toqiah. Am I even saying that right?"

"Yes, that's right," Nara said, her manner unflappable. "Al toqiah is a belief held by some Muslims that it's okay to use deception in order to advance the cause of Allah. The lies will be forgiven if Allah's cause is advanced and his will is done."

"Does your father believe in the doctrine of al toqiah?" The host asked the question pleasantly enough, but the implications were devastating. Could it be that all this reform rhetoric coming from Khalid was merely a way for him to enter this country? Was Khalid really a radical supporter of Hezbollah merely masquerading as a moderate?

Nara's hesitation surprised Alex. She began by repeating the question. "Does my father believe in al toqiah?" She turned her head a little to the side. "My father has *never* spoken in support of this doctrine, to my knowledge. But most religions, while they condemn lying, also recognize that there are sometimes bigger issues at play. For example, in the Jewish and Christian traditions, there is the story of Rahab and how she lied to protect the Jewish spies. She was commended for it, not chastised. Sort of like sacrificing the lesser good for the greater good."

"Some would call that the end justifying the means," the host countered.

"If you're suggesting that my father has somehow engaged in a thirteen-year deception just to gain people's trust so that he could then commit these heinous acts, you are mistaken. He became a reformer while living in Lebanon, long before he considered coming to the United States."

But Nara's indignation did not entirely assuage Alex's concerns. He hoped Taj Deegan wasn't watching. She may have just discovered a wonderful tool for cross-examination.

Al toqiah. Lying for the cause of Allah. Deegan could use it to cast doubt on everything Khalid and Nara said.

Even Alex found himself considering Khalid's statements in a whole new light.

42

JONESY MAXWELL had been in charge of maintenance at Grace Coastal Church in Los Angeles for as long as anyone could remember. He'd seen the good times and the bad. Lately, with the installation of a friendly young pastor who also had a decent dose of humility, the Lord had chosen to bless.

Grace Coastal was overwhelmingly white and suburban, and Jonesy was from the inner city, but the church members accepted him as a brother. He sensed it was almost a point of pride for the congregation—*Look, we have black members too!* So Jonesy played his part, sitting in the first or second row, raising his hands and singing loudly during the worship time, tossing a few amens toward the pastor during the stronger moments of the sermon.

The amens had been flying fast and furious yesterday because the church had baptized a total of thirteen new converts during three separate worship services. Jonesy was especially fired up when a young woman from a prominent Muslim family walked boldly through the waters of baptism. "She risks persecution and alienation from her family for her decision to follow Christ," the pastor had said. "Now, what's holding *you* back?"

Yes, sir, yesterday had been Grace Coastal Church at its absolute finest.

On Monday morning, Jonesy had to contend with the earthier part of being a church janitor. There would be bulletins and papers left in the pews, bathrooms to clean, and if he had time, a lawn to mow. Jonesy had intended to start work at eight, but his knees were acting up, and he couldn't drag his tired body to the building before nine.

He planned to empty the baptismal first. He would pull the plug, do some other work while the water drained, then come back to rinse it out. He climbed the steps behind the stage, felt the knifelike pain in his right knee, and wondered if he should break down and get a total knee replacement after all. He caught his breath and limped toward the baptismal. A few feet away, he stopped dead in his tracks, mouth open in a silent scream. Before he could look away, he felt his breakfast rising, and he turned to the side and hurled. He knelt on his left knee, dizzy at what he had just witnessed.

There was a dead body in the baptistry!

He tried to catch his breath and look back—he needed to confirm the picture now seared into his mind. A second glance brought a second round of vomit, this time in a nearby trash can.

After he had wiped his mouth with the back of his hand, he tried to make sense of it all.

The head of the young woman who had been baptized yesterday was floating in the bloody water—severed from her body.

Somehow, Jonesy composed himself and found the urge to pray. "Lord, have mercy," he said over and over. "In the name of Jesus, bring her killer to justice."

43

BY MONDAY AFTERNOON, news of the honor killing at Grace Coastal Church had exploded across national television. There was no hard evidence linking Khalid to the murders, but that didn't stop commentators from noting the similarities in the methods used by the executioner and the fact that Khalid Mobassar was out on bond. Before long, legal "experts" began a renewed assault on the decision by Judge McElroy to free Khalid. "This might never have happened if Judge McElroy had one ounce of common sense," one of them suggested.

Alex resorted to the hunker-down strategy, retreated to his office, and gave Sylvia strict instructions that he was not to be disturbed. He knew he needed to get ready for the preliminary hearing on Friday. Instead, he spent his time second-guessing whether he should even stay on the case. Nara Mobassar was right. At this rate, her father would be convicted before the opening statements began.

It didn't help that Shannon had filed Ghaniyah's personal-injury case earlier that same morning. Legally, they could have waited. But the firm desperately needed the cash flow, and both Alex and Shannon thought it might help in the sympathy department for the Mobassars. That was before the California honor killing. Now, Alex and Shannon were being portrayed as greedy ambulance chasers who took Khalid's criminal case only because they didn't want to lose Ghaniyah's civil case.

Alex knew things were bad when his grandmother called to second-guess his strategy. "Whose idea was it to file that personal-injury case today?"

"Shannon's," Alex said. "And mine," he added.

There was silence. "Well, if Shannon is on board, then I guess I can't be too critical."

Alex looked up and noticed a reporter and a cameraperson standing at his office door. *How did they get past Sylvia?*

"I've got to go, Grandma," Alex said. "It looks like I've got company."

Alex spent the next several minutes escorting the news team out of his office suite. Because he refused to grant them an interview, that night's telecast would run clips of Alex prodding them into the hallway and closing the door behind them. What they didn't record was the young lawyer's exchange with his receptionist afterward.

"Why'd you let them back to my office?" Alex asked, his voice sharp and accusatory.

"I tried to tell them," Sylvia protested, "but they kept insisting. I figured a few questions wouldn't hurt."

"'A few questions wouldn't hurt'?" Alex repeated. He couldn't believe anyone could be so incompetent. But before he could launch into a serious lecture, Sylvia started to cry.

"Look, why don't you just take the rest of the day off?" Alex said.

After she left, Alex locked the outside doors and retreated to his office again.

Shannon had been the smart one. After filing the personal-injury lawsuit, she had spent the rest of the day working from home.

44

GOOD LAWYERS DIDN'T COME CHEAP, especially on a case with as much negative publicity as Khalid's. Though Ghaniyah's case would almost certainly be profitable, Alex knew he and Shannon would most likely burn through all that money and a whole lot more by the time they finished defending Khalid. For this reason, they called a meeting on Tuesday morning to request a $50,000 retainer from Khalid and to give him one important stipulation—no Hezbollah funds could be used to pay his lawyers. For Alex, it was a last-ditch effort to extricate his firm from the case. If Khalid refused to pay the retainer, even Shannon wouldn't argue that they should take the case for free.

Alex had decided not to turn on the television this morning. Given the developments in California, he felt like his firm and Khalid were under siege. Forensics experts had already determined that the same sword used to sever Ja'dah's head had been used in California. Young lawyers dream about high-profile cases, but Alex had always pictured himself wearing the white hat, not the black one. In this case, Alex felt as if he were wandering aimlessly in the fog of war, bullets flying all around him, and he couldn't even tell where they were coming from.

He had a one-word strategy for these next few weeks of negative publicity: *survive*.

He checked his phone messages on the way to work and was surprised to discover that his critics had somehow discovered his cell number. He had already deleted dozens of hate-filled e-mails, including more than a few death threats. But there was something different about actually listening to the voices of his harshest critics; hearing the raw anger unnerved him. He thought about Shannon—the one lawyer in the firm who'd actually had the guts to speak out at Khalid's bond hearing. She hadn't said one word about death threats, but Alex was sure she must have received twice as many as he did.

He began to wonder if $50,000 was enough.

When he arrived at the office, Sylvia was behind her desk but looked like she might not last the day. She gave him a tortured look— her migraine face—and groaned out a "Good morning."

For heaven's sake, suck it up! Alex wanted to say. Instead, he also mumbled, "Good morning" and headed straight to his office.

Five minutes later, Sylvia was in his doorway, talking softly and moaning about her headache and the threats she had received as the firm's receptionist. She had called the police, but all they did was take another report. As she talked, Sylvia would occasionally stop and squeeze her temples just to make sure that Alex realized how much pain she was in.

"Do you need to go home?" Alex finally asked.

"I don't want to leave you stranded. But I can hardly keep my eyes open without the pain becoming just unbearable."

Alex sighed. "Hold on a second."

He walked down the hall to Shannon's office, closed the door, and admitted defeat. It was time for Sylvia to go. It was lousy timing, with everything happening on the Mobassar cases, but Alex couldn't handle it any longer. Shannon was happy he had finally discovered the obvious; she even volunteered to do the honors but also expressed caution. "Whoever fires her shouldn't mention the headaches," Shannon counseled. "They might be covered by the Americans with Disabilities Act."

Alex rose from his chair. "I need to do it," he said. "I'll let you figure out how to replace her."

Alex returned to his office and tried to let Sylvia down gently, but she did not cooperate. She had a spasm of crying, which only made the headache worse. Alex tried to comfort her but also kept glancing at his watch. It took thirty minutes of coaxing and sixty days of severance pay to send Sylvia packing with any kind of positive attitude.

Alex shuffled back to Shannon's office and plopped down in one of her client chairs. It felt like the end of a long day, but he knew the challenges were just beginning. He was giving Shannon a full report on Sylvia's situation when the phone rang. It was Alex's line, but Shannon picked it up. "Mr. Madison's office," she said.

She told the caller that Alex was busy, took a message, and returned the phone to its cradle. Less than a minute later the phone rang again. This time, it was Shannon's number, an outside line that Alex didn't recognize. If Shannon answered the phone, she'd get stuck speaking with the person even if she didn't want to.

She gave Alex a sideways glance—*What are you waiting for?*—and Alex picked up the phone. "Ms. Reese's office," he said. "How may I help you?"

Welcome to the big time, he thought.

45

THE MEETING with Khalid and Nara started heading downhill from the moment Nara opened her mouth.

She was upset about the coverage of Khalid's case she had seen on the news that morning. The ties with Hezbollah had been exaggerated. Plus, the media kept associating her father with the California case when there was absolutely no evidence he was involved. "How can they get away with that?" she asked.

Alex loved her commitment to the case, but she didn't know the first thing about the American legal system. Shannon gave Alex one of those *Who invited her?* looks.

"We'll have a chance to make our case in court," Alex reminded her. "There's no sense even watching the news coverage right now."

He could tell from the volcanic look in Nara's eyes that he was wasting his breath. She had her hair pulled up today, emphasizing her long neck and sharp cheekbones. She looked every bit as striking as the first time Alex laid eyes on her, but her exotic Middle Eastern appearance was decidedly less enchanting today. In fact, Alex would have traded her in a second for a mundane-looking daughter who was ten times less intense.

But intensity was part of her DNA and her culture. She emphasized the consonants when she spoke in a way that made her speech seem hard-edged—almost guttural. She couldn't hide a disapproving frown when somebody said something she didn't like. She seemed to speak her mind without filtering her thoughts, and she evidently expected others to be equally blunt with her.

In order to pacify Nara, Alex suggested that the firm issue a statement condemning the rush to judgment by the press and denying that Khalid had anything to do with *any* honor killings. But Nara wanted more. "This is racial profiling," she pressed. "Sensationalism. They make it sound like all Muslims are the same. We need to show them that my father is a *reformer*. He's a sworn enemy of the radicals. He's being set up by the fundamentalists."

Shannon had heard enough. "We're not a PR firm," she said. "We're lawyers. And we're good at what we do."

Not surprisingly, Nara frowned. Shannon turned to Khalid. If anyone had earned credibility with Khalid, it was Shannon. "You've got to trust us, Khalid. If you don't, then get somebody you do trust."

Khalid glanced down at the table for a second and then at his daughter. When he turned back to the lawyers, Alex knew bad news was coming.

"I do trust you," Khalid said, his voice measured yet firm. "But I've been thinking about the wisdom of having the same firm represent both myself and Ghaniyah.

"I *am* innocent. I detest the notion of violence in the name of religion, and I especially abhor the concept of honor killings. Nara is right—I've been set up by some very powerful enemies. But I also realize I could easily lose this case and spend the rest of my life in jail." Khalid looked haggard, and Alex knew that this infighting wasn't helping. He felt a little ashamed that he hadn't provided better leadership.

"If that happens, I'll need money to hire someone to look after Ghaniyah. I do not want Nara to sacrifice her work in Lebanon to come back and spend the rest of her life as an unpaid nurse for her mother."

"I disagree with my father on that," said Nara. "I see it as my duty to do so, and I would gladly fulfill it."

"Nevertheless," Khalid continued, his eyes becoming a little moist, "I'm very concerned about the impact on Ghaniyah's case if the same firm that represents me also represents her. That firm could become demonized before my case is over. And that could certainly hurt Ghaniyah's case."

Khalid took a deep breath before continuing. "It seems this case has made me a bit of a celebrity in the Muslim world. There are two Muslim law firms in Detroit that are willing to represent me—how do you say it?—pro bono. Nara has talked to the firms. . . . They actually contacted her, right after her appearance on national television. They've been pleading with us to turn both cases over to them."

"I have nothing against your firm," Nara quickly interjected. She was looking decidedly less attractive to Alex right now. Perhaps the nose *was* a little too sharp after all. "I can only assume that you are both gifted lawyers. But these other firms have more experience in high-profile criminal cases. And they are willing to launch a defense that will capitalize on my father's reformist tendencies."

"It's a mistake to use out-of-town lawyers," Alex insisted. *Especially Muslim ones.* "We need to focus on the evidence in this case—not turn this into a referendum on Muslim theology."

"I disagree," Nara said, as if she were an experienced criminal defense attorney. "This is not a gang killing; it's an alleged *honor killing.* We can't avoid the religious issues."

"I'm not saying we *avoid* them," Alex protested.

"Please," interrupted Khalid. "May I finish?"

Alex bit his tongue and quickly analyzed his own emotions. Until now, when he realized he might get fired from the case, Alex had not appreciated how much he wanted to stay in it. Yes, he hated the publicity. And yes, his client's uppity daughter was going to be a pain. But Alex's grandfather had been right. Something about defending an accused man when the whole world wanted to string him up made Alex feel noble.

"I understand Nara's misgivings with regard to your experience," Khalid continued. "But I personally have great faith in your legal skills and think I would be well-served to be represented by both of you. And forgive me, Ms. Reese, for being so blunt. But neither one of these Muslim firms has a strong female attorney who could help try the case, and I believe that's an important consideration.

"But I need to ask you both a question, and you don't have to answer it right now. In fact, I would like you to take the night to consider this."

Alex and Shannon were on the edge of their seats. Alex had never had a client quite like Khalid. "If I determine, in my capacity as guardian for my wife, that I should have a different law firm handle her case than the firm that represents me, which of the two cases would you prefer to handle?"

"If we could only pick one?" Alex asked.

"If you could only pick one."

◁ ▷

After Khalid and Nara left, Alex listed all the reasons he and Shannon should take Ghaniyah's case. There was serious money to be made in the personal-injury suit. On Khalid's case, they would get paid by the hour, if they were lucky, and they would have to endure the constant second-guessing of Nara Mobassar. Plus, Alex pointed out, civil cases were their specialty. They knew how to strong-arm insurance companies into big settlements. What's more, if they dropped Khalid's case, Alex's problems with his church would be over.

Shannon sat there frowning as Alex laid out his arguments.

"I'll take your silence as agreement," Alex said.

She shrugged. "I just think Khalid would be making a big mistake by going with a Muslim firm on his case. He'd be playing right into the prosecution's stereotypes. Even if we get Ghaniyah a million dollars, what good will it do her if Khalid's in jail?"

"Are you saying we should take Khalid's case and dump Ghaniyah's?"

"No. I'm just saying that Khalid is making a big mistake."

They decided to wait until the morning so it would seem like they had given it a great amount of thought. In truth, they both knew where the decision was headed.

"You're sure about this?" Shannon asked.

Alex was surprised to feel a tinge of regret. *How often do you get to try a case where you can really make a difference?* But that regret was nothing compared to the burden that would be lifted from his shoulders.

"I'm sure," Alex said.

"One hundred percent?"

He hesitated. "A good ninety-nine."

46

ON WEDNESDAY MORNING, for the third day in a row, Hassan Ibn Talib followed Taj Deegan to work. The prosecutor made it almost too easy. She drove her kids to school every morning in a Chrysler minivan, taking the same route to school and then work. She parked in the same public parking lot in approximately the same spot, as close as possible to the commonwealth's attorney's office. Her court appointments were a matter of public record. She never left the building for lunch. But most importantly, when she parked the van, she tossed the keys into the center console and locked the door. When she returned, she unlocked the door using the keypad on the outside.

His first step would be to obtain the access code for the keypad.

Using a telephoto lens, Hassan had watched her work the code— left, right, left, right, middle. He recorded a video of her working the keypad. She managed to keep the precise numbers hidden, but Hassan had a solution for that as well.

In the early morning hours he had paid a visit to her house and washed off the keypad with a solution that would erase all fingerprints. Now, one hour after she disappeared into the office, he checked the parking lot and made his way to her van. He quickly dusted the pad for prints and found that three of the buttons had been pushed—the 2/3 button, the 6/7 button, and the 8/9 button.

Armed with that information, he returned to his car and watched the video he had taken earlier. Deegan's shoulder was in the way, but it wasn't hard to figure out. Based on the movements of her hand and the information he had just gained, he narrowed it down to two or three combinations. He memorized the combinations, put on a pair of plastic gloves, and walked to her van a second time. Two minutes later, he was in.

Somebody was angling toward him in the parking lot, so he sat in the driver's seat and pretended to talk on his cell phone. After the person ambled by, he grabbed the garage door opener and returned to his car.

Later, he would gain access to Deegan's garage, disable her alarm, and enter her house. From there, the plan was simple. If she had a spare key, he would simply make a copy. If not, he would unscrew one of the window locks, cut off the bottom of the screws, and replace the lock and screws. The window would look secure, but he would be able to break in anytime he wanted.

He would inform his superior and wait for further orders.

The American justice system was no match for the zealous disciples of Mohammed.

◁ ▷

Alex worked from his condo until almost ten. He and Shannon had agreed to call Khalid at eleven, so Alex headed to the office so they could use the speakerphone.

When he entered the waiting area at 10:45, he was surprised to see his grandmother sitting behind the reception desk. He blinked, trying to make sure he wasn't seeing things.

"Must be nice to keep banker's hours," she quipped. "You're just in time for lunch."

"What are you doing here?"

"I heard about Sylvia's . . . departure, and I thought you could use a little help until you find a new assistant."

By now, Shannon had joined them. "Did you know about this?" Alex asked.

"I found out when I got to work," Shannon said. "Of course, that was several hours ago."

Alex wasn't an emotional person, but for some reason, he had to blink back tears. "Thanks," he said to his grandmother.

Ramona pointed to the sign on the wall, listing the firm's hourly rate. She had crossed out $200 and listed the starting rate at $250. The sign now said that the firm charged $400 "if you want to advise us on how to do our job."

"From what I've heard about the imam's daughter, you're going to earn every penny," Ramona said.

Alex smirked. "I see you've been talking to Shannon."

"She told me about your meeting yesterday," Ramona said. "And if you want my opinion, Mr. Mobassar obviously has no idea what he's doing."

"Can we talk before we call him?" Shannon asked. From the look in her eyes, Alex knew what was coming. She probably couldn't sleep last night. She would want to take the criminal case and pass on the civil one. How could they let an innocent man go to jail?

Before she even made her argument, Alex had calibrated his response. He would put up token resistance, only because he wanted to be able to say "I told you so" if the case went south. In truth, Alex was ready to take the criminal case too.

◁ ▷

Twenty minutes later, Alex and Shannon broke the news. Khalid should get someone else to handle Ghaniyah's case. The firm would need a retainer of $50,000 for his. The billing rate was $200 an hour. *Unless Nara stays involved,* Alex wanted to say. But this was no time for levity.

There was silence on the other end for a few moments. "I'm not surprised you made that decision," Khalid eventually said. "I told Nara you would . . . and I'm glad you didn't make a liar out of me."

"So am I," said Alex.

Khalid cleared his throat. "Can I share a little secret with you?"

Shannon gave Alex a look. "Of course," Alex said tentatively.

"There were some people in my community—even some in my own family—who questioned whether you were truly committed to my case. They thought that perhaps you only wanted a lucrative settlement in Ghaniyah's case and would then drop mine. I decided to take a Solomonic approach to the issue."

Alex immediately picked up on the reference to King Solomon. To determine which of two women was the real mother of a baby, Solomon threatened to split the child in two. He knew that the actual mother would give away the baby before she would allow the child to be harmed.

"By demonstrating your willingness to forgo Ghaniyah's case, you've proven that you were not just in this for the money," Khalid concluded.

"Are you saying you don't really see a conflict with our firm handling both cases?" Alex asked.

"I just need a firm committed to proving my innocence."

At that moment, Alex wasn't quite sure how to respond. On the one hand, he wanted to reach through the phone and strangle his client. On the other, he was relieved that they could handle Ghaniyah's case as well. But Alex knew one thing for sure: he would keep a skeptical eye on Nara Mobassar. Everything seemed to have turned chaotic from the moment she came on the scene.

He thought maybe he should confront Khalid about lying to his lawyers but decided to let it go. For now, there was nothing else that needed to be said. It was time for Madison and Associates to get to work.

47

ON THURSDAY MORNING, Alex received a frantic call from Khalid.

"They've got a search warrant for the mosque," his client said. Alex could hear loud voices in the background. "They've already taken my work computer."

Alex pictured the cops ransacking the mosque, emptying out Khalid's drawers and filing cabinets, creating the same mess they had at the imam's house. "Get the officer in charge and give him your phone," Alex said.

"It's Detective Brown," Khalid said.

A few minutes later, Khalid was back on the line. "She said she can't speak to you now."

"Sit tight and don't touch anything. I'm coming over."

Before he left his office, Alex told his grandmother to call the local television stations. Perhaps Alex could gain a little sympathy for his client.

◁ ▷

Alex stood next to Khalid Mobassar on the steps of the Islamic Learning Center and faced the two camera crews who had bothered to show up. The wind was blowing hard, and a slight drizzle had started. But Alex ignored the conditions.

"If separation of church and state means anything, it means the police cannot storm into your church or mosque and confiscate your computers and financial records. Yet that's exactly what they did here. If this had happened at a Baptist church, the moral outrage would be deafening. Why should it be any different at a Muslim place of worship?"

Alex paused and reminded himself to keep it short. Sound bites, not lectures. "I'll be filing a motion to suppress any evidence the police might try to use from this unconstitutional raid. The Free Exercise of Religion clause is no respecter of faiths."

He turned toward his client. "I'm going to ask Mr. Mobassar to show you the inside of the mosque and the complete lack of respect shown by the police officers who conducted the search."

Later, Alex's little press conference would be broadcast around the world. The most disturbing footage included video of Khalid's office, where the Qur'an had been tossed on the floor.

The Muslim community reacted with outrage, calling on the federal government to intervene. Legal experts accused Alex of playing "the Qur'an card." They expressed concern about security at Khalid's trial.

Harry Dent wasted no time getting Alex on the phone. The head deacon got right to the point. "I can't believe you're trying to get this guy off on a technicality. My phone's been ringing off the hook all day. If you're going to stay on this case, it's time for you to step down as our pastor."

Alex had been getting kicked around all day by complete strangers. He didn't need his own deacons piling on.

"The Constitution is hardly a technicality," Alex said, his tone every bit as strident as Dent's. "As for stepping down, that won't happen unless the congregation votes me out."

48

KHALID AND NARA came to the office on Friday morning so that everybody could ride together to the preliminary hearing. Alex hadn't slept
much the night before. Even Nara, dressed conservatively in a blue skirt
and white blouse, looked tired. Khalid wore a gray business suit that
looked out of place on a man with a long, straggly beard and short black
hair befitting a Muslim cleric.

Alex reminded Khalid and his daughter not to expect a strenuous
defense *at this stage*. The prelim was a chance to discover the government's case, nothing more. Alex could tell by Nara's pursed lips and
body language that she didn't like the plan. To her credit, she didn't
object. Shannon, who would be handling the majority of witnesses,
looked especially tired and stressed.

Only Khalid Mobassar seemed relaxed, under control, and preter-
naturally calm.

◁▷

Alex knew that Judge McElroy had received so much flak for allowing Khalid Mobassar out on bond that he would bend over backward to look tough at the preliminary hearing. Alex therefore wasn't
surprised when McElroy gaveled the proceedings to order and proceeded
to lecture the entire courtroom about proper decorum, promising to
throw any violators in jail. The tension in the hall was off the charts.

After his lecture, McElroy turned to Taj Deegan. "Call your first
witness."

As Taj stood and announced that Dr. Marnya Davidson would be her first witness, Alex thought about why Taj was the perfect prosecutor for this case. She was a minority and would be less vulnerable to the claim of racial profiling. A woman, she could bring a fair amount of righteous indignation on behalf of the victims. She was totally unpretentious—even today she had dressed in a loose-fitting cotton dress with a gray vest—just the right balance of professionalism and common touch. Her voice was deep and melodic. She had a reputation for being as tough as nails.

Her first witness was equally battle tested. Dr. Marnya Davidson was a crusty old medical examiner from Virginia Beach who had testified in more than a thousand cases. She was legendary for her gruesome and colorful descriptions of corpses. When defense attorneys tried to cross-examine her, she turned on the sarcasm and gave them an incredulous look over the top of her wire-rimmed glasses. Before long, her dry wit would have the jury snickering at the lawyers.

Under questioning from Taj Deegan, the medical examiner provided all the gory details about the beheading of Ja'dah Mahdi and the asphyxiation of Martin Burns. She described the severing of the various arteries in Ja'dah's neck and the amount of blood that would have gushed out "like water from a garden hose." Based on the weight of the lungs and the fluid buildup, she also described the slow pain Burns would have endured as he struggled for breath over an extended period of time. When Davidson finished, Alex had no questions.

Deegan's next witness was a man named Christopher Long, an FBI special agent who worked in the terrorist surveillance unit. He had a buttoned-down appearance accentuated by black plastic glasses and a solid jaw that made him look determined. He could have passed for Clark Kent. Long gave an overview of the Patriot Act surveillance program, including the software used to filter calls and text messages and to flag calls of special concern. Because of manpower shortages, the FBI and DOJ couldn't review *every* call, only those from certain individuals or those calls that contained notable keywords or phrases. At the time of the murder of Ja'dah Mahdi, the word *honor* was not a phrase that triggered follow-up. That had recently changed.

Though none of Mr. Mobassar's calls or texts had been flagged at the time, the software archived each call and text so it could be accessed later. Agent Long testified that he had personally reviewed every phone call and text message sent or received by Khalid Mobassar in the month prior to the deaths of Ja'dah Mahdi and Martin Burns.

At this point, Alex lodged an objection to any evidence garnered from phone taps under the Patriot Act. "We believe the Patriot Act, as applied to Mr. Mobassar, is an unconstitutional violation of the Fourth and Fourteenth Amendments," Alex explained. "If the charges against my client are certified today, we'll be filing a motion to suppress."

McElroy nodded his head and overruled the objection. He knew that Alex was just preserving the record. The motion to suppress would be taken up by a circuit court judge.

After laying the proper foundation, Taj Deegan introduced the text messages into evidence. She then had Agent Long read them out loud.

"'Ja'dah Fatima Mahdi has converted to the Christian faith. She has defiled herself by consorting with an American man, disgraced her family, and dishonored Allah. She must be given only one opportunity to repent and return to the faith. If she refuses, the honor of her family must be restored.'"

The second message, Long explained, had an attached photograph of Ja'dah Mahdi and Martin Burns. "The text itself reads: 'If you attend Beach Bible Church on Saturday night, you will find her there. May Allah guide you.'"

"What were the dates and times of the text messages?" Deegan asked.

"The first was received at 2:03 p.m. on Wednesday, June 2," Long replied. "The second message came approximately two minutes later."

"Dr. Davidson determined that the death of Ja'dah Mahdi occurred on Saturday night, June 12, at approximately 10 p.m.," Deegan said. "Were there any text messages received by Mr. Mobassar's phone shortly after that time?"

"Yes. There was a one-word message from another cell phone sent approximately two and a half hours after the death of Ja'dah Mahdi."

"And what did that message say?"

"'Finished.'"

49

THE PROSECUTION'S NEXT WITNESS was a pencil-thin Indian man named Dr. Kumar Santi, a specialist in cell tower and satellite technology. After boring the judge with a long list of qualifications, Dr. Santi explained the concept of cell phone triangulation, based on the location of cell towers relaying signals for a phone at any given time. By plotting successive calls using this technology, it was possible to trace the general movement of a cell phone.

As a result, Santi was able to provide three important opinions. First, when the original messages were sent from Khalid Mobassar's cell phone on June 2, they were sent from the vicinity of the Islamic Learning Center in Norfolk. Second, the phone that received the messages, which Santi referred to as "John Doe cell phone number one," was in the Seven Corners area of northern Virginia. Third, the cell phone that sent the one-word "finished" message back to Mobassar's cell phone shortly after the murders on June 12, called "John Doe cell phone number two," was in the Sandbridge area. That same cell phone had been purchased earlier in the day in the vicinity of Petersburg, Virginia, and had been carried to Virginia Beach before being brought to Sandbridge.

Dr. Santi also testified that both John Doe cell phones one and two had been purchased using fake identities the police had not been able to trace.

A few times during Santi's testimony, Alex leaned over and reminded Khalid not to look so glum. "Take notes," Alex suggested. "Wipe that 'guilty' sign off your forehead."

Alex tried hard to look upbeat himself, but he felt like Deegan had just placed the lid on his client's coffin and was pulling out her hammer and nails.

When Santi stepped down, Deegan called Special Agent Christopher Long, who played for the court some of Khalid's phone calls from a few days after the murder, with Khalid's voice clearly identifiable on the recordings. This was done, Alex knew, because the cell phone had disappeared by the time the police had questioned Khalid. It was a preemptive strike by Deegan—taking away any defense based on the allegation that somebody had stolen Khalid's phone and sent the messages ordering the killings.

Special Agent Long was followed by a local banker who had access to the Islamic Learning Center accounts. She testified to the irregularities in the mosque's deposits and the $20,000 that had been wired to a bank in Beirut, authorized online by someone using Khalid's password. Another path of bread crumbs that led to Khalid's door.

Following the lunch break, the prosecution called Fatih Mahdi to the stand, and a murmur of anticipation floated through the spectators. Mahdi stepped forward looking swarthy and somber, his eyes on the judge as he stood in the well of the courtroom. Mahdi was a short man with broad shoulders and a thick waist. He had receding black hair and wore the white cloth hat and long white robe of an orthodox Muslim.

"Do you swear or affirm to tell the truth, the whole truth, and nothing but the truth?" Judge McElroy asked.

"I affirm," Mahdi replied.

He took the stand and stared at Khalid. Alex's client returned the stare without flinching.

It quickly became obvious that Mahdi did not want to be there. He answered Deegan's questions with short sentences that he spit back at her, a perpetual scowl lining his face.

"At some point, did you become aware that your wife, Ja'dah Fatima Mahdi, was attending Beach Bible Church?"

"Yes."

"How did you find out?"

"I followed her."

"Why did you follow her?"

Mahdi sighed. "Because I had suspicions."

"Based on what?"

"Changes in her behavior and the fact that she was making excuses to be out alone every Saturday night."

For thirty minutes, Taj Deegan asked carefully scripted questions, and Mahdi gave his grudging answers. Mahdi testified that he had secretly followed his wife to Beach Bible Church and watched her meet up with Martin Burns. Later that night, Mahdi had confronted his wife and learned that she had converted to Christianity. Not knowing what else to do, Mahdi had turned to Khalid Mobassar for counsel. Mobassar was the *only* person Mahdi had talked to about his wife's conversion.

"What did Mr. Mobassar say?" Taj Deegan asked.

Mahdi glanced at Khalid and turned back to Deegan. "He worried about what this might do to the reputation of my family and the mosque. He said he would like to meet with Ja'dah. He urged me not to tell anyone else." Mahdi stopped, his face tight with tension. He started to speak but paused to gather himself. "Khalid said to leave it to him—that he would take care of it."

Khalid leaned over and whispered in Alex's ear. "That's a lie."

"What did you take that to mean?" Deegan asked.

Mahdi thought about this. "At the time, I thought it meant that he would talk to Ja'dah . . . help her see the error of her ways. Ja'dah was young and impetuous. I never thought it would mean . . ." Mahdi stopped again and looked accusatorily at Khalid. "In retrospect, it appears that I was wrong."

Taj Deegan sat down sharply. "No further questions."

50

THOUGH THE RESULT of the hearing was already a foregone conclusion, Taj Deegan ended her case by calling Detective Terri Brown to the stand. Most of Brown's testimony was a regurgitation of facts already known to Alex. She detailed the results of her investigation and stated that the police were still exploring the funding for the Islamic Learning Center to see if there were any ties with Hezbollah. But she had found one piece of interesting information on Khalid's work computer.

Alex sat up a little straighter, bracing himself for the worst.

"Please tell the court what you discovered," Deegan said.

Brown looked at Judge McElroy. "We found a Google search on March 29 for Sandbridge rental properties."

"Was one of the results pulled up during this search the listing for 112 Kingfisher Drive?"

Alex held his breath. That was the address of the property that had been rented for cash the week of Ja'dah Mahdi's murder. The CSI teams had found trace amounts of Ja'dah's blood on the premises.

"Yes," Detective Brown replied. "The third property listed was 112 Kingfisher Drive."

◁ ▷

After the commonwealth rested its case, Judge McElroy ordered a ten-minute recess.

Nara elbowed into the huddle at counsel table. "Put me on the stand," she said to Alex.

"We've been through this," Alex replied, his patience wearing thin.

"We're saving our case for trial. The commonwealth has already put on enough evidence to win this hearing."

"I know that," Nara snapped. "But after that last bit of testimony, every potential juror in Virginia Beach is going to assume that my father ordered this horrible crime."

With good reason, Alex thought. *How else do you explain it?*

"We'll make our case at trial," Alex insisted.

Nara blew out a breath of frustration. She softened her tone. "My father could go to prison for life, Alex."

"I know that."

"We've got to make him seem human." She was pleading now, rather than demanding. "I can do that. I can talk about my brothers, my dad's efforts to reform the faith, how he always gave me permission to ask questions. Mahdi lied about his meeting with my father. My father would have *never* said that."

"We can't." Alex's tone was apologetic, but he wasn't open to persuasion. "I'm sorry."

Khalid took a half step forward, his voice hushed. "Alex is calling the shots here," he said to Nara, putting his hand gently on her arm. "Fatih did lie. But we have to trust our lawyers to expose those lies at the proper time."

Nara started to say something but apparently thought better of it. Her dark eyes glowered at Alex, her lips pursed in frustration. "Your call," she said to Alex. "But I'll be sitting right here in the front row if you need me."

Don't hold your breath.

"Thanks," Alex said.

◁▷

When court reconvened, Alex told Judge McElroy that the defense did not intend to call any witnesses. As soon as Alex sat down, McElroy issued his ruling.

"The court finds probable cause for both counts of conspiracy to commit murder," he said. "My clerk will be calling counsel to coordinate a trial date."

After court was adjourned and Alex started packing his bags, Nara moved close enough so only he could hear.

"Are we ever going to fight back?" she asked.

Alex didn't need this. There were lots of people gunning for him already. Why couldn't his own client's daughter trust him?

"At trial," he said. Nara stared at him, and Alex stopped packing. He glanced up at her. "Let me do my job."

"And let me help," Nara replied.

Alex fought the urge to lash out at her. She undoubtedly meant well. "Now's not the time to have this discussion," he said.

◁ ▷

That night, Alex went for a long walk on the Virginia Beach boardwalk, losing himself in a mass of summer tourists. The adrenaline from the hearing had long ago seeped out of his body, leaving him spent and emotionally raw.

What if Khalid is guilty? Criminal defense lawyers weren't supposed to ask those questions, but how could he help it? Taj Deegan had two text messages from Khalid's phone ordering the deaths. There was a one-word confirmation back from the killer. Prior to the killings, Khalid had used his computer to search for the rental property in Sandbridge where Ja'dah's beheading had occurred.

After the hearing, Khalid had assured Alex that he didn't know anything about the Google search. Was he lying? Just because Khalid was a committed reformer didn't mean he was innocent. If everything kept pointing back to Khalid, how could Alex keep defending him?

Somebody had ordered the beheading of Ja'dah Mahdi and this other young woman in California as well as the slow and painful murder of Martin Burns. Whoever it was deserved to die.

How did I get myself into this mess? Alex wondered. Things had seemed so much more black and white when he was reading law under his grandfather's supervision.

51

ALEX HAD ONE SUIT that fit perfectly—a black pin-striped suit that he liked to wear with a red power tie and a light blue shirt. It was his most traditional outfit. Old school. He normally reserved that suit for his rare appearances in federal court.

On Sunday morning, he donned the suit and slipped on a pair of black loafers. He'd once owned a pair of wingtips, but they were so uncomfortable that he'd tossed them two weeks after purchasing them. He preferred the loafer look—casual enough for the beach, dressy enough for a lawyer. His hair was still fairly short from when he had buzzed it a few weeks ago, and he was beginning to like the clean and streamlined look.

He couldn't find the thin black belt he had worn to court on Friday, but he found a thick one that barely fit through the belt loops and looked a little funny because the buckle was too big. Oh well. He could button his suit coat in church, and no one would notice. As a final concession to the importance of the occasion, Alex had even slipped on a pair of black dress socks. Many Sundays he would go without socks, and the old folks would tease him about it. But today, there was too much on the line. His congregation needed to know he was taking this seriously.

They might vote him out of a job today, but at least he would look good leaving. He checked his reflection in the mirror one last time, stuffed his notes into his thin Bible, and smiled at the thought of the Scripture passage he had chosen for the morning's sermon.

The most controversial story in the New Testament. At least nobody would accuse him of going down without a fight.

◁ ▷

On Easter Sundays, South Norfolk Community Church attendance might crack a hundred. But most weeks, Alex preached to a smattering of about seventy people in a sanctuary designed to hold three hundred. Most of the people would sit near the back, especially the third row from the back, where the hearing-aid plugs were located. The hard-of-hearing parishioners liked the aids because they could turn them up—or down—depending on the contents of the sermon.

When Alex stood to preach, he looked out over a full crowd of nearly two hundred. Many were either curiosity seekers, members of the press, or members of South Norfolk who hadn't attended in years but had been dragged to church by friends to help stack the vote. Like most small evangelical churches, the only way that somebody got eliminated from the rolls at South Norfolk was by their own death, and even then the odds were about fifty-fifty.

At the request of the ever-hungry media, Alex had authorized television crews to set up tripods along the back wall—though only after a lengthy conference call with the deacons on Saturday. Harry Dent had been adamantly opposed to the idea but had a hard time countering Alex's argument that this might be God's way of broadcasting the worship service to the entire world.

"It just feels like somebody's asking to come into my house and broadcast a family feud," Dent argued.

"Then let's show them a family lovefest instead," Alex countered.

Dent cast the lone dissenting vote on the camera issue.

Before beginning his message, Alex took a deep breath to calm his nerves. His eyes landed for a split second on Nara Mobassar, seated on the aisle in the second-to-last row. She looked more stunning than ever and gave Alex a subtle nod. *What's she doing here?*

"Our text this morning is a passage of Scripture that many people say should not even be in the Bible," Alex began. In preparing this message, Alex had decided not to ignore the elephant in the room. "Naturally, since this might be my last sermon, I went straight to the most controversial passage I could find. Would everyone turn to the Gospel of John, chapter eight?"

Alex heard the rustle of Bibles among the congregants while the reporters looked clueless. Nara stayed locked on to what he was saying.

"My Bible, like most modern translations, contains a note just above this chapter that states, 'The earliest manuscripts and many other ancient witnesses do not have John 7:53–8:11.' I'll bet many of you didn't even know that there was this chunk of Scripture, right in the middle of the Gospel of John, that many scholars believe doesn't even belong in the Bible."

A few parishioners gave Alex a quizzical look—he was right. Nara's expression didn't change. Alex knew that Muslims believed the Bible had been corrupted during its copying and translation. If anything, she was probably thinking, *Why should I be surprised?*

"While Jesus was teaching at the Temple," Alex explained, "the religious leaders brought a woman before him who had been caught in adultery. They said to Jesus, 'Teacher, this woman was caught in the very act of adultery. The Law of Moses commands us to stone her. Now, what do you say?'

"Most of you probably already know Christ's response. He wrote in the dirt with his finger a couple of times and told the religious leaders that whoever was without sin should cast the first stone. One by one, the leaders dropped their stones and left. When only Jesus and the woman remained, he looked at her and asked where all her accusers were—'Hasn't anyone condemned you?' And she said, 'No one, sir.' Jesus responded to her with these words: 'Then neither do I condemn you. Go now and leave your life of sin.'"

Harry Dent was squirming. Bill Fitzsimmons, located one row behind Harry, looked down at his Bible and frowned. He probably thought it wasn't fair for Alex to use this passage today. It wasn't hard to figure out who the religious leaders were in the analogy.

"So I want to ask two questions about this passage," Alex said, stepping out from behind the pulpit. He wanted no barriers between him and his congregation. "What did Jesus write in the dirt? And should this passage even be in the Bible?"

Alex walked down from the platform and into the center aisle. Even with two hundred in attendance, the first few rows were empty.

"Keep in mind that this woman was caught *in the very act* of adultery. There was no question about her guilt or innocence." Alex paused and surveyed the congregation. The loudest complainers had been questioning all week about Alex representing someone he *knew* was guilty. "And Jesus didn't offer a substantive defense. Instead, he knelt down and wrote something in the dirt."

Alex knelt now and pretended to write on the floor. He spoke in soft tones. "What did he write? We don't know. Perhaps . . ." Alex looked up at his congregation. "Perhaps he wrote a list of sins the religious leaders had committed—maybe even the names of women they had slept with. Perhaps he was sending a message to the leaders that if they stoned this woman, their sins would be exposed as well." Alex couldn't help taking a quick glance at Harry. The man's neck was turning crimson.

"Perhaps this is a reminder to all of us that we should be slow to judge and that every sin—even our own sin—is an affront to a holy God."

Alex stood and walked a few rows deeper into the congregation. Nobody was scribbling pictures on the bulletin today. If his entire ministry hadn't been on the line, this might have been fun.

"Or perhaps what he wrote in the dirt was the Roman statute that made it illegal for anyone but Rome to impose capital punishment. That's why the Jewish leaders had to get the sanction of Pontius Pilate before they could crucify Christ. But whatever he wrote in the dirt was not what we would call a substantive defense. Though none of us like to think of it this way, Jesus defended this woman on a technicality."

Ramona could not have looked more proud. Her posture, as always, was impeccable. On the other side of the sanctuary, Nara slowly nodded her approval.

"As to my second question—'Does this passage even belong in Scripture?'—we have to determine whether this passage was added by the early church leaders or whether it was contained in the original manuscript of John and for some reason removed by the early church. As you all know, we don't have the original manuscript. And so we must judge based on what we know about the early church and based on the thousands of ancient copies that we do have."

Alex was starting to lose them a little. Nobody had ever accused his congregation of getting mired down in theological details. "You should know that this story *is* contained in a fifth-century Greek manuscript, one of our oldest copies, and in the original Latin Vulgate. The story is also referenced in several writings of the early church fathers in the third and fourth centuries.

"We know that the early church was adamant about the sin of adultery. In fact, when an early Christian literary work called *The Shepherd of Hermas* suggested that persons who committed major sins such as adultery could be forgiven only one time, it was roundly criticized by church leaders for being *too lenient*. Tertullian called it 'The Shepherd of Adulterers.' Given this judgmental attitude of early church leaders, it's hard to believe that those leaders added this story rather than deleted it.

"And if that's the case, we ought to pay careful attention to a story that is so poignant that the early church fathers couldn't quite embrace its radical message of mercy and forgiveness. Maybe they had forgotten that Christ's entire message was based on God's willingness to forgive our sins, not just one time, but for *all* time. There is no better picture of such forgiveness than this story."

Alex hesitated before he dove into the next part. He didn't want to make the sermon all about him, but he knew his own future was the issue foremost on everyone's mind.

"At the end of today's service, you'll have a chance to vote on whether I should remain as your pastor. Many of you are upset with me because I've chosen to defend a man of another faith who I believe is innocent. Many of you have already decided that he is guilty."

Alex was getting some hard looks. He had gone from preaching to meddling. "But even if you want to assume that this man is guilty, does that mean I shouldn't represent him? Did Christ make you prove your innocence before he died for your sins? If this story about the woman caught in adultery stands for anything, it stands for the proposition that we are never more like Jesus than when we're defending those persons who have been rejected by everyone else. This is a story about grace. A story about forgiveness. And if you decide to fire me as your pastor, then I would urge you to do what the early church leaders seem to have done. . . ."

Alex spoke softly now, though he knew his words were landing with nuclear force. One thing that South Norfolk Community Church believed was that you didn't mess with Scripture. So Alex reached into the back of a pew and pulled out the nearest Bible that the church had placed there next to the hymnals. "If you decide to vote against me, have somebody take a pair of scissors, open each Bible to John chapter eight, and cut that chapter out. And along with it, some other teachings on grace in the New Testament."

Harry Dent was actually shaking his head from side to side, the equivalent in church of a declaration of war. Ramona had a thin but pleased smile on her lips.

Alex hoped that his message today had given her some good ammunition for the business meeting that would take place after the service. An hour from now, he would know whether it was enough.

52

ALEX WAITED IN THE FOYER as the church members deliberated. Anyone who was not on the current membership roll—including all members of the press—suffered the same fate. When Alex declined to answer questions from the reporters and told them the meeting could last an hour, they decided to leave. Alex promised to call them when he found out the results of the vote.

Despite receiving many accolades about the sermon from the regular church members, Alex was pessimistic about the vote. Harry Dent and his cohorts had invited people to church who hadn't darkened the doors for two years. They were undoubtedly planning to vote Alex out.

Alex thanked Nara for coming and was surprised when she told him that she was going to wait it out with him. After most of the visitors left, Alex and Nara found a seat on the steps at one end of the foyer.

"You want anything to drink?" Nara asked. "I can run to the store. This meeting might take a while."

"Democracy at work," Alex said.

"Only in America do you determine God's will by majority vote."

"Good point," Alex said. He was too emotionally drained to argue. Preaching wasn't easy when your job was on the line.

"That was a good message," Nara said. She hesitated, clearly wanting to say something more. "I've been pretty pushy—especially in court on Friday." She turned to him, then added, "I think I might have judged you too swiftly."

The admission surprised Alex. His mind was still on the proceedings in the sanctuary, but when he looked at Nara, he was struck by the sincerity in her eyes.

"Don't worry about it," he said. "If I was in your shoes and it was my grandmother's preliminary hearing, I probably would have fired my lawyer on the spot."

"I can do that?" Nara asked.

Alex smiled. He liked that about Nara—the smart-aleck attitude. "Fortunately for me, you most certainly cannot."

"I'll try to behave myself from now on."

"Promises, promises."

"No, really."

Alex turned serious. "For what it's worth, Nara, you've already done a lot to help your father's case."

Nara thought about this for a moment, as if weighing how much she should share. She glanced around the foyer to make sure nobody was within earshot. "I know you're focused on the vote right now, and you should be. But when this is over, we need to sit down with my father and have a very frank discussion. You need to ask him about the Islamic Brotherhood in the United States and who provides their funding."

Alex looked at her, measuring the earnestness in her eyes.

"It will all go back to Hezbollah, Alex. Beheading women. Terrorizing Americans. These honor killings have Hezbollah fingerprints all over them. I think they're using the Islamic Brotherhood as a conduit."

◁▷

When Harry Dent came to fetch Alex, the look on his face said the news was glum. Whether it was glum for Alex or glum for Harry, Alex couldn't tell. Harry led Alex to the front of the church and launched into a little speech about how much everyone in the church appreciated Alex's ministry. Alex felt like he was listening to his own ministerial eulogy.

"Not one person in this church has anything against you personally," Harry said, oozing with hypocrisy. "We all think—including any-body who voted against you—that you've done an *excellent* job."

When Harry looked out over the congregation, Ramona was cir-cling her hand—*move it along*. Harry took the hint.

"By a vote of seventy-eight to seventy-six, South Norfolk Community Church has voted to keep you as our pastor."

There was a smattering of applause, and it surprised Alex when he felt his knees buckle a little. He had expected the worst. Instead, Ramona was beaming.

Alex felt himself choking up. He had made a decision earlier in the week about what to do next, though he was suddenly having second thoughts about it. But he didn't trust himself to think clearly under these circumstances, so he decided to stick with the original plan.

"That means more to me than I can ever say," Alex began. "It really does." He swallowed, and his voice became a little hoarse. "I never meant to hurt this church or have my law practice become a distrac-tion. But I thought it was critical that I allow this vote to proceed so that all of you could define the type of church you want this to be. And I've never been more proud of you than I am right now."

A few folks started clapping, but Alex held up his hand. As he looked around the sanctuary, memories flooded him. The members he had visited in the hospital. The ones he hugged every Sunday morn-ing. Ramona and her friends. His deacons.

"Having said that, I must also say that I believe it's in the best interest of South Norfolk Community Church for me to step down, at least until this case is over." He paused, and the gasps were audible. Somebody in the back shouted, "No!"

"If I win this case and prove the innocence of Khalid Mobassar, I hope that you might consider taking me back. The church has already proven that it values grace and forgiveness over legalism, and that may be the most important verdict to come out of this whole mess."

He thanked the members profusely and walked down the aisle to vigorous applause.

53

SHANNON REESE got to work early Monday morning, outlining the questions she intended to ask witnesses during her interviews later that week. Nara could worry about the media, and Alex could worry about the big picture, but Shannon believed that cases were won or lost in the trenches. On the details. And the most important details in every case were the ones surrounding the dollar signs. Follow the money, and you will find the culprit.

After a few hours at the office, Shannon met Khalid Mobassar at the Islamic Learning Center. He introduced her to the mosque's bookkeeper—an elderly woman named Riham El-Ashi—who had made herself available for a couple of hours of questioning.

Riham was soft-spoken, petite, and no-nonsense—the type of person who would make a credible witness at trial. Shannon talked to Riham in her office, where the bookkeeper sat hunched over her computer, checking her spreadsheets for answers to Shannon's detailed questions. When she did so, Riham moved her face so close to the screen that Shannon suspected the bookkeeper needed new glasses.

Riham seemed embarrassed by the financial details that had emerged during the investigation. She was unquestionably loyal to Khalid and felt that her own negligence had somehow exacerbated the evidence against him.

Riham explained the concept of zakah, one of the five pillars of the Muslim faith, requiring true believers to give a percentage of their income to the mosque and the poor. Though the Qur'an did not specify an amount, Khalid had always taught that Muslims should give no less than 2.5 percent.

Donations were made through a secure donation box located at the back of the mosque. According to Riham, most of the donations came by check, although about 10 percent came in the form of cash. Each night, one of the imams would place the donations from the box in a small leather zip bag, which was then locked in a safe. Only the imams had access to the donation box. When Shannon asked, Riham also listed the three other leaders in the mosque, including Fatih Mahdi, who had access to the safe.

Each morning, Riham pulled the money from the safe, counted the checks and cash, stamped the back "For deposit only," and entered the amounts on a ledger for each contributor. The cash and checks would then go back in the safe until Riham made the weekly deposit into the mosque's operating account.

The mosque typically took in more than $20,000 a week. But during the three weeks prior to the murder of Ja'dah Mahdi, the deposits had been approximately half that amount, and the cash had fallen from more than $2,000 a week to less than a thousand.

After Khalid's arrest, Riham had discovered that someone had deposited nearly $30,000 over the course of three weeks into the mosque's building fund, using a deposit stamp for that account. Just before Ja'dah Mahdi's murder, $20,000 had been wired from that account to an account in Beirut, Lebanon, which had since been closed.

The name of the account holder in Beirut was not familiar to Riham. The wire had been authorized pursuant to an online transaction. The person authorizing the wire had signed in under the user name and password assigned to Khalid Mobassar.

"How many people have online access to the accounts?" Shannon asked.

"Only the three imams. But the bank says that the user sign-in was for Khalid."

Shannon had already questioned Khalid about the way he stored his passwords. He had them all in a single document on his computer named "FAQs" that was not password protected.

"How did you communicate the user names and passwords to the imams?" Shannon asked.

"By e-mail."

Shannon liked it. Another possible leak.

"Did anybody have access to Mr. Mobassar's e-mail or computer?"

"You should probably ask him," Riham said. "But I do know of one assistant who helps all the imams with their scheduling and other administrative tasks."

"I talked to him," Shannon said. "Khalid had not given him access to the computer."

Still, the commonwealth's case was not airtight. Somebody could have gone on Khalid's computer when he wasn't looking or hacked into his e-mail or even hacked into Riham's e-mail. Shannon wasn't trying to blow up the commonwealth's financial case. She just needed to sow a few seeds of reasonable doubt.

But even if she could poke holes in the financial evidence, there was still the text message ordering the killings. And the return text message from the killer. And the search for the Sandbridge property listings. And the conversation between Khalid and Fatih Mahdi. And the Hezbollah connections.

Shannon was making progress. But in the grand scheme of things, she and Alex were still hoping for a miracle.

Maybe she would find one at her next stop.

◁ ▷

When Shannon pulled up to Fatih Mahdi's house in the Ghent section of Norfolk, nobody knew she was coming. She had learned from previous cases that surprise visits early in the case could prove profitable, especially if you caught people off guard with questions they didn't expect.

Mahdi lived in one of downtown Norfolk's nicer neighborhoods. The homes were a mixture of stone and brick fortresses nestled on small lots. The lawns were manicured, and Shannon saw a fair number of Lexus and Mercedes cars in the driveways. She wondered what the neighbors thought about having a fundamentalist Muslim living on their street.

It was three o'clock in the afternoon and unmercifully hot and humid. Shannon wore a modest dress and two-inch heels so she would seem taller. She stared at the house for a few seconds from inside her air-conditioned car and felt sweat forming on the back of her neck. She knew that in any honor killing, the husband would always be one of the first suspects. She also believed that Fatih had lied in court about his conversation with her client. Could Fatih be the one who had orchestrated his own wife's death? The thought of going face-to-face with someone like that both infuriated her and scared her. She thought about Ja'dah and ratcheted up her courage.

She walked confidently to the front porch, knocked, and waited. After a few seconds, she noticed the doorbell and rang it. The front door opened slowly, and Shannon found herself a few feet away from Fatih Mahdi.

She had seen him in court, but he had looked less intimidating in his traditional Muslim garb. He stood before her now in jeans and a white T-shirt, powerfully built with a barrel chest. Like everyone else, he towered over her. His hair was unkempt. He eyed her up and down for a second before speaking.

"What do you want?"

"I'd like to ask a few questions about your wife's murder."

Mahdi's eyes betrayed his sadness—not the reaction Shannon expected. She had steeled herself for anger. Instead, he gave her a look of fatigue and resignation. "I have talked to the police and to the common-wealth's attorney. I can only hope that my friend Khalid had nothing to do with Ja'dah's death."

"It would help Khalid Mobassar a lot if you'd let me ask you a few questions," Shannon responded. "We both want the same thing—the person or persons who are responsible for Ja'dah's death brought to justice."

Mahdi looked down for a second, considering Shannon's request. When he faced her again, he seemed more resolute. "The news reports say that you will be filing motions to keep the text messages out of evidence based on technicalities. Is this true?"

"We'll be filing a motion to suppress the wiretap evidence because it violated our client's constitutional rights—hardly a 'technicality.'"

"Nevertheless," said Mahdi, "a strange way to get at the truth about who killed Ja'dah. A strange way to bring the killer to justice."

"My job is to defend my client," Shannon said, trying not to be argumentative. "And just because he happens to be an imam whose mosque in Lebanon used to support Hezbollah's relief work does not mean the government should be allowed to tap his phone."

"I'm sorry," Mahdi said. "But I know how the American system works. The best way for you to try to prove Khalid's innocence is to build a case against me."

Shannon sensed that Mahdi could cut through any pretense. She decided to play it straight. "That's one way. But if somebody else ordered the killing of your wife, we would have a better chance to catch him if we worked together."

"What evidence do you have that my wife's murder was ordered by someone other than Khalid?"

The sun was beating down on Shannon's back, but a slight breeze floated out from the air-conditioned house. Lawyers liked to ask questions, not answer them. She needed to get inside with Mahdi and become the interrogator again. "May I please come in and ask you a few questions? It would only take about thirty minutes."

"As I thought," Mahdi said sadly. "Your only defense is to blame the husband. And you expect me to help you dig my own grave?"

"It's not like that," Shannon said quickly. Too quickly.

"For me," said Mahdi, "it is precisely like that. If you find real evidence that points to someone other than Khalid, I would love to talk. Until then, it appears to me that our conversation would only help my wife's killer finesse his freedom."

Mahdi started to close the door and paused for a second. "I hope you are right about Khalid," he said. "The thought that my imam and good friend ordered the death of my wife has made this ordeal unbearable." With that, he politely dismissed Shannon and closed the door.

The whole encounter left her with an unsettled feeling. She hadn't really expected him to answer her questions. But she thought the man would be angry and condescending. Instead, he acted like he was still mourning. And to be honest, he didn't seem like the type of man who would order the beheading of his own wife.

Was Mahdi also a victim? Was there someone else out there pulling all the strings so that Mahdi would suspect Khalid and Khalid would suspect Mahdi? If so, what could be his motive?

Though Shannon hadn't thought this visit would provide a lot of answers, neither had she expected it to generate so many questions. She left with her stomach in turmoil. It would be harder to point the finger at Fatih Mahdi than she originally thought.

54

ACCORDING TO THE NEUROPSYCHOLOGIST, it was Khalid's job to help Ghaniyah return to the normal routines of life. She was still having a little trouble with short-term memory and with what the doctor called "executive functioning." The doctor had encouraged Ghaniyah to write down anything that came to her mind throughout the day that she needed to do. The lists would help her remember.

On Tuesday night, Khalid took it upon himself to make a list of all the things they needed at the grocery store and then went shopping with Ghaniyah. He drove to the local Harris Teeter and walked the aisles with his wife, checking off items as they put them in the cart.

Things went smoothly in the store until the Mobassars stepped into the long checkout line with their cart full of groceries. A moment later a few young men stepped into line behind them wearing cutoff jeans, work boots, tank tops, and frayed ball caps. Khalid could smell alcohol on their breath.

They were talking in the loud and obnoxious fashion of men who had downed one too many beers and therefore overestimated their own wittiness. The language was vulgar, and Khalid did his best to ignore it. He didn't want any trouble. He just wanted to check out and get home with his groceries.

Things started escalating when one of the men apparently recognized Khalid. "Hey, ain't that the towelhead who ordered those women beheaded?"

Khalid flinched but stared straight ahead. He could read the tension in Ghaniyah's features. Her temper had always been more explosive than his.

"That boy right there oughta be in jail," one of the men said. "The other prisoners would teach him a thang or two about submission."

The men laughed; Khalid pretended not to hear.

"I'd have my wife wear one of those head coverings too if she looked like that."

Khalid felt his face redden with rage, his muscles tensing. It took every ounce of self-control not to react. Others around him glanced nervously at Khalid and the men behind him.

"If the man had any guts, he'd turn around and say somethin'." Khalid felt the speaker literally breathing down his neck. The man was taller than Khalid by a couple of inches.

Khalid wanted to turn around and nail the guy—make sure the first punch was a good one. But this evening, his focus was on Ghaniyah. Stress like this wouldn't help her recover.

He took her by the elbow. "Let's go," he whispered, then began walking with her to the front of the store, leaving the full grocery cart in the line.

"Come on back, big man!" one of the men called out. "You want a piece of this?"

Ghaniyah didn't say a word as Khalid led her to the car. He could tell she was irate. He thought about calling the cops, but that might end up as a black mark against his probationary status.

He started the car and turned to back out of the space. To his surprise, one of the men had followed him and was standing directly behind Khalid's vehicle with his arms crossed.

"Wait here," Khalid said to Ghaniyah.

He put the car in park and stepped out of the vehicle. "I'd appreciate it if you'd get out of my way," he said. "I don't want any trouble."

The man laughed. "You already found trouble." He moved toward Khalid as one of his buddies appeared from a different direction.

Khalid considered his options. There was a car parked directly in front of his. Within seconds, a pickup driven by the third man came screeching around the parking lot and stopped sideways behind Khalid's vehicle, pinning him in.

"Call 9-1-1," he said to Ghaniyah. "And lock the doors."

He kicked his door shut and took a step toward the first man in front of him. "This is the part where you walk away quietly before the police get here," Khalid said.

"No, this is the part where I kick your butt," the man said. He was about six-two and easily weighed more than two hundred pounds. He waited while the third man climbed out of the truck and joined the first two.

"Why don't you just go back to Afghanistan with the other towel-heads?"

The man on Khalid's right took a jab step at him, and Khalid jumped back. All three of Khalid's tormentors laughed and spread out around him, forming a semicircle. Other customers in the parking lot watched but kept their distance.

"We ought to put him in Abu Ghraib so a female guard can strip him down and lead him around on a leash like the other dogs," one of the men said.

Hearing no sirens, Khalid decided he had no choice. As the men taunted him, Khalid planned his move. He would go after the man on his right first—the smallest of the three. A quick blow to the crotch, and then whirl around toward the big guy in the middle.

"Yeah, get down on your knees and bark," the guy on Khalid's left said.

Khalid pivoted quickly and kicked the man on his right, bringing him to his knees. He spun toward the attacker in the middle, but the man was quicker than Khalid had expected. He caught Khalid with a hard right that cracked against Khalid's cheekbone just as the third man came in with a flying tackle that drove Khalid to the pavement. Instantly all three men were on him, slamming their fists into his face and body. Khalid tried to curl into a fetal position for protection, but one man knelt over him and pounded Khalid while the others kicked the imam. He tasted blood and felt himself losing consciousness.

"What the—?" His attacker's words were lost in a squeal of tires and the crash of metal. Khalid looked up. Ghaniyah had backed their car into the men's truck.

"Are you crazy?" one of them yelled. The guy on top of Khalid jumped up just as Ghaniyah slammed the car into drive, pulled forward a few feet, then slammed it into reverse and floored it again. She crashed into the truck a second time, bending more metal and breaking more glass. The truck bounced back.

She had the full attention of Khalid's attackers now. The driver of the truck scrambled toward it. "You freakin' idiot!" he yelled.

Before he could get there to move it, Ghaniyah slammed into the truck a third time, pushing it out of the way. She jumped out of the car and started cursing at the men like a possessed woman. They gaped at her, astonished by her brazenness.

"Look what you've done!" she screamed, pointing to Khalid. "May your souls burn in hell forever!"

None of the men seemed to know what to do with a woman who was certifiably nuts.

"Get out of here!" she shreiked, taking a menacing step at one of the men. He held his ground but didn't argue. The look in her eyes said Ghaniyah was ready to kill. She had always been intense before the accident, but Khalid hadn't seen her show this much emotion since.

Khalid struggled to his feet and moved next to Ghaniyah. "C'mon," he said. "They're not worth it."

Khalid could hear the sirens coming in the distance. "Look at my truck!" the biggest man yelled. "I'll sue you for every dime."

Only in America, thought Khalid, *can you get beat up by someone who then threatens to sue you.*

One of the attackers picked up his hat, dusted it off, and put it back on. "You're quite the man," he said to Khalid. "Had to have the old lady bail you out."

The sirens were getting closer. The men glanced around and yelled at the people in the parking lot who had stopped to stare. "Show's over, people! Get back to your pitiful lives!"

All three climbed into the truck. The man on the passenger side leaned out the window and promised Khalid that he had not seen the last of them. Then the driver squealed the tires, and the truck pulled away.

As the adrenaline began to fade, Khalid started feeling the intense pain in his face and ribs. "You're going to the hospital," Ghaniyah said.

He didn't even try to argue.

55

ALEX WAITED SEVERAL DAYS while Khalid mended before asking his client to meet with his lawyers and provide answers to most of the questions they had been asking. The imam brought Nara with him to the conference room at Madison and Associates.

For Alex, Khalid's appearance was a grim reminder of how danger-ous this case had become. The imam's right eye was swollen nearly shut with a large half-moon of black-and-blue bruises around the out-side and four stitches just above the eyebrow. His right upper lip was twice its normal size. Khalid winced when he took his seat and shifted around a little until he got comfortable. "It only hurts when I breathe," he quipped. Fortunately, the X-rays had shown no broken bones.

By contrast, Nara looked composed and well rested. She wore a light blue blouse with a matching skirt and heels that accentuated her long, slim figure. She had used just the right touch of makeup to high-light her alluring eyes and full lips. Alex caught himself staring at her as she talked. Out of his peripheral vision, he could see that Shannon was giving him a disapproving look. *Jealous?*

He had to admit that having Nara around had become less of a burden after their talk on Sunday. Now, sitting in the same room with her, he had to force himself to concentrate on the case.

There had been no further developments in the tepid investigation of Khalid's beatdown. Alex's firm had issued a press release explaining that Khalid had been assaulted in the parking lot of his local Harris Teeter. Neither the press nor the police seemed to care very much.

Once Alex and Shannon convinced Khalid that the conference

room was not bugged, he agreed to detail the connections between the Islamic Learning Center, the Islamic Brotherhood, and Hezbollah.

The mosque in Norfolk was part of a grand strategy to build at least one flagship mosque in every major American city. According to Khalid, the Islamic Brotherhood had helped fund the mosque through a spider-web of charitable organizations and NGOs it secretly controlled. Though Khalid didn't know for sure, there were rumors that the Brotherhood received much of its funding through a maze of international NGOs that could be traced to various donors in Saudi Arabia and certain terrorist groups. You can't build a $13-million mosque in Norfolk, Virginia, without some outside funding, Khalid explained.

Khalid had been asked to help lead the mosque because he was a prestigious professor at Old Dominion University and because he had been a high-profile leader in Lebanon. In the beginning, the Islamic Brotherhood also paid a stipend to other mosque leaders such as Fatih Mahdi.

Shortly after the mosque was completed, Khalid had a falling-out with the Islamic Brotherhood. The Brotherhood wanted to grow the attendance by using the tactics they had used in other cities, the same tactics used by Hezbollah in Lebanon. Brotherhood members would go door-to-door in the inner city and find families in need. They would provide groceries and assistance with rent. They would claim that Allah had sent them to bless the family. They would say that Christians, Jews, and Muslims were all pretty much the same theologically, all people of the Book, all worshiping the same God. They would tell single moms that Islam would teach their sons discipline and help them stay out of trouble in school.

"Mosques are being built all over the United States in this manner," Khalid explained.

"What about yours?" Shannon asked.

"Not ours," Khalid said. "Ours was different. From the beginning, we appealed more to university students and restless young professionals and those who had grown tired of the materialistic Christianity of the West. By that, Alex, I mean no disrespect."

"None taken," Alex said.

"We had professionals from as far away as Richmond and even northern Virginia who would come to our Friday salats," Khalid explained. "When I began preaching serious reform, the Islamic Brotherhood withdrew all support. Yet at the same time, moderate Muslims started showing up in force. There were, of course, those in the mosque who were disappointed by my teaching. At first, the whispers were quiet. But after the Israeli-Hezbollah war of 2006, my critics started making their displeasures known."

"Was Fatih Mahdi one of your critics?" Shannon asked.

Khalid thought about this for a moment, which gave Nara a chance to interject. "Most definitely," she said. "Fatih was one of the most outspoken critics. He's been vehemently opposed to many of my father's teachings. And I'm sure—though Father has never said this to me— that Fatih was also extremely upset that my father would allow me to speak so openly about women's rights."

"It is true," Khalid admitted. He was contemplative, not angry, speaking in the way family members talk about a loved one who has run into hard times. "But Fatih would always talk to me privately before he criticized me publicly. Even when we disagreed, we were friends. More like brothers. I cannot believe that Fatih is to blame for what has happened."

"But you know he recruited for Hezbollah when we lived in Beirut," Nara protested. "He's still part of the Brotherhood. Even today, he's recruiting for mosques all over the United States."

"I know," Khalid conceded. He said it with a tone that indicated the facts did not change his mind.

"It's one of the challenges with my father," Nara explained, as though her dad were not in the room. "He always sees the best in everyone. He can't imagine that anyone would have anything but his best interest in mind."

"Well . . . somebody was out to get him," Shannon said. She flipped a page in her legal pad and took a sip of bottled water. "Can I ask a few questions about the flow of money?"

She spent the next several minutes questioning Khalid about church procedures and how he protected his passwords. Alex listened appreciatively for a while. This was Shannon at her best. Taking notes. Uncovering nuances. Drilling down for details that might escape others.

When she started asking about access to Khalid's work computer, Alex began losing interest. He was busy studying Nara as she intensely followed the conversation. He had so many questions about her. What kinds of things made her smile? What did she like doing when she wasn't crusading to free her father? Were there any men in her life? Was there anything she feared? How deeply committed was she to the Muslim faith?

When Shannon turned her focus to the recipient account in Lebanon, Alex began to focus again. They had to find out who owned that account. Yet even if they did, there was no way they could subpoena an account in a foreign country.

Khalid seemed like he wanted to share something but kept holding back.

"What is it?" Shannon asked. "Do you know something about this account?"

The imam looked at his daughter and shifted painfully in his seat. He winced, either from the pain of his bruises or the subject matter at hand—Alex couldn't tell. "I've thought a fair amount about this," he said. "I still have one very close friend inside the Hezbollah organization who plays a key role in the financing of the Islamic Brotherhood." He pursed his lips and breathed in through his nose, as if he didn't want to say anything else right now.

"What's his name?" Shannon prodded.

"They need to know," Nara said. "It's the only way they can help."

"Can we keep his name confidential?" Khalid asked.

Shannon looked at Alex. If Khalid gave them the name of a friend who could help, they would be duty-bound to procure that testimony by whatever means possible.

"I can't promise anything," Alex said. "But we'll try."

Khalid thought about this. "I would rather exhaust all other channels first," he said. "The men who control the financing for the Islamic Brotherhood are ruthless and unforgiving. I am not willing to jeopardize my friend except as a last resort."

204 || FATAL CONVICTIONS

"We're already at last resort," Shannon said. "In fact, we passed last resort about two weeks ago."

"Then I'll contact him myself," Khalid said, "and see if he's willing to get involved."

Alex and Shannon wanted to play it differently. "Let me contact him," Alex said. "He's got to know that your freedom is on the line."

But Khalid wouldn't yield. Alex and Shannon both tried to dissuade him, but they were wasting their breath. The Mobassar family had stubborn down to an art form.

When the meeting was over, Nara pulled Alex aside in the hallway. "I'll get that name for you," she said.

"If you do, and if he's willing to testify, we may have to go to Lebanon to depose him," Alex said.

"I'll go with you," Nara said.

The intensity in her dark eyes was nearly impossible for Alex to resist. If he did go to Beirut, it would be smart to have someone with him who knew her way around. But his instincts were on red alert. The fifth admonition on his grandfather's list read *This is a law firm, not a dating service. Don't get emotionally attached to the clients.* But there was a spark of adventure in Nara's eyes, and she was hitting all the right chords.

So Alex began doing what lawyers did best—rationalizing. Technically, Nara wasn't even his client; Khalid was. And Alex was doing this for Khalid.

At least that would be his story when he explained it to Shannon. He pushed aside the mental picture of the framed yellow legal paper with his grandfather's handwriting on it. "Why not?" he said.

◁▷

Two days later, Nara came through on her end of the bargain.

"His name is Hamza Walid," she said. "My father talked with him. Walid's lawyer should be giving you a call."

Alex smiled. It was the first real break in the case in weeks. "I've heard Beirut is beautiful this time of year."

56

THE PROBLEM with any high-profile case was that sooner or later all the excitement and attention degenerated into hard work. Alex and Shannon spent the two months after the preliminary hearing interviewing witnesses, reviewing documents, and working on a motion to suppress key parts of the prosecution's evidence.

In addition, Alex obtained court approval to take the videotaped *de bene esse* deposition of Hamza Walid in Beirut, Lebanon, that could be used at the trial. Alex arranged the deposition through a Beirut lawyer named Nijad Abadi. Though Abadi would not let Alex speak with Walid directly, Abadi did say that he thought the deposition would be worth Alex's time. He also insisted that Alex not take the deposition until just before trial, in case the parties worked out a plea bargain that might make the deposition unnecessary. Alex hoped Walid would be able to provide the missing details linking Fatih Mahdi with both the Islamic Brotherhood and Hezbollah.

Shannon spent large chunks of her time trying to move Ghaniyah's personal-injury case forward despite the strident opposition of two defense attorneys, one hired to represent Country-Fresh, Inc., the company that owned the produce truck identified by Shannon, and a second hired to represent the driver.

The company's lawyer, a cranky, old-school practitioner named Mack Strobel, was a plaintiff lawyer's worst nightmare. Mack never agreed to anything. He fought every motion and defended every deposition tooth and nail. He was especially condescending and combative with young lawyers and saved his greatest disdain for young women. The first time Shannon met him, during a court hearing over one of the many objections Mack had filed to her discovery requests, he treated her as if she had just graduated from elementary school. Even when she won the hearing, it didn't seem to put a dent in his superiority complex.

The other defense lawyer, a young buck named Kayden Dendy, was the antithesis of Strobel. Kayden landed the case because he and the truck driver were in the same motorcycle club. At the first deposition, Kayden showed up about ten minutes late, riding a hopped-up Harley with bagger exhaust pipes that Shannon could hear from inside the building. When he strolled into the conference room wearing his leather jacket, Mack Strobel couldn't resist a snide comment.

"Is this a deposition or a biker's convention?" Strobel asked.

Dendy stared at Strobel, a dumbfounded look on his face. Then he formed his mouth into a small circle. "Oh . . . I get it! You're making a joke!" He gave a fake chuckle. "A good one, too, Mack. And they said you didn't have a sense of humor. That you were just some nasty old coot."

"Sit down and shut up," Mack Strobel said. "You've already kept us waiting ten minutes."

Just for spite, Dendy stood for the first half hour of the deposition.

About the only thing that Mack Strobel and Kayden Dendy had in common was a shared belief that Shannon didn't have a case. They denied that a Country-Fresh truck had anything to do with the accident even after Shannon deposed the truck driver and was able to place him on North Landing Road at the time of Ghaniyah's accident. They denied that Ghaniyah was seriously hurt, emphasizing the lack of "verifiable damage" on the MRI or CT scan. And they turned every deposition into a battle of wills.

The most contentious deposition was the day Ghaniyah's neuropsychiatrist testified. Based on his evaluation, he had little doubt that Ghaniyah had suffered diffuse axonal injury to the orbital frontal cortex and the anterior temporal lobes, causing noticeable changes in her social behavior, emotional status, decision-making skills, and executive functions. Strobel and the expert battled back and forth for hours, throwing around terms that were largely unfamiliar to Shannon. When he concluded, Mack Strobel had a self-satisfied grin on his face, as if he had just Perry Masoned the witness and forced a tearful admission on the stand.

Dendy followed up with a cross-examination that was more down-to-earth. He emphasized that Ghaniyah's symptoms were all subjective and that the imaging tests designed to show structural damage didn't reveal any. "Isn't this pretty much the same as a football player who suffers a mild concussion?" Dendy asked.

"It's more serious than that," the doctor said. "I'm seeing more long-term effects."

"Based on what Mrs. Mobassar tells you, right?"

"In part. But also based on my own clinical evaluation."

"Which, again, is based on how well Mrs. Mobassar does on the questions you ask her."

"Of course. That's the way all neuropsychological exams work."

Following the expert's deposition, Strobel subpoenaed all of Ghaniyah's medical records, even those that had nothing to do with her traumatic brain injury. He also tried to get the Mobassars' financial records, on the theory that maybe they were in so much financial difficulty that Ghaniyah was faking the accident. At the hearing on this issue, which Shannon won, she was indignant beyond words.

"Fake the injury?" she had asked, looking first at Strobel and then back at the judge. "Is he seriously claiming that Ghaniyah Mobassar ran her car into a tree so that she could fake a traumatic brain injury? That's like putting a loaded revolver in your mouth and pulling the trigger to *fake* a suicide."

"She's got a good point," Kayden Dendy mumbled.

The judge sent Strobel away empty-handed. At least somebody in the case was using a little common sense.

◁▷

While Shannon battled the lawyers on the civil case, Alex dug in on the criminal matter. He studied the financial records of the Islamic Learning Center, attempting to decipher if there was any connection with Hezbollah. He questioned members of the mosque about Fatih

Mahdi: What were his views on the role of women? What kind of temper did he have? What kind of marital problems with Ja'dah? What about his first wife?

Alex found himself craving his opportunities to work on the case with Nara. One hot Friday afternoon they sat in a conference room, reviewing documents and chatting about things unrelated to the case.

"You're a surfer, right?" Nara asked.

Alex looked up from the document he was reading. "Yeah."

"Ever do any stand-up paddleboarding?"

Alex was surprised she even knew about paddleboarding. "I've tried it a few times."

"I used to do it in Beirut," Nara said matter-of-factly. "The Mediterranean waves aren't huge—so they're perfect for paddle-boarding. One day, I went paddleboarding in the morning and snow skiing in the mountains that same afternoon."

Alex didn't quite know what to make of this. He had grown to appreciate Nara and had even learned to relish their occasional—okay, make that frequent—disagreements. Iron sharpens iron, and all that. But he had never seen her without makeup and her hair done just right, dressed for the office. She seemed like the furthest thing from a surfer he could possibly imagine.

"I could get my hands on a couple of paddleboards," Alex suggested. He owned a surfboard, not a paddleboard. But he could rent them if he had to.

Nara perked up at the suggestion. "That might be fun. I'm starting to feel pretty cooped up with my parents."

They scheduled a time to meet the next day. And Alex started formulating a plan. Paddleboarding in the early afternoon. After that, maybe he'd rent a couple of Jet Skis so they could ride together and have dinner at Chick's.

Khalid's case had been wearing on Alex, his nerves becoming increasingly frazzled as he thought about everything he needed to get done. But that day, he left the conference room feeling ten pounds lighter.

Paddleboarding with the imam's daughter. Go figure.

57

SATURDAY WAS WARMER than normal for late August with a high predicted to hit the upper nineties. There was a slight southeast breeze, and the air seemed humid enough to wade through. The waves were mostly wind swells, a mediocre day for surfing but a perfect day for paddleboarding. Early in the afternoon, Alex rented two boards from the Freedom Surf Shop and tied them into the back of his truck. Three o'clock couldn't come fast enough.

He and Nara had planned to meet on the beach at 65th Street, a location far enough north that there would be relatively few tourists. It was an area popular with surfers, partly because the lifeguards didn't patrol that far north. Though Alex couldn't remember the last time he had been anyplace early, it was only 2:30 when he threw on a pair of board shorts and a tank top and headed out.

He predicted that the paddleboarding would go pretty quickly. Nara would have difficulty staying up in the choppy surf of the Atlantic. He would give her a few lessons. She would get frustrated. Then he would suggest they hop on the Jet Skis and head to Chick's.

Alex arrived early and staked out a place where nobody else was swimming or surfing. He decided to take a quick swim before Nara arrived, body surfed a few waves to the beach, and then walked along the wet sand. He kept an eye peeled toward the footpaths over the sand dunes that led to the streets, walking up and down the beach until about three fifteen before he started getting nervous. He went a little farther in each direction in case Nara had gotten confused about the exact spot of their rendezvous.

By 3:25 he was sure he had been stiffed. She would probably have some lame excuse on Monday morning and ask him to reschedule. He would tell her that they really needed to focus on getting the case ready for trial. If she begged him, he *might* acquiesce to one more attempt to meet up at the beach.

When 3:30 rolled around, he was ready to leave. He checked his watch and decided to give her five more minutes. Exactly three minutes later, he finally saw her. She came over the sand dunes carrying her towel and sandals, wearing a two-piece bathing suit, shorts, and designer sunglasses. She shook her long, dark hair away from her face and gave Alex a big smile, stepping quickly across the hot sand.

The wait was worth every minute.

"Sorry I'm late," she said. "My mom's having a bad day, and I couldn't leave until almost three. I tried to call your cell phone."

Alex hadn't brought his cell phone, but he was no longer worried about starting a few minutes late. Nara looked like she had been born for the beach. Her skin was naturally bronze, and she was tall and lithe with muscular legs that Alex assumed came from skiing. He had not imagined that the daughter of a Muslim imam would look so much at home on the sands of Virginia Beach.

Nara expressed her surprise at how beautiful and secluded this part of Virginia Beach was. They chatted for a few minutes, and then Alex launched into his paddleboard-for-dummies lecture. Nara smiled as he rambled on and finally interrupted. "Let's just give it a try," she said. "I've done it a few times in Lebanon."

She took off her sunglasses and shorts, picked up the paddleboard and graphite paddle, and headed toward the water. The paddleboard itself was nearly eight feet long, and Alex was a little surprised at how easily she handled the thing. He expected her to watch him navigate the waves a few times, and then he could help her get out beyond the breakers. Instead, Nara led the way. On that point, Alex was not surprised.

She waded out until the water was thigh-deep, slapped her paddle-board down, and crawled on top of it. The water was cold, but Nara didn't flinch. She paddled on her knees until she had navigated just beyond the first line of breakers and then stood like a pro, her balance impeccable. She played around in the breakers until she found the one she wanted, pivoted her paddleboard, and dug in on the front face. Alex noticed the slight definition in her biceps and deltoids as she skimmed across the face of the wave, even cutting back to extend the ride. *The girl must work out.*

After a ride that took her almost to shore, she cut out, using the paddle as a brace while she pivoted toward the next set of waves.

"Not quite Beirut," she yelled over her shoulder, "but these aren't bad!"

"You sure you don't need that lecture?" Alex called out.

He had been standing in the water—at first because he wanted to help her when she crashed and burned, and then because it was a good vantage point from which to watch. He suddenly realized that he was supposed to be surfing with her, not just playing the role of a gawking teenager. He quickly headed out himself.

Though Alex was at home on surfboards, he didn't paddleboard much and at first felt a little shaky. There was a different rhythm to the sport, standing and paddling as he looked for the perfect wave. His timing on his first ride was a little off, and he bailed when it fizzled behind him.

"You need to be more patient!" Nara called. "Don't get out in front of it."

As if he needed coaching from a Beirut girl. Alex grunted and pivoted his board around. This time, less shaky and more determined.

For nearly an hour, they played in the waves. Nara had the slight advantage because she was lighter than Alex and thus her paddleboard had more buoyancy. But Alex was stronger—though not as much as he'd thought he would be—and could pick up speed faster. He was also a little more reckless.

Showing off, he decided to drop in on a wave Nara was already riding. He cut in right next to her, forcing her to lean hard away from him, her edge nearly hitting his board. Unfortunately for Alex, the break on the wave caught the back of his board, throwing him off balance and causing a spectacular wipeout—elbows, knees, and paddleboard tumbling in the surf. He scrambled to his feet, the board tugging at his ankle strap and his paddle several feet away.

Nara had a huge grin on her face. "You okay?" she asked.

"Next time we're using surfboards," Alex yelled.

They left the beach at four thirty, paddleboards under their arms. Alex couldn't remember the last time he'd had so much fun. Nara had on her sunglasses, the sun glistening off the moisture on her skin, her dark hair tangled and probably full of sand. Just another surfer girl at the beach.

"Where'd you learn how to paddleboard?" Alex asked.

"First time out," said Nara.

"Right."

When they reached the truck, Alex sprung the second part of his plan. "If you're hungry, we could rent a couple of Jet Skis and go down the Lynnhaven to a place called Chick's," he suggested. "Best seafood at the beach." He didn't tell Nara that he had already made reservations.

"You mean like a date?" Nara asked.

"I don't know. Maybe." Alex hated this part. "More like a ride on Jet Skis and dinner at Chick's. Some might call that a date."

"I'd love to," Nara said. Her face fell. "But I don't think it's a good idea." She had the look of genuine disappointment. "I think we need to be a little more careful."

Alex wanted to argue the point, but he knew Nara was right. The two of them had been brought together by a case with relentless media scrutiny. Alex's first job was to defend Nara's father. He was not being paid to entertain his client's daughter. And that was a shame. Under different circumstances, he could definitely see something developing between himself and Nara. After all, how many women this beautiful and this smart also knew how to surf?

◁ ▷

He had been staring at the two surfers all afternoon through his telephoto lens. He must have taken more than a hundred shots, but none of them was exactly what he needed. It wasn't until this final moment, just before they parted ways, that Nara stepped in and did exactly what the photographer had been urging her to do under his breath all afternoon.

She gave Alex a quick hug.

In real time, it looked rather harmless, the soft embrace of friends. But through the still lens of his camera, and after framing the picture from the waist up, it would look like something entirely different. Except for Nara's bathing suit top, it was bare skin against bare skin. It could be interpreted a hundred different ways. It was not exactly a passionate kiss, but it wasn't a sterile handshake either.

He squeezed off three quick shots and checked the digital images on his camera.

Perfect. The paparazzi couldn't have done it better.

58

THE RINGING OF HIS BLACKBERRY woke Alex out of a sound sleep Sunday morning. Without opening his eyes, he patted the nightstand to locate his phone. Success. He cracked open an eyelid and looked at the caller ID. Why was Shannon calling at 7:30 a.m.?

"Remember the Sabbath day and keep it holy," Alex said when he answered the phone. His voice was hoarse and gruff. "Tell me you're not calling about work."

"What were you *thinking*?" Shannon asked, her voice in midday form. And the energy . . . It sounded like she'd already chugged three cups of coffee.

"About what?"

"Have you been on the Internet?"

Alex dropped his legs over the side of the bed and ran his hand across his face. "I was sleeping," he said.

"Alone?"

"What's that supposed to mean?" He was waking up now and getting a little perturbed.

"There's a picture of you and Nara on the Internet." Shannon's voice was cold. "Lots of bare skin. Doesn't look like it's been Photoshopped. You're definitely in some kind of embrace."

Alex grunted. "We went paddleboarding yesterday. That photo was probably taken at the end of the day—late afternoon. She gave me a sympathy hug after rejecting my dinner invitation."

"*She* gave *you* a hug?" Shannon said, as if she was certain that Alex had mauled Nara instead. "She's the daughter of a Muslim cleric, and *she* gave *you* a hug?"

"Come on, Shannon. I already told you it was just a friendly hug. . . . She felt sorry for me after standing me up for dinner."

"That's not the way the press is playing it."

"I'm sure it isn't." Alex was ready to get off the line. Go back to sleep. Crisis averted. "I've hugged women before, Shannon. I might've even hugged you a time or two."

Shannon let out an exasperated sigh. She launched into a rapid-fire lecture about fraternizing with a client or a client's daughter. She even referenced his grandfather's list. Alex put the BlackBerry on speaker, placed it on the bed next to him, and crawled back under the sheets.

"Do you know why an honor killing is typically a beheading?" Shannon asked.

Where did that come from? "Some verse in the Qur'an, I guess," Alex replied.

"Not really," Shannon said. "Beheadings invoke terror. Honor killings are terrorist acts, Alex. They don't just kill women; they *decapitate* them. They want to strike the fear of God into anyone thinking about leaving the Islamic faith. And, Alex, they don't just kill the women, either. The men die too."

Alex stared at the phone for a second. Maybe Shannon had a point. The last thing Alex wanted to do was put Nara in danger. "I'm sorry," he said, though it came out grudgingly. "I guess I wasn't thinking."

"I've noticed that about men," Shannon said. "Their brains shrink in direct proportion to the size of the bikini."

If Alex hadn't been so tired, he might have thought of a good comeback. Instead, all he could mumble was that it wasn't a bikini.

He promised Shannon he would be more careful, hung up the phone, got out of bed, and surfed the Net. The picture was everywhere.

"Forbidden Romance?" one of the sites asked.

The caption on another was even more demeaning.

"All in a Day's Work," it read.

◁▷

As if on cue, the next honor killing occurred four days later in the suburbs of Cleveland, Ohio. A young Muslim woman had disappeared along with her alleged American boyfriend. The police manhunt concluded after forty-eight hours, when the bodies were discovered in a shallow grave not far from an evangelical church the two had been attending. As in the other killings, the woman had been beheaded. The man's body was badly charred. The authorities grimly concluded that he had been burned alive.

The experts speculated with abandon about the religious symbolism. In the first honor killing, Martin Burns had been buried alive. Was this a mockery of the Resurrection? The second killing involved baptism. And the man in the third had been burned alive—probably an allusion to the fires of hell.

The nation was terrified—and angry. The hate mail to Madison and Associates quadrupled.

59

THE FLAP OVER THE PICTURE proved to be relatively short-lived. Still, it changed the way Alex and Nara acted around each other. They now kept it über-professional. No touching. Little time alone together. Certainly no platonic hugs. You never knew when someone might be watching.

Alex normally enjoyed the fall, a time of year when the tourists left and the locals reclaimed the beach, but this year was different. It seemed he spent every waking moment at the office. Khalid's case clung to him like a shadow, sparking pangs of guilt whenever Alex tried to relax and take some time off.

Though the media attention dissipated somewhat, Shannon still argued that she should now be the one to go with Nara to Lebanon to take Hamza Walid's deposition. But even Khalid didn't agree with her about that. They were already getting signals from Walid's lawyer that he was skittish. He was a traditional Muslim. He would want a man asking the questions. And Alex wasn't about to stay home on this one.

Alex did concede that he and Nara should fly separately. She left first so she could spend a few days with her friends. Three days later, on the second Sunday in November, Alex checked in for his flight to Beirut with layovers in New York and Paris. The deposition started Tuesday.

◁▷

When he landed at the Beirut-Rafic Hariri International Airport around 10 a.m. on Monday, Alex felt as if he had been flying in planes for two straight years. It was great to stand up straight and stretch his legs, back, and neck.

He saw signs in French, English, and Arabic, but most of the words spoken around him were indecipherable. He had coffee breath and a stiff neck, and his face felt puffy. Like a lost sheep, he followed the herds of strangers through customs, picked up his luggage, and looked around for Nara.

He felt disoriented by both the jet lag and the unfamiliar culture buzzing around him. As he listened to the Lebanese men and women speak to each other in their hard-edged Arabic, he suddenly felt a little vulnerable. He was now officially in the land of Hezbollah. He didn't know the language. He had no weapons. His American street savvy would be of little use. He was a surfer from Virginia Beach stepping onto the gigantic stage of a distant and dangerous world.

He spotted Nara, straightened his shoulders, and summoned a little of that famous Madison bravado.

"How was your flight?"

"Piece of cake."

She almost gave him a hug but pulled back. "Welcome to Beirut," Nara said with a proper and firm handshake. Her enthusiasm quickly chased away any lingering apprehensions Alex felt. "The Paris of the Middle East."

Nara helped him with his luggage and hailed a small car at the curb that looked like a taxi. "It's called a ser-veese," Nara explained. "S-e-r-v-i-z. It's basically a small car with a wild man for a driver who will ignore all traffic signals."

After they threw Alex's luggage into the trunk, Alex and Nara climbed in the backseat. "Taxi," Nara said. Then she spoke to the man in Arabic.

"These cars operate as either a taxi or a serviz," Nara explained to Alex. "A taxi costs a little more, but it means the driver doesn't pick up other passengers along the way. A serviz means he stops and picks up others during the trip."

On the way to the hotel, Alex found out that Nara's original description of a serviz had been uncannily accurate. Traffic lights apparently served no purpose other than to illuminate intersections. Lines on the road were merely decorative. In twenty-five minutes, Alex saw remnants of five different accidents.

One ploy by the driver was particularly unnerving. On one of the streets in downtown Beirut, the driver stopped right in the middle of the road, got out of the car, walked to the sidewalk, and started talking in animated Arabic to one of the shopkeepers. Other drivers blew their horns and gave Alex and Nara dirty looks. Nara let this go on for about thirty seconds before she got out of the car and started yelling at the taxi driver. He talked back for a few seconds, then returned to the car, hopped in, and pulled away.

"What was that all about?" Alex asked.

"He was lost," Nara said.

They eventually found the Ramada where Alex was staying, and Nara promised to return that afternoon to show him the sights. He checked into his room, threw his gym bag on the floor, and lay down on the bed to relax. The bed was lower than most American beds and hard as a rock. The only other furniture in the room consisted of two plastic chairs. The walls were painted a muted orange. The bathroom looked decent, though Alex had been told that you didn't flush the toilet paper in Beirut; you placed it in the trash can.

He missed America already.

He turned on a small television set and surfed through the channels. Most of the programs were in Arabic. CNN had an English-speaking program, but the stories seemed to center around Europe. He kicked off his shoes and stretched out on the bed. Within minutes, he was sound asleep.

60

ALEX WOKE UP at three o'clock to the annoying sound of his BlackBerry alarm. He felt like he had been run over by a Mack truck. He had been sleeping so hard there was drool on his pillow.

He staggered out of bed and into the bathroom. He had the air conditioner set as cool as it would go, but he had still been sweating in his sleep. He brushed his teeth, showered, and threw on a fresh pair of shorts and a T-shirt. When he got to the lobby, Nara was waiting for him.

"Good nap?" she asked.

"Like I was drugged."

Fifteen minutes later, they were walking on the Corniche—the concrete walkway along the coast atop the cliffs of the Mediterranean. It wasn't quite Virginia Beach, but Alex had to admit that this place had its charms. People lined the railings along the Corniche—talking, fishing, or just hanging out watching other people. Some folks were dressed in conservative Muslim garb and others wore next to nothing. Runners would occasionally pass by. Small groups of people smoked something through a long hose attached to a decorative bowl sitting on the sidewalk.

"What's that?" Alex asked.

"It's called sisha," Nara replied. "They're smoking fruit-flavored tobacco through a water pipe."

"Sounds awful."

"I've tried it a few times," Nara admitted. "Tastes like perfume."

As they strolled along and took in the sights, it seemed like Nara was walking closer than normal, their arms occasionally brushing against each other. Alex had an urge to reach for her hand, but he remembered the uproar created the last time they had touched.

They talked about Hamza Walid's deposition. Alex explained how the process worked. He and Taj Deegan would both be there. Walid's own attorney would also be present. A court reporter would take down the testimony, and a videographer would tape the entire deposition. Though Nara couldn't go in the room, she could wait outside, and Alex promised to consult with her during breaks. He also knew that it would probably help fortify Walid if he realized that Khalid's daughter had made the trip.

"There's a lot riding on his testimony," Alex said.

"Let's talk about something else," Nara suggested.

◁▷

A few hours later, Alex and Nara got out of a serviz at Martyrs' Square. The statues there were riddled with bullets and missing large chunks where mortar blasts had ripped them apart. Nara pointed out a nearby shell of a building that had been decimated by bombs during the civil war.

"That was a Holiday Inn," Nara explained. "We're standing in the Green Zone—the epicenter of the fighting. That building became the headquarters for one faction and then another, depending on who controlled this area."

"How many years ago was that?" Alex asked.

"1980."

"And they haven't rebuilt it?"

"There are some things left as a reminder," Nara said. "But in most areas, Beirut rebuilds quickly. My people are a resilient people."

They sat on the concrete at the base of a statue, and Nara started talking about her family. "I was very young during most of the civil war, but I've heard the stories. My mother's brother was killed not too far from here. It made her bitter and angry, in part because my father didn't harbor the same level of hatred that she did."

Nara leaned back and shook her hair out of her face. The sun was beating down on them, unhindered by clouds. "I can hardly remember a time when my parents didn't fight at home. In public, my mother played the silent and obedient wife. But in private, she questioned my father's commitment to the Muslim faith. When I grew up and rebelled against the oppressive rules in our home, my mother blamed it on my father."

"I've never really seen your parents fight," Alex said.

"That's because you didn't know them before the accident."

Nara leaned forward, picked up a pebble, and tossed it absent-mindedly. She gazed into the distance. "Any other Muslim man would have divorced my mother twenty years ago. That's why this whole thing seems so bizarre and unfair. My father is the last person who would try to hurt a woman."

"I know that." Alex said. "And I intend to prove it."

Spending time in Beirut seemed to be relaxing for Nara, causing her to open up more than usual. She talked about losing both of her brothers. Omar had been working in a refugee camp when he was killed by an Israeli bomb. "Naturally my mother blamed the Jewish infidels, even though it was Hezbollah who instigated the hostilities and stationed their soldiers among innocent refugees."

Less than two years later, Ahmed was killed as part of a Hezbollah raid north of the border. "He was only sixteen," Nara said sadly. "I felt like I never had a chance to tell him good-bye."

Nara's mother again blamed the Israelis. But Nara held Hezbollah and the radical imams responsible. "They brainwashed him, Alex. They had him running missions that they didn't have the guts to do themselves.

"My mother rejoiced that her son had been found worthy to be a martyr. But after that, she was never the same. She had lost both sons, and she was left with a rebellious teenage daughter who despised her."

Alex listened in silence. He sensed that Nara hadn't been this vul-nerable in a long time. Perhaps ever.

"I more or less left the Muslim faith when my brothers died," Nara admitted. "Not physically, but emotionally."

Alex had never heard Nara state it so bluntly.

"I studied your Jesus for a while, but I ultimately decided I should work within my family's faith to help women find a voice," Nara continued. "I believed then, and I believe now, that radical groups like Hezbollah and the Taliban have hijacked a faith that could have been a great blessing to the world."

"A lot of Americans agree with that," Alex said.

Nara turned to him. The contemplative look was gone. Therapy over. The spark was back in the almond eyes. "Yes," she said with a tinge of sarcasm. "The enlightened Americans. How many female presidents have you had?"

"None. They're too emotional."

She swatted him.

"Case in point."

61

THE LEBANESE KNEW how to eat. Multiple courses spread over two hours. Exotic Mediterranean cuisine. The food was served mezze—in small dishes that formed a colorful array of textures, aromas, and tastes. For Alex, an eat-fast-food-in-the-car, I-don't-have-time-for-dinner guy, it was an eye-opening experience. Two hours spent with Nara in the soft light of a restaurant overlooking the Mediterranean was not quite heaven. But it was close.

He didn't get back to his hotel room until nearly nine, and he still needed to review some things before tomorrow's deposition. He kicked off his shoes and lay on the bed. He was jet-lagged and now had a full stomach in a warm room. He didn't quite have the emotional energy to deal with the upcoming deposition right now. Alex closed his eyes. Maybe he would take a short nap first. Just a half hour or so . . .

The BlackBerry always sounded twice as loud when it woke Alex out of a sound sleep. He jerked awake, disoriented in a room that he didn't immediately recognize.

The next feeling that hit was a sense of foreboding. Nobody ever calls late at night with good news.

"Hello," he said, his voice scratchy. He checked his watch. The display said 10:37 p.m.

"Alex, this is Nijad Abadi," the voice said. He had a heavy Lebanese accent, and it took Alex a second to place the name—Hamza Walid's lawyer. "I am sorry to disturb you so late."

"It's all right," Alex said, but his stomach had dropped to his knees. This could mean only one thing.

"I am very sorry to inform you that my client will not be able to be deposed tomorrow. I just learned of this myself and wanted to let you know immediately."

"What?"

"My client—Mr. Walid—he will not be coming in for his deposition tomorrow. I am very sorry that we must cancel on such short notice."

Alex was fully awake now. "You can't cancel. I came all the way from America."

"I know. And I am terribly sorry. But as we both know, his testimony is entirely voluntary. And Mr. Walid has had a change of heart."

"What happened?" Alex demanded. "You at least owe me an explanation."

"I am not at liberty to say anything more," Nijad said. "However, I am authorized on behalf of Mr. Walid to reimburse you for your expenses."

"I don't want my expenses reimbursed!" Alex said, practically shouting. "I need to take Walid's deposition. A man's life is on the line. A friend of your client."

"I am sorry. That cannot happen."

"Let me talk to him." Alex had quickly gone from confused to furious. How could they do this?

"That is not possible, Mr. Madison. He has asked that you communicate only through me."

The rest of the conversation was a blur. Alex expressed his frustration in no uncertain terms, trying his best to put a guilt trip on the Beirut lawyer. When he got off the phone, he quickly called Khalid to see if Khalid could get in touch with Hamza and talk him into showing up. When that didn't work, Alex called Abadi back and said that he would show up at the lawyer's office tomorrow morning at nine anyway, just like they had planned. If Hamza reconsidered, Alex would be there.

"I'm afraid that would be a waste of time," Abadi said. "When I spoke to Ms. Deegan, she said that she would be taking the first plane back to the United States."

Of course, Alex thought. Taj knew the deposition couldn't go forward without her.

It was time to face the facts. There would be no deposition.

The one person Alex didn't call that night was Nara Mobassar. He didn't want her to find out over the phone. He would tell her face-to-face, first thing in the morning.

62

THEY WERE STANDING next to a concrete bench outside Abadi's office when Alex broke the news. He had already gone inside, demanding to at least meet with Abadi, and had been told that the lawyer was not in. Alex had left the building and waited for Nara outside. When she arrived, he walked her to the bench and asked her to have a seat.

She froze instead, eyeing Alex suspiciously. "He's not coming, is he?"

Alex shook his head. "No. He's not."

There was fire in Nara's eyes as she tried to keep a stiff upper lip. "When did you find out?"

"Last night."

"And you didn't call me?"

"I didn't want to tell you over the phone."

Nara seemed to be on the verge of crying—they both had harbored high hopes for this deposition. She pursed her lips and set her jaw defiantly, but Alex could see tears forming in her eyes. He told her about the phone calls the previous night and his attempts to get the deposition back on track.

At some point, though he didn't really notice when, Alex and Nara both sat down. She sniffed a few times and used a finger to brush some tears from the corners of her eyes. "I'm sorry," she said, as if she wasn't allowed to cry. "I just knew that Hamza's testimony would get the truth out there. It's so unbelievably frustrating."

"I know." Alex wanted to hold her and offer some comfort, maybe let her cry on his shoulder, but he knew how that would look in the tabloids. "I feel the same way."

They talked for a few minutes about what to do now. Alex tried to stay positive, but he also sensed that Nara liked it best when he played it straight. "What if we can still find Walid?" she asked. "What if he tells me who the bank account belongs to? Can I testify about that?"

"It's actually kind of complicated," Alex said. "If Hamza talks with us, we might be able to use whatever *information* he gives us so long as we can verify it in some other way that is admissible in court. But what he tells us would be hearsay. So the statements themselves would generally not be admissible."

"Generally?" Nara asked, picking up on the loophole. "What are the exceptions?"

Alex grunted. "There are tons of exceptions. But the only one that might apply to Walid is if he said something that could be regarded as an admission against interest. In other words, he admits something that might subject him to criminal liability or might be against his own financial interest. Those statements are generally deemed reliable because people don't incriminate themselves unless it's true. But even if he made statements like that, we'd have to prove that he's not available to testify, and we would need corroborating circumstances."

Nara was silent for several moments, processing this information. Alex could see that she had latched on to this angle as a thin ray of hope.

"I'm going to call my father," Nara said. "Find out who knows Walid. Maybe we can still meet with him."

"Okay," Alex said, though he was not very enthusiastic about the plan. It was one thing to take Walid's deposition in the safety of another lawyer's conference room. It was another thing to set up a clandestine meeting with a witness who had obviously been intimidated from testifying by Hezbollah leaders.

"Be careful," Alex said.

Nara looked at him and nodded. "Do you want to go for a walk?" she asked. Resolve had returned to her moist eyes. The resignation and despair of just a few minutes ago had been replaced by the new possibility, slight though it might be, of a secret meeting with Walid.

"Sure," Alex said, amazed at how quickly Nara had rebounded.

"My people are a resilient people," she had said. Alex thought about

the amazing contrast he had seen between the bombed-out buildings around Martyrs' Square and the glitzy new downtown where they had dined last night. Beirut knew how to rebuild. Today he had learned that even the areas devastated during the 2006 war had been reconstructed in ways that made them better than before.

Maybe he could learn from that.

He walked in silence with Nara for a while, thinking about the case and the ways he might still be able to win even without Walid's testimony. They would challenge the Patriot Act. Plus, there was Khalid's exemplary record as a reformer. They could blame Fatih Mahdi, a controlling husband with a misogynist view of the world.

He found himself hopeful for the first time in the case, as if maybe the pluck of the Lebanese was rubbing off on him. Or maybe it had more to do with Nara. Somehow, he felt more optimistic just being around her. Stronger. More courageous.

"We'll figure this out," he said. "With or without Walid, we're going to be fine."

"I know we will," Nara replied.

◁ ▷

It didn't shock Alex when he got a call from Nara later that day. "I've found somebody who thinks he can set up a meeting with Walid. Can you be ready in an hour?"

Alex was ready now. But he thought he had detected just a hint of nervousness in Nara's voice. "Where are we going?"

"To the Hezbollah district," she said.

63

ALEX DREW CONSIDERABLY more stares in the Hezbollah district than he had in downtown Beirut. There were not many blond American males walking the streets with pretty Lebanese women. The old men sitting in front of the shops leered at Nara as she walked by. Occasionally, some would call out, *"Yalla habibi."*

The first time, Alex glared at them, and Nara chuckled. The men were smiling, too.

"What does that mean?" Alex asked.

"'Come on, baby' or 'let's go, baby'—that type of thing."

"Smooth," Alex said.

The signs in downtown Beirut had been in both Arabic and English, but in the Hezbollah district there were few English signs. Large billboards contained gigantic faces of men Alex assumed were Hezbollah leaders. Most of the women they encountered were totally covered and averted their eyes when Alex looked at them.

Buildings still showed the lingering effects of the 2006 war with Israel. As Nara had explained during the serviz ride, the Hezbollah leaders made their headquarters in the middle of civilian neighborhoods, and the Israelis had destroyed entire city blocks with their bombs. Several years later, the rebuilding still had a long way to go.

"The Lebanese government is corrupt and slow," Nara explained. "One of Hezbollah's greatest strengths is disaster relief and the rehabilitation funds it deploys."

They eventually found a cramped little restaurant that reminded Alex of a New York deli. There was a counter for ordering food and just enough room on the opposite wall for a line of small tables. Nara talked in rapid Arabic to the proprietor and introduced the man to Alex. Alex didn't catch his name, but the big man reached over the counter and shook Alex's hand with the strength of a vise grip.

"I'm going to order for both of us," Nara said in English.

"Great," Alex answered. "I'll take a Big Mac."

"Ugly Americans," Nara said.

The dish that Nara actually ordered was like nothing Alex had ever tasted. It featured chickpeas, olives, and radishes mixed with a creamy substance that had the texture of yogurt. All of this was wrapped inside some kind of dough. Alex ate the food with a smile and a few approving grunts. Truthfully, it didn't compare to last night's dinner, but Alex wasn't about to complain at a restaurant in the Hezbollah district.

He chatted with Nara as they ate, and at least twice the owner came over to see how the guests were enjoying their meal. Alex lied about how great everything tasted, and Nara translated his compliments.

Just before they left, the man came back one last time and talked to Nara. When they finished chatting, she stood and gave him a hug. Alex also stood and shook the man's hand. He gave Alex a good-natured slap on the shoulder.

When Nara tried to pay for the meal, another animated discussion ensued, and it was obvious that the man wasn't going to let her. Alex smiled and nodded in appreciation. "Thanks," he said. The proprietor smiled back.

After they left the restaurant, Nara looked for a serviz.

"What's the deal?" Alex asked.

She unfolded a piece of paper that the man had apparently slipped into her hand. The writing was in Arabic.

"Hamza Walid is going to meet us tonight," Nara said in a whisper.

"Where?"

"I don't know. It just says where his driver is going to pick us up."

64

HASSAN IBN TALIB was a teenager at a Hezbollah training camp when he first held an AK-47. He had been in training for three weeks before the leaders handed him and the other recruits their very own assault rifles. The adrenaline pumped through Hassan's body as he smelled the steel and oil. The gun felt cold and hard in his hands.

The leaders showed the boys how to load the gun, how to fire it, and how to care for it. After what seemed like an interminable amount of time, they allowed each of the young recruits to fire at some cardboard targets shaped like human silhouettes.

When Hassan's turn came, he knelt down, placed his finger on the trigger, and pulled. At first, he fired tentatively, slowly. Few targets fell. But then he started firing faster, one blast after another, and the targets began to drop. His heart started beating quicker. He pulled again and again, faster and faster. Shell casings flew to the ground as Hassan blew through an entire magazine of bullets. The steel became hot in his hands, and the roar of the gun rang in his head.

When he stopped firing, the silence seemed deafening. Somehow, Hassan knew that things would never again be the same. He had started this day as a boy. Now he was a man. The gun had a mystical power unlike anything Hassan had ever felt.

He was born for this.

He looked at his leader, a man who rarely smiled. The man was grinning now.

"Very good, my son. Soon you will be ready."

65

AT 11 P.M., an old BMW pulled up to the curb in front of the Ramada, and the driver stepped out.

"Nara Mobassar?" he asked.

Nara responded in Arabic and told Alex that this was the one. They climbed into the backseat, and Nara had another exchange with the driver.

"Where are we going?" Alex asked.

"He wouldn't say," Nara responded. "Apparently Hamza is big on secrecy."

"Are you sure about this?" Alex asked.

"For the third time, *yes.*"

Alex had lots of misgivings about the trip, but Nara, true to form, had an answer for everything. Alex didn't like going without knowing the destination. But as Nara pointed out, they didn't have much choice in the matter. What if it was a setup, Alex had asked. Nara said she trusted her sources. Plus, she had enlisted the help of several friends. She would send them text messages, updating them on her location. If they didn't hear from her at least once every five minutes, they would call the police.

Alex could shoot a thousand holes in the plan. What if the police were slow to respond? What if somebody took her cell phone? What if Hezbollah thugs blew up their car or shot them without warning?

But he didn't bother asking more questions. Nara was going, with or without him. If necessary, she would take someone else. And Alex wasn't quite ready to admit that this woman from Lebanon had more guts—or a greater commitment to the case—than he did.

The one thing that still bothered him as they wound their way through the streets of Beirut was Nara's insistence that they not tell Khalid. "If my father finds out, he'll make us promise not to go," Nara had explained.

That should have told Alex everything he needed to know.

Fifteen minutes into the trip, even Nara started looking a little nervous.

"Where are we?" Alex asked. He was afraid he already knew.

"The Hezbollah district."

"And whose idea was this?"

Nara didn't answer. She was too busy texting one of her friends.

The driver eventually veered off the main street, navigated a few side streets, and pulled into an abandoned parking lot.

"Here?" Nara asked.

The man nodded without turning around.

Alex looked at Nara and twisted his face. *Are you sure about this?*

"It's an old train station," Nara said. "The trains in Beirut haven't been running for years."

Without turning around, the driver said something in Arabic, and Nara replied. Alex heard tension in her voice. Nara and the driver argued for a few minutes before she turned to Alex.

"He says that Hamza will meet us down at the tracks. There are three abandoned railcars. I'll tell you a legend about them on the way."

Nara spoke to the driver in Arabic again. "I told him to leave the lights on and wait for us to get back," she said to Alex. She typed out another text message. "You ready?" she asked.

"Not really."

"Neither am I."

Nara was the first to get out; Alex followed. They walked to the far corner of the parking lot and headed down a path toward the tracks. Abandoned buildings and overgrown weeds lined the walkway on both sides. In a few seconds they were beyond the lights from the BMW. Alex used the glow from his BlackBerry screen to shed some pale light on the path. Nara edged closer, and for some reason they found themselves whispering.

"They say that during the civil war, train cars like these were used to house prisoners and hold trials," Nara said softly. "The legend is that the militia would hold the prisoners captive in one train car, give them a five-minute trial in the next, and execute them in the third. When that car was full, they'd haul it away to a mass grave."

"I could have gone all night without hearing that story," Alex said.

They were closing in on the train cars now, the noise of the city faint in the distance. Nara and Alex stepped over an old power line. Dead leaves crunched under their feet. There was an abandoned masonry building on their left, the shells of the three train carriages on their right. The place smelled like urine, and Alex imagined it was probably a hangout for the homeless.

"Hamza?" Nara called softly. "Hamza?"

Alex felt his heart race a little faster. The night was hot and muggy, but a cold bead of sweat ran down the back of his neck. They waited a few minutes in silence.

"I'm going to take a look inside those cars," Alex said.

Using his BlackBerry again for light, Alex peeked inside all three cars. They were rusted and covered with debris, but there was no sign of anyone waiting for them. Nara stayed within arm's length the entire time.

"I don't like this," Alex said. "Hamza could be leading us straight to the slaughter."

"Three more minutes," Nara said. "If Hezbollah wanted to kill us, we'd be dead by now."

"That makes me feel better."

There was a rustle in the bushes behind them. Alex turned and froze, staring at the spot where the noise originated.

Nara grabbed his arm and froze too. "Probably just rats," she whispered.

"Rats," Alex said, his voice skeptical.

"Stop being a wimp."

Alex exhaled, but his heart was still trying to beat its way out of his chest. This kind of thing looked glamorous in the movies. In real life, you'd never hear the bullet that took you out.

Nara sent another text message.

"Are you ready to go?" Alex asked.

Nara nodded. "I don't understand this." It was the first time Alex had heard real concern in her voice. "Maybe something happened to him on the way here."

Before Alex could respond, there was a flash behind them, and Alex pivoted. He stepped in front of Nara and was blinded by a spotlight. He shaded his eyes and saw something in his peripheral vision. But before he could grab Nara and run, he was broadsided by a man who hit him with the explosiveness of a linebacker, driving Alex into the ground. Alex tried to scramble free, but another man jumped on. They quickly had Alex facedown, his arms wrenched behind him as they slapped on some plastic ties as handcuffs.

He heard Nara scream, and he yelled her name just before they pulled a hood over his face.

Strong hands grabbed his arms and jerked him to his feet. He called Nara's name again, and one of his captors punched him in the gut, doubling him over. They quickly straightened him up and pulled him along, speaking to each other in Arabic. Alex was struggling for breath but tried to concentrate. There were at least three or four voices, as far as he could tell.

They made him climb some steps into one of the railcars and pushed him into a seat. He heard a commotion next to him and the frightened breathing of Nara.

His captors stopped talking, and Alex felt the indent of a round barrel against his temple. He tried to look out the bottom of the hood, but everything was black. The only sound was his own heavy breathing.

He was certain he would die right there in that abandoned railcar in Beirut. Nobody in America would ever know the details. A lawyer and an imam's daughter—never heard from again.

"Nara, are you okay?" he asked. He flinched, anticipating another punch.

"I'm fine," she said, though her voice was breathless. "Watch what you say—they probably know English."

There was no panic in her voice, and the sound of her composure steeled him. For the sake of Nara, he needed to be brave. He needed to show her that Muslims weren't the only ones who knew how to die. He wanted to make a joke or some sarcastic comment that demonstrated his bravado. But words failed him as the gun jammed harder into his temple. His captors spit out more Arabic phrases, and Alex felt utterly helpless.

"It's going to be all right," he said to Nara, but his voice betrayed the truth.

He didn't believe it himself.

66

NARA TALKED TO THEIR CAPTORS in Arabic—argued with them, as far as Alex could tell—and their captors seemed to respond with growing frustration. Through it all, Nara kept her voice measured but firm, even as the men spoke louder, their words biting and harsh.

A noise startled Alex, as if somebody had kicked over a box. He tensed, waiting for the blows to start.

"What are they saying?" he asked.

"Not now," Nara snapped.

She engaged them again, her voice more cautious this time. But her words engendered the same angry response.

It sounded to Alex like there were three or four male voices in the room. He had a gun pointed at his head and his hands cuffed behind his back. He assumed that Nara was in the same position. For whatever reason, she didn't seem to be backing down. She talked for a long time, uninterrupted, and this time the response seemed less angry. Like maybe they were seeing her point. She answered again, and they didn't respond at all.

And then, just as Alex began to relax just a little, Nara shrieked. There was the sound of wrestling and a muffled groan.

The room grew quiet.

"Are you okay?" Alex asked.

A hand grabbed Alex's hood and yanked it off. Alex blinked and looked around. A lantern in the corner of the carriage car provided dim light and cast long shadows. There were four men, each wearing a hood, the slits revealing hard eyes and eerie-looking mouths. Three of the men held AK-47s. One had the barrel of his gun within inches of Alex's temple.

Nara was sitting across the aisle with her hands cuffed behind her back. Her captor had wrapped white cloth around her face, but there was an opening for her eyes. The man behind her had gathered the white linen in his fist behind her head and was pulling on it, tilting her head back and exposing her neck. With the other hand, he held a long knife, its blade touching the side of Nara's neck. Her eyes were wide with terror.

"Have you ever seen a beheading?" asked the man standing in the aisle a few rows in front of Alex. He spoke English, just as Nara had predicted.

Alex shook his head.

"Unless you do as we say, you may get your chance with your pretty girlfriend."

Alex glanced at Nara, whose dark eyes were pleading with him to do this right. He turned back to the man in the aisle. "Tell your buddy to take the knife away from her neck," Alex said.

The man clenched his teeth and shook his head, his eyes narrowing. He held his index finger and thumb an inch apart. He mumbled something that made Nara close her eyes and tense; then the man behind her sliced the blade ever so slightly into Nara's neck, creating a small sliver of blood.

"Do not think you give the orders here," the first man said.

Alex tried not to panic. He watched the blood trickle down Nara's neck. "What do you want?" he asked, his voice shaking.

"We have a little script for you to recite," his captor said. "If you perform it flawlessly, you will save two lives."

Alex looked at Nara; she gave him the slightest nod. The man pulled her head back tighter, and she winced. The blade rested against her artery.

"Okay," Alex said quickly. "Just tell me what you want me to do."

67

THEY CUT THE PLASTIC HANDCUFFS from Alex's wrists, and he rubbed the raw skin there. Nara's eyes followed his every move. The man with the English proficiency, the tallest of his captors, handed Alex a piece of paper with a script and demanded that Alex memorize it. "We don't have much time."

Alex looked at the paper, angled it toward the lantern, and read it quickly. "Word for word?" he asked.

"As close as possible."

Alex pretended to focus on the paper, mumbling to himself, secretly considering the possibilities for escape. Four captors. Two AK-47s pointed at him. One knife at Nara's neck.

He wasn't James Bond. There would be no escape.

After a few minutes, the tall captor reached out and grabbed the paper. "Enough. Move to the front. We start filming now."

He pushed Alex to the front of the car, positioning him in front of a nondescript wall. One of the other captors focused a video camera on Alex. A third pulled out the battery-operated spotlight they had used earlier. He turned it on and blinded Alex.

Alex closed his eyes and tried to visualize the script. He opened his eyes, squinted at the light, and started speaking. He used a wooden monotone, making sure the words were devoid of any emotion.

"My name is Alexander Madison, and I'm the attorney for Khalid Mobassar. The date is November 16. Mr. Mobassar's trial for conspiracy to commit murder begins in approximately three weeks.

"Later tonight, I will upload this video to the Internet and password-protect the site. If anything happens to me . . ."

Alex took a deep breath and tried to remember the next line, then shook his head and rubbed his temples. Having spent most of the few minutes they gave him for memorization trying to think of ways to escape, he drew a blank. "I don't remember. Can I see that paper again?"

One of the men grumbled something in Arabic, and another turned off the spotlight. While Alex struggled to adjust to the new lighting, the English-speaking captor thrust the paper at Alex and poked the barrel of his AK-47 against Alex's chest. "Three minutes."

This time, Alex worked furiously to memorize his lines, glancing occasionally at Nara. At the end of a quick three minutes, his captor grabbed the paper and Alex began take two.

The spotlight came on again. Alex slipped into the same monotone. "My name is Alexander Madison, and I represent Khalid Mobassar. The date is November 16. Mr. Mobassar will be on trial for conspiracy to commit murder in approximately three weeks.

"Later tonight I will upload this video to the Internet and password-protect the site. I will give the password to one of my friends with instructions that he should circulate the video to the appropriate authorities if anything should happen to me. As long as I remain alive, the attorney-client privilege prevents me from sharing what I know. But if I die, I want people to know the truth."

When Alex had first glanced through the script, he realized immediately what his captors were doing. If Alex or Khalid tried to blame the beheadings on Hezbollah at trial, they would kill Alex and release this video on the Internet. Everything would point to Khalid Mobassar as the man responsible for both the honor killings and Alex's death.

"My client has confessed to me that he ordered the honor killing of Ja'dah Mahdi as well as two other Muslim women who converted to Christianity. He also ordered the deaths of the men who convinced two of these women to reject the Muslim faith. He has instructed me to defend his case by blaming other possible suspects, including those associated with Hezbollah. Mr. Mobassar's hope is to discredit Hezbollah and its allies while ensuring his own rise to prominence as a reformer of the Islamic faith. That is the sole reason he ordered the honor killings in the first place—to bring attention to his reform proposals so that he can become the voice of Islam."

Alex shifted his weight and stared at the back wall, past the blinding spotlight. He was almost done, and he was pretty sure he had gotten most of it right. "If you are watching this video, it means that my client considers me too high a risk to allow me to live. It is ironic that in trying to protect himself from exposure, Mr. Mobassar has sealed his fate."

The spotlight cut off, and Alex blinked to adjust, his pupils dilating. "How did I do?"

"That will work."

The captor standing behind Nara unwrapped the linen strips from her face and cut the plastic handcuffs from her wrists. They spoke to Nara in Arabic—harsh and angry tones—and she replied with her composure still unshaken.

"We need to leave," she told Alex. She walked down the aisle and headed for the door. None of her captors made a move to stop her. Alex followed close behind, glancing nervously at the AK-47s pointed at him. When Nara and Alex stepped out of the train car, she grabbed his hand and started running. They stumbled through the dark, sprinting away from their captors as quickly as possible.

"Why did they let us go?" Alex asked as they darted toward the parking lot.

Nara was nearly out of breath but kept running. "I'll explain everything later."

They didn't stop running until they made it to the lot. The driver of the BMW was gone. Nara looked around and grabbed Alex's hand again. "Let's go." She took off running toward one of the side streets, glancing behind in the direction of the train cars.

"Do you know where you're going?" Alex gasped.

"As far away from here as we can get."

68

NARA AND ALEX EVENTUALLY hailed a serviz, and Nara gave the driver instructions in Arabic. During the ride, Alex used his shirt to wipe the blood away from Nara's neck.

They discussed their options, but Nara was dead set against reporting the incident to the authorities. The police in Beirut were not going to take on Hezbollah. Reporting the kidnapping would only make the terrorist organization more aggressive.

"More aggressive?" Alex asked. "How can they possibly get more aggressive?"

Nara made a motion with her hand for Alex to keep the volume down. She nodded toward the driver. "He picked us up in the Hezbollah district," she whispered. "And a lot of these guys speak pretty good English."

"Sorry."

Nara leaned closer. "To answer your question—if Hezbollah wanted us dead, we'd be dead. They wanted to scare us, Alex. They don't really care if Hezbollah gets blamed for these killings. But we were obviously onto something with the deposition of Walid. My guess is that they thought we were getting close to one of Hezbollah's top leaders. This must go pretty high up the chain."

What Nara said made sense. "Then let's report it to the American authorities," Alex suggested. "As soon as we get back."

Nara looked at him like he'd lost it. "You don't think Hezbollah can get to us in America? And what are the American authorities going to do? File a report? Call their counterparts in Lebanon? Stir things up just enough to get you and me killed?"

They were talking in hushed tones so as not to be overheard by the driver. "You got a better idea?" Alex asked.

"Let's talk later."

When they got to the Ramada, Nara insisted that Alex check out of the hotel and find another place. The driver had picked them up at the Ramada; their attackers knew that's where he was staying.

"I thought they were just scaring us," Alex said.

"Why take chances?"

After paying for the room, they snuck out the back and found an out-of-the-way place near the shore named the Regis Hotel. It was a nondescript backpackers' dive with the room rate listed on a white board near the Formica front desk. The sign listed the cost in Lebanese pounds and American dollars. For a single room, someone had crossed through $34 and discounted the rooms to $25.

They went to the room together so they could talk over a plan.

"Nice place," said Alex.

"Just don't touch anything," Nara responded.

The room felt more like a dorm than a hotel. The plaster walls were off-white with water stains in three or four spots. The carpeting was threadbare. There was a small single bed next to a window. Alex quickly closed the curtains. The bathroom had a black-and-white checked tile floor and small black tiles on the wall. A radiator sat idle in one corner. Air-conditioning was apparently not included.

Nara sat at the end of the bed, and Alex took a seat in the lone plastic chair in the room.

"What were you saying to those guys?" Alex asked.

"I told them that my friends knew exactly where we were and knew that we were meeting with Hezbollah. If they didn't hear from me in five minutes, they were going to call the police and the U.S. embassy."

"And they bought that?" Alex asked.

"Not really. But I came up with another story that they liked better." Nara rolled her neck and rubbed a spot on her left shoulder.

"I told them that we would not be implicating Hezbollah at trial. I told them that you were a very good lawyer and that your first line of defense would be to attack the Patriot Act. I argued that this could be a major victory for Hezbollah and its allies."

Alex admired Nara's quick thinking, but he wasn't fond of her reasoning. Would a victory by Alex really be a win for all of America's terrorist enemies? He knew he should think only about Khalid's innocence—but at what cost to the country? He quickly put the thoughts aside. The soul-searching could wait.

"I also told them that if the court ruled against us on the Patriot Act, I had another defense that did not involve Hezbollah. This one did involve a small lie, however. You remember the doctrine of al toqiah?"

"I remember," Alex said. *How could I forget?*

"I told them that I had convinced you I was a Christian and that my father had accepted my decision to abandon the faith. I told them that I would be the last witness called at my father's trial and that this evidence would establish his innocence even without pointing the finger at Hezbollah."

Nara looked sheepishly at Alex. "Sorry," she said.

"You saved our lives," Alex said. "No need to apologize."

"They never really intended to kill us," Nara said. "Think about it. They had the video and the script ready to go. They just wanted to scare us . . . and create evidence that would convict my father if they decide to kill us later."

The logic seemed sound, but Alex was in no shape to figure things out. The adrenaline was gone. So, too, was most of the terror. In their place was a bone-weary fatigue. He rubbed his face and stretched his back.

Nara must have felt it too. She sighed and lay back on the bed, her legs dangling over the edge. She stared at the ceiling for a minute and then shut her eyes. "They're the ones responsible for killing these women, Alex. They want to pin it on my father because he's a reformer and they're afraid of him—afraid of his ideas."

Nara opened her eyes and looked at Alex. "Put me on the stand in my father's trial," she said. "I'll tell the world what happened tonight. We can expose Hezbollah for who they are."

Alex had a million reasons why that was a bad idea. The rules of evidence, for starters. But perhaps the biggest reason was Nara's own safety. He had a duty to Khalid. But he would not sacrifice Nara to fulfill it.

He moved over and sat next to her on the bed. "Let's talk about it later."

Nara sat up, and Alex put his arm around her shoulder. As she leaned in, he could smell the shampoo in her hair. He pulled her closer. She wrapped her arms around his waist, burying her head on his shoulder. They sat like that for a moment, and then he felt her begin to cry.

He reached down and brushed the tears from her cheek.

"Alex," Nara said softly, her voice so low that he could barely hear her, "I really should go now."

"I know."

It was hard to let her go, but he knew it was the right thing to do.

After she left, he kicked off his loafers and lay on the bed, staring at the ceiling. Given everything he had just been through, it would be impossible to fall asleep.

It took Alex two minutes to prove himself wrong.

69

THE DAY AFTER THE KIDNAPPING, Alex and Nara talked over breakfast about what they should do. They agreed that going to the authorities right now would be counterproductive. They also agreed that they should keep the matter between themselves. Nobody else could know—not even Shannon or Khalid.

But they disagreed vehemently on whether Nara should testify about their capture at her father's trial. Alex didn't think the testimony would be allowed. And if the judge did allow it, he was fearful that Hezbollah would retaliate against Nara.

And maybe against him as well, though he didn't voice that particular concern.

Nara insisted on taking the stand. In fact, she wanted to be the last person to testify in her father's case. That way, she could cast aspersions on Hezbollah and leave the commonwealth very little time to counter. Alex said the only way he would consider that was if she agreed to enter the witness protection program.

She found the suggestion laughable. "Let me get this straight. The same government that's trying to convict my father of something he didn't do is going to protect me?"

"Actually," Alex said, "the state's prosecuting your father. The witness protection program would be the feds."

"A distinction without a difference."

At the end of the day, they agreed to disagree. They would have three weeks to figure it out.

◁ ▷

When Alex returned to the United States, Shannon picked him up at the airport. He hadn't been in the car two minutes before she started firing away with the questions.

Alex chose his words carefully. He felt sleazy about misleading Shannon, but he knew it had to be done. Shannon played everything by the book. If she found out about the train station incident, she would insist on going to the authorities. She would argue that, as Khalid's lawyers, they had a duty to put Nara on the stand and have Nara describe what happened.

The ride to the office from the airport usually took about twenty-five minutes. With Shannon asking one question after another, it seemed like an hour. Plus, she wasn't satisfied with generalities and made Alex describe his Beirut experience day by day. He made mental notes of the fibs he told so that he and Nara could be on the same page. He kept trying to change the subject.

Finally, on the third try, he was able to shift their conversation to the upcoming motion to suppress.

"Did you finish the research?" Alex asked.

"Yes. It doesn't look good."

"Impossible or highly unlikely?"

"Closer to impossible."

Alex forced a tired smile. "The difficult we do immediately; the impossible takes a little longer."

Shannon groaned. "Madison and Associates—we specialize in cheesy clichés."

◁ ▷

Judge Gerald Rosenthal was the newest of the nine Virginia Beach Circuit Court judges. His main qualification was that he had donated enormous amounts of campaign funds to both Republicans and Democrats at a time when the legislature was looking for a compromise candidate.

Judge Rosenthal was a thin wisp of a man with a strong type A personality, a rounded spine, and a pack-a-day cigarette habit. He'd quit smoking at least seven times but, at the age of sixty-two, figured he had already beat the odds.

Rosenthal started his career as a mass tort lawyer who sued most of the big companies in Hampton Roads. He made a killing from the asbestos litigation and somehow got the lion's share of Virginia's fen-phen cases as well. His advertisements were everywhere, and they were classier than most plaintiffs' lawyers' ads, at least in Rosenthal's opinion. He had a pretty narrow focus when it came to politics. Tort reform was bad. Accordingly, Democrats were good.

Once he made his millions, Rosenthal became less of a Democrat and started discovering his Republican tendencies, especially the ones that despised high taxes on the rich. To make up for lost time, he supported Republican candidates with a vengeance, and thus, when the legislature deadlocked on all the more qualified candidates, Rosenthal found himself appointed to the bench.

When Alex learned that the Honorable Gerald P. Rosenthal had been appointed to hear the motion to suppress, it was not welcome news. To broaden his appeal on the Republican side of the ledger, Rosenthal had catered to law-and-order groups, earning the endorsement of the Fraternal Order of Police. In addition, he hated young personal-injury attorneys like Alex, who were stealing clients from Rosenthal's old firm.

It didn't surprise Alex that the rookie judge had drawn the shortest straw and been assigned this complicated hearing. What worried Alex was that Rosenthal might get locked into the case and serve as the trial judge. It would be a little like showing up for a basketball game and learning that your opponent's grandfather had been chosen to ref.

"At least we'd get a lot of smoking breaks during the trial," Shannon said. "His hands start shaking after an hour."

70

ALEX STUDIED THE PATRIOT ACT and associated case law for a solid week after returning from Beirut. Shannon knew the issues better and probably should have argued the motion, but Alex felt like he had no choice. Nara had promised their captors in Beirut that Alex would launch a full-scale assault on the Patriot Act. It wouldn't do for him to sit back silently and let his law partner take the lead.

Of course, he used a different reason to convince Shannon. "You're going to be lead counsel on Ghaniyah's case," he told her. "And this will be a very unpopular motion. I don't want Ghaniyah's jury biased against you."

Shannon looked at him as if he had lost his mind. "What's the real reason?" she asked.

Alex made a face and resorted to his second tier of lies. "Because we're going to lose, and I'm a man. Khalid will accept it better if I'm the one who argues it."

That excuse was even more lame. They both knew that Khalid respected Shannon.

"Not to mention the fact that the hearing will draw nationwide media coverage," Shannon said.

Alex smiled sheepishly. If that's what she wanted to believe . . . fine.

"Busted," Alex said.

◁▷

A soggy nor'easter could not keep the crowd away from the motion to suppress hearing in *Commonwealth v. Mobassar*. The small courtroom was crammed with reporters, lawyers, and onlookers trying to drip-dry from their dash through the rain. The tight quarters and abundance of bodies generated a musty smell that reminded Alex more of a locker room than a court of law. The pool camera for the live video feed was set up in the jury box—a good vantage point to film both the lawyers and the judge.

Alex took off his trench coat and bunched it up next to the front rail. He took a seat beside Khalid at the counsel table.

"You doing okay?" Alex asked, trying to ignore the lens of the TV camera.

"I'm fine. You?"

"A little nervous," Alex admitted.

A few minutes after Rosenthal gaveled the proceedings to order, Alex's nervousness disappeared. He believed in both his client and his argument. So what if everybody in the courtroom wanted him to lose?

"This is not the first time the Patriot Act has been used to target a leading moderate Muslim," Alex argued. "Tariq Ramadan was named by *Time* magazine as one of the top one hundred innovators of the twenty-first century. Professor Ramadan taught at Notre Dame and used his position of prominence to denounce violence in the name of Islam. His visa was revoked under Section 411 of the Patriot Act."

"Is the government trying to revoke Mr. Mobassar's visa?" Judge Rosenthal asked.

"No. But my purpose in mentioning it—"

"I didn't think so," Rosenthal said, cutting Alex off. "So let's stick to the issues in *this* case."

"The government *is* trying to use wiretapping and electronic surveillance evidence against Mr. Mobassar," Alex countered. "And the way that evidence was gathered violates the Fourth Amendment to the U.S. Constitution."

Alex launched into a detailed explanation of the Foreign Intelligence Surveillance Act, something that Alex referred to as "FISA," an act that was later amended by the Patriot Act. FISA established a special court comprised of eleven district court judges with authority to grant or deny applications by the CIA and other federal agencies for electronic surveillance when "a significant purpose" of the request was to obtain foreign intelligence information. According to Alex, this violated the Fourth Amendment to the U.S. Constitution, which requires that the government establish "probable cause" that a crime had been committed before obtaining the authority for wiretaps or searches.

He quoted language from a Supreme Court case that dealt with a different set of circumstances but articulated a principle that applied here: "'We cannot forgive the requirements of the Fourth Amendment in the name of law enforcement. . . . It is not asking too much that officers be required to comply with the basic command of the Fourth Amendment before the innermost secrets of one's home or office are invaded. Few threats to liberty exist which are greater than that posed by eavesdropping devices.'"

Under normal circumstances, Alex explained, the government would have to provide a magistrate with facts supporting probable cause. But under FISA and the Patriot Act, there was no need to show a crime had been or was being committed, so long as the surveillance involved foreign intelligence.

More than fifty thousand surveillance authorizations a year were issued pursuant to the Patriot Act. The government eavesdropped on hundreds of thousands of conversations and intercepted millions of e-mails just to establish patterns of communication aimed at smoking out illegal international activity. The Act even authorized "sneak and peek" searches where agents could break into the homes of persons under surveillance and secretly search through their stuff without ever telling them.

"When the federal government first started the surveillance of Mr. Mobassar's phone calls and text messages, there had been no honor killings. Their only justification for doing so was the *suspicion* that the Islamic Learning Center was sending funds to organizations associated with Hezbollah to help in the rebuilding of Beirut following the 2006 war. The government does not even claim it had probable cause to believe a crime had been committed."

Alex paused for a moment and placed his legal pad on the table.

He looked Judge Rosenthal squarely in the eye. "I know a ruling in my favor won't win any popularity contests, Judge, but the Fourth Amendment has served this nation well for 220 years as the last line of defense against the type of mob mentality we see in this case. I'm asking Your Honor to declare the Patriot Act unconstitutional and to suppress the evidence gleaned from the text messages allegedly sent by my client."

"Thank you, Mr. Madison," Judge Rosenthal said. He made a few notes because that's what judges were supposed to do when they wanted to look fair. Alex knew he had done his best, but that feeling in the pit of his stomach was back. He was pretty certain that his best hadn't been good enough.

Rosenthal told Taj Deegan he was ready to hear from her.

"The Ninth Circuit Court of Appeals is probably the most liberal court in the nation," Taj began, "and even that court was not willing to do what Mr. Madison just requested. The Patriot Act has resulted in over four hundred convictions arising out of terrorism investigations since September 11, 2001.

"The government has always had the authority to gather foreign intelligence information without meeting the probable-cause requirements of the Fourth Amendment. Our Constitution is a wonderful thing. But it should not be used to strip the government of its ability to protect the United States from foreign enemies, including terrorists.

"Mr. Madison is correct in his assertion that the original basis for the wiretap on his client's phone was the mosque's suspected support of Hezbollah. I will not apologize for a government that conducts surveillance on those suspected of supporting terrorist organizations. Reduced to its simplest form, Mr. Madison's argument is this: You tapped my phone because you thought I was in league with terrorist organizations. As a result, you discovered that I ordered honor killings of Muslim women. Therefore, you should throw out the evidence."

When phrased that way, it sounded ludicrous even to Alex.

"In other words, suspected terrorists can get away with murder so long as their crimes are not technically terrorism," Taj Deegan continued. "I'm pretty sure that's not what our founding fathers had in mind when they passed the Bill of Rights."

The prosecutor reminded Rosenthal about the war on terror and the numerous court decisions upholding various provisions of the Patriot Act. She must have said the word *terrorism* fifteen times, *justice* ten times, and the phrase *law and order* at least five. After she finished by asking Judge Rosenthal to uphold every single provision of the Patriot Act, Alex half expected "Yankee Doodle" to start playing.

Instead, the judge announced a ten-minute break.

◁▷

Ten minutes turned into twenty, and Alex figured the judge must have had time to burn through at least three cigarettes. During the wait, Khalid told Alex that his argument was "compelling."

Nara pulled Alex to the side. "We're going to lose, aren't we?"

"Probably."

Alex was right. Judge Rosenthal returned to the bench, posed for the media camera, and promptly denied the motion to suppress. He reminded everyone that the country was still at war with terrorists. He held that the Patriot Act contained adequate safeguards to ensure that the CIA and Justice Department did not go overboard in their surveillance and searches. He even added a bonus that Taj Deegan had not requested—saying that the honor killings in this case might themselves be acts of terror. He didn't just rule against Alex's motion; he annihilated it.

The day could have been a complete loss. But Alex had one more trick up his sleeve.

"Is there any other business for the court?" Rosenthal asked. It was meant to be a rhetorical question; his gavel was already raised, ready to come down and signal an end to the proceedings.

Alex jumped to his feet. "Actually, there is one thing."

Judge Rosenthal sighed and laid his gavel down.

"Since the court has just held that wiretaps under the Patriot Act can be used against my client, I am requesting a subpoena to the Department of Justice to reveal any phone conversations, text messages, or e-mails they might have obtained under that same act for Fatih Mahdi's phone and computer."

From the look on the judge's face, Alex's maneuver had caught him totally off guard. *Take that!*

"If surveillance under the Patriot Act can be used to convict a defendant," Alex continued, "then certainly that same defendant is entitled to surveillance under the act if it might prove his innocence."

Taj Deegan sprang up. "We don't even know if there is any such surveillance."

"Let the Department of Justice tell us that," Alex responded. "All I'm asking for right now is a subpoena that would allow me access to such surveillance if it does exist."

"That might compromise national security," Deegan countered. "That's the whole purpose of the act."

"Then I'll agree to a confidentiality order so that only my client and I can look at the information," Alex suggested. "I'll clear it with the court before I use any of the information at trial."

The lawyers both paused, and all eyes turned toward Rosenthal. Stymied, he did what judges do when they have no idea how to rule. "That's an interesting issue, Counsel. I'll need both sides to submit any authorities they want me to consider within seven days. I know the trial is scheduled to start on the third of December. I don't intend to postpone the case based on this last-minute request. But I'll need some time to research this point."

This time, Rosenthal didn't ask if the lawyers had any other business. He banged his gavel and called it a day.

71

WITH KHALID'S TRIAL only eight days away, Thanksgiving was just another working day at Madison and Associates. The only member of the firm who didn't come to the office on Thanksgiving was Ramona Madison. She had been serving the homeless Thanksgiving dinner for twenty-five straight years, and she wasn't about to skip a year now. Alex gave her the full day off but made her promise to cook dinner for everyone else.

By six o'clock, the firm was sitting down at Ramona's dining room table, ready to dig into the feast. Shannon generally spent Thanksgiving with her folks in Alabama, but this year she couldn't get away. The fourth member of the group, Nara Mobassar, had never shared a Thanksgiving meal with anyone. Alex had also invited Khalid, but Ghaniyah had been reluctant to participate, so Khalid decided to stay home with his wife.

Ramona had put her best china on the table and made Alex mute the football game while they sat down to eat.

"Do you mind if we hold hands and say a brief prayer?" Ramona asked Nara. "We won't be at all offended if you choose not to join us."

"That's fine," Nara said. "Actually, I'd like to join you." She held out her hands, and the others took the cue.

"Alex?" Ramona said, once they were all holding hands. "You're the minister here."

"*Former* minister," Alex reminded her.

He kept the prayer short, focusing on the things for which they were thankful. At the end, he couldn't resist a quick petition for success

258 || FATAL CONVICTIONS

on Khalid's case. After his amen, the others echoed the word, and the feast began.

"How did you have time to cook all this stuff and work at the feeding kitchen too?" Shannon asked as she passed around the main courses.

Ramona gave Shannon a sly smile. "I donate five hundred a year to their Thanksgiving feedings. That should entitle me to a few leftovers."

Alex's head jerked up from slapping the mashed potatoes on his plate. "You took food from the homeless?"

"They had plenty," his grandmother said, somewhat defensively. "And if I do say so, I think they got the better end of the deal."

Undeterred by the source of the bounty, the Khalid Mobassar legal team dug in with great enthusiasm while Alex periodically ribbed his grandmother about her wonderful cooking. Ramona had established one firm rule for Thanksgiving dinner—no talking about the case. Alex could tell that it was killing Shannon.

Just before dessert, with Ramona clearing the dishes, Nara provided Shannon with an opening.

"When is my mother's case going to trial?" Nara asked.

"January tenth," Shannon said. "But your mom will be deposed a week from Saturday. I've been pushing for depositions of the defendants, and the judge ruled last week that the defense lawyers get to depose Ghaniyah first."

"I still can't believe Judge Lewis did that," Alex said. "I think he got intimidated by Strobel."

They had had this same conversation around the office several times. Mack Strobel and Kayden Dendy were anxious to depose Ghaniyah. Shannon had resisted, knowing that her client wasn't yet ready. Recently, Strobel had gone to court to complain, and Judge Lewis had ordered Shannon to make Ghaniyah available for deposition. Shannon refused to miss a day of Khalid's trial, so a compromise was struck. Ghaniyah's deposition would take place on a Saturday.

"She'll make a terrible witness," Nara said.

The comment seemed a little out of line, and for a few seconds, nobody responded. "Actually, the problem we have is that your mom might make too *good* a witness," Shannon responded. "Her recovery is coming along great, which is a good thing. But if she does too well in her deposition, the jury might not believe she's suffering from a serious brain injury."

72

THEY FINISHED EATING BY SEVEN, and Alex was pretty sure that Shannon would head back to the office. Because Nara had ridden to Ramona's house with Shannon, Alex offered to give her a ride home. Shannon raised her eyebrows but apparently wasn't willing to make a scene.

Ramona had no such reservations. "Try to avoid making out in public," she said.

"You're fired," Alex replied.

On the way to the Mobassars' place, Alex had a brilliant idea. "Do you have a few minutes to go to the Virginia Beach boardwalk with me?" he asked Nara.

Nara gave him a puzzled look. "Why?"

"This time of year, they line the boardwalk with Christmas lights. You drive your car down the middle of the boardwalk and see all kinds of cool stuff." In truth, the Christmas lights were not that spectacular, but Alex was looking forward to time alone with Nara.

"Sounds great," she said. And just like that, Alex felt as light-headed as a middle schooler on his first date.

The night was clear and cold, with a stiff breeze blowing in from the ocean. Alex paid the ten dollars at the end of the boardwalk and turned off his headlights. There was a little hot chocolate stand just before the vehicles pulled onto the boardwalk, and Alex bought a cup to share with Nara.

Because it was Thanksgiving night, there was a steady stream of traffic. The cars were moving at a snail's pace, but Alex was in no hurry. Five miles per hour felt just about right.

He put in the CD that came with the experience—the sounds of the season. Hotels rose skyward on their left, and the sands of the beach spread out to the right. The sponsors of the event had done a clever job of constructing innovative light displays on each side. Santa Claus was surfing. Moving lights made it seem like sharks jumped in and out of the sand. There was a monster truck decorated in lights and fish jumping over the boardwalk in a lighted arch.

Alex occasionally glanced at his passenger. The light from the moon and stars reflected off the ocean and glimmered in her hair. Her features were silhouetted against the beach, and she looked more beautiful than ever.

He was thinking romance, but Nara apparently had other things on her mind.

"Have you researched the issue of whether our encounter with Hezbollah would be admissible?" Nara asked. The question came out of the blue while they were in the middle of a long display depicting the Twelve Days of Christmas.

Alex forced his thoughts back to the mundane matters of the law. "Technically, the statements of our captors are hearsay," Alex said. He could have left it at that, but he didn't want to lie to her.

"However, there are some exceptions that might apply. As I mentioned in Lebanon, statements against interest are admissible if there is corroborating evidence. We could argue that the statements our captors made to you were statements against their interest. I mean, they pretty much admitted Hezbollah's involvement."

Alex felt like he had just converted a romantic ride down the boardwalk into a law school lecture. Talk about breaking the mood.

"What kind of corroborating evidence do we need?" Nara asked.

"Anything, really. We took some pictures of the cut on your neck—that might work. It'd be even better if we could get some geek to hack into the hidden Internet site where they posted that video of me indicting your dad.

"We can always figure out the corroborating evidence, Nara, but that's not the point. I'm not willing to put you on the stand unless you agree to go into the witness protection program."

It wasn't the first time Nara had heard this. But tonight, she didn't reject it out of hand. Instead, she stared out the side window for a few minutes. Alex drove on in silence—the lights had lost their allure.

"The problem is that I don't trust your government to protect me," she said softly. Alex turned the music down a little. "This is the same government that is prosecuting my father for murder. The same government that has taped every one of his phone calls and monitored every one of his e-mails. Your government has declared war on those of us who hold my religious beliefs, and now you are asking me to trust them."

"It's a different part of the government," Alex responded. "We're talking about the U.S. Marshals, not the CIA. And they know how to keep their witnesses safe."

"How would you know that? Do you think they actually tell you when they let a witness get killed?"

"Which proves my point," Alex said. He kept his tone as understanding as possible, but he wanted to let Nara know he was firm on this. "I can't put you on the stand if you don't agree to this. No matter what happens after the trial, you would be in too much danger."

"My father is your client," Nara reminded him. "Your only duty is to decide whether I help or hurt his case. Am I not right about that?"

Alex kept his eyes straight ahead. This woman knew all the right buttons to push. And she happened to be right—defending Khalid was *supposed* to be the only issue. But it wasn't.

"I don't want to lose you," Alex said.

His admission surprised him as much as it seemed to surprise Nara. She turned from the window and looked at him. "That's very sweet," she said.

She leaned over and, before he knew what had happened, gave him a kiss on the check.

His mind immediately raced to the pictures of him and Nara embracing after their paddleboarding adventure. He checked his rearview mirror and glanced at both sides of the boardwalk. It was dark, and there was no one around.

Nara smiled. "We're safe," she said. "I checked."

She was right. The only things in the sand on the right were five golden rings. The car behind them had its headlights off. There was not a soul on the left between them and the hotels.

Keeping his left hand on the wheel, Alex reached over with his right, gently cradling the back of her head. He leaned toward her, and this time he was the one who initiated the kiss, something he'd wanted to do for a very long time. The alarm bells sounded—she was a client's daughter; she worshiped a different god; he shouldn't get emotionally involved in the middle of a case.

But he turned off the alarms and enjoyed the moment, tasting the hot chocolate on her breath, losing himself in her kiss. When she finally pulled back, she took a deep breath, smiled, and looked at him with a mixture of surprise and affection.

Alex realized that he had just crossed every acceptable social and professional boundary—not to mention biblical. He started to say something—maybe an apology—but Nara put a finger on his lips. "Let's just enjoy this moment," she said. "We can analyze it later."

She was right again. He reached over and placed his right hand on top of hers, and they intertwined their fingers. They rode in silence for a few minutes, and for the first time in weeks, Alex forgot about the case. He focused instead on the electricity that seemed to flow from her hand to his. He smiled to himself at the absurdity of it all.

Bing Crosby was playing on the CD, dreaming of a white Christmas amid the shimmering sand of Virginia Beach. They were passing two turtledoves on the left, approaching a partridge in a pear tree on the right, and Alex was falling in love with a woman from the other side of the world whose culture was practically at war with his own.

And in one week, he would be defending her father in the biggest murder case Virginia Beach had ever seen.

◁▷

Hassan Ibn Talib could not have been more disgusted. He drove slowly through the holiday lights display on the boardwalk, two cars behind Alexander Madison's truck. It didn't surprise him that Nara Mobassar was spending time alone with her father's American lawyer. Her liberal views had never represented the true Muslim faith. It seemed to Hassan that she was close to taking the final step and rejecting the faith altogether.

She certainly knew better. There would be a special place in hell for those like Nara who led so many people away from Allah. Hassan had already beheaded women who had done far less damage.

As far as Hassan was concerned, Nara Mobassar was a Muslim in name only. Sure, she claimed to be a follower of Mohammed. She prayed five times a day, and she said all the right things. But it was only a facade—all designed to hide the heart of an infidel.

She had fooled many people. Hassan was not one of them. He knew better. Often, the most dangerous deception was the one that looked the most like the truth.

73

THE DAYS BETWEEN THANKSGIVING and the start of Khalid's trial passed in a giant blur of paperwork and trial prep. Alex arrived at the office every day by 8 a.m. and was typically the last person there, frequently leaving after midnight. He had witness notebooks to prepare, subpoenas to issue, exhibits to review, and an opening statement to write. Meanwhile, Shannon took the lead on pretrial motions, jury instructions, and collecting information on the prospective jurors.

Alex spent three entire afternoons preparing Khalid for his turn on the stand. During one of those afternoons, Shannon conducted a mock cross-examination, and they videotaped Khalid's answers.

Complicating matters was the fact that Alex was not as focused as he needed to be. Though he and Nara both tried to act as if the Thanksgiving night kiss had never occurred, he couldn't get her out of his thoughts. The others on the trial team could apparently sense that things had changed dramatically between Alex and Nara. For one thing, they were no longer constantly at each other's throat about trial strategies. In fact, Nara was so supportive of Alex that it became a little awkward for everyone else. All of this only made Shannon more businesslike; Alex thought he detected a slight tinge of jealousy in the air.

Late one afternoon, Alex's grandmother mentioned something about it. "It's really none of my business what goes on between you and Nara," Ramona said, "except I do know that your grandfather had some pretty strict rules about fraternization with clients."

"I'm not fraternizing with her," Alex said. *And it is none of your business,* he felt like adding.

Ramona took a quick glance around. Alex could sense that she had been debating whether to say anything at all. "I just don't want to see you mess up things with Shannon," she said. "I always thought you two would make a great pair."

The comment caught Alex a little off guard. He and Shannon had developed an amazing friendship. But even before Nara had arrived on the scene, he had decided not to ruin a special friendship by making another attempt to date her. "Shannon and I are really good friends, Grandma. And we work great together. But we've kind of got an unspoken pact that we won't jeopardize that by trying to turn it into something more."

"I see," Ramona said. "And like I said, it's really none of my business. I'm just not so sure that Shannon remembers signing that pact."

◁▷

Three days before trial, Judge Rosenthal surprised Alex by ordering the federal government to immediately turn over Fatih Mahdi's telephone calls, text messages, and e-mails. Boxes of CDs and documents arrived the next day. Ramona and Nara immediately began the mind-numbing task of listening to every telephone conversation and reviewing every e-mail and text message Fatih had sent or received.

As the trial grew closer, Alex vacillated about whether to put Nara on the stand. The torment of that decision was exacerbated by the fact that he couldn't discuss it with anyone except her. On the eve of trial, they agreed to play it by ear. Nara would take the stand only if it looked like they might otherwise lose the case.

74

LIKE HER COUNTERPARTS on the defense side, Taj Deegan had been working late every night. She hated not seeing the kids, but it was part of the price she paid. And so, on the night before trial, when the babysitter's number showed up on Taj's phone screen at work, it was a welcome break. It would give her a chance to tell the kids how much she loved them before they settled in for the night.

But when she answered and heard the panic in her babysitter's voice, Taj Deegan's blood ran cold. For an instant, it felt like her heart had literally stopped.

"You need to come home right away." The woman was breathless. She refused to tell Taj what was wrong. "You just need to see this. The kids are both okay."

The fifteen minutes it took Taj to get home seemed like five hours. When she arrived, her daughter was crying. Her son, only in the fourth grade, tried to keep a stiff upper lip. The babysitter pulled Taj aside and showed her the note.

> If Khalid Mobassar is convicted, there will be at least
> one more beheading.

"I found this on your daughter's pillow," the sitter told Taj.

Taj felt the rage boiling within her as she struggled to maintain her composure. The sitter had handled the note and had probably destroyed any fingerprint evidence. "Pack an overnight bag for the kids," Taj said. "I want you to take them to my mom's. I'll have several police cruisers sitting outside her house tonight. I'll be there myself by midnight."

Taj immediately dialed Chief Stargell and told him about the threat. She made it clear that she wanted to personally work with the CSI team.

Once the call was completed, Taj slipped into mom mode. She pulled the kids together on the living room couch and tried to reassure them. She put her arms around both of them and held them close.

"I'm scared," her daughter said. Tears rolled down her cheeks.

"There's nothing to be scared about," Taj said. And she meant it. "Mommy's going to make sure this guy spends the rest of his life in jail."

75

ALEX WOKE UP ON FRIDAY, December 3, feeling like he hadn't really slept. When he left the office after midnight, his grandmother and Nara were still poring over Fatih Mahdi's records. His grandmother's endurance had been amazing to watch. Alex hoped he had half her energy when he was her age. But he knew he needed some sleep or he would be irritable and slow-witted the first day of trial.

Alex shaved and put on his one suit, gulping down two cups of coffee along the way. He already had the jitters. He was chilled, his stomach was upset, and he couldn't sit still to think things through. It was a good thing Shannon would be in charge of picking the jury for the next few days. It would take Alex that long just to calm down.

◁ ▷

Lawyers know to expect the unexpected on the first day of trial, so Alex tried not to be thrown when the sheriff's deputy requested that he, Shannon, and Khalid Mobassar meet with Judge Rosenthal in his chambers.

"What's this about?" Khalid asked.

"I don't have the foggiest idea," Alex admitted.

They followed the deputy through the door behind the judge's bench. Another deputy fell in behind as they walked down the hallway and turned into Rosenthal's chambers. The judge was sitting at his desk smoking a cigarette, the air stale and thick with smoke. He welcomed them and, in a solemn tone, asked all three to take a seat. Taj Deegan and Detective Derrick Sanderson were already in the chambers, and Alex knew that something big was about to happen.

"Where's the court reporter?" Judge Rosenthal asked. He took another drag on the cigarette and tapped off some ashes.

"She's on the way," the deputy replied. The man had stationed himself right next to Khalid.

Judge Rosenthal turned his attention to some papers on his desk.

"What's this about?" Alex asked.

Rosenthal looked up. "I'll let you know as soon as the court reporter gets here."

They waited for several minutes in absolute silence. Alex glanced at Shannon, who shrugged. Alex knew her stomach was probably doing somersaults just like his.

After a few minutes, the court reporter arrived and set up her stenographic machine. Rosenthal stated the case name for the record, noted the persons present, and turned the floor over to Taj Deegan.

"Last night, I received a call from my babysitter, who had found a note on my daughter's pillow." Taj stared at Khalid for a second. "Detective Sanderson is here to testify about the subsequent investigation. I actually have the note in a plastic bag and would like to have it marked as Exhibit A for this hearing."

"What hearing?" Alex asked. "I wasn't put on notice about any hearing."

"Let her finish," snapped Rosenthal. The venom in his voice surprised Alex.

"I'd also like to read the note into evidence," Taj continued. She seemed unnaturally composed, her voice cold and hard. "It says, 'If Khalid Mobassar is convicted, there will be at least one more beheading.'"

The words sucked the wind out of Alex. Shannon went pale. Khalid remained stoic, as if he hadn't even heard what the prosecutor said.

"Detective Sanderson can fill you in on the details of his investigation," Deegan continued. "At this point, the police have no hard leads other than the obvious connection to the defendant. My kids are under 24-7 surveillance, and they are understandably scared to death."

Deegan paused for a moment, holding her anger in check. "It's obvious that the defendant or someone associated with him is trying to disrupt this trial by intimidating me and my family. Who knows? He may have already made similar threats against potential jurors or witnesses. Accordingly, I'm asking that the court revoke his bond and sequester the jury."

"*What?*" The word was out before Alex even knew he had said it. He turned to Taj Deegan. "What evidence do you have that *my client* was behind this?"

"Who else do you think did this?" she shot back. "Open your eyes, Alex. You think somebody did this for a prank? Maybe I just got 'punked' by someone in my office?"

Rosenthal put his cigarette in an ashtray and held up his hand. "That's enough. I don't need you two at each other's throat before we even pick the jury." The judge sighed and snuffed out his cigarette. "Let's stick to the issue at hand. Mr. Madison, what's your response to the commonwealth's motion to revoke bail and sequester the jury?"

"It's ridiculous," Alex said. "Mr. Mobassar was sitting at home last night with his disabled wife, wearing a court-ordered electronic ankle bracelet. Why would he do something like this? *How* could he? Next thing you know, Ms. Deegan's going to march into court with a confession pasted together from cutout magazine letters and claim that she should be able to introduce it into evidence."

"I don't need your sarcasm," Taj said. Her voice was as biting as Alex had ever heard it. She turned, eyes flaring, neck muscles taut. "Nobody messes with my kids. If you're right and this is just a setup, you ought to join me in asking for Mr. Mobassar's confinement so that nothing else gets blamed on him."

The judge held up his hand a second time. "Okay," he said, drawing the word out as he thought. "I've heard enough. Here's what we're going to do: As far as I'm aware, there is no specific evidence linking this note to Mr. Mobassar." Rosenthal looked at Detective Sanderson. "Is that right?"

"Other than the reference to the case," Detective Sanderson said.

"Yes, I get that," Rosenthal said. "And even without the existence of a direct link, the court has wide latitude when it comes to the issue of bail. I tend to agree with Ms. Deegan that it is far better to err on the side of safety in these matters. I cannot let this case get derailed by intimidations and threats."

The judge turned squarely toward Khalid. "If you're behind any of this, sir, you need to know that neither the prosecutor nor this court will be intimidated." The judge paused for a moment before continuing. "And if you're not behind this, then revoking your bail will protect you from blame for things you didn't do.

"Accordingly, I'm going to grant the commonwealth's motion to revoke Mr. Mobassar's bail during the pendency of the trial and restrict his communications to only his attorneys and family—"

"She didn't even ask for that," Alex interrupted.

The judge gave him a nasty look. "She doesn't have to ask for it. I have the absolute power to impose my own terms, and that's what I've just done."

"We understand, Your Honor," Shannon said. She apparently realized that Alex was too emotional right now to respond and would only dig himself a deeper hole if she let him. "Please note our objection."

"So noted," Rosenthal said. His tone had become more reasonable. "Given this occurrence, I also feel that the court has no choice but to sequester the jury."

"We object to that as well, but we understand the court's concern," Shannon said quickly.

Rosenthal nodded at her. "I thought it best to conduct this hearing in my chambers so that the media didn't catch wind of what happened and publish a story during the jury selection process. We're going to have enough trouble picking an unbiased jury as it is. If either side objects, I'll be happy to go into open court and state the reasons for my rulings on the record." Rosenthal looked from Taj to Alex and back.

"We don't want to make this any more complicated than it already is," Taj said.

"Fine by us," Alex said, though his tone said, *What's the use?*

Rosenthal thought about this for a moment. "I'll have to say *something* in open court. The issue of sequestering the jury is an easy one. It's often done in cases like this to protect the jury from the press. But I won't tell them they're going to be sequestered until the end of the day so that we don't have more than the usual number trying to get off the panel.

"But with regard to the revocation of bond, my intent is to simply say that some matters have come to the court's attention that would justify revocation of bond pending trial. I'll probably get an FOIA request about this hearing from the press by the end of the day, but I'll take that up if and when it's filed."

◁ ▷

When Rosenthal convened court that morning, he matter-of-factly announced that some things had been brought to his attention that made it prudent for him to revoke Mr. Mobassar's bail. He then had the deputy sheriff bring in the prospective jury members and launched into an explanation of the jury selection process. For the rest of the morning, Judge Rosenthal and the lawyers went about the business of trying to find unbiased jurors to hear the case.

The media lawyers wasted no time. By lunch, they had filed their motions to obtain a transcript of the hearing held in Rosenthal's chambers. The judge said they could argue the motion on Monday morning, and he would rule shortly thereafter.

The rest of the day on Friday was taken up with the tedious process of questioning individual jurors about their perspectives and biases. Every one of them had heard about the beheadings. Most promised they could be unbiased despite what they had seen or read.

But several of the jurors—especially those who were self-employed, Alex noted—were more blunt about their ability to be unbiased. "It'd be hard," one juror admitted. "My understanding is that they have a text message from his phone." Another took a swipe at Alex and his motion to suppress. "Actually, Judge, in my gut I'd have a hard time listening to somebody who's already challenged the Patriot Act in order to find a loophole for his client."

In order to keep any one juror's opinions from poisoning everyone else, much of the questioning was done with individual jurors while the others waited in the deliberation room. Shannon had a clever way of talking to the jurors so that they would lower their guards and let some of their prejudices slip out. She and Deegan would then argue at length about whether this juror should stay or that juror should go. By the end of the day, the parties had sifted through only eighteen prospective jurors and had dismissed fifteen of them for cause. Not one of the three remaining jurors was a member of the Muslim faith.

"At this rate, I won't be giving my opening statement until Tuesday," Alex whispered to Shannon.

"You want an unbiased jury or a lynch mob?" Shannon whispered back.

"So far, it's hard to tell the difference."

76

ALEX PRACTICALLY LIVED at the office from the time court adjourned on Friday until court reconvened Monday morning. But no matter how early he arrived or how late he left, Shannon was there before him and stayed later.

The rest of the world was getting into the holiday spirit, but for Madison and Associates, there was not a Christmas card or decoration anywhere in the office. There was certainly no tree. Those types of things all took time—the one thing that Khalid Mobassar's legal team did not have.

By Monday morning, there were documents scattered throughout every square inch of the office. They still needed about ten more days to prepare for the case—and ten more lawyers. And when Alex dragged his weary body out of bed Monday morning, he couldn't remember the last time he had managed more than five hours of sleep.

Judge Rosenthal used the morning session to resolve the issue of whether to release the transcript from the hearing in his chambers. Media lawyers filed thick briefs and argued at great length. Alex and Taj Deegan both said that there was no reason to release the transcript while they were picking the jury. Judge Rosenthal ultimately decided to take the matter under advisement until the next day.

Alex smiled to himself. The judge would release the transcript, but he would wait until after the jury had been safely selected and sequestered.

By Tuesday afternoon, a jury of twelve members and two alternates was in the box, and Judge Rosenthal promptly released the transcript.

Alex made his team, especially Nara, promise not to read or watch any media coverage. Things were about to get even more nasty, and they didn't need the distraction.

The jurors were predominately white, and eight of the twelve main jurors were women. There was not a Muslim or a person of Middle Eastern descent in sight.

"You call this a jury of his peers?" Alex whispered to Shannon.

"Next time, you pick the jury," Shannon replied.

◁ ▷

At 10 p.m. on Tuesday, Alex gathered his team in the conference room and cleared off the table. He stood at one end while Shannon, Nara, and Ramona got comfortable in the chairs scattered around the room.

"Ladies and gentleman of the jury, it is my honor to represent Khalid Mobassar. . . ."

It took Alex twenty-five minutes to get through the first dry run of his opening statement. When he finished, the others took turns critiquing his performance. Nara loved it, and Alex could tell that Shannon wanted to roll her eyes. Ramona thought Alex should punch it up a little and give it the kind of drama he brought to his sermons. Shannon said Alex sounded too argumentative. "I don't want the judge sustaining an objection against us right at the start of the case. I'd rather see you in storytelling mode as opposed to presenting an argument."

Alex gave the opening a second time, and more critiques followed, sometimes contradicting the first set of critiques. Even Nara pitched in with some suggestions for improvement. Alex tried to keep all the feedback straight for round three.

By the time the clock struck midnight during his third practice session, Alex could feel himself wearing down. His critics, it seemed, were just getting warmed up. Ramona finally broke in and declared that her grandson needed to get some sleep or he might doze off during his own opening. The others agreed, and court was adjourned at 1:10 a.m.

On his way out of the office, Alex glanced at the list on the wall and allowed himself a moment to miss his grandfather. This was the kind of case that John Patrick Madison would have loved. Being the underdog. The world hoping you would lose. A client's future in his hands. Alex wondered how his grandfather would have approached the opening.

Alex read through the list, though he knew it by heart.

> Never sue a client over a fee.
> Even drunk drivers deserve a lawyer; they just don't deserve us.

Sentence number six, Alex knew, was the result of the tragic accident, caused by a drunk driver, that had killed Alex's parents. John Patrick Madison had been a firm believer that everybody was entitled to a lawyer, but as he often said, "that doesn't mean they're entitled to *us*." His grandfather took cases he could believe in. Cases like this one.

And then there was sentence number eight, the one that seemed particularly appropriate tonight:

> For every case, pray like a saint, and then go fight like the devil.

Alex had certainly been saying his prayers. Tomorrow the battle would begin in earnest.

77

ALEX WORE A WHITE SHIRT and yellow tie with his suit for his opening statement. The textbooks said not to alienate the jury by the way you dress.

Taj Deegan apparently didn't read the same textbooks. The prosecutor displayed a classy nonconformist streak—pressed gray dress slacks with a wide leg, a hunter green suit jacket, gold chandelier earrings, and layered gold chains. Alex admired the attitude. If the jury didn't like it—tough. Taj did, and that was all that mattered.

When she stood to give her opening, she took a sip of water and walked without notes to the jury box. All eyes were on her, and the prosecutor seemed to like it that way.

"Every year, dozens of fires are set by volunteer firefighters. John Orr, for example, headed a large California arson squad and had a reputation for uncanny instincts about how fires started. It turned out that it wasn't instinct at all. It was inside knowledge. Orr set the fires himself."

Alex had been so surprised by Taj Deegan's opening remarks that he didn't object until Shannon leaned across Khalid and prompted him.

"I object, Your Honor. If I'm not mistaken, John Orr is not even on trial here."

Judge Rosenthal looked as confused as Alex. "Sustained," he said. "Let's stick to the facts of *this* case."

Taj Deegan looked at him and smiled. "Sorry, Your Honor. I just thought it might help to provide the jury with a little context."

She turned back to the jury, and they were even more attentive than before. "Why would a firefighter start a fire?" she asked. And then quickly added, "And what's that got to do with *this* case?"

Alex half-rose to object, but Taj veered in a new direction before he got the words out.

"The defendant, Khalid Mobassar, ordered the beheading of Ja'dah Fatima Mahdi and the execution of her friend Martin Burns," Taj said. She had that authoritative prosecutor's voice going now, deep for a woman, a voice that said, *Trust me*. "The commonwealth will present overwhelming evidence linking the defendant to these gruesome murders. We will show you text messages from the defendant ordering the killings, text messages from the killer's phone to the defendant confirming the killings, money diverted from the defendant's mosque to pay for the killings, and an Internet search from the defendant's computer to find the place for the killings. It's like he gave us a digital blueprint... digital DNA, if you will. All that evidence points to only one person."

Taj Deegan paused for a moment so that the jury could take all of this in. She half-turned and looked at Khalid. Alex had coached his client to meet her stare and not blink.

"That evidence alone would be enough to convict Mr. Mobassar beyond a reasonable doubt," she said, turning back to the jury. "I will go into that evidence in great detail in a few minutes. But that evidence doesn't answer the question of *why* he did this. And though the commonwealth doesn't need to answer the *why* question in order for you to convict the defendant of conspiracy to commit murder, it sure helps when you're trying to fit all the pieces together.

"I like to use the analogy of a puzzle." Taj walked in front of the jury box now, a little chat with her friends who had promised to do justice in this case. "The various pieces of evidence are like the pieces of the puzzle. And when you fit them together, they'll form a picture of the defendant. But if we understand motive, it's like looking at the picture on the puzzle box. It helps us understand where the pieces go and how they relate. So let me talk to you first about that puzzle box. *Why* would somebody order such gruesome crimes?"

Taj had everyone's attention, including Alex's, though he tried hard to look disinterested. He scribbled a few notes, the picture of calm. Inside, his stomach was in knots.

"The defendant is an imam at the Islamic Learning Center in

Norfolk, Virginia. He is an outspoken critic of fundamentalist Muslims. In fact, he has a very important book that he was about to publish when these honor killings occurred. That book represents the culmination of his entire life's work. It is his attempt to reform the Muslim faith, a religion that claims 1.5 billion adherents.

"When I sit down, I suspect that Mr. Madison is going to stand up and tell you that his client could not possibly have ordered these murders. That you should ignore the evidence against him because the defendant is not the type of religious leader who would ever order the gruesome act of beheading someone just because they converted to Christianity."

Taj twisted her face as if she was deep in thought. "And on the surface, that makes a certain amount of sense. Mr. Mobassar *is* a reformer. He detests violence in the name of Islam. But think about it for a moment on a deeper level. In fact, let me show you something."

Taj walked back to her counsel table and picked up a few books that Alex recognized.

"When we executed a search warrant at Mr. Mobassar's house, we found some fascinating books in his library. There were books on the lives of reformers like Dr. Martin Luther King Jr. and Gandhi and Nelson Mandela. The defendant had marked these books and dog-eared the pages. He apparently saw himself as someone who stood in their tradition—a reformer of the highest order."

Taj took one of the books to the jury box, showing the jury some highlighted portions. "We'll introduce these into evidence, and you can look for yourselves. You'll want to take special note of the sections Mr. Mobassar highlighted. He was apparently fascinated with the fact that these men were persecuted and imprisoned for their efforts. And when that happened, it jump-started their movements, giving them a louder megaphone so their ideas could spread faster. In other words, a little controversy can catapult a reformer onto the front pages of the papers and the feature slots on the television news shows. Just like it takes a fire for a firefighter to become a hero."

Again, Alex wanted to object. But if he did so now, it would only highlight her point.

"Unfortunately for Mr. Mobassar, there were a few things he didn't know. He didn't know that his phone was being tapped under the Patriot Act. He didn't know that the Internet searches he conducted on his computer were under surveillance as well. He didn't know that his past association with terrorists allowed the government to scrutinize his every move."

As Deegan continued, Alex lost focus on what she was saying. Instead, he was frantically trying to process the implications of her masterful opening statement.

In five short minutes, she had just gutted the entire theme of his case. In his opening, Alex was going to emphasize that Khalid was a true reformer. But somehow, Taj Deegan had now twisted the logic so that Khalid's penchant for reform had become his worst enemy. The more Alex emphasized Khalid's desire to reform the Muslim faith, the more he was playing into Deegan's hands.

"The defendant knew that Ja'dah Fatima Mahdi's husband had strong fundamentalist views about the roles of women in the Islamic faith," Deegan continued. "They were views that the defendant detested. And he knew that Fatih Mahdi would be an easy target to blame."

Taj paused, looked down, and gathered her thoughts. She delivered her conclusion full force, looking the jury straight in the eye, summoning a silent pact that she would do her part for justice if they did theirs.

"Firefighters don't start fires; they put them out. And reformers don't commit honor killings; they rail against them.

"So why would the defendant order the honor killing of someone in his own mosque, especially when that someone was the wife of a friend? Because every reform movement needs a hero. And every hero needs a controversy. And sometimes, it's necessary to sacrifice the lives of a few in order to change the course of history."

She let the statement hang out there for a moment and then returned to her seat, heels clicking against the hardwood floor.

Judge Rosenthal turned to Alex. "Does the defense wish to present an opening statement?"

78

ALEX FELT SLIGHTLY DISORIENTED. It wasn't like this was his first trial, but it was certainly the first time he had been so terribly wrong about the other side's theory of the case. Taj Deegan had turned the trial on its head. The opening statement that Alex had carefully scripted, almost memorized, no longer made sense.

He had expected Deegan to hammer Khalid's alleged ties with Hezbollah. He had thought Deegan would try to paint Khalid as a closet radical. Alex's opening would emphasize that Khalid was a true reformer. But now, Taj had preempted Alex's theme. He felt like he had been sharpening his sword for days just so he could hand it to Taj Deegan to use against him—to carve him up.

"Does defense counsel wish to give an opening statement?" Rosenthal asked for the second time.

"Could we take a brief recess, Your Honor?"

Deegan's opening had been surprisingly short for a murder case, and any other judge would have scoffed at Alex's request. But this was Judge Rosenthal, and Alex could tell by the look on his face that he was craving his sixth cigarette of the day.

"Ten minutes," Rosenthal said, cracking his gavel.

As soon as he left, Alex turned to Shannon. "What do I do now?"

"Stick with the plan," Shannon said. "We can't throw our entire opening out the window just because the prosecutor changed her theory of the case."

"Then help me revise it."

For the next ten minutes, they worked furiously on the revisions. Alex scratched through text and made handwritten notes in the margins. He tore a page from a legal pad and inserted a whole section. But as the recess ended, he was more confused than he had been before. Now they were talking out of both sides of their mouths—Khalid Mobassar was a committed reformer but not so passionate that he would set up something like this. Yes, he had spent years writing his book, but no, he certainly wouldn't order honor killings just to gain nationwide attention.

As the jury shuffled in and Rosenthal called the court to order, Alex still felt unsettled. He thought back to his days as a pastor. Whenever he gave sermons with this level of ambivalence, they always bombed. How could a jury believe what Alex was saying when he couldn't figure it out himself?

"Mr. Madison . . . ," Judge Rosenthal prompted.

Alex stood. "We would like to reserve our opening until the beginning of the defendant's case."

"*What?*" Shannon whispered.

Although defendants technically had the right to reserve their opening until they put on their own evidence, it was unheard of for a lawyer to actually do so. No decent defense attorney wanted the jury to hear from the prosecution for several days before the defense lawyer even put his theme out there. Yet Alex felt in his gut that it was the right thing to do.

"If that's what defense counsel wishes." Judge Rosenthal turned to a stunned Taj Deegan. "You may call your first witness, Ms. Deegan."

Alex sat down, and Shannon leaned over the back of Khalid, who was seated between them. "I hope you're ready to explain this to Nara when we break for lunch," she whispered.

Nara, like all potential witnesses, was not allowed in the courtroom until she testified. Alex hadn't thought about how she might react, but it was too late to consider that now. She would understand. She would have to.

"The commonwealth calls Dr. Marnya Davidson."

Dr. Davidson walked into the courtroom, took the oath, and settled into the witness stand with the authority of someone who had done this hundreds of times before. She glanced quickly at Alex and gave him a nod, as if she looked forward to his cross-examination. Alex pulled his legal pad closer and started taking notes.

Davidson's testimony mirrored what she had said during the preliminary hearing except that she added a few bells and whistles. When Taj Deegan trotted out the autopsy photos, Alex offered to stipulate to the cause of death. Deegan whirled and looked at him, wise to his ploys. "Unless you're also willing to stipulate that the defendant ordered the killings, I think I'm entitled to show the jury the photographs," she said.

She turned to Judge Rosenthal. "Your Honor, these are not theoretical killings; these are real victims murdered in the most cowardly and cold-blooded way imaginable. While it gives me no pleasure to present these photographs, the jury needs to know all of the facts in this case, including the gruesome nature of the crimes. Plus, I intend to show that these murders are related to other honor killings, thereby proving a pattern of conduct that makes it clear the murders were religiously motivated."

Alex had just sat down when Taj Deegan mentioned other honor killings. He jumped back up as if his seat were electrically charged. "I object, Judge! That has no place in this trial!"

To Alex's great dismay, the jurors were leaning forward. Dr. Davidson had an eccentric personality that had already intrigued them. And now the lawyers were adding yet another twist. *"Other honor killings."* This case was getting juicier by the minute.

"Approach the bench," Rosenthal ordered.

On the way up, Alex glared at Deegan. She knew *exactly* what she was doing. Even if the judge sustained Alex's objection, she had planted the specter of the other honor killings in the minds of the jury.

"I can't believe you stooped to that," Alex whispered to her, just out of earshot of the judge.

"Spare me," Deegan shot back. "We both know he did it."

The lawyers huddled around Rosenthal's bench and engaged in a furious argument. Deegan wanted to ask Dr. Davidson about two additional honor killings that had been committed using the same sword. "The exact same sword, Judge. Under the rules of evidence, other crimes are admissible if they show a pattern of conduct."

"That's ridiculous," Alex countered. "Our client hasn't even been charged with those killings. Plus, even if the commonwealth could prove that the murders were all committed by the same person, how does that prove a pattern of conduct by *our* client? Nobody's saying that our client actually carried out the beheadings."

As the lawyers argued back and forth, their voices rising with each volley, Rosenthal decided it was time for another break. He announced a fifteen-minute recess so that he could study the issue in more detail. Alex watched the jury shuffle back into the jury room, knowing that the main thing on their mind was exactly how many honor killings the defendant had ordered. And whether they would get to hear about them.

"Now would be a good time to go out in the hallway and tell Nara that you waived your opening statement," Shannon said to Alex.

"Later," Alex said.

◁▷

After a two-cigarette recess, Rosenthal came back to the bench recharged. Before he called the jury back into the courtroom, he announced his ruling. "Mr. Madison is right. The law requires more than a pattern of conduct. It requires a pattern of conduct that is unique to the defendant, and the commonwealth hasn't shown that here. For example, it could be that the defendant and another party just use the same 'triggerman,' so to speak. The fact that the sword is the same reflects on the triggerman's pattern of conduct, not the defendant's."

Alex requested a curative instruction, and Rosenthal promised that he would tell the jury to disregard the question they heard before the break. As if that would make everything better.

When the jury returned, Rosenthal mumbled something about disregarding the last question asked by the commonwealth's attorney. "As for defense counsel's objection about the admissibility of the photographs, I'm overruling that," Rosenthal said.

To Alex's surprise, everyone managed to keep his or her breakfast down while Taj Deegan displayed blowups from the crime scene and autopsy. Juror 5 looked pretty pale, and Alex thought she might pass out. Juror 10 had to put her hand over her mouth at least twice. But nobody hurled on the spot, a minor victory for the defense.

Just before lunch, Taj Deegan finished her direct examination of Dr. Davidson, and Judge Rosenthal again turned to Alex.

"Does defense counsel have any questions?"

"Not at this time, Your Honor."

When the judge and jury had left the courtroom, Shannon let her frustrations show. "A great morning for the defense team," she said sarcastically.

The deputies were coming over to take Khalid to lockup, and Alex felt the need to reassure his client. He put a hand on Khalid's shoulder. "Don't worry. We're saving our ammo for when it counts."

"I trust you," Khalid said.

At least somebody does, Alex thought.

79

NARA WAS WAITING IN THE HALLWAY when court recessed for lunch. She fell in stride with Alex and Shannon as they made their way down the escalators and out of the building. As they were heading toward the cars, Nara asked how things went that morning.

"I'm going to peel off," Shannon said, heading toward her car. "I'll just grab a quick salad and meet you back in the courtroom."

"Do you really think it's a good idea for Nara and me to do lunch together?" Alex asked. "We might get the tabloids talking."

"If you avoid body contact, you should be okay," Shannon said over her shoulder.

Alex drove down Princess Anne Road until he found a Subway. He needed something quick so he could get back to court and prepare for the afternoon witnesses. Alex looked around to make sure no reporters had the same idea. He and Nara each ordered a sub and found a booth toward the back.

Nara took a few bites and leaned forward. She took a sip of her drink and kept her voice low. "How did it go this morning?"

"I'm really not supposed to say," Alex said.

"The judge said you couldn't talk to me about the *witnesses*. How did your *opening statement* go?"

Sometimes the woman was too smart for her own good.

Alex chewed a bite of sub and eventually swallowed. He looked at Nara and decided that he couldn't lie. She trusted him. If they were ever going to have any kind of relationship, he needed to be straight with her.

"I didn't give it."

Nara froze mid-bite and stared at him. "What?"

"I didn't give it. Taj Deegan took the case 180 degrees from where I expected she would go with her opening. I decided it would be best if I waited until we begin our case to give mine."

Nara looked at him as if he had sprouted a third eye. "Are you serious? You didn't say *anything*?"

Alex shrugged. "It's not like I won't be able to give an opening. I just *delayed* it for strategic reasons until the commonwealth's case is over."

Nara's face grew stormy. "Why do you keep holding back on us? What could Taj Deegan possibly have said to make you throw away your entire opening?"

"Shh," Alex said. People were starting to look at them.

"I'm tired of sneaking around and being quiet, as if we're ashamed of our case. The least you could have done was to deliver the opening statement that we all worked so hard on last night."

Alex felt like he was in the middle of an E. F. Hutton commercial as the other conversations in the sub shop suddenly receded. He kept his own voice low, hoping that Nara would catch the hint. "I can't tell you everything that Taj Deegan said. But, Nara, I'm not holding back . . . and I think by now you should cut me a little slack."

Alex turned and glared at some of the people who were staring at him and Nara. The onlookers quickly looked away. He returned his attention to Nara and leaned forward. "Frankly, after putting my life on the line, I hoped I might get a little more trust. Why isn't anything ever good enough for you?"

Nara snorted. "Don't turn this on me. Every time we disagree on something, you go into your 'trust me' routine." She wrapped her half-eaten sandwich and crinkled up the bag of chips as she talked. "'I'm the lawyer, Nara. I know what's best.' Do you know how condescending that sounds?" She gave him no chance to answer. "I think I'll just wait outside."

Alex tried to dissuade her, but Nara threw her trash away and walked out the door. She stood in front of the Subway looking out at the parking lot with her arms crossed. It was early December and probably forty degrees, but Alex no longer cared. He took his time and ate the rest of his sub. Then he stood in line to get a cookie for dessert.

It was a long, silent ride back to the courthouse.

80

THE FIRST WITNESS Taj Deegan called that afternoon was the mosque's diminutive bookkeeper, Riham El-Ashi. She walked down the aisle, affirmed that she would tell the truth, and gave Khalid a look of empathy. Deep lines of concern furrowed her brow.

Alex felt sorry for the woman. He also relaxed a little; Shannon would be cross-examining this witness.

Riham lowered the mic and stated her name for the record. During her direct examination, Judge Rosenthal had to remind her several times to speak up. To compensate for the witness's lack of enthusiasm, Taj Deegan seemed to ask her questions louder and move around the courtroom more. Alex noted that some of the jurors were starting to struggle with heavy eyelids.

Riham testified about the importance of the zakah to Muslims. She explained the mosque's system for securing donations and how the money was counted and deposited. She listed the persons who had access to the funds at every step in the process, including Khalid Mobassar. Riham also testified that only she and the three imams had the authority to wire funds from the mosque accounts.

Next, Taj Deegan asked questions about the donations in the weeks prior to Ja'dah Mahdi's murder. Deegan had prepared a few charts and graphs, which Riham reluctantly agreed were accurate. The charts demonstrated that donations to the general operating account were about half their normal amount during the weeks leading up to the murders. The building fund, on the other hand, increased dramatically during that same time frame.

"Did somebody authorize a transfer of $20,000 from the mosque's building fund to an account in Beirut, Lebanon, two days before the murders?" Taj Deegan asked.

"Yes."

Deegan turned to the judge. "This might be a good time to inform the jury of a stipulation between the commonwealth and defense counsel."

Shannon stood. "No objection."

Taj Deegan grabbed a piece of paper from her counsel table and turned to the jury. "In order to avoid the inconvenience of having the commonwealth subpoena an officer of the Bank of Virginia, both sides have stipulated that the $20,000 wired from the mosque's building fund was authorized in an online transaction from an unknown computer. The user who authorized the transaction signed in with the user name and password assigned to Khalid Mobassar."

Before sitting down, the prosecutor turned back to the witness. Deegan apparently wanted to remind the jury that they could expect Riham to help the defendant if she could. "Thank you for being here today," Deegan said, as if the witness had a choice. "I know you're very close to the defendant and that this has been very difficult for you."

"You're welcome," Riham said, falling for the prosecutor's trick. Alex wanted to gag.

Shannon, however, didn't seem to be the least bit bothered by it as she bounced to her feet. "Good afternoon, Ms. El-Ashi."

"Good afternoon."

"As I understand it, you're basically saying that about half the donations normally intended for the operating account instead got put in the mosque's building account during the three weeks prior to Ja'dah Mahdi's death. Is that right?"

The witness nodded. "Yes, that's correct."

"And that could have been done by anyone who had access to the safe, because they could have come in at night and taken some of the checks and the next day deposited them in the building account using a deposit stamp. Is that correct?"

"Yes, that's also correct."

"Then let's list on this easel all the people who had access to the mosque's safe."

In almost flawless handwriting, Shannon made a list of the three imams and the three other individuals named by Riham. Both Khalid Mobassar and Fatih Mahdi were on the list. "Now we don't know for a fact which of these men may have been diverting the mosque's money. Is that correct?"

The witness furrowed her brow. "Yes . . ." She hesitated, a desire to be 100 percent truthful. "But we do know that the transfer was authorized using Mr. Mobassar's user name and password."

"My point exactly," Shannon said. She seemed confident. Perky. As if she was getting ready for a tumbling pass that she knew she would nail. "Do you know how Mr. Mobassar protected his password?"

"No."

"Would it surprise you to know that he had all of his user names and passwords on his computer in a Word document entitled 'FAQs' and that the document was not password-protected?"

The witness thought for a moment. "No, this wouldn't surprise me. Mr. Mobassar is a very trusting person."

"Did you know that anyone could find that document by simply searching Mr. Mobassar's computer using a search term like *password*?"

"Objection!" Taj Deegan was on her feet. "This witness already said she didn't know how Mr. Mobassar stored his passwords. How could she possibly know this?"

"Sustained," Judge Rosenthal said.

"Did Mr. Mobassar always close his door and lock his office when he wasn't there?"

"Not in the middle of the day. Only when he left for the night."

"So people could just walk right into his office in the middle of the day and access his computer?"

The witness thought about this. "I guess so."

"And if we made a list of all the people that could have done that, the list could include virtually everyone who is a member of the mosque. Is that right?"

"Many members come back to our office complex—yes."

Shannon checked her notes and started asking questions about how Khalid Mobassar received his user name and password. The witness testified that she had personally set up the passwords several years ago and communicated them to the three imams via e-mail.

"Did you use special encryption on the e-mail?" Shannon asked.

"No."

"Are you aware of all the ways e-mail can be hacked into these days?"

"No, I'm afraid I am not."

Shannon made a check on her notepad, and Khalid leaned over to Alex. "She's very good," Khalid whispered.

Alex nodded. "You haven't heard her punch line yet."

Shannon stationed herself in the middle of the courtroom and pushed a stray strand of hair behind her ear. She looked down at the floor for a moment, deep in thought. "Can you think of any reason, if you were going to pay someone to do an honor killing, that you would wire funds from the mosque's account using your *own* user name and password?"

Taj Deegan wasted no time on this one. "Objection! Calls for speculation. Maybe Mr. Mobassar didn't know his user name and password could be traced. Maybe he didn't think the government could gain access to the accounts of a mosque. There may be a thousand reasons, but this witness is the wrong person to ask."

Shannon turned to the prosecutor. "If you want to testify, perhaps you should get sworn in."

Rosenthal banged his gavel. "I don't need counsel talking to each other," he snapped. "The objection is well-taken and will be sustained."

The witness looked sheepishly at the judge. "Does that mean I should not answer?"

"Yes."

But Alex didn't care about the answer, and he knew Shannon didn't either. The question had been planted in the jury's mind. It was the tactic defense lawyers always used when a circumstantial case against them seemed overwhelming. They would argue that the case was *too* perfect. Why would anyone make so many stupid mistakes? Doesn't it seem more consistent with a setup? It was like a judo expert using his opponent's weight and momentum to throw him.

"That's all I have for this witness," Shannon said.

81

ALEX AND SHANNON both knew that Special Agent Michael Long would be a tougher witness than the mosque's sheepish bookkeeper. Long took the stand with an air of crisp authority. He was clean-cut, articulate, and handsome enough to have the single women on the jury drooling. Alex had no doubt that Taj Deegan would draw out his testimony as long as she could.

Long's role was to authenticate the text messages sent from Khalid Mobassar's cell phone. To get there, he would have to explain the ins and outs of the Foreign Intelligence Surveillance Act and the Patriot Act, as well as the reasons that the Department of Justice had been tapping Khalid Mobassar's phone. Since Agent Long had a law school education, Taj Deegan turned his testimony into a tutorial on the legal basis for national-security wiretaps.

"So long as the primary purpose of the eavesdropping is to obtain foreign intelligence information, the special court will allow the wiretaps to take place," Long explained. He discussed the government's concern that mosques like the Islamic Learning Center were sending funds to Hezbollah to help in the rebuilding of Beirut following the 2006 war. "Hezbollah is a known terrorist organization with a history of attacking innocent civilians and American soldiers. It is one of the two or three most dangerous terrorist organizations in the world," he testified.

He talked about the specific authorizations that were obtained under FISA and the Patriot Act to record phone conversations and intercept text messages and e-mails sent and received by leaders of the Islamic Learning Center.

"Did those leaders include Mr. Khalid Mobassar and Mr. Fatih Mahdi?" Deegan asked.

"Yes, ma'am, those men were included."

Shannon stood and addressed the court. "At this time we would renew our earlier objection to the admissibility of any information obtained under the Patriot Act on the grounds that the act is unconstitutional as applied to our client. The Patriot Act does not require probable cause—"

"I know the argument," Judge Rosenthal said, cutting her off and motioning her back to her seat. "And I'm overruling the objection for the reasons previously stated in my opinion."

"After the murders of Ja'dah Mahdi and Martin Burns, did the local authorities request access to the phone records and e-mails of the imams at the Islamic Learning Center as well as Mr. Mahdi?" Taj Deegan asked.

"That's correct. They did."

"And were you part of the team that searched those records?"

"Yes, ma'am. I supervised that team."

"Did you find any text messages, e-mails, or phone conversations related to the murders of Ja'dah Mahdi and Martin Burns?"

Long testified about running searches through the digitized programs that recorded conversations and text messages. He explained the various search terms and parameters the authorities used to unearth the messages related to the murder investigation.

Once the technicalities had been covered, Taj Deegan made a Hollywood production of introducing the text messages into evidence and having them read to the jury. She had reproduced them on posterboard blowups that she placed on easels so the jury could read along. After she milked the testimony for all it was worth, she asked the witness whether he personally ran searches on text messages, e-mails, and phone conversations by Fatih Mahdi.

"Yes, ma'am, I did."

"And did those searches reveal any text messages, e-mails, or phone conversations that would in any way implicate Mr. Mahdi in the murder of his wife or Martin Burns?"

This time, Special Agent Long hesitated for a second or two so that he could have the jury's undivided attention.

"No, ma'am, they did not."

"Your witness," Deegan said.

82

SHANNON REESE BOUNCED UP even before Deegan had settled into her chair. "Just to be clear, what you've shown us are text messages and not phone calls; is that correct?" Shannon asked.

"Yes, ma'am."

"So you don't technically know who sent them; you just know that they came from Khalid Mobassar's phone?"

"That's also correct, ma'am."

"Have you run the phone for fingerprints?"

"No, ma'am. The phone turned up missing."

Shannon raised her eyebrows, and Special Agent Long apparently thought he ought to elaborate. "We have photographs showing the phone in the possession of Mr. Mobassar on dates before *and after* the text messages in question. We also have recorded phone conversations from Mr. Mobassar both before *and after* the text messages, some from the very day the text messages were sent. The phone did not turn up missing until several weeks later."

Shannon gave the officer a quizzical look. "I'm sorry. Did I ask you when the phone turned up missing?"

Special Agent Long gave her a glittering smile, dimples in full display, and Alex thought the guy could have had a career in Hollywood. "No, ma'am. But I thought it might be helpful information to the jury."

A few of the jurors smiled along with the witness, but Shannon didn't seem amused. "Maybe you could let the lawyers be the judge of that and just answer the questions."

"Objection!"

"Sustained."

Shannon walked back to her counsel table and picked up a document. She asked if she could approach the witness. Once granted permission, she handed a copy of the document to Taj Deegan and the original to Special Agent Long. She turned so that she was facing more toward the jury than the witness.

"Can you tell me what that document is?"

Long looked confused. "It appears to be a copy of the Wikipedia page about the Patriot Act."

Deegan stood, her tone indicating confusion. "Objection, Your Honor. There's no relevance to a Wikipedia page on the Patriot Act. Even if there was, there's been no foundation laid as to its accuracy."

Judge Rosenthal leaned forward on his elbows and looked down at Shannon. "Are you serious? You want to introduce a Wikipedia page as an exhibit?"

"Does that mean that the objection is sustained?" Shannon asked innocently.

"Absolutely."

Shannon bit her lip and acted like she was thinking for a moment. "Then let me ask it this way—are the provisions of the Patriot Act a secret?"

Long looked more confused than before. "Of course not. They're part of the United States code."

"And anybody who can read the U.S. code—or even Wikipedia for that matter—would know that the federal government can tap the phones and intercept e-mails and text messages of people who have even loose connections with suspected terrorist organizations. Is that right?"

"Objection; calls for speculation."

"Sustained."

Who cares? Alex thought. *Point made.*

"Let's talk about the cell phone that *received* the text messages," Shannon said. "That phone was registered under a fictitious name. Is that correct?"

Long didn't seem like the epitome of confidence anymore. "That was my testimony."

"Is it difficult to register a cell phone under a fictitious name?"

Again Taj Deegan objected, and Rosenthal sustained the objection.

"Well, it's safe to say that at least somebody associated with the killings of Ja'dah Mahdi and Martin Burns knew how to register a cell phone to a fictitious name; is that correct?" Shannon asked.

Taj Deegan was on her feet again but apparently could think of no reasonable objection. She sat down.

"Yeah. I think that's clear."

"Can you think of any reason why my client, knowing that his mosque was providing funds to humanitarian organizations helping to rebuild Beirut, and knowing that his phone was probably tapped under the Patriot Act—"

"Objection!" Taj Deegan yelled, cutting Shannon off midsentence.

"Sustained," Rosenthal said quickly.

Shannon stood there for a moment, as if she couldn't figure out what to do next. "May I have a minute?" she asked the judge.

"One minute."

She walked to her counsel table and huddled up with Alex. "Do you think the jury got the gist of what I was implying?" she whispered.

"You can never be too sure," Alex said.

Shannon gave him a cold stare. "Easy for you to say."

She returned to the center of the courtroom and crossed her arms for a moment, deep in thought. "In your experience, Special Agent Long, do criminals typically like to get caught?"

Long shook his head as if Shannon were an idiot. "Of course not."

Shannon took a deep breath and then spit the next question out as quickly as possible. "Then why would my client use his own cell phone knowing that it was probably tapped?"

"Objection!"

Rosenthal banged his gavel and stared at Shannon Reese, clearly perturbed. "I told you that question was objectionable." He turned to the jury. "Please disregard that question. Counsel will have sufficient time to argue her case during the closing argument."

Shannon turned and looked at Alex. He gave her a subtle nod. *I'm pretty sure they got it that time.*

"No further questions," she said cheerfully.

When Shannon sat down, Taj Deegan stood and announced she had only one question on redirect.

"Do you have any reason to believe that Mr. Mobassar, a Muslim cleric who specializes in Islamic studies, was intimately familiar with the details of the Patriot Act?"

"Absolutely not."

Shannon leaned over and whispered to Alex, "Unless he could read Wikipedia."

83

BEFORE THE DEATH of his brother, fifteen-year-old Ahmed Obu Mobassar had been living a double life. During the day, he went to school and learned how to be a productive Lebanese citizen. But each evening, he attended the salat at a local mosque and became indoctrinated in the elements of jihad.

His father led a different mosque, one more conciliatory in its views. But his father was a tolerant man and wanted Ahmed to discover his own path to Allah. He often quizzed Ahmed about what he was learning and cautioned him about certain teachings, but he never prevented Ahmed from attending the more radical mosque.

Ahmed had learned not to tell his father everything. He also learned what it meant to be a true Muslim—one committed to completing the conquest Mohammed had started and establishing a global caliphate. Allah would be glorified. The Great Prophet would be pleased. *Jihad* was the way!

Ahmed was taught that true Muslims should hate the enemies of Allah with all their hearts. He was taught that Sharia law must be established in every nation inhabited by true Muslims. And his instructors extolled the glory of martyrdom over and over. At the first drop of your own blood, you would redeem your soul. By laying down your life, you would redeem your family. Martyrdom. Paradise. Redemption. There was no other way for a true believer to die.

While the imams filled his mind with the elements of jihad, Hezbollah warriors trained his body. Ahmed learned how to assemble explosives, how to handle and shoot an assault weapon, how to lay a land mine and turn an automobile into a bomb. He learned how to destroy others in hand-to-hand combat.

But the week after Omar died in the Palestinian refugee camp, Ahmed's double life came to an end. His father's views changed overnight. With his parents' full knowledge and the help of his father's friend, Fatih Mahdi, Ahmed moved into a Hezbollah training facility on the outskirts of Beirut. His first mission into Israel would be less than a month later.

Before Ahmed and the others embarked on that mission, a revered imam gathered the teenagers and looked each of the young men squarely in the eye, as if searching for any chinks in their courage. "Today you will become men," the imam said. "Today you will fight for the glory of Islam. Today you will fight for the glory of Lebanon. Go with courage and for the glory of Allah!"

"Allahu akbar!"

The shouts echoed as adrenaline surged through Ahmed's body. He and the others were mighty warriors for Allah, though many of them did not yet shave. Still, he had no doubt that each one would strap explosives to his body and trigger the fuse if he could take out twelve Israelis. These were the greatest warriors in the Middle East. They were dead men with nothing to lose and everything to gain. Allah would be glorified! Family members would be redeemed! At their funerals, there would be rejoicing.

It was only a matter time.

84

ALEX AND HIS TEAM were cautiously optimistic Wednesday night. It seemed to Alex that the jury was bothered by the same thing that had struck him about this case—why would Khalid send text messages from his own cell phone?

There were, of course, a number of possible explanations. Perhaps Khalid really didn't know about the particulars of the Patriot Act. Perhaps Khalid didn't think he would ever be a suspect because the police would zero in on Fatih Mahdi. Perhaps Khalid did it precisely because it would seem too obvious and he could later argue that it created reasonable doubt, like a killer signing the crime scene in blood. Who could be that stupid? Maybe Khalid had outsmarted everybody, including his own lawyers.

Alex preferred not to think about that last alternative.

Nara seemed upbeat when she showed up at the office after visiting her father. "My dad says you guys really know what you're doing," she said.

They were sitting around the conference table preparing for the following day's witnesses. Shannon merely looked up when Nara made the comment and then went back to work. Alex took it as Nara's way of apologizing for the way she had acted at lunch. The words *I'm sorry* were not a prominent part of Nara's vocabulary.

"Shannon did a great job on cross-examination," Alex said. "And as you know, I made no mistakes in my opening statement."

"So I heard," Nara said. She flashed a beautiful white smile.

Apology accepted, Alex thought.

Later, Alex had a few minutes to talk with Nara in the privacy of his office. "I'm ready to testify," she said.

"We'll make that call this weekend," Alex responded. "The commonwealth should rest its case on Friday. I'll know better after I cross-examine Fatih Mahdi whether we'll need you."

"Alex," Nara said, waiting for Alex to look in her eyes before she continued. "If there's any chance we might lose this case, I need to take the stand. Promise me."

Alex didn't respond. He still believed that if he put Nara on the stand, it would only be a matter of time before Hezbollah took her out. Even the witness protection program was no guarantee against an organization with as many tentacles as Hezbollah.

"Promise me," she insisted.

He looked down. "If I think we need your testimony, I'll put you on the stand."

"Thank you, Alex." Nara rose from her seat, approached Alex, and kissed him on the cheek. She paused a few inches away from his face. "If I have to testify, I'll be okay. I've got a place to go. After a few years, I'll come back."

Looking directly into her eyes, Alex wanted to believe her. He wanted to believe that she would be all right. He wanted to believe that she would come back for him. But during their trip to Beirut, Hezbollah had already demonstrated its ability to know things it shouldn't know.

He had the uneasy feeling that she was only telling him the things that she knew he wanted to hear. Al toqiah. Anything for the sake of the cause.

But two could play this game. Unless the case fell completely apart, Alex had no intention of putting her on the stand.

And then, a split second later, none of that mattered. Who could think of such things when a woman like Nara leaned in for a serious kiss?

◁▷

Even the juiciest trials get bogged down in details, and Thursday was that day for the Mobassar trial. Dr. Kumar Santi took the stand and gave the jury a lesson in cell phone triangulation. To keep the jury somewhat awake, Deegan showed PowerPoints with lots of colorful charts and maps. When Santi stepped down, there was little doubt that the text messages from Khalid's cell phone had been sent from the vicinity of the Islamic Learning Center in Norfolk. The message from the killer's cell phone had been sent from Sandbridge.

Santi was followed by someone from the CSI lab who testified about the traces of Ja'dah Mahdi's DNA at the Sandbridge rental property. Next came a Sandbridge rental agent who explained how she had left the key to the property under a mat because of the occupant's plan to arrive late at night. A signed rental agreement under a phony name had been sent previously via mail. In other words, the rental agent never laid eyes on the killer.

The deputy sheriff who had found the bodies testified next. He told the jury all about the elaborate search and the carefully trained dogs who actually located the bodies. Just before lunch, Taj Deegan again grossed out the jury with the pictures of the bodies.

It was all very interesting, Alex thought, but not particularly damaging. A tale of sound and fury, signifying nothing.

After lunch came more of the same. Taj Deegan might as well have passed out pillows and cots as the jurors listened to a computer technician testify about the way he had searched the hard drive of Khalid Mobassar's work computer. The witness had a monotone voice, an expressionless face, and a unique way of making a murder trial seem as exciting as high school calculus.

After about twenty minutes, Judge Rosenthal clearly needed a cigarette break, and some of the jurors looked like they needed alarm clocks. Eventually the technician meandered around to the point of his testimony—someone had used Khalid Mobassar's work computer to search for Sandbridge rental properties on March 29, just a few months prior to the killings. Other searches and e-mails made it pretty clear Khalid was the only one using his computer that day, and in particular during the time frame surrounding the search.

Shannon had no questions for the witness on cross-examination, and Rosenthal mercifully decided that it was time for a break.

The rest of the afternoon was taken up with the testimony of Detective Terri Brown. The detective explained how she had first focused on Fatih Mahdi as the primary suspect. The crime fit the profile for a religiously motivated honor killing, and the husband would therefore be the primary suspect. But, according to Brown, all the hard evidence pointed toward the defendant.

They had also caught the defendant in a couple of lies. For example, during her interviews with Mr. Mobassar, the imam denied knowing anything about a search for Sandbridge rental listings. Brown also noted that the defendant had been less than forthcoming about his conversations with Fatih Mahdi and had been a supporter of Hezbollah in the past.

During Brown's testimony, Taj Deegan introduced copies of the books she had waved around during her opening statement and a copy of the manuscript for Khalid's new book. The jury was also shown video of Khalid talking on Hezbollah television shortly after Omar was killed and on American television after the Israeli strikes against Lebanon in 2006.

Brown was a seasoned witness, so Shannon conducted a limited and cautious cross-examination. She scored a few points about why Fatih Mahdi had been a suspect and asked Brown numerous questions about Mahdi's radical philosophy and belief in Sharia law. Then she carefully returned to the same theme she had introduced earlier: why would somebody as intelligent as Khalid Mobassar use his own cell phone to send text messages ordering an honor killing?

"I have no reason to believe that the defendant knew his text messages were being monitored under the Patriot Act," Brown responded. "I believe that the defendant thought we would focus on the husband and therefore never seriously investigate the defendant. Plus, I've been a detective long enough to see murder suspects do some incredibly stupid things."

Alex could tell from the look on Shannon's face that she regretted asking the question. But she was a pro and quickly moved on to the next line of questioning.

By the time court adjourned at five o'clock, one thing had become obvious to everyone in the courtroom: the case would rise or fall on the testimony of two men—Fatih Mahdi and, if he took the stand, Khalid Mobassar. That knowledge kept Alex at the office until well after midnight on Thursday. He probably would have stayed all night if his grandmother hadn't chased him out.

"You can't think straight if you don't get any sleep," Ramona said, setting some papers on his desk.

"Ten more minutes," Alex said. He really needed two more hours but didn't have the strength to argue with anyone, especially his grandmother. He would take the documents home and finish his work there.

"You said that an hour ago," Ramona reminded him.

Alex sighed and rolled his eyes. "Didn't I already fire you once? Now go home and let me finish getting ready."

Ramona told Alex that she needed to get a few more documents copied and a few more things organized. Not once in the last week had Ramona left before Alex. She headed out of his office but stopped at the door and turned back toward Alex.

"I'm proud of you, Alex Madison. Your parents and your granddad are proud of you too."

85

FRIDAY MORNING, after a few hours of restless sleep, Alex threw his legs over the side of the bed and sat there, contemplating what lay ahead. A few more days and it would all be over. He had been so immersed in the "trial tunnel" for the past few months that any semblance of a normal life had disappeared. He woke up thinking about the case. He went to bed thinking about the case. It seemed like he spent every waking moment working on it.

He allowed himself a few minutes to think about how great it would be when the trial was over and he could enjoy the holiday season. He could sleep in. He could decorate his condo and buy some presents. By Christmas Day, Khalid would be either a free man or facing life behind bars. Nara would either be safe and free to live her life, or she would be in hiding, constantly looking over her shoulder for the deadly agents of Hezbollah.

Today's witness would probably decide both Khalid's and Nara's fate.

The pressure of the challenge started squeezing in on Alex, constricting his chest. He blew out a deep breath and tried to relax.

It was time for some strong coffee.

◁▷

Fatih Mahdi looked like he had aged ten years since the preliminary hearing. He stood in the well of the courtroom dressed in his traditional Muslim garb and affirmed that he would tell the truth. He had dark circles under his eyes and looked at once both sad and determined. His black beard, dark complexion, and receding hairline played into

310 || FATAL CONVICTIONS

the Muslim stereotype. But when Mahdi testified, he mumbled softly, and the spectators in the courtroom leaned forward and strained to hear. Several times, Taj Deegan asked him to speak up.

The prosecutor made every attempt to personalize Mahdi, but he was not cooperating. He never looked at the jury and didn't allow himself to relax. His broad shoulders slumped forward, and he hunched over the microphone.

The substance of his testimony was about what Alex expected. He told the jury how he met Ja'dah and how devoted she had been to the Muslim faith. He described their life together.

"Did you love her?" Taj Deegan asked.

"Very much."

Mahdi's life centered around his work and the mosque. Deegan did a good job of portraying him as deeply religious but not fanatical.

Mahdi testified about his friendship with Khalid and Ghaniyah Mobassar. They had been through a lot together in Lebanon. He had helped Khalid mourn the loss of two sons, and he described the way those losses affected Khalid.

He also testified about how Khalid's views as the imam in the Norfolk mosque became increasingly unorthodox. Though Khalid was his dear friend, Fatih Mahdi had led the opposition to certain doctrines that Fatih considered heretical. According to Fatih, the more resistance Khalid Mobassar encountered, the more strident and adamant he became. Those in the mosque who opposed Khalid were usually forced out.

"About six months before the death of your wife, it seems you stopped being critical of Mr. Mobassar. Can you tell the jury what happened?"

Fatih hesitated at the question, looking down to collect his thoughts. "I sensed that all of the dissension and turmoil was driving my wife away from the faith," Fatih said. He kept his eyes on Taj Deegan, who had stationed herself next to the jury box.

"I still believed that Khalid was wrong, but I realized that if I continued to fight, I might lose both a friend and my wife. I continued to debate things with Khalid privately, but I chose to cease any public criticism. I prayed instead that Allah would show him the way."

As Fatih testified, Alex studied the jury and didn't like what he saw. The whole tenor of the courtroom seemed to be one of empathy and respect. The man certainly didn't come across as a jihadist who would order an honor killing of his own wife.

"I'd like to turn your attention now to the events surrounding the death of your wife," Taj Deegan said. She spoke softly, helping to sustain the courtroom mood. "Please tell the ladies and gentlemen of the jury how you learned that Ja'dah had converted to the Christian faith."

For the next several minutes, Fatih talked about the changes he saw in his wife and how he had followed her one Saturday night to Beach Bible Church. He seemed genuinely ashamed of what he had done. When he talked about seeing Ja'dah with Martin Burns, his face reflected the lingering memory of the heartache he had experienced. She had rejected both her husband and her faith, Fatih said, but he still loved her.

One of the reasons he had sought counsel from Khalid was because he hoped Khalid's more progressive view of the faith might break through his wife's strong reservations. In Fatih's mind, he had brought his wife to America in order to help Americans find the Muslim faith. Instead, he felt like the American culture and the Western brand of Christianity had corrupted *her*.

Taj Deegan had the witness describe in detail his conversation with Khalid and his reaction when he learned that his wife had been beheaded. Fatih spoke in soft and measured tones about learning of his wife's death and the evidence that pointed to his good friend as the one who ordered her killing. He shed no tears but seemed like a man who was still in shock. If he had broken down and cried during his testimony, it would have come across as phony. But to Alex's great chagrin, Mahdi's subdued answers and perplexed demeanor came across as very genuine.

Shannon leaned over to Alex. "He makes a better witness than I thought he would."

"I know," Alex whispered back.

Taj Deegan checked her notes to ensure that she hadn't missed anything. "One last question. There are those who say your brand of the Muslim faith is demeaning to women and fosters honor killings. What do you say to that?"

Fatih Mahdi squared his jaw and looked directly at Taj Deegan. "The great Prophet Mohammed, peace be upon him, was most respectful to women. True followers of Mohammed would never oppress women and would certainly never sanction something as heinous as honor killings. Only those who falsely claim the name of Allah and distort the Qur'an engage in such things."

"Thank you," Taj Deegan said. "I have no further questions."

"Does defense counsel have any cross-examination?" Judge Rosenthal asked.

"I might have a few questions," Alex said.

The judge gave Alex a wry smile. "Perhaps before we get started, we should take a ten-minute break."

86

WHEN ROSENTHAL GAVELED the court back to order, the spectators fell unnaturally still. There was none of the usual whispering or shuffling around. The jury leaned forward, knowing the case could well be decided in the next few hours.

Alex felt his own palms moistening with sweat, his heart hammering against his chest. *Breathe deeply; stay calm.*

"Good morning, Mr. Mahdi."

"Good morning."

The jitters would go away when he drew first blood. Hopefully that wouldn't take long.

"In your view, America should be governed by Sharia law; isn't that right?"

Mahdi furrowed his brow. "America has a long tradition based on English common law," he said. "It would not be practical to suggest that the laws of this country be overhauled to reflect the religious beliefs of a small minority of Muslims."

"Nice tap dance," Alex said, "but let's try it again."

"Objection!"

"Sustained."

Alex thought about how to best phrase the question. To him, a sustained objection was never the final word; it was only a suggestion to rephrase. "Isn't it a goal of the Islamic Brotherhood to have every country where their members reside governed by Sharia law?"

Mahdi appeared to relax, as if he had just discovered the cause of an unfortunate misunderstanding. "Perhaps as an organization, that is one of the Brotherhood's stated goals. But the Brotherhood is only espousing the belief that the Muslims who live in that country should have their own affairs governed by Sharia law in Sharia courts. And this vision is for sometime in the future, perhaps at a time when many in this country have turned to the Islamic faith and desire to have certain parts of their lives—such as marital disputes or financial disputes with other Muslims—resolved in Sharia courts."

When Mahdi stopped for a breath, Alex started his next question, but Deegan jumped up to protest. "The witness wasn't finished," she said.

"Let the witness finish his answer," Rosenthal admonished.

Alex waited, frustrated that the judge was interfering with his questioning.

"It's the same idea the original colonists had in America," Mahdi continued. "Blue laws. Prayers before legislative sessions. Even the oath most witnesses take before testifying. These are all reflections of the Christian faith. The Brotherhood is just saying that Muslims ought to be able to follow their own faith on certain legal matters. It may, for example, interest you to know that the Archbishop of Canterbury proposed that Britain should consider just such a system."

"Are you done?" Alex asked.

"Yes."

"Good. Now let me ask you a yes or no question. Do *you* personally believe—not the Islamic Brotherhood and not the Archbishop of Canterbury but *you*, Fatih Mahdi—that America should be governed by Sharia law?"

Fatih shook his head. "At this time, no. Maybe someday—but only for those citizens who desire to be governed by Sharia."

Not exactly a yes or no. But it was an answer Alex could live with.

He walked back to his counsel table and retrieved a copy of an e-mail that Mahdi had sent to a Chicago-area imam in 2008. Ramona had found it in her review of the mountain of Patriot Act documents produced by the government.

Alex handed a copy to Taj Deegan and had the clerk give a copy to the witness. Mahdi studied the document as if he had never laid eyes on it before.

"What is this document?" Alex asked.

"An e-mail I wrote to a leader of a mosque in Chicago."

"At the time, the recipient of this e-mail was supporting Khalid's ideas for reform; is that true?"

Mahdi looked at the document. "Yes."

"Could you please read the first two sentences in the second paragraph?"

Mahdi mumbled his way through it, a sharp contrast to his clear enunciation of a few minutes ago. "'It is the duty of every member of the Islamic Brotherhood to be an advocate for Sharia law. Your support for Mr. Mobassar is in direct conflict with that duty.'"

Mahdi looked up when he finished, and Alex let the silence hang there for a moment. "And those were your words, correct?"

"Yes. But that sentence does not imply that we will usher in Sharia law immediately. Like your church, Mr. Madison, our Brotherhood seeks to convert others to our faith. Only among those true converts would it be possible to implement some tenets of Sharia law."

"Where does the e-mail say that?"

Mahdi took a sip of water. "It does not explicitly say that. As they say, you must read between the lines."

Alex picked up another document from his table, and Mahdi eyed him suspiciously. This was one of Alex's favorite tricks—get the witness in trouble with a document early in his testimony, and for the rest of the time, the witness would watch with trepidation as Alex picked up other documents. It kept the witness honest. He would never know whether Alex had something else in writing to impeach him with, should the witness waffle on the truth.

"Let's talk about Sharia law and specifically the rights of women," Alex said, looking at the new document. "Can a man be convicted of rape based on the victim's testimony alone?"

Taj Deegan jumped to her feet. "Nobody's claiming rape here, Judge."

"But we *are* trying to determine who committed an honor killing— in other words, who places such a low value on the life of a woman that he would order her killed just to restore the honor of her family."

Rosenthal thought about this for a moment. "I'll allow it."

Alex took a step or two toward the witness. "Can a man be con-victed of rape based on the testimony of the victim alone?"

"No."

"How many witnesses does it take?"

"Four."

"Do they have to be eyewitnesses?"

"Yes."

"Do they have to be men?"

"Yes."

"And how many witnesses, in addition to the alleged rapist, does it take to clear a man accused of rape?"

"One."

"So if the rapist and a friend testify that it was consensual sex, then the man goes free?"

"Yes."

"And the woman could be whipped for committing forni-cation—true?"

"Under Sharia law, fornication can be punished by whipping."

"How many times have you seen a *man* whipped for fornication?"

Mahdi lowered his voice. "None."

"Under Sharia law, a man can divorce his wife by simply saying the words, 'I divorce you.' Isn't that true?"

"Like America, fault is not required for divorce."

"Is fault required to be shown if the person who wants the divorce is a woman?"

"It is."

"But a man can divorce his wife even by sending her a text message, if he so desires, so long as the text message is clear. Am I right about that?"

"A divorce can be granted by any means of communication."

"And the children—under Sharia law, they're considered the seed of the man, and he is entitled to custody if he so desires. Is that correct?"

"Yes."

"Judge," Taj Deegan pleaded, "is this a quiz on Sharia law, or will we ever get around to relevant testimony for this case?"

"You have a point," Judge Rosenthal conceded. "Mr. Madison, let's move on."

"Yes, sir." Alex consulted a document and glanced at the jury. The empathy he had seen on their faces earlier was fading. The women especially seemed to be cooling toward the witness. Also disappearing was the nervousness that Alex had felt before he started the cross-examination.

"You divorced your first wife after only four years of marriage; is that correct?"

"Yes. I am sorry to say that it did not work out."

"And the children stayed with you?"

"They did. They are grown now, but I raised them. They wanted to stay with me. My wife just wanted out of the marriage and out of the home."

"Did you accuse your first wife of infidelity?"

Mahdi started to speak and caught himself. He glanced at Taj Deegan, apparently looking for a bailout, and then turned to the judge. "Must I discuss the conduct of my first wife in open court?"

"Answer the question," Rosenthal said. There was no sympathy in his voice.

Mahdi sighed. "She *was* unfaithful. With several men. I tried to handle the divorce with dignity and compassion—never accusing her publicly."

"Did you ever hit her or abuse her?"

Mahdi straightened with indignation. "Absolutely not."

"How many witnesses did you have for her infidelity?"

"I didn't need witnesses," Mahdi said quietly but with conviction. "She admitted the affairs."

"Did you split the assets with her?"

"No, Mr. Madison. My wife wanted out of the marriage. She didn't want the responsibility. She didn't want me. I granted her that wish by seeking a divorce, and I kept her unfaithfulness quiet."

Alex shifted gears and spent some time grilling Mahdi about his access to the mosque's safe. He established that Mahdi was at the mosque nearly every day and could walk into just about any office.

"Did you ever borrow Khalid's cell phone on the pretense that you needed to make a call because your own phone wasn't charged?"

"Never."

Rosenthal had a short—but loud—coughing fit, and Alex glanced at his watch. "Would this be a good time for a break, Your Honor?"

The jurors seemed appreciative, and Rosenthal looked as if he could hardly wait to clear them out so he could rush away for another cigarette.

After the jurors and judge left, Alex sat next to Shannon. "You've got him on the run," Shannon said.

But Fatih Mahdi didn't look like a man on the run. He was staring at Alex. The look in his eyes promised that this was not over yet.

◁▷

After the break, Alex turned his attention to the theological disputes between Fatih Mahdi and Khalid Mobassar. Step-by-step, Alex walked the witness through the history of the dispute, highlighting Mahdi's vocal opposition to the imam's teachings.

"And then, about six months ago, you abruptly stopped criticizing Mr. Mobassar publicly. Isn't that correct?"

"I don't remember the exact day. But yes, there came a time when I ceased my public opposition to your client's teaching."

"That's when you decided to stop him another way—that's when you decided to set him up for the honor killing of your wife. Isn't that true?"

"Absolutely false," Mahdi said. "I didn't even know about Ja'dah's conversion to Christianity at that time. I thought she was still committed to the Muslim faith."

Alex walked in front of Taj Deegan's table and parked himself at the same spot next to the jury rail that she had occupied earlier.

"You are aware that in Virginia, if you seek a divorce, your wife is entitled to equitable distribution—half of the marital estate?"

"I was not aware of that. I did not seek a divorce from Ja'dah. Instead, I went to my friend, Khalid Mobassar, hoping that he could talk to my wife and restore both her faith and our marriage."

"How much are you worth, Mr. Mahdi?"

The witness turned crimson. "What does that have to do with anything?"

"Just answer the question," Alex said.

Mahdi hesitated and looked at Taj Deegan. But Alex knew she wouldn't object. This line of questioning was absolutely relevant. Mahdi collected himself. "My net worth, including retirement accounts, is approximately $460,000."

"And you worked your entire life to save that amount; is that correct?"

"I've worked very hard. Yes."

"So you concocted a plan to save half that sum, restore the honor of your family, and put an end to the reforms of Khalid Mobassar, all in one swing of the sword."

Taj Deegan was on her feet. "That's not a question; that's a closing argument. This isn't *Perry Mason*."

"Sustained," said Rosenthal. "You should know better, Counsel."

"That's a lie," the witness said.

"Mr. Mahdi," Judge Rosenthal barked, "I sustained the objection. You are not to answer the question."

"Let me phrase it differently," said Alex. His strategy was working perfectly. Every objection just drew more attention to the question. "Do you now possess, all by yourself, every penny of the $460,000 that you previously shared with your wife?"

"Yes."

"Has Khalid Mobassar been discredited as a result of the charges against him?"

"That is not for me to say. That is for this court and jury to decide."

"And under Sharia law, has the honor of your family been restored as a result of the death of Ja'dah Mahdi?"

The witness leaned forward and glared at Alex. "I would do anything to get my wife back. Your question is an insult to the memory of a woman I loved very much."

"Is that right?" Alex asked. He walked back to his counsel table, and Shannon handed him a large pile of documents. Alex had been waiting the entire cross-examination for Mahdi to reiterate his love for his wife.

"May I approach the witness, Your Honor?"

Rosenthal nodded. Alex walked to the witness box and handed the documents to Mahdi. "These are transcripts from cell phone calls you had with your wife in the six months prior to her death. Why don't you point out to me how many times in those calls you told your wife that you loved her."

Mahdi didn't even look at the documents. "It was something I told her in person. It was something I showed her by my actions."

"I guess we'll let the jury decide," Alex said.

87

ALEX'S TEAM SHARED lunch at a nearby Mexican restaurant, and Alex had to use every ounce of restraint to keep it from becoming a premature celebration. Shannon and Ramona had been in court to see Alex's masterful cross-examination of Fatih Mahdi. As a potential witness, Nara had been sequestered but was now getting the blow-by-blow.

Technically, Nara was still a potential witness and should not have been hearing about Mahdi's testimony. But Alex wasn't worried. He had already decided that it wouldn't be necessary for Nara to take the stand now. Why take unnecessary chances? They had already created reasonable doubt.

So Alex half-smiled as Shannon and Ramona recounted the more interesting parts of Mahdi's testimony and described the look on his face when Alex had plunked the transcripts of his telephone calls in front of him.

"Let's not give him a big head," Ramona said, referring to her grandson. "We've still got a long way to go."

"Yeah, this case is far from over," Alex said. In truth, he was enjoying the accolades. He was especially pleased that Nara was hearing all this.

After lunch, Alex invited Nara to ride back to the courthouse with him, while Shannon hitched a ride with Ramona. He wanted a few minutes alone with Nara so he could talk to her about not testifying.

"This isn't about protecting you from Hezbollah," Alex said. "Even if your safety weren't a factor, I wouldn't call you as a witness. Not after Mahdi's testimony. You don't take chances when you're winning."

Nara had a lot of questions, but she eventually seemed satisfied with Alex's advice. "Does this mean I can watch the trial now?" she asked.

Alex had already considered this. He expected Taj Deegan to rest her case that same afternoon. He would then give his opening statement, and it would be better now than it would have been at the start of the case. He definitely wanted Nara there to hear it.

"I don't see why not," Alex said.

Nara reached over and put a hand on Alex's forearm. "I'm glad you're my father's lawyer."

◁▷

Rosenthal was noted for long lunch breaks, but on Friday he set a record. The lunch recess had begun at 12:30, and the judge didn't appear on the bench until 2:15. He made no excuses for being late. But then again, he was the judge. Everyone knew that judges were *never* late.

"Ms. Deegan, your next witness," Rosenthal said.

"The commonwealth would like to recall Fatih Mahdi."

Alex felt a stab of anxiety. He liked the way Mahdi's testimony had ended before lunch. Taj Deegan was up to something.

Mahdi walked into the well of the courtroom with downcast eyes. "Your prior affirmation still applies," Judge Rosenthal reminded him, "under penalties of perjury."

"Yes, Your Honor." Mahdi climbed into the stand again and hunkered forward. He looked like he had been waterboarded over the break.

Taj Deegan positioned herself in the center of the courtroom and interlaced her fingers. She pondered the wall just above the judge and then looked at the witness. "Mr. Mahdi, you testified earlier as to why you stopped criticizing Mr. Mobassar's reforms about six months before your wife died. Do you recall that testimony?"

"Yes, I do."

"You said that you decided your friendship was more important than opposing Mr. Mobassar's reforms. Do you recall that?"

Alex stood. "I object, Judge. She's just rephrasing his testimony."

"I'll allow it," Rosenthal said. The way he said it made Alex think that the judge knew something Alex didn't.

"I think I said that I didn't want to lose our friendship *or my wife*," Mahdi said.

"You're right; I stand corrected," Taj said calmly. "But, Mr. Mahdi, are those the only reasons you stopped opposing Mr. Mobassar?"

The witness shifted in his seat and glanced at Taj Deegan. He looked back down and studied his hands. "No. Those were not the only reasons."

"Please explain to the jury what happened six months before your wife died that caused you to stop criticizing Mr. Mobassar."

Mahdi looked at the jury. He inhaled and blew out a breath. "I had a meeting with Mr. Mobassar. It was when the rift in the mosque was growing severe and our disagreement was very intense. Mr. Mobassar urged me to support him as my religious leader in the mosque. He said we were like brothers and that brothers should not treat each other this way."

"Is that all he said?" Deegan prompted.

"No. He told me that we had been through a lot together and that he had protected me in the past in ways I did not know. He told me . . ." Mahdi paused and frowned. After a few seconds, he found the courage to continue. "When I was a young man, around twenty years old or so, Lebanon was in the middle of its civil war. I had nothing but contempt and hatred for the Christians. I was a warrior for Allah.

"During that war, Khalid Mobassar's wife lost a brother. The Christian Phalange killed him and disemboweled him. I was furious and wanted revenge. Ghaniyah was in mourning and equally furious. But Khalid reacted differently. He wanted to work through diplomatic solutions and broker an end to the violence. He called it 'pointless bloodshed.' It put great strains on his marriage."

Mahdi looked at Khalid Mobassar, and Alex felt his own heart in his throat. The same witness who had been despised by the jury this morning was now in some type of confessional mode. And the jury was hanging on his every word.

"Khalid's wife turned to me in her pain and anger. I was young, not yet married. I slept with her."

The revelation caused a few gasps and a buzz of excited murmuring in the courtroom. Judge Rosenthal rapped the gavel. "Silence!"

Out of the corner of his eye, Alex tried to gauge the impact on his client. Khalid looked stunned, staring at the witness, his gaze vacant. Then he looked down at the table.

"Did you think that Khalid Mobassar knew about this?" Taj Deegan asked.

"No, I didn't. Not until that meeting six months before Ja'dah died. During that meeting, he told me that he had protected me in the past in ways I would never know. He said—"

"So the record is clear," Taj interrupted, "tell us who you're referring to when you say 'he.'"

"Khalid Mobassar, the defendant."

"Thank you. Please continue."

Fatih hesitated for a second while he recaptured his train of thought. "Mr. Mobassar told me that he knew about my affair with Ghaniyah. He said that he had kept it to himself all these years out of his great respect for our friendship and his desire to stay married to his wife."

"That's a lie," Khalid whispered to Alex. He had a hand on Alex's elbow. "This whole thing is a lie. Ghaniyah would never do that."

Alex held up a hand. He needed to hear the testimony.

"What did you do?" Taj asked.

"I was stunned. I did not deny the affair and I did not admit it. I thanked him for his friendship. We embraced. I told him that I considered him closer than a brother. I told him that he was a better man than I was. I left with a deep appreciation for the pain he must have felt at such betrayal and at his nobility for keeping this to himself."

"That's not true," Khalid whispered. "None of it."

"Is that why you stopped criticizing Khalid's teaching at the mosque?" Taj asked.

Fatih nodded. "Yes, it is. I realized that our friendship was more important. I realized that he could have destroyed my reputation but chose not to. I decided the least I could do was stop attacking his."

Taj Deegan appeared to be thinking about this for a few seconds, but Alex knew she was just letting the information sink in. In five minutes of testimony, the entire complexion of the case had changed. For Alex, the lunchtime celebration suddenly seemed like a distant memory.

"Why did you really go to Khalid Mobassar for advice when you discovered that your wife had left the Muslim faith?"

"Because I knew he had dealt with his own wife's unfaithfulness. My situation wasn't exactly the same, but it wasn't completely different either. I felt rejected and humiliated. I thought Khalid could help me work through those issues. Instead, I believe he saw it as an opportunity to exact revenge and advance his agenda."

Alex leaped to his feet. "Objection! That's just raw speculation."

"The jury will disregard the last part of the witness's answer," Judge Rosenthal ruled.

"Mr. Madison and Ms. Reese have been asking several different witnesses whether they have any idea as to why Khalid Mobassar would send text messages ordering an honor killing from his own phone. Do you have any information about that?"

Alex was up again. "Objection. That calls for speculation too."

"It might," Judge Rosenthal conceded, "but Ms. Deegan is correct. You've been asking the same question throughout the case. Objection overruled."

Mahdi glanced toward Khalid Mobassar, then turned back to Taj Deegan. "Mr. Mobassar knew that I was ashamed of what I had done in 1980 and didn't want it made public. He probably believed that I would never tell police that I had a meeting with him to discuss my concerns about Ja'dah."

Alex stood again, hands spread. *This is ridiculous.* "Judge, that's pure speculation. How can he possibly know what my client was thinking?"

"Ladies and gentlemen of the jury, please disregard the witness's answer. He can only testify as to facts within his own personal knowledge."

Alex sat down but knew it was a hollow victory. The jury was thinking the same thoughts that Fatih Mahdi had just expressed.

"Why didn't you tell the jury about this during your testimony this morning?" Deegan asked. She obviously knew that Alex would hammer that issue on cross-examination, so she wanted to put it on the table first.

"I hoped it would not be necessary. I am deeply ashamed of what I have done. But after my testimony this morning, I realized that the man who ordered my wife's death might go free if I didn't come forward and tell the truth."

"No further questions," Taj Deegan said.

88

"DID IT TAKE YOU ALL LUNCH to think that up, or did it come to you right away?" Alex asked as he rose to his feet.

"It is the truth," Mahdi said. His gaze was level, his voice steady.

"Very convenient for you that it's a truth hard to verify. I mean, it just so happens that the only two people who were part of these conversations were you and my client—your word against his."

"Your client's wife can confirm or deny this," Mahdi said.

"When did you divorce your first wife?" Alex asked.

"In 1989."

"So you divorced your first wife for unfaithfulness nine years after you had slept with another man's wife?"

"I divorced her because she wanted to leave. I was simply fulfilling her wishes."

"Let's see—you didn't tell the truth the first time you testified, you cheated with another man's wife, you lied about loving your second wife, and now you expect the jury to take your word that these alleged conversations with my client took place?"

"I did love Ja'dah. What I did with Ghaniyah was wrong. Why would I make something up that is so publicly humiliating?"

"Perhaps because your hatred for Khalid Mobassar consumes you and trumps everything else," Alex shot back.

"Objection!"

"Sustained." Rosenthal glared at the witness. "You are to answer Mr. Madison's questions, not ask your own."

"Yes, Your Honor."

"I have nothing further for this witness," Alex said.

Taj Deegan stood behind her counsel table. "The commonwealth first learned about Mr. Mahdi's affair over the lunch break. When we did, we had the sheriff's deputy serve a subpoena on Mrs. Mobassar, requiring her immediate attendance in court. We would request a brief recess until she arrives."

Alex felt like he had just been run over with a bus. Ghaniyah was coming to testify? If she confirmed the affair, there was a good chance the jury would believe everything else Mahdi had just told them.

"Court will stand in recess until Mrs. Mobassar arrives," Judge Rosenthal said. "And I'm instructing both sides not to have any contact with her prior to the time she takes the stand."

"Yes, Your Honor," Taj Deegan and Alex said in unison.

89

GHANIYAH MOBASSAR took the stand looking nervous and frazzled. She wore the long, flowing robes of the traditional hijab Alex had seen her wear around the house, complete with a matching head scarf. Her eyes were wide with confusion and distrust.

She stole a glance toward Khalid, and he gave her a reassuring look as Taj Deegan began her questioning.

"Please state your name for the record."

"Ghaniyah Mobassar."

"Please slide a little closer to the mic," Judge Rosenthal said.

Ghaniyah inched closer. "Ghaniyah Mobassar," she repeated. This time everyone in the courtroom could hear.

"Are you the wife of the defendant, Khalid Mobassar?"

"Yes."

"Mrs. Mobassar, I am sorry that I have to ask you this next question, but it has become an issue in the case. Did you have an affair with Fatih Mahdi shortly after your brother died in the Lebanese civil war in 1980?"

Ghaniyah stared at Taj Deegan as if she couldn't believe that the prosecutor had the gall to ask. It felt like the entire courtroom inhaled and held its collective breath. Ghaniyah didn't utter a word.

"Mrs. Mobassar, you need to answer the question," Deegan prompted.

Alex wanted to bail her out, but he couldn't. After a thirty-minute argument in the judge's chambers, with Alex claiming that Ghaniyah shouldn't take the stand because of her brain injury, Rosenthal had personally called Ghaniyah's neuropsychiatrist. After a brief phone conversation, he denied Alex's motion.

Ghaniyah shook her head. "I will *not* answer the question," she said indignantly.

You just did, Alex thought.

Judge Rosenthal leaned toward the witness. "Mrs. Mobassar, I know this is uncomfortable, but you have no choice. You are instructed to answer the question."

Ghaniyah looked longingly toward Khalid and then turned to face Taj Deegan. She stared at the prosecutor as if she wanted to gouge Deegan's eyes out. "I have always been faithful to my husband."

Alex exhaled. To his surprise, the prosecution's strategy had backfired. The jury may not believe Ghaniyah because she had been so hesitant to answer. But her testimony could not have been more clear.

Yet Taj Deegan did not seem deterred. She took a few steps closer to the witness. "Mr. Mahdi claims that Ahmed was his child. Do you deny this?"

"Objection!" Alex called out. "Mr. Mahdi gave no such testimony."

"Counsel is right," Judge Rosenthal said to Deegan. "I don't remember any such testimony."

"He said it to me," Taj Deegan responded. "I didn't want to make that fact public if I could help it."

"He didn't testify to it," Rosenthal said. "So rephrase the question."

Alex turned to Khalid, who looked like a ghost, his face reflecting betrayal and utter defeat. Alex needed to reassure him somehow. But what could he say? How much more would Khalid have to endure?

"Mrs. Mobassar, I understand that this is hard for you, but it is important that you tell the truth," Deegan said. "Your son Ahmed was killed on a bombing mission inside Israel in 1996. Is that true?"

"Yes."

"And the authorities had to use DNA to identify him. Is that also true?"

Ghaniyah looked pained, her voice cracking and barely audible. "Yes, that's true."

"I want you to know that if I must, I will ask Judge Rosenthal to suspend this trial so that we might obtain those DNA results. But first,

I want to ask you the question one more time—is Fatih Mahdi the father of Ahmed Mobassar?"

Ghaniyah's facial expression went from contempt to shame. For an interminably long time, she didn't answer. Then she blinked back the tears and rubbed her eyes. Hardly moving her lips, in a barely audible voice, she said, "Yes, Fatih Mahdi is Ahmed's father."

The revelation created a stir in the courtroom, and the judge banged his gavel. Ghaniyah gave Khalid a despondent look. "I'm sorry," she mouthed.

Alex suddenly remembered that Nara was also in the courtroom, and he turned to look at her. She was sliding past the others in her row, trying to get to the aisle, tears filling her eyes. He watched as she walked down the aisle and out of the courtroom without once looking back.

"Thank you, Mrs. Mobassar," Taj Deegan said. "I'm sorry this has been so difficult. I have no further questions."

Alex put his arm on his client's shoulder. The imam looked like he was in shock. "Did you know this?" Alex whispered.

Khalid just shook his head. The man's eyes were wet, and he refused to look at his wife. The pain on his face was not something he could manufacture.

Alex didn't bother to stand. He wanted the jury to look at him and see his client sitting next to him in obvious distress. He kept his tone low and understanding as he began his questions. "Had you ever mentioned this to your husband?"

Ghaniyah looked down at her folded hands. "No."

"Did you have any reason to think that your husband knew about this affair?"

"No. It was something that happened in the distant past. I was angry because Khalid did not seem to care about my brother's death. I made decisions that I still regret."

Alex looked at Ghaniyah and felt nothing but sympathy. Regardless of how this trial ended, her relationship with Khalid would never be the same.

"No further questions."

90

TAJ DEEGAN rested her case, and for the second time, Alex was confronted with giving an opening statement that suddenly seemed irrelevant. This time he had no choice.

He stood and faced the jury, clutching his legal pad. He followed his notes and summarized the evidence in favor of Khalid Mobassar. But the question on everyone's mind had now shifted. *How does the affair fit into this puzzle?* Alex felt like everyone had the same sense of the matter he did—the key to the mystery was right in front of them but somehow just out of reach.

He finished his planned opening, walked back to his counsel table, and left his notepad there. He turned toward the jury, contemplative, as if he had just thought of one more thing.

"I'm still trying to process the testimony we just heard, and you probably are as well. What does it all mean? I don't have that figured out yet, but there is one thing I know for sure. When Ghaniyah Mobassar sat right there on that witness stand and told her husband that she was sorry, that was no act. It wasn't technically part of her testimony, but I know some of you saw her say that."

Alex was standing next to his client, and he put a hand on the back of Khalid's neck. The imam was studying the table in front of him, too embarrassed to even look at the jury.

"And when I saw the look on my client's face during this afternoon's testimony, I knew it was the first time he had heard about the affair. Many of you glanced at him. Judge for yourselves. Was this the first time that Khalid Mobassar heard about this? And if so, how could Fatih Mahdi possibly be telling the truth?"

Alex took his seat, leaving them to ponder that question. Under the circumstances, it was the best he could do.

◁▷

After a brief smoking recess, the judge told Alex to call his first witness. There was only an hour left in the day, and Alex and Shannon still couldn't decide whether they should put Khalid on the stand. Over the break, they had devised a stalling strategy that would give them the weekend to make that decision.

Alex would call Nara as his first witness. Fatih's revelation and Ghaniyah's testimony now made leaving her off the stand impossible. He could easily fill the hour or so until court adjourned for the week with background information about her father and his views on Islam. Then Alex would have the weekend to decide whether he wanted to ask Nara to testify about the events in Lebanon. Besides, he had to discuss that testimony with Shannon before he made the call.

But when Alex announced Nara Mobassar as his first witness, Taj Deegan objected, noting that Nara had been in the courtroom when Fatih Mahdi and Ghaniyah testified. Alex countered by explaining that he had decided not to call Nara as a witness until the surprise revelation about the alleged affair. The lawyers argued for about ten minutes in hushed tones at the judge's dais, just out of earshot of the jury.

Rosenthal decided that Alex should have an opportunity to put Nara on the stand, but when the deputy went into the hallway to call her, she couldn't be found. Cell phone calls proved futile, so finally Judge Rosenthal gave up and adjourned court for the weekend.

"You'd better have all your witnesses ready to go first thing Monday morning," he warned Alex.

"I will," Alex promised.

After court, Alex and Shannon fought their way through the reporters without making any comments. Shannon headed to Ghaniyah's home to provide their client with some comfort. Alex headed home. He had a splitting headache, and the last thing he wanted to do was spend time with Khalid's unfaithful wife.

He changed clothes and turned on ESPN. He tried in every way possible to distract himself from the day's events but eventually ended up pacing around the condo trying to make sense of it all. It felt like the case was in serious jeopardy now, and he needed to pull out all the stops. Ghaniyah had corroborated Fatih's testimony about the affair. And Fatih's question kept churning through Alex's mind—"*Why would I make something up that is so publicly humiliating?*"

Had Khalid really threatened to expose Fatih? That could explain a lot, including Fatih's abrupt decision to stop criticizing his imam six months prior to Ja'dah's death. But if that was true, Khalid was an incredible actor. The look on his face today was one of genuine shock and devastation.

Either way, Alex resigned himself to the fact that both Nara and her father would need to testify on Monday. If he held anything back and Khalid was convicted, Nara would never forgive him.

He couldn't get Nara off his mind, knowing the heartache she must be feeling. He tried calling her and left messages. It was nearly eight o'clock when she finally returned his calls. She had been visiting her father at the jail. He had talked to her about forgiveness and tried to calm her down. She needed to talk. Could they meet at his condo?

Alex wanted to say yes, but he'd learned his lesson. The only thing worse than being seen alone in public with Nara would be to have her seen entering his condo. "Why don't we meet at Catch 31? Do you remember where that's at?"

Catch 31 was a swank restaurant and bar on the ground floor of the Hilton Hotel on the boardwalk. The place had a stone patio outside with chairs gathered around brick fire pits. That night, for the first week of December, was relatively mild. Alex thought they might be less conspicuous outside.

"I can be there in twenty minutes," Nara said.

"Wear something warm."

◁▷

Nara wore a heavy overcoat with the collar pulled up and a wool cap pulled down to her eyebrows. Alex wore a down jacket and a baseball cap. There were not many people outside by the fire pits since the temperature was hovering around forty-five degrees with a stiff wind from the ocean. The two of them sat close together and propped their legs up on the edge of the fire pit. Alex ordered a diet soda; Nara went for a vodka and tonic.

Alex wanted to put his arm around Nara and keep her warm, but he didn't know if a telephoto lens might be snapping shots from one of the balconies of the rooms above them or from a hundred other locations with a direct view.

"I hate that woman," Nara said when Alex asked how she was doing. "She's always pretended to be so pious and such a woman of faith. Now her affair may well cost my father his freedom."

Alex couldn't argue and didn't really want to. Instead, he let Nara vent until she had poured out all the venom. When she started to softly cry, Alex could no longer help himself. He reached over and put his arm around her, and she placed her head on his shoulder.

"Your father is a good man," Alex said. "The jury's going to believe him when he says he never knew about the affair. And even if they don't, think about it this way—why would Khalid order an honor killing when his own wife was unfaithful and he did nothing but love her for the next thirty years?"

Nara burrowed in a little closer and wiped some of the tears with the back of her hand. "I know," she said softly. "I'm just so scared."

"There's nothing to be afraid of." But it was lie. He was just as concerned as Nara.

"I may need you to take the stand after all," he said softly. "Once the jury finds out about what happened to us in Beirut, this case should be over."

Nara turned her head and looked at him, her moist eyes pleading. "When it's finished, will you go away with me?"

Alex wanted to say yes. They were sitting by a fire looking at the Christmas lights on the boardwalk and the moon over the ocean. One of the most beautiful women Alex had ever met was leaning against his shoulder with her eyes full of tears asking him to spend his life with her. What kind of man could say no under these circumstances?

"Let's take it one step at a time," Alex said, surprising himself with his answer. Was he really ready to leave the beach and Ramona and Shannon behind?

"Okay." She snuggled a little closer, and Alex could feel the warmth. For several minutes neither he nor Nara said a word. Monday morning was a long way off. For now, Alex would relax, enjoy the fire, and dream about what life with Nara might be like.

91

ON SATURDAY, Nara showed up at the office just before noon to work on her trial testimony. Before leaving Catch 31 the night before, Alex and Nara had agreed to start at ten, but that was before she had downed three vodka and tonics. She looked, Alex had to admit, like she hadn't slept at all.

"I can't go back to my parents' place tonight," she told Alex during a break in their preparation. "I don't know if I'll ever be able to forgive my mother, but right now, I can't handle being around her."

They talked about Nara's feelings for a few minutes until Nara finally got up the nerve to ask the question she had apparently intended to ask all along. "Could I stay at your place tonight, Alex?"

He hadn't really expected that question. His heart said absolutely. He cared deeply about Nara. She was hurting. He could help.

But his head told him that this could be one of the dumbest moves he had ever made, especially in the middle of a huge trial. "Why don't we get you a room at the Hilton and see if Shannon can stay with your mom tonight?" Alex asked.

Nara's face reflected her disappointment. The dark eyes were downcast, but she immediately tried to recover, forcing a thin smile. "You're right. I'm sorry I asked. I just need a little space."

◁ ▷

Alex spent most of Sunday at the Virginia Beach City Jail in a small interview booth, talking to Khalid Mobassar through the sound slits at the bottom of the bulletproof glass. Khalid swore he knew nothing about the affair between Ghaniyah and Fatih Mahdi. He asked Alex

337

how Nara was handling things, and Alex gave him the truth. The dark circles under Khalid's eyes and the deep wrinkles on his face evidenced his grave concern.

The revelations of the last twenty-four hours seemed to have thrust Khalid into a zombielike state of mourning. His voice had no energy. Alex could hardly imagine putting him on the stand like this. The only time Khalid showed any emotion at all was when he inquired about Nara. Nevertheless, they rehearsed his testimony and practiced cross-examination for nearly six hours, until Khalid was so exhausted that his answers made little sense.

"You'll do fine tomorrow," Alex assured him.

Khalid gave him a lifeless look. "Even if we win the case, my family will never be the same."

He was right about that, and Alex had no response to offer except, "I'm sorry."

◁▷

By 9 p.m., Alex, Shannon, and Ramona were still at the office preparing for the final stage of trial. Alex didn't particularly want to go home. Misery loved company, and right now he liked being around Shannon and Ramona.

Nara had sequestered herself in the Hilton at the oceanfront, a tempting short drive from Alex's condo, but a drive he had resisted on Saturday night and was determined to resist again tonight. Shannon had arranged for some friends of Ghaniyah to stay with her.

The temperature was hovering in the low forties with a threat of rain, but apparently Kayden Dendy didn't bother checking weather reports. It was nearly nine thirty when the team heard his Harley pull up and stop in the parking lot outside their building. "That's got to be Dendy," Shannon said. "I'd recognize those mufflers anywhere."

She went to the window and confirmed her suspicions. "Wonder what he's doing here on a Sunday night."

Less than a minute later, they had their answer. Shannon looked at Alex when she heard the loud knock on the reception area door. "Just what I don't need right now," she said.

"I'll handle it," Alex said.

When Alex opened the door, Kayden was there in all of his leather-clad glory, holding his gloves in his right hand. "You got a minute?" he asked.

"Actually, we're kind of busy," Alex said.

But Kayden took a few steps into the reception area anyway. "This'll only take a minute. Is Shannon here?"

He found his way to the conference room, greeted Shannon, and asked if he could meet with the lawyers in private. As Ramona was leaving, Kayden had the gall to ask her if she could get him some hot chocolate.

Ramona stopped and glared at him for a second. "No," she said, and then turned and walked away.

"I'd fire her," Kayden said to Alex.

Alex ignored the comment.

"You're probably wondering why I'm here," Kayden said. He walked over and closed the door. "It won't take long. I know you've got a big day tomorrow. Which, actually, is the reason I'm here."

He looked at Alex. "Your partner has been doing a good job on the Mobassar civil case, by the way. But I will say that Max Strobel knows how to push her buttons."

"Look," Alex said, "we really don't have a lot of time."

"That's good, 'cause neither do I." Kayden took off his leather coat and threw it over a chair. He started pacing next to the table. "Do you know what a pen register is?"

"No." Alex didn't try to hide the frustration in his voice. He didn't need this guy pontificating and taking up valuable time the night before a busy day of trial.

"Didn't think so," Kayden said. "A pen register is an electronic device that records all numbers dialed from a particular telephone line. Law enforcement used the devices for decades to find out what numbers somebody was calling. They could get court orders for a pen register easier than they could to tap phone lines because with a pen register, they were only getting phone numbers called and not the actual content of the conversations."

"And this is relevant why?" Shannon asked.

"I'm getting there," Kayden admonished her. "Section 216 of the Patriot Act expanded the definition of a pen register to include devices or programs that provide the same kind of function with regard to Internet communications. In other words, under the Patriot Act, the government can find out all the Web sites visited by a specific computer or by a router at somebody's home if they meet the same criteria they would need for a pen register on a phone line. Here's where it gets interesting."

It better get interesting fast, Alex thought.

Kayden stopped pacing and leaned forward on the table. "When you guys subpoenaed the information that the federal government had on Mr. Mobassar under the Patriot Act, you asked for copies of all phone calls, text messages, and e-mails the government had monitored. But your subpoena didn't ask for the pen register information. Am I right?"

Alex didn't have the foggiest idea.

"I drafted the subpoena," Shannon said. "I didn't even know about pen registers, so I'm sure I didn't include that in the request."

"Well, in the civil case, Max Strobel did," Kayden said. "And he turned that information over to Taj Deegan this weekend. And, well, I've been wrestlin' all weekend with whether I should tell y'all what's in there."

This sounded to Alex like it was going to be more bad news. He wasn't sure he could take anything else right now.

"I finally decided to stop by and tell you on one condition." Kayden looked directly at Shannon. "You can't say where you got this information."

Shannon looked at Alex, and they both shrugged. After this big buildup, they had to know what he had. "Agreed," Shannon said.

"When I tell you about this evidence, you're gonna wanna dismiss your civil case against my client and Country-Fresh, Inc. But I didn't think it was fair to have Mr. Mobassar spend the rest of his life in jail just because you got ambushed by this."

Kayden turned back to Alex. "You are puttin' your client on the stand tomorrow, aren't you?"

"I haven't decided for sure," Alex answered. He still didn't trust this guy.

"You may not want to after you hear this." Kayden reached into his back pocket and pulled out a piece of paper. He unfolded the paper and spread it on the table in front of him. "The commonwealth confiscated the computers at your client's home, searched the hard drives, and gave you a copy of what they found. Am I right?"

"That's right," said Alex.

"But that only gives you the Internet search history and downloads for the computers that were actually found in your client's home. The pen register information under the Patriot Act gives you the Internet searches for any computer using the wireless router there. So if your client buys another computer for the sole purpose of conducting searches that he doesn't want the authorities to later find out about, those searches will still show up on the pen register information even if your client tosses that computer. Do you follow me?"

Alex nodded and braced himself for the bombshell. He had a sinking feeling in the pit of his stomach.

Kayden tapped the paper in front of him. "This here's a list of searches and Web sites visited during the two months prior to Ghaniyah Mobassar's accident. I didn't copy all of them, but I did put down all the searches and sites relating to—" he looked up at Alex and Shannon and said the next words slowly—"closed . . . head . . . injuries."

Alex was so stunned he couldn't speak. The color drained from Shannon's face. "You mean . . . ?" she managed.

"That's right." Kayden slid the paper across the table to Shannon. "Mr. and Mrs. Mobassar were researching closed head injuries in the two months *before* she had her accident. They must have bought a new computer specifically for that purpose and disposed of it afterward, because those searches don't show up on the hard drives of the computers seized by the commonwealth. Unfortunately for the Mobassars, they didn't know that every Internet site they visited and every search they conducted was being recorded on a pen register pursuant to the Patriot Act."

Alex thought about the evidence in the civil case. There was no brain damage shown on the MRIs or the CT scans. Ghaniyah had definitely run the car head-on into a tree, but the major damage had been to the passenger side. She did have a nasty bump on her head and some swelling around her eyes. But was it possible she did that to herself? Could she be faking the head injuries? Had Khalid and Ghaniyah been scamming *everybody*?

"Taj Deegan now has this information," Kayden said to Alex. "She didn't have to give it to you because it's not exculpatory. But if you put your client on the stand tomorrow, she'll shred him with it."

Shannon had been studying the list. She typed some of the sites into her computer and pulled them up. From the look on her face, it must have been bad.

"Why did you bring this to us?" Alex asked.

"Because the evidence won't go away just because you now have it. I can still use it in the civil case if you decide to keep going forward. But I've been following Mr. Mobassar's case the last couple of days, and even though your client might be a liar and even though he tried to rip off the insurance company, I don't think that makes him a killer."

"Thanks for your vote of confidence," Alex said.

His own view of Khalid had just taken a serious hit. Alex thought about how much he had put on the line for this client. He had resigned from his church. He had staked his reputation on this case. In Alex's mind, he had been Atticus Finch defending an innocent man whom the rest of the world wanted to lynch. And he had been winning the admiration of his client's beautiful daughter in the process.

But in a few short minutes, Kayden Dendy had blown that story-book fantasy into tiny little pieces. Instead, it now seemed that Khalid Mobassar was a con artist willing to risk serious injury to his wife in order to steal hundreds of thousands of dollars. Kayden was right; that didn't make him a murderer. But it sure made Alex feel dirty representing the man.

Alex looked at Shannon, who simply shook her head.

"Whose idea was it to take this case?" Alex asked.

92

THERE WERE WAYS FOR HASSAN to abduct Nara Mobassar from her hotel room, but that would have required a little luck and could have gotten messy. His orders on this one were very specific. It would be the hardest assignment of Hassan Ibn Talib's violence-ridden life.

He prayed to Allah for courage, favor, and faithfulness. Those prayers were rewarded on Sunday night, when Nara paid a visit to her father at the Virginia Beach City Jail. Hassan used a slim jim to unlock her car and then waited in the backseat, shivering in the cold. He blocked out thoughts of his childhood as he prayed to Allah and recited the portions of the Qur'an that he had committed to memory. He murmured the hadiths.

He waited two hours for Nara to return. When she did, she climbed into the driver's seat and closed the door. She started the car but hesitated before buckling her seat belt. She stared straight ahead and began to sob quietly, wiping the tears from her cheeks. Hassan steeled himself to act before he lost his nerve.

He leaned over the seat and pulled a cloth tight across her face, stifling her screams and causing her to inhale the chloroform. She resisted and pushed the horn with a free hand, but Hassan quickly chopped across her forearm and pinned her arms to her sides with his left arm while he pulled the cloth tight with his right. She was stronger than he anticipated. Fortunately, there was nobody around them in the parking lot. After a few seconds, she lost the will to fight. Within a minute, she went limp.

Hassan climbed out of the back and opened the front passenger-side door. He dragged Nara into the passenger seat, buckled her in, and climbed into the driver's seat. He drove the car to a deserted parking lot, where he pulled over and cuffed her ankles and wrists, duct-taped her mouth, and gave her a shot of Rohypnol. The "date rape" drug would keep her unconscious for at least four hours and would cause partial amnesia about tonight's events.

By tomorrow, it would no longer matter. Nara Mobassar would be dead.

On the trip to the Outer Banks, he kept his eyes focused on the road in front of him. He glanced over at her once, and guilt flooded him like a tsunami. He started reciting his chants with renewed fervency. Doing the will of Allah was never easy. But Hassan had died to his own comfort and his own desires a long time ago.

The only path now was one of total submission.

◁▷

FOURTEEN YEARS EARLIER
BEIRUT, LEBANON

The funeral of Ahmed Obu Mobassar was nothing like the service for his brother Omar.

Eighteen months before, Omar's body had been returned from the Palestinian camp and cleansed the same day in accordance with the Islamic rituals for ceremonial washing. His corpse had been covered with a plain white shroud and displayed in the courtyard outside the mosque. The young man's father, Khalid Mobassar, had led friends and relatives in the salat al-Janazah—a funeral prayer that was part supplication for Omar and part praise to Allah. Mourners had been allowed to cry but not wail or sob uncontrollably. Allah was good. His will was perfect. Fifteen-year-old Ahmed had been reminded that a good Muslim must accept the way of Allah even when he did not understand it.

Omar's burial had taken place in a common grave site, his body placed into an open grave without a casket. They had laid him on his right side, facing Mecca. Three small spheres of hand-packed soil had been placed under him—one under the head, one under the chin, and one under the shoulder.

Ahmed and his father had sprinkled three handfuls of soil on top of the body and recited the traditional words: "We created you from it, and return you into it, and from it we will raise you a second time." The men had prayed and professed their faith. The women had not been allowed to attend the graveside service.

Ahmed had wanted to linger. He could not bear the thought of saying good-bye to his older brother. But he had clenched his jaw and fought back the tears and left with the other men.

Omar had been killed by an Israeli rocket while doing humanitarian work. But a year and a half later, when word came to the same mosque that Khalid Mobassar's younger son had died, the circumstances were very different.

Omar had been a victim; Ahmed had died a martyr.

The mosque buzzed with a mixture of sadness and pride as the word spread. Ahmed had been conducting a raid with other Hezbollah warriors. He had detonated an explosive device strapped to his body, taking more than a dozen Israeli soldiers with him. His remains had been identified only through DNA.

The courtyard was packed for the victorious salat al-Janazeh offered on behalf of Ahmed Obu Mobassar. Curiously, the boy's own father had elected not to lead the prayer ceremony. While many who attended seemed to walk a little straighter and pray a little more fervently knowing that Ahmed had died the glorious death of a martyr, Khalid Mobassar was not among them. Rumors swirled that he saw nothing but tragedy and a senseless waste of life in the loss of his second son.

Ghaniyah Mobassar, on the other hand, held her chin high throughout the ceremony, reciting the Shahadah more fervently than ever. "I testify that there is none worthy of worship except Allah, and I testify that Mohammed is the messenger of Allah." The look on her face said it all. Her son was, at that very moment, enjoying the fruits of paradise. And he had redeemed his family members as well.

Ahmed's sister did not seem to share that conviction. She stayed in the courtyard long after the other mourners had finished their prayers and departed. She refused to leave with her mother. She knelt on the baked dirt, tears rolling down her face, murmuring her brother's name.

After a time, she rose to her feet and wiped the tears from her eyes. "I love you, Ahmed Mobassar," she said. "I'm sorry I never told you."

The video camera that captured every second of the service celebrating the glorious martyrdom of Ahmed Obu Mobassar was not close enough to record the sound of the words spoken by his sister, but reading her lips was not difficult.

The next day, as Ahmed watched his own funeral in the privacy of a Hezbollah hideout, the video unleashed a flood of emotions. He held them mostly in check until he saw the look of sadness and regret on his teenage sister's face. They had always fought. He had never known how much she cared about him. She had always acted as if she didn't care at all.

Truthfully, she was probably just putting on a show. Nara Mobassar always had to be the center of attention. The two siblings had become polar opposites. He had dedicated his life to serving Allah, to becoming a warrior like Mohammed. His sister, on the other hand, preferred to sit in the luxury of her Beirut home and criticize those who sold out for the glory of Allah.

When the video was over, Ahmed promised himself that he would never watch it again. He was a new man. The boy named Ahmed Obu Mobassar was dead.

He had excelled in his training as a Hezbollah warrior. He had professed his total submission to Allah and his death to his own fleshly desires. His actual martyrdom was coming; it was only a matter of time. By staging his death now, Hezbollah leaders could help Ahmed forge a new identity that would allow him to go places he could never have gone as the son of a high-profile leader in a prominent Beirut mosque. Ahmed felt heartsick about deceiving his family, but the leaders who had orchestrated the deception reminded Ahmed that it was all for the glory of Allah.

Al toqiah.

Watching the video had fortified Ahmed's sense of destiny as a shahid—a martyr for the faith. He had already experienced the praise and celebration of a shahid funeral. How could he back out now?

His new identity was rich with significance. Hassan Nasrallah had been the leader of Hezbollah since 1992. Ali Ibn Abu Talib was a cousin of the Prophet Mohammed and a respected imam who had become the successor to the Great Prophet. Ahmed's new name was a combination of the two legendary leaders: *Hassan Ibn Talib.*

That name filled him with pride, devotion, and a sense of destiny. The imams expected great things of him. He would demand no less of himself.

93

HASSAN PULLED INTO the driveway of the beach house a few minutes after midnight. He had taken his usual precautions and lined the basement floor and walls with plastic. He had used plastic gloves and walked around in shoes that were a size and a half too big for his feet.

The Outer Banks area was largely deserted during the second week in December, especially this late on a Sunday night. After he prepared the room, he carried Nara in from the car and placed a hood over her head. It may be Allah's will that his sister die, but nothing said he had to look into her eyes as he killed her.

The plan had been laid out in excruciating detail. Tomorrow, after court started, Hassan would send an e-mail from Nara's iPhone to Taj Deegan at work. Afterward, he would toss the phone into the North Landing River.

By the time he sent the message from the Chesapeake area, Nara would already be dead in the Outer Banks. But he would make sure they didn't discover the body until he was ready. By then, it would be impossible to pinpoint the time of her death.

In Hassan's opinion, the e-mail struck just the right balance between caution and desperation. It would be the final nail in Khalid Mobassar's coffin:

Ms. Deegan:

Last night, I told my father that I was not willing to
take the stand and lie on his behalf. Now, I'm afraid to

go home or anyplace where the men who work for my father might find me. I heard one of them say that if I was killed like the others, the jury would never believe that my father was the one behind all the beheadings.

I'm scared and I have nowhere to turn. Can we meet? I would be willing to testify about some things you need to know if you would put me and my mother in the witness protection program. I can be reached at this e-mail address.

Nara Mobassar

Hassan returned to Nara's car and opened the trunk. He pulled out a second syringe and needle along with his sword and sharpening stone. Leaving the items in the room with Nara, Hassan went into the bedroom to retrieve a pillow and blanket. He placed the pillow under Nara's head and covered her body with the blanket, then set the needle onto the end of the syringe and gave Nara a second shot designed to keep her unconscious until four or five in the morning.

Hassan went into a different bedroom and retrieved another pillow and blanket, making a mental note to take everything with him when he left. Tonight he would lie next to Nara on the hard tile floor. In the morning, one hour before dawn, he would awaken, perform a ceremonial cleansing, say his morning prayers, and end Nara's life.

It would be a dramatic blow for Allah. Khalid Mobassar's reforms would be fully discredited. His daughter would not be around to pick up the mantra. Instead, two days later, her headless body would be found on the altar in Alex Madison's former church.

◁ ▷

The nightmares haunted Hassan throughout the night, more vivid and real than ever. They started not with Hassan fighting in triumph against the infidels, but with a glimpse into hell. Flames leaped and engulfed shrieking men and women whose faces contorted with pain as the fire melted their skin. Hassan tried to look away but could not.

Most horrifying of all were the faces he recognized. Not just friends who had been weak in the faith, but members of his own family. The man who had raised him was there, looking grim and determined, not crying out like the others. Khalid Mobassar refused to admit he was wrong even in the depths of hell. Nara was there as well, reaching out to him, but a large gulf separated them. Her eyes were dark and pleading.

And then her face transformed. The melting skin hanging from her skull was restored to the classic beauty that had stirred the hearts of so many men. The flames disappeared, and she was dressed in white, sitting on a black stallion. Like Hassan, she held a sarif in her right hand, her horse stamping and snorting beneath her. *"Allahu akbar!"* she shouted.

She turned to Hassan, and he nodded as they spurred their horses and charged ahead together. Just before they plunged into the horde of infidels before them, Hassan stole a final glance at his sister. She had the same look of fierce determination he remembered from their days growing up together. But this time, it was not the rebellious fire that he had seen so often in her eyes. It was the fire of complete devotion.

They rode side by side, swords swinging in every direction, infidels dropping around them in a futile attempt to dislodge the warriors from their horses. Hassan wielded his sword with all his might, his muscles glistening with sweat and growing weary as he struck blow after blow. As always, the infidels kept coming, mostly Americans and Jews with possessed eyes and heinous laughs. There were Sunni Muslims opposing him as well, including some faces he recognized from his childhood. An arrow dropped him from his horse, and he was swarmed by hundreds of infidels. But Nara had circled back, creating a swath through the enemy as she tried to rescue her brother. Just as he reached out for her, an infidel's sword swung through the air, slicing toward his neck. . . .

Then came the calm. He was standing on the golden carpet, before the magnificent throne of Allah. This time, he was not alone.

He stood next to Nara, her chin held high, and Allah smiled at them both. He placed a crown of virtue on each of their heads. The crowd began to chant—*"Allahu akbar!"*—but the noise could not drown out the words of Allah himself.

"Welcome to your reward!"

94

HASSAN AWOKE WITH A START well before dawn. He was clammy
with sweat, and it took him a moment to get his bearings. The dream
. . . He focused immediately on the vivid details of the dream before
it left the recesses of his memory. Dreams were a gift from Allah, clarity of purpose in a world filled with confusion. He struggled to recall
every facet.

He tried to reconcile the dream with the theological realities he
knew. Khalid Mobassar would be in hell unless he was redeemed by
a member of his family. Nara, always rebellious, would surely follow
him, but in Hassan's dream she had become a warrior like him. Could
this be her lot in life?

The Sunnis in his dream reminded Hassan of his cowardice as a
child. But this morning, they also brought back memories of why the
bullies had ceased their relentless attacks.

After the day Mukhtar was beaten and Hassan ran away scared,
the two boys had started taking an alternate route home. But the next
week, even on this new route, Mukhtar and Hassan found themselves
walking down the sidewalk heading straight for the same gang of boys
one block away on the other side of the street.

Hassan quickly reached into his pocket and found the money that he
hoped would satisfy the bullies. This time, he and Mukhtar would run
together. If they caught Mukhtar, Hassan would stop and offer them his
money. If it wasn't enough, Hassan would take a beating along with his
friend. He had learned that the emotional wounds of cowardice hurt
more than any physical wounds the Sunnis could inflict.

But for some reason, the Sunnis only glared at Hassan and Mukhtar and never crossed the street to confront them. They talked among themselves and narrowed their eyes, putting the fear of Allah into Hassan's heart, and yet they allowed the Shia boys to walk by unmolested.

Two months later, when Hassan got into an argument with another kid at school, he found out why the Sunnis had backed off. The kid taunted Hassan, asking, "What are you going to do—get your sister to fight your battles again?"

When Hassan confronted Nara, he learned that his sister had indeed walked up to the Sunni gang and called out the leader in front of all his friends. She had challenged him to a fight, and when he tried to laugh her off, she attacked. Perhaps because of Nara's rage, or perhaps because the boy felt awkward fighting a girl, she more than held her own. The boy eventually retreated, claiming that he did not want to hurt Nara. Nara shouted curses at him as he left.

When Hassan initially learned about his sister's actions, he was humiliated and furious. But now, as he looked at Nara lying motionless on the floor, he felt only gratitude and sympathy.

Allah had never revealed his will to Hassan in a dream before—at least not the way he had last night. Hassan had heard of other great warriors who had received a direct word from Allah. In some ways, it made Hassan jealous. Wasn't he every bit as passionate for Allah as the others?

But last night, on the tile floor of this deserted vacation home in the Outer Banks, Hassan had experienced his own encounter with the ruler of the universe. The orders from his superiors no longer mattered. Allah had spoken.

The dream called for a new plan. One of Hassan's own making. One that fulfilled the prophecies in the dream.

Nara was destined to be a great warrior and a passionate follower of Allah. His first order of business would be to convince her that her father's ways were wrong. Someday, according to the dream, she would follow him to paradise. Like her brother, Nara would arrive on a river of blood.

But what thrilled Hassan even more was the certain knowledge that today was his day to bring great glory to Allah. This was the day he had been dreaming about his entire life. Events had transpired that now demanded he pay the ultimate price. For the sake of stopping the heresy of his traitorous stepfather. For the sake of preserving the legacy of his real father.

But most of all, for the sake of Allah.

Today, he would fight. Tonight, he would enjoy the fruits of paradise.

95

ALEX MET WITH HIS CLIENT at the Virginia Beach City Jail at 6 a.m. on Monday. Khalid was still in his orange jumpsuit and flip-flops. All the conviction and fire were gone from his demeanor. He seemed to be a mere shell of the man who had been sitting next to Alex when the case started. He spoke barely above a whisper, and his bloodshot eyes reflected the sad recognition that one of the things he valued most—his relationship with his wife of thirty-three years—had been damaged beyond repair. He was hanging on by a few tattered threads of his devout faith.

"Until Friday, I believed deep in my soul that we would win this case and justice would be served," he told Alex. "But now, whether we win or lose is of no great consequence to me. I've already lost the most important things."

Alex tried to fortify his client for the day ahead. He wanted to say something encouraging. But the sad truth was that things were about to get worse for Khalid, not better.

"We've got to discuss some things I learned last night," Alex said. "You're not the only one who didn't get any sleep."

◁▷

Hassan knelt next to his sister and removed her hood. Her eyes were still closed and her breathing was steady. As soon as the drugs wore off and she recognized him, he would be committed to his new plan.

He went to the bathroom and completed the ceremonial cleansing. He came back into the tiled game room and performed the morning salat. The rhythmic ritual of the prayer put his mind and soul at peace. When he finished, he sat in a corner and waited. He had to leave by 8 a.m. whether his sister had regained consciousness or not. He could leave a note behind, but he wanted to see the look on her face.

Allah had given him a new mission. Hassan had always been the consummate soldier, carefully executing the orders of the Islamic Brotherhood and Hezbollah without ever wavering. But today was different. This plan had come straight from Allah's lips to Hassan's heart. He prayed that Nara would wake up soon. She needed to hear what Allah had given him to say.

Thirty minutes later, she stirred. He wanted to go over and shake her but instead stayed in the corner and prayed. It wouldn't be long now.

A few minutes later she groaned and moved again. Another minute and she opened her eyes. She squinted and closed them quickly. She opened them a second time, and it seemed like she was trying to pull her hands from behind her back when she realized they were handcuffed together. When she noticed Hassan sitting in the corner, she blinked and wiggled into a sitting position.

Hassan stood without talking.

She stared at him with a confused look, as if she thought maybe she was dreaming. Her eyes were glazed and somewhat distant, the residual effect of the Rohypnol. Hassan took a few steps toward her. Her gaze grew clearer.

Then, in a moment of sudden recognition, Nara's eyes flew wide. She tried to say something, but the duct tape turned it into a murmur. She squirmed and turned her head left and right, eyes darting around the room, a look of panic taking over. When Hassan moved in front of her and knelt, she tried to scoot back. Her face was wild with fear.

"It's me," Hassan said softly. "And I'm not going to harm you."

She was in a state of shock, woozy from the drugs, but there was no mistaking the recognition in her eyes.

"I've been working for your father," Hassan said. He was down on one knee in front of her. "He knows that I am still alive. He has been ordering the beheadings of those who convert to Christianity in order to advance his own vision for the Islamic faith. It is exactly as the prosecution claimed in their opening statement."

Nara shook her head. She spoke louder into the duct tape, but Hassan could not decipher the muffled words.

"Listen to me!" he said. Nara flinched and shuffled back a little. "Your father is not who you believe he is. He sent me here to *kill* you. He said if I did that, the jury would never believe he was guilty. He'll take the stand and testify about how much he admired you, but in truth, he thinks you've discovered his true agenda, and he sent me to eliminate you and restore the honor of the family."

Hassan could tell that Nara didn't believe a word he was saying. But he knew beyond any doubt that she would one day come back to the faith. And when she did, it would happen with a vengeance.

"Your father knew from the beginning that I didn't die," Hassan explained. "He helped me gain a new identity because my fake death helped propel his cause forward. It's hard to ignore a man who lost both sons to the Israelis."

Hassan stood and Nara looked up at him. There were tears in her eyes, and he sensed her fear. He would have to trust Allah to change her heart.

"Do you remember when we were kids and the Sunnis would beat me up on the way home from school?"

Nara nodded. She tried to say something but couldn't.

"You fought *my* battles then. Today, I will fight yours. When I am done, those who wish to harm you, and those who wish to despise the name of Allah and his Prophet, will no longer be a threat."

He thrust out his jaw and spoke the words with as much conviction as possible. "After I die, you must take up the cause. Allah will give you wisdom enough to see the truth and courage enough to one day lay down your life."

Nara shook her head and lifted her chin, as if she was willing to die on the spot for what she believed. Her eyes pleaded with him to remove the duct tape, but he knew better. She would argue and protest. She would anger him and endanger her own life. He was doing this for her! Why couldn't she see that?

He would have to give her another shot of Rohypnol and then secure her to the bed so that when she woke, she would not be able to squirm away. During his mission, he would carry the rental agreement for this property in his pocket. After his death, they would come for her.

He reached out and put his hand on Nara's shoulder. She stared and tried to shake the shoulder free. But this did not bother him. He had heard from Allah. Who could stand against the will of God?

He smiled at his sister, remembering how she had cried at his funeral, how she had ridden next to him in the dream. "One day, you will follow me to paradise."

96

"DO WE HAVE ANY HOUSEKEEPING items before I bring in the jury?"
Judge Rosenthal asked. It was the same question he asked every morning, a perfunctory inquiry that always generated a "No, sir" from the lawyers. But this morning, Alex had a few surprises.

"There is one thing, Judge." Alex handed a two-page document to Rosenthal and gave a copy to Taj Deegan.

"It's on a related case," Alex explained. "It's a motion to nonsuit the civil case of *Ghaniyah Mobassar v. Country-Fresh, Inc., et al.*"

Rosenthal looked at Alex as if the lawyer had lost his mind. "You want me to sign an order to nonsuit your civil case?"

"Yes, sir," Alex said, as if this type of thing were done every day.

"Do you mind telling the court why?"

"As a matter of fact, I do."

Rosenthal tilted his head back as if Alex had just taken a swing at him. But on this point, Alex knew he was entirely within his rights. Under a unique aspect of Virginia law, every plaintiff in a civil case had the opportunity to nonsuit the case one time as long as the request was made before the judge granted a motion to strike or the jury retired for deliberations. A nonsuit was a voluntary dismissal, after which the plaintiff was entitled to start fresh by refiling the case anytime within the next six months. It was one of the many things Alex loved about Virginia. Judges had no choice in the matter; they had to grant a nonsuit if the plaintiff requested one.

"It seems a little peculiar, but I guess my hands are tied," Rosenthal said as he peered down his nose at Alex. He grabbed a pen and scribbled his signature on the order. He handed it to the bailiff, who in turn gave it to Alex.

"Is there anything else?" Rosenthal asked. "And maybe this time it could have something to do with *this* case."

"Just so the record is clear, Your Honor, my firm no longer represents Mrs. Mobassar. Because of a perceived conflict of interest, we have given her a letter of resignation that became effective once the court granted our nonsuit."

"That's fine," Rosenthal said. "But it makes no difference to the court in this case. Bailiff, bring in the jury."

When they were seated, Rosenthal turned to Alex. "Call your next witness, Counsel."

"The defense calls Ghaniyah Mobassar."

◁▷

Hassan arrived at the Virginia Beach Courthouse at 9:25. He was wearing a gray suit under a long overcoat and carrying a black leather briefcase. As he approached security, he flashed a Virginia bar card he had created several months earlier and a Virginia driver's license. The deputy waved him into the line for attorneys, and he placed his briefcase on the belt for the scanner. Hassan passed through the metal detector without incident, picked up his briefcase, and told the deputy to have a nice day.

"By the way, what's all the commotion about?" Hassan asked.

"You're not from around here, are you?"

Hassan shook his head.

"Big murder trial on the third floor. A Muslim imam accused of ordering honor killings."

"Sounds interesting," Hassan said.

He rode the escalators to the third floor and found his way to Courtroom 8, where the trial of Khalid Mobassar was under way. The courtroom had reached capacity, but Hassan explained to the guards that he was there to represent Fatih Mahdi, who had been subpoenaed as a witness. Hassan flashed his bar card and was allowed to pass through the metal detector that had been set up outside the courtroom doors.

Once Hassan entered the courtroom, he kept his head down. He didn't think anyone would recognize him, but he didn't want to take unnecessary chances. He found a spot against the back wall next to a TV cameraman and placed his briefcase on the floor. He crossed his arms and leaned against the wall to assess the situation.

His mother, Ghaniyah Mobassar, was on the witness stand. She was dressed in her traditional hijab and head covering, though she was not wearing a veil. She looked tired and haggard and was answering softly enough that the judge told her to speak up. Alexander Madison was prowling around the well of the courtroom, asking questions.

There were two deputies stationed against a wall toward the front, not far from Khalid Mobassar's counsel table. The larger one watched everything in the courtroom like a hawk. There was a third deputy by the door Hassan had just entered through, but he was preoccupied, whispering to a man who looked like a lawyer. Each of the deputies had a Taser, handcuffs, and a pistol on his belt.

The gun used by the courthouse deputies was a Glock 17, a light-weight pistol that chambered 9 mm bullets. Hassan would have pre-ferred larger-caliber bullets, but he liked the fact that the magazine capacity was seventeen rounds. The only safety on the gun was an internal trigger safety designed to prevent accidental discharge.

The spectators all seemed transfixed by the testimony on the witness stand. Ghaniyah was focused on Alexander Madison, and Hassan was not in her direct line of sight. Fatih Mahdi sat in the second row right behind the prosecutors. Hassan had been told that the lawyers had sequestered witnesses until after they testified. If Fatih was now allowed to watch the rest of the trial, his time on the stand must be over.

Hassan was pleased by his own calm demeanor as he sequenced the best plan of attack. He had trained for this moment; he was ready. His heart was not racing, and he felt entirely clearheaded. But it was more than just his training; his serenity came from a sense of destiny. He had been a dead man walking for years, ready to sacrifice his life for the sake of Allah at a moment's notice. Finally, that day was here.

The Islamic Brotherhood had adopted a Trojan horse strategy

for America, the idea that the best attack always came from within. They had infiltrated the country and were using America's arrogance and sense of invulnerability against her. Hassan had used the same approach to infiltrate this courtroom.

Americans considered the open court system a great cornerstone of their democracy. Today, Hassan would exploit that openness. He was already in the same room with every person who knew the truth about the honor killings and could therefore deal a crippling blow for the cause of Mohammed. He calmly determined the minimum number of rounds he would need. Three for the deputies. One for Taj Deegan. One for Alexander Madison. One for Shannon Reese.

And one for the man he once thought was his father—Khalid Mobassar.

Hassan listened to the testimony of his own mother. He was concerned that Madison may have discerned the truth. Hassan reached down to his briefcase and removed a yellow legal pad and a pen. He began writing his final note.

> My name is Ahmed Obu Mobassar, the son of Ghaniyah Mobassar and the stepson of Khalid Mobassar. Several years ago, my stepfather orchestrated events to make it appear as if I had died so that I might become an anonymous agent for the cause of Allah. I have always been the Sent One—the messenger who restored honor to families when their women rejected the Muslim faith. I have done so at the order of my stepfather, a prophet who has promised to lead us in a new direction. But first, he said, we must purify our ranks.
>
> As this trial has unfolded, I have sadly learned that my stepfather cares nothing about the glory of Allah. Instead, his desire is to elevate his own name above the name of Mohammed.
>
> On this day, as a messenger of Allah, I have come to restore the honor of my own family.

97

KAYDEN DENDY HAD ARRIVED at court early enough to stake out the location he wanted—outside aisle, last row. The windchill that morning had been in the thirties, so he'd left the Harley at home in the garage. Because he was coming to court, he wore a tie and leather jacket. One of his personal rules was that he only wore a real sport coat when he was arguing a case himself.

Alex and Shannon had done as they had promised. In exchange for Kayden's help the prior night, they had agreed to nonsuit Ghaniyah's case. Kayden's client would be happy; his work here was done. But Kayden was a trial lawyer. And he could never resist some good fireworks. He'd known that Alex intended to call Ghaniyah Mobassar to the stand. That would be interesting enough by itself. But he also had a pretty good idea about who the second witness might be.

That one would be worth waiting for.

Kayden sent a few text messages on his BlackBerry and listened as Alex fired questions at his former client.

◁ ▷

Alex felt like he had stepped through the looking glass this morning and walked into the courtroom of the bizarre. *Alex in Wonderland*—grilling a woman who had been his own client a few short hours before. Ghaniyah followed his every move, her bloodshot eyes broadcasting a mixture of confusion and distrust.

"Do you know what a pen register is?" Alex asked.

Ghaniyah shook her head. Judge Rosenthal reminded her that she needed to answer the question verbally.

"No."

"You know that Detective Brown and the other officers confiscated all of the computers at your home during their search, right?"

"Yes, I was there."

"And you know that they examined the hard drives from those computers to look at all the Internet sites you visited?"

"That is what you have told me. Yes."

"But did you know that under the Patriot Act, the federal government can also monitor the ISP address for your home network and see what Internet sites you visited even if you used a computer that was not seized in the search?"

Alex thought he detected a microsecond of panic flash across Ghaniyah's face. But if he did, her calm and vacant demeanor quickly returned.

"I have no idea what you mean."

"A pen register is a listing of all Internet sites visited by *any computer* that used your home wireless router. Do you understand that?"

"Objection," Taj Deegan said, her voice expressing annoyance.

"On what basis?" Rosenthal inquired.

"For starters, Mr. Madison is testifying, not asking questions. Plus, there's absolutely no foundation for this line of questioning."

"I have Detective Brown under subpoena, Your Honor. I intend to put her on the stand later this morning and have her authenticate the pen register for the Mobassar household. I would like to question the witness subject to linking that up later."

Rosenthal looked at Deegan again. "Any objection to that?"

Deegan was now in a tight spot. If she objected, she might not be able to introduce the same evidence herself. After all, this was supposed to help her case. "Subject to that stipulation, I'll withdraw my objection."

Alex walked back to his counsel table and tried to avoid eye contact with Khalid. When Alex had extracted a promise of trust earlier that morning, he knew his client hadn't anticipated *this*.

He picked up a document from the table and handed a copy to

Taj Deegan. He passed the original to the witness and kept a copy for himself.

"I'll represent to you that this is a pen register for all the Web sites accessed through your wireless Internet router in the sixty days prior to your automobile accident. I want to ask you some questions about the highlighted entries."

Ghaniyah studied the document and furrowed her brow. She looked up at Alex as if he had turned into a snake. "Okay," she said guardedly.

"Alex," Khalid whispered. Alex ignored his client and took a step closer to the witness.

"On June third of this year, you had an automobile accident in which your vehicle hit a tree. Is that right?"

"Yes."

"A few weeks later, you filed a lawsuit claiming that a Country-Fresh, Inc. tractor trailer had run you off the road and that you had suffered a brain injury. Is that right?"

A flash of anger crossed Ghaniyah's face. "Of course. You represented me in that lawsuit and encouraged me to file it."

Alex turned to the court. This next statement would be addressed to the court but was actually for the benefit of the jury. "Judge, that's the lawsuit we dismissed without prejudice earlier this morning."

"I'm aware of that," Rosenthal said sharply.

Alex turned back to the witness. "Only last night, I came into possession of this pen register. Have you seen it before?"

"Objection! Please tell Mr. Madison to stop testifying and just ask questions."

Rosenthal leaned forward and glowered at Alex. "She's right, Counsel. Just ask the witness your questions."

"Okay," Alex said good-naturedly. "Do you see how this pen register has a list of Web sites along with the date and time each one was visited?"

Ghaniyah pretended to study the document. Alex knew she was probably buying time to figure out what to say. "It appears that way."

"All of the ones I've highlighted were visited in the sixty days before your accident. Is that right?"

Ghaniyah took her time and scanned both pages. "That is correct."

Alex twisted his face and thought. The jury eyed him with confused looks. He knew they were struggling to piece this together. "Did your brain injury show up on CT scans or MRIs?" Alex asked.

"No. But a neuropsychologist confirmed it."

"Were we able to find any other witness who confirmed that the accident happened the way you described it?"

"No."

"Here's what I don't understand," Alex said. "Why would somebody in your home be visiting Web sites about brain injuries in the two months *prior* to your accident?"

Ghaniyah stared at him for the longest time. "I have no idea why anyone would do so. My husband spends more time on the computer than I do, but I can assure you that this was not him or me."

"Does anybody else live with you?"

"No."

"Did somebody from your mosque have an accident and suffer brain damage in the sixty days prior to your accident?"

"No."

"Do you know *anybody* who suffered brain damage at that time?"

"No."

Alex cocked his head and looked at the jury, as if he had just discovered a great mystery. Perhaps the next witness could help them straighten it out.

"No further questions," Alex said.

Taj Deegan stood. "I don't have any questions, Judge. It seems that Mr. Madison has already asked all of mine."

Alex glanced over at Fatih Mahdi. Alex had purposely decided not to object to Mahdi remaining in the courtroom even though Alex intended to call him next. He wanted Mahdi to hear every word of Ghaniyah Mobassar's examination.

"Next witness?"

"The defense would like to recall Fatih Mahdi," Alex announced. He turned to where Fatih was sitting. "I see that he's right here in the courtroom, and we would request that I be allowed to examine the witness before we take a break."

Rosenthal gave Alex a look of contempt. Alex could guess what the judge was thinking. It was one thing for a hotshot young lawyer like Alex to push the rules of evidence a little when he examined witnesses. It was another thing altogether to interfere with the judge's sacred smoking breaks.

"How long do you intend to take?" Rosenthal asked.

"Ten minutes max," Alex promised. "If I'm not done in ten minutes, you can cut me off mid-sentence."

"I'll hold you to that," Rosenthal said. "Mr. Mahdi, please take the stand."

98

HASSAN SAW A FEW EMPTY SPOTS along the wall halfway up the right side of the courtroom. He grabbed his briefcase and moved there as Fatih Mahdi took the stand. Hassan was enjoying an unusual sense of clarity and peace in these last few minutes of his life. It seemed like the world had slowed down and he could now peer into other men's souls.

Mahdi settled into place, his square jaw thrust out in defiance. Hassan thought Mahdi knew what was coming. Allah would be honored. The judge, on the other hand, was self-absorbed, oblivious to the danger right under his nose. Alex Madison, like a snake, slithered into the well of the courtroom for his final examination.

Soon all of his words would be meaningless.

◁▷

"Did Ghaniyah Mobassar ever embrace her husband's reformist views?" Alex asked the witness.

Mahdi was in combat mode this time, his face etched in a scowl. He gave Alex a look that made it clear the infidel was not worthy of his time. "To my knowledge, she adhered to a more orthodox view of the faith."

"Would you call her a true believer?"

"It makes no difference what I would call her. Allah will be the sole judge."

"So you were married to a woman who had embraced Christianity, and Ghaniyah Mobassar was married to a man who had rejected orthodox Islam. Is that right?"

Mahdi looked at Taj Deegan, but no objection was forthcoming. "That is correct, but I see no relevance to this case."

"Maybe this next question will help you," Alex said. He took a few steps, eyes on the floor as he framed the question. "Do you love her?"

Mahdi feigned indignation. "Ghaniyah Mobassar?"

"Yes, Ghaniyah Mobassar. The woman you had an affair with years ago. Do you still love her?"

Taj Deegan started to stand for an objection, but Judge Rosenthal looked at her and gave a small shake of the head. Deegan sat down, and the witness stared at Alex in defiance. Alex was determined to wait him out.

"No. I have always appreciated her commitment to the Muslim faith, but I do not love her. It is insulting for you to even ask these questions."

Now Alex was getting someplace. Mahdi's face was flushed with anger. Rage bubbled just below the surface.

"Did you conspire with Ghaniyah Mobassar to kill your wife and frame her husband for the crime?"

"Objection!"

"That's a lie!" Mahdi snapped. He looked at the judge. "Why do you allow him to insult me without so much as a shred of evidence?"

The veins in Rosenthal's neck pulsed at the rebuke. He didn't like it when witnesses called him out. "Objection overruled. Answer the question."

"It's a lie."

"Isn't it true that you ordered the honor killing of your own wife, Ja'dah Mahdi?" Alex asked, his voice tinged with disgust.

"Another lie," Mahdi hissed.

"And after researching the Patriot Act, did you not tell Ghaniyah Mobassar to send text messages from her husband's phone to the killer's phone so that Khalid Mobassar would be blamed?"

"Absolutely not," Mahdi said. The answer did not surprise Alex, but he was startled to hear his own client interject.

"She would never do that," Khalid Mobassar blurted out, loud enough for Alex to hear. Alex glanced over his shoulder and saw Shannon put a hand on their client's arm.

To the witness, Alex said, "And didn't you tell Ghaniyah to obtain her husband's password for the mosque's financial accounts and do a search on his office computer for Sandbridge rental listings?"

"You have a vivid imagination," Mahdi said. "But none of this is true." The witness had regained his composure. He attempted to brush off the questions as if they were nothing more than the ravings of a lunatic.

"And then you and Ghaniyah decided that she should fake an injury so she would never be suspected?"

Mahdi smiled and gave a little chuckle. "You are truly mad," he said. "Ghaniyah Mobassar is going to run her car into a tree so that she won't be suspected?"

"You don't trust Ghaniyah to navigate the in-depth police interviews without a crutch, so you concoct a plan that will minimize her interrogation. And if she forgets something or gets mixed up, you can blame it on the brain damage."

"Objection! That's a speech, not a question."

"Is it true?" Alex asked, without waiting for Rosenthal's ruling.

"It is *ludicrous*," Mahdi sneered. "Where do you come up with such things?"

"I'll show you." Alex walked to his counsel table, and Shannon handed him a packet of documents. Before he could turn back to the witness, Khalid grabbed Alex's arm and pulled him closer.

"You've got to stop," Khalid whispered, his voice desperate. "I don't want another word said about Ghaniyah. I don't care if I go to jail."

Alex nodded. He looked into his client's desperate eyes and reminded himself that the highest duty of a lawyer was defending an innocent man . . . even when that man wanted no defense. "No more questions about Ghaniyah," he promised Khalid. "But I've got to finish my job."

99

HASSAN HAD HEARD ENOUGH. While Alex Madison retrieved something from his counsel table, Hassan locked eyes with Fatih Mahdi. He knew Allah had brought him here for this very moment.

Mahdi stared back at him, his face composed and confident. Alex was back in the well, holding some papers and asking another question, but Mahdi ignored him, looking directly at Hassan. Slowly, almost imperceptibly, he nodded.

Hassan walked toward the back of the courtroom and approached the lone deputy stationed there. Hassan showed the deputy his bar card and leaned in so his voice wouldn't be heard by others. "Excuse me. I'm representing Mr. Mahdi. A minute ago I was standing against the wall on the right side of the courtroom." Hassan pointed to the place where he had been a few seconds earlier. "A man who had been there earlier left a briefcase and exited the courtroom after my client took the stand. Can you come check it out?"

The deputy looked around the back of the courtroom and nodded. He followed Hassan toward the briefcase as the testimony continued.

◁▷

"Were you here when I questioned Ghaniyah Mobassar about her pen register?" Alex asked.

"You know I was," Mahdi said. "I was sitting in the second row."

Alex hadn't had time to subpoena the pen register associated with Mahdi's wireless router between the time of Kayden Dendy's visit last night and the start of court this morning. But that small detail wouldn't

370

stop him. Instead, Alex glanced down at the documents he had retrieved from his table and hoped Mahdi would remember his testimony earlier in the case when Alex had used other documents to discredit him. Sometimes, you just had to bluff it.

"The authorities confiscated your computers and hard drive when they conducted a search of your property. Isn't that right?"

"That's correct."

"And they didn't find anything on those hard drives that was suspicious. True?"

"Of course not. I had nothing to hide."

"But now you know that under the Patriot Act, there are also records kept of every Web site visited by any computer hooked up to your home's network. Do you understand that?"

"That is what you said in court this morning. I have no independent knowledge as to whether it's true."

Mahdi was being cagey, but Alex could see the calculating look in his eyes. Alex took a step closer to the witness, but not close enough so that Mahdi could see the writing on the documents. "Would you care to explain to the jury why you were looking at Web sites about brain injuries in the sixty days *prior* to Ghaniyah Mobassar's accident?"

The witness stared at Alex for a long time without answering.

"Mr. Mahdi?" Rosenthal prompted.

"I do not know. Perhaps your client came to my house and used his laptop."

"That's the best you can do?"

This brought Deegan to her feet. "Your Honor, he's badgering the witness."

◁▷

Hassan pointed out the briefcase, and the deputy looked it over. When the deputy bent down to get a closer look, Hassan made his move. He slammed his knee into the deputy's face, crushing the man's nose. At almost the same moment, he brought his elbow down hard on the back of the deputy's neck. The crack of bone told Hassan he had landed the perfect blow. In less than a second, he had the deputy's revolver in his hand and whirled to face the infidels, feet spread wide in a combat stance.

A few spectators screamed. Somebody yelled, "Gun!" as Hassan squeezed off his first two shots in rapid succession. Though there was chaos in the courtroom, the world moved in slow motion for Hassan, presenting itself in vivid Technicolor—the vibrant hues of his childhood dreams.

He winged one of the deputies with his first bullet and put the second bullet into the neck of the other deputy at the front of the courtroom. The man crumpled to the floor in a lifeless heap. In the same motion, Hassan swung the gun toward Khalid Mobassar and his legal team, sitting ducks in a shooting gallery.

The noise in the courtroom became the din of his childhood battles, the sound of paradise calling. He was astride his horse, his nerves calm as he took aim at the infidels: Taj Deegan, Alex Madison, Khalid Mobassar, and Shannon Reese. He had a bullet for every one of them. His own bullet would come from the deputies who would eventually enter the courtroom to provide reinforcements.

100

ALEX HAD BEEN SO FOCUSED on the witness that he didn't know anything had happened behind him until he heard the shots. There was instant chaos, people screaming and scrambling for cover. In his peripheral vision, he saw Taj Deegan take a hit. He whirled toward the back wall just as Shannon lunged from her seat and knocked Khalid Mobassar to the floor. Alex froze. *Where are the shots coming from?*

He dove for the floor, but that split second of hesitation cost him. He saw the flash of a gun and had time to register that it was held by a Middle Eastern man on the side wall with an eerily calm look in his eyes. Before Alex even heard the noise, he felt the slug explode in his left side and drive him backward, sucking the wind out of his lungs with the most intense pain he had ever experienced. There were more screams, but they seemed distant now as Alex gasped for air and the edge of his vision started going black.

◁▷

Hassan had trained his whole life for this. He felt an almost supernatural ability to process all the stimuli at once, slowing the world like a frame-by-frame video. He had hit Taj Deegan and Alex Madison, but the little gymnast had reacted too quickly, tackling her client to the floor and pulling him behind the safety of the solid wood rail that separated the spectators from the counsel area.

Everyone else in the courtroom reacted the way Hassan had predicted for the weak-kneed Americans. Hysteria. People screaming and diving for the floor. There were no heroes in this bunch.

He swung the pistol in a wide arc and started quickly moving toward the front of the courtroom so he could stand over Khalid Mobassar and see the look of fear in his eyes before Khalid met his maker. Just before he got there, the back door burst open, and two deputies rushed in, guns drawn. Fortunately for Hassan, it took them a fraction of a second to locate their target. By the time they realized that Hassan was their man, he had unleashed a flurry of shots, dropping both of them as more screams filled the courtroom.

He was at the rail now and put his left hand on the top to sidestep over when he noticed a blur from just over his shoulder. He whirled quickly enough to see a man in a leather jacket diving into him with a jarring tackle that sent both of them crashing over the wooden rail and sprawling across the floor. Hassan held on to his Glock and whipped it across his assailant's face, cracking the man's cheekbone and spraying the area with blood. The man's eyes rolled up in his head. Hassan scrambled to his feet and into his shooter's stance.

He now had a point-blank shot at both Shannon Reese and Khalid Mobassar. *"Allahu akbar!"*

But before he squeezed the trigger, he felt something slam into his chest, driving him back to the floor in an explosion of pain. He struggled to stand, but his movements were sluggish. His thoughts were cloudy; the world seemed to spin as blood poured from his chest wound. As he staggered to his feet, he saw Taj Deegan pointing a gun at him. Out of the corner of his eye he saw more deputies rushing through the back door. He saw a flash of gunpowder and felt more bullets tear into his chest and side.

Blood spattered the wall and carpet. One bullet exploded part of his face.

But Hassan was no longer there. In that last moment of life, he was riding through the infidels again, swinging his sword in a large arc, the arrows of the enemy piercing him from every direction.

His last thought was the grim certainty that he had allowed Khalid Mobassar to live. His last emotion was the fear of an angry Allah, condemning him, telling him that he should have done more.

At first there was calm. Then fire. And faces melting like wax.

The sound of wailing was deafening.

101

ALEX FELT AS IF AN ELEPHANT were stomping on his chest; the courtroom was now at the end of a long tunnel back to reality. The shooting had stopped, but people were still yelling and shouting orders. He watched in a semiconscious state, as if he were stationed above it all, his mind separated from his body.

Shannon crawled to his side and patted his cheek. "Don't you dare quit on me, Alex Madison!" she said, nearly hyperventilating. "Listen to me. . . . No! Don't shut your eyes!"

Alex tried to obey, but the debilitating pain in his side was shutting down every shred of consciousness. Taj Deegan pulled off her blazer and stuffed it into his wound, applying pressure that Alex could barely feel. Just before the blackness completely took over, he felt Shannon pinch his nose and tilt his head back.

"Get an ambulance!" she yelled, then blew the first breath into Alex's lungs.

◁▷

Shannon was numb on the ride to the hospital. Detective Sanderson had the siren on and the lights flashing, and he tried to encourage her. "You did an amazing job with that CPR," he said. "You probably saved two lives today."

His words barely registered. Shannon had never seen so much blood. Alex, Kayden Dendy, and two sheriff's deputies had been whisked to the hospital by the paramedics. Three other deputies and Ahmed Obu Mobassar had been pronounced dead at the scene. Taj

Deegan had taken a shot to her back, but a bulletproof vest had saved her life. Khalid Mobassar was in shock but unharmed. Deputies had taken him back into lockup.

When Shannon arrived at the hospital, she followed Sanderson into the ICU like a zombie. A nurse informed them that Alex was already in surgery.

A resident checked Shannon out, cleaned her up, gave her some drugs, and released her to join the others standing vigil in the ICU waiting room. For two hours, Alex's friends and family stared at the floor and spoke in hushed whispers. Ramona led them all in prayer. Officers came and took statements about the chaos in the courtroom. The television in the corner of the waiting room played nonstop coverage of the day's carnage until somebody turned it to a game show.

Detective Sanderson left the room periodically to check with the ICU nurses. It was one o'clock in the afternoon when he came back and stopped in the doorway.

Shannon looked up. "Any news?"

Sanderson managed a smile. "Your boy's a lot tougher than he looks. The bullet entered the left side of Alex's chest and missed his heart, major arteries, and stomach by a few centimeters. It hit his left lung and did some minimal damage to the liver. The doctor says that Alex will probably have some lung damage, but fortunately for him, the lung didn't collapse. He says the liver has an amazing way of repairing itself. Basically, he's going to be all right."

Relief flooded the room, and Ramona summed up the feelings of pretty much everyone there. "So basically, it's a miracle."

102

ALEX HEARD THE VOICES before he opened his eyes. The sounds were familiar and comforting, but he couldn't understand most of what they said. They were voices from another world, soft tones with an occasional laugh or chuckle.

He felt the wooziness of lingering anesthesia and high doses of painkillers. He couldn't bring his thoughts into focus; his mind felt mushy and unresponsive. He tried to open his eyes but quickly closed them again. He was aware of an uncomfortable tube in his nose and other tubes hooked up to his arms and something packed against his left side.

The voices stopped for a moment, and there was an excited murmur. "He moved. I think he's waking up."

He tried to wake up—he really did—but the voices were still so very far away. He could only make out bits and pieces of what they were saying, as if he were underwater and people were calling to him from the surface. His mouth was dry. So dry. He tried to lick his lips; they felt like sand.

But none of this bothered Alex. Not even a little. He was floating in a wonderland of drugs and semiconsciousness, enjoying the warmth of his hospital bed. There was a nagging sense of something not quite right in the back of his mind, something he should be worried about. For a moment he struggled to place it. But the worries of the world could gain no traction in Alex's state of narcotic bliss. He closed his eyes and relaxed.

"It's okay, Alex. Get some more sleep."

The voice was right. He was tired. Everything else could wait.

◁▷

Sometime later—he had no idea how long—Alex managed to open his eyes and clear some of the cobwebs from his head. The room was dark except for the glow from a television set. The objects around him were strange and unfamiliar. He still felt detached from his body and struggled to break clear from his mental fog. He turned his head slowly to the left and saw his grandmother sleeping in a reclining chair. On the same side, toward the foot of the bed, Shannon was lying on a cot, her back to the bed, curled up with a thin hospital blanket over her.

He tried to say something, but his tongue was too thick, and he couldn't form the words. His mouth was bone dry; his throat felt like it had swollen shut. He groaned and Ramona stirred. He tried to increase the volume, and this time she sat straight up, turning toward him. She stared for a second and then grabbed his hands. He spoke again, did his best to say, "Thirsty," and his grandmother put a straw to his lips so he could suck down some water.

"Shannon! Shannon! He's awake."

Shannon quickly climbed off her cot, rubbed her face, and came to hover over Alex as well. He was remembering a few things now. The courtroom. The shooter. A sudden blast and a bolt of pain.

His side. He must have been shot in the side.

"I'm glad to see you guys here," Alex said, his voice husky and dry. "But I always thought that heaven would be a little more plush."

◁ ▷

Over the course of the next twenty-four hours, Ramona and Shannon filled Alex in on the details he had missed. They often had to tell him the same fact on two or three different occasions as he struggled to regain his lucidity.

Ramona informed him that the shooter was Ahmed Obu Mobassar, the son of Ghaniyah and Fatih Mahdi. "He faked his own death years ago so that he could work undercover," Ramona explained. She told Alex the authorities had found Nara tied up in a vacation home in the Outer Banks, traumatized but unhurt. Ahmed had tried to convince Nara that Khalid Mobassar ordered the honor killings, and he also tried to frame Khalid with a suicide note, but none of that worked.

Taj Deegan had immediately gained access to the pen register for Fatih Mahdi's home and checked out the two months prior to Ghaniyah's automobile accident. Just as Alex had suspected, they found sites explaining various aspects of closed head injuries. They also found searches for Sandbridge rental properties and numerous visits to the Beach Bible Church Web site. Most importantly, the pen register for Fatih showed that he was on the bank's Web site at the exact moment that someone used Khalid Mobassar's password to wire funds to Beirut.

It was enough to arrest Fatih and Ghaniyah, according to Shannon. In confidence, Taj had told Shannon that Ghaniyah's lawyer was already talking about cutting a deal. She would testify against Fatih in exchange for a reduced sentence.

Alex remembered the shots that preceded the one that hit him and asked about fatalities. Three deputies had died and two were seriously wounded, Shannon told him. Kayden Dendy had undergone reconstructive surgery on the left side of his face. Because of the threat she had received prior to trial, Taj Deegan had been wearing a Kevlar vest, or she might be dead as well. Ahmed had died from numerous gunshot wounds, including a bullet fired from a gun Taj Deegan kept in her briefcase.

"There were lots of heroes," Shannon explained.

"Including Shannon Reese," Ramona added.

The drugs kept Alex on an even keel as he absorbed the news. His mind told him that the deputies were somebody's father and somebody's husband. But his emotions barely registered, suppressed by the magic of narcotics and the calm demeanor of the nurses and doctors who took care of him.

It wasn't until evening on the second day that the full force of the tragedy began to register. Shannon peeked into the room and asked Alex if he was ready for some visitors.

Honestly, he just wanted a little peace and quiet. Visitors made small talk until Alex could no longer keep his eyelids open. When he responded, he sometimes caught himself rambling in and out of cohesiveness, depending on his level of fatigue.

But Shannon apparently wasn't asking for permission. She disappeared and a few seconds later returned, followed by Khalid and Nara Mobassar.

103

KHALID AND NARA APPROACHED Alex gingerly, and it dawned on Alex how awful he must look. He hadn't showered in two days. He had that forty-eight-hour unshaven look and a scummy taste in his mouth that came from sleeping so much. He felt like he was getting behind on his pain medication, despite his efforts to push the button on the morphine drip every time he woke up. His side throbbed. It felt like somebody had taken his insides out and beat on them with a hammer before sewing him back together.

He reached over and took a quick sip from his water bottle. "Thanks for coming by," he managed. He smiled, but he knew it looked halfhearted.

Shannon stood on the left side of his bed, and Khalid and Nara stood next to his tray table on the right. Khalid started to talk and then swallowed hard to regain his composure. Alex was still a little groggy for this much emotion.

"I feel like I owe you my life," Khalid said.

"She's the one who knocked you to the floor," Alex said, rolling his eyes toward Shannon.

"I don't mean just that," Khalid said. The sadness etched into his eyes made Alex remember how much this man had lost in the last few days. "I mean the way you stood by me in court and believed in me. There's no way I can repay you for that."

As Alex looked up at his client, he realized that he had never seen Khalid cry, even after everything the imam had been through. But there were tears in his eyes now, and he placed a hand on Alex's forearm.

"You are one of the bravest men I've ever met," Alex said. "If I had half your courage, I'd be unstoppable."

Khalid shook his head slowly. "I've heard it said that success is when those who know you best love you most. By that standard, with the exception of Nara, my life has been quite a failure."

Nara reached over and held her father's hand.

"That's not your fault," Alex said. "People make choices. Even when you love them, they make choices we don't understand. Nara is your legacy."

Alex locked eyes with her. Nara looked tired, but her expression conveyed a deep sense of gratitude . . . perhaps not only for what Alex had done but for what he was saying now. He tried to concentrate, but his thoughts started running together.

"I'm sorry I doubted you, Khalid. There were times . . . I don't know . . ." The sentence seemed to fall off a cliff. Alex wanted to somehow convey his admiration for this man's unwavering convictions and for his trust in Alex as his lawyer. But he couldn't quite string the words together.

"I'm sorry. . . . I forgot what I was trying to say. But what I meant was that you can't blame yourself. What you've done, and the way you handled yourself in this case, is amazing. And you've also got a pretty amazing daughter."

The comment actually made Khalid smile. A thin smile, with a trace of irony, but it helped Alex realize that the only things Khalid had left were his faith and his daughter.

A nurse walked in and took some notes about Alex's vital signs. While she did this, Shannon and the Mobassars chatted as if Alex had left the room. By the time the nurse finished, the mood in the room had lightened. Khalid and Nara asked the expected questions about Alex's injuries and how he was feeling. Alex started fading fast, and after an awkward silence, Khalid said that he and Nara should probably be going.

"I'd like to stay in touch," Alex said.

"I would like that very much," Khalid responded.

Nara looked apprehensive and turned to Shannon. "Would it be

382 || FATAL CONVICTIONS

okay if I had a moment with Alex?" she asked. Shannon looked a little surprised but didn't object. Khalid touched Alex on the shoulder and thanked him again. He promised to come by the next day.

104

WHEN ALEX AND NARA WERE ALONE, he started to tell her how thankful he was that she was okay, but she cut him off. "I need to say something, Alex. And I need you to just listen. Is that okay?"

Alex was losing strength, but he sensed the importance of this moment to Nara. He nodded and focused on her eyes, those alluring eyes that had first drawn him to her.

"I'm going back to Beirut, Alex. My mother will be in prison for a long time, and my father is committed to finishing his book and rebuilding his mosque. I have to finish my studies, and I believe that I have been given a special opportunity to speak about the plight of women in the Muslim faith. Right now, the whole world is listening. I can't walk away from that responsibility."

Alex wanted to tell Nara that she could do that here in Virginia Beach. What about Hezbollah? What about the men who had threatened them both with death if they tried to tie Hezbollah to the honor killings?

"It's not safe there," Alex said.

"Beirut's my home."

"Make your home here with your father. Your voice can be heard from America." Alex turned up his palm and reached out for her. "I was hoping we could spend some time together."

She took his hand in both of hers and moved a half step closer to the bed. "You're one of the most remarkable men I've ever met, Alex Madison, and the things that happened between us were real." She stopped herself and thought for a moment. Alex could tell she had more to say, and he squeezed her hands for reassurance.

"But our relationship was built on a common goal of defending my father. We're very different people from very different worlds."

She looked down at their hands and shifted her weight. "I don't know how to say this, Alex, so I'm just going to put it out there. The Hezbollah agents in the train car in Beirut were a setup." She stopped and gauged the effect on him.

"After Hamza Walid cancelled his deposition, I was sure that my father would be convicted of something he didn't do. I knew we didn't have the evidence we needed. So I set the whole thing up with some close friends to make it seem like we had been kidnapped and threatened by Hezbollah. I trusted you, Alex, to do your best. But I knew, if all else failed, I could testify about our kidnapping and plant reasonable doubt in the minds of the jurors."

Even in the mellow world of the opiates, the revelation shocked Alex. He had been envisioning a future together, and she had been deceiving him all along. Not only that, but she had put him in mortal fear of death in order to manipulate a verdict in favor of her father.

Not to mention the fact that one of her friends had punched him.

The train incident had caused him weeks of apprehension and paranoia. If he had put Nara on the stand, she would have perjured herself. She had been lying to Alex. She was prepared to lie to the court.

And then it hit him. Al toqiah. His head churned with the implications.

"Why did you tell me now?"

Nara shrugged. "I couldn't go back to Beirut *without* telling you. I'm tired of all the lies and deception and everything it's done to my family."

She bit her lip and gently rubbed his forearm. "I wish we weren't separated by half the world and this religious divide and everything else. . . ."

Alex knew he should be angry. She had lied to him! Used him and misled him for her own purposes. But somehow, none of that really mattered.

"It doesn't have to be that way."

"But it *is* that way. I've seen you preach, and you believe what you say. You live it, Alex. And I can't abandon my faith and my father after all that we've been through."

Alex felt the tears pooling in his eyes, the wet tracks forming in the corners and running down the sides of his face. The last thing he wanted was for Nara to see him cry.

She reached out and gently wiped the tears away. "I'm sorry, Alex." She leaned over and kissed him on the forehead. Then she stood and waited, holding his hand one last time.

She squeezed his hand, placed it gently on the bed, and turned to walk away.

"The waves are better here," Alex said. "We've got wide beaches and white sand."

Nara turned and gave him that lopsided smile he had come to love so much. "But we can go surfing in the morning and skiing in the afternoon," she countered. "Come over sometime and give it a try."

"Maybe I will," said Alex. But they both knew he was lying.

He watched her go, then lay back on the pillow and closed his eyes. He felt empty. Maybe it was the drugs. Maybe it was the sense of betrayal. Maybe it was just the grim reminder of his own mortality that the would-be assassin's bullet had provided. Whatever the cause, Alex felt a profound sense of sadness settle into his psyche. The carefree and noncommittal surfer who had inhabited his body earlier that year had been irrevocably replaced by a more serious and melancholy man.

Maybe in a few weeks he would get back on his feet. Maybe in a few months he would be surfing again. Maybe someday the Alex Madison mojo would return.

But for now, he mourned quietly and faded off to sleep.

EPILOGUE

ALEX MADISON PULLED his pickup into the designated clergy parking area, grabbed his Bible, and walked briskly toward the emergency room door. Last year, the Mobassar case had consumed his December, and Christmas had totally snuck up on him. This year, he was determined to enjoy every moment of the holiday season.

He walked through the automatic doors, feeling a little like Scrooge at the end of *A Christmas Carol*, determined to make up for lost time. "What's up, Bones?"

The old man with the wiry gray hair looked up from his magazine. "Bah, humbug," he said.

Alex reached into the pocket of his down jacket and pulled out two tickets to the Old Dominion basketball game on Saturday night. "Merry Christmas to you, too," he said, handing the tickets to Bones.

"Good message Sunday," Bones said. "Except it was about twenty minutes too long. I think I read someplace that Jesus' Sermon on the Mount was only ten minutes."

Bones had been coming to church for the last three months. When he first came, he told Alex that he hadn't darkened a church door in nearly forty-two years. Now he was a faithful attender, and he never missed a chance to complain about the length of Alex's sermons.

"If I were Jesus, I could get it done in ten minutes too," Alex said. "But then again, if he were in my shoes, preaching to the folks in my congregation, he might take forty-five."

They bantered for a while, and Bones gave Alex the room number for Billy Canham, a church member who had just endured a total hip replacement. Billy only came to church on Easter and Christmas and to watch the grandkids in the vacation Bible school program, but his wife was a longtime member. Alex had been by earlier, before the surgery.

When Alex got to Billy's room, Judy Canham hugged him and told him how thankful she was that he had come. "They've had trouble getting his blood pressure back up, so they can't give him enough pain medication," Judy explained. "He's in a lot of pain."

Billy was squirming on the bed, his face contorted. "Get me out of here," he demanded. "Preacher, my back and hip are killing me."

"He's got to relax," Judy said.

Billy gritted his teeth. "Easy for you to say. Get that doctor back in here! I can't take this!"

It took every ounce of Alex's patience to get Billy calmed down as nurse after nurse came in to check his vitals and determined his system was still not ready for drugs. Eventually, his blood pressure stabilized enough for the anesthesiologist to start pumping him full of morphine. By the time the medication had circulated, the tight lines on Billy's face had relaxed. Soon he was sleeping like a baby.

"I'm so glad you came," Judy said.

"I should have just given him Sunday's sermon," Alex said. "That would have put him to sleep."

Alex left the room and chatted with some of the ICU nurses he had befriended a year ago during his own hospital stay.

Before leaving, Alex made his traditional rounds to the two rooms that had changed his life.

Room 4103 was where it all started. Ghaniyah Mobassar had been supposedly recovering here from her car accident nearly eighteen months ago. She was now serving a fifteen-year term in the state correctional system. Alex thought about her courage and determination, however misplaced. Here was a woman who had crashed the passenger side of her car into a tree at nearly forty miles an hour so she could fake a brain injury. Alex still shook his head in disbelief at the thought of it.

Tonight there was an older man in the room recovering from a perforated bowel that had occurred during a colonoscopy. Alex talked to the man for a few minutes and prayed with him for a full recovery. He left a copy of his business card. One-sided. *Reverend Alexander Madison, South Norfolk Community Church.* He invited the man to come visit when he got back on his feet.

At the other end of the hall, in Room 4154, was a single mom who had fractured her sternum in a car accident. "A drunk driver pulled into her lane," one of the nurses told Alex.

This was the room where Alex had rehabbed just last year. The room where Nara Mobassar had walked out of his life, leaving him confused and melancholy. Alex smiled to himself when he thought about that day. It might have been the drugs, or the intense emotions of the case, or the fact that he had come so close to dying. Whatever the reason, his reaction to Nara's confession and departure confirmed to Alex that he should never try to make major life decisions while semiconscious and lying in a hospital bed.

At the time, Alex had desperately hoped Nara would not go back to Beirut. He had asked her to stay. Somehow, he had thought, the two of them could make it work. In hindsight, he recognized just how incompatible they would have been. And the more he thought about her deception, the more he realized that she had probably never cared for him as much as he had cared for her.

Alex and Khalid had stayed in touch. The imam had published his book and was now a leading voice in the effort to discredit those who had hijacked the Muslim faith with their violent interpretation of jihad. Nara had returned to America only once, to testify at the sentencing hearing for Fatih Mahdi. The jury had given Mahdi multiple life sentences without parole; his case was now winding its way through a labyrinth of appeals.

During Nara's visit, Alex and Shannon had eaten lunch with Nara and Khalid and had listened to Nara's recounting of her advocacy work in Lebanon. Alex was happy for her, and they parted with a polite hug. But the spark was gone. Alex had moved on. He sensed that Nara had as well.

They promised to keep in touch. But the only time she popped into his mind was on days like today, when he headed to Room 4154. And even now, he had no regrets about the direction his life had taken.

Alex Madison had never been happier. He had left the practice of law and thrown himself into his work at the church. Over the past year, the small congregation had turned into a medium-size fellowship, with all the good problems that accompanied growth. At first Alex felt guilty leaving his grandfather's firm. Slogan number ten on his grandfather's list came to mind often: *If you've been called to be a lawyer, don't stoop to be a king.* But eventually he realized that the sentence really wasn't about practicing law at all. It was about finding your calling—the one thing that God created you to do.

And Alex had found his.

Rosa Gonzalez, the patient in Room 4154, was a wiry woman with a swollen face and the usual assortment of tubes hanging from her body. Given the amount of painkillers flowing through her veins, she was surprisingly lucid and talkative. She opened up to Alex about the challenge of raising her two sons, and she teared up when she admitted that she didn't know what she would do now.

Alex stayed ten minutes longer than he had planned and assured Rosa that everything happened for a reason. He said it with the conviction of someone who had been in that very bed, recovering from serious trauma himself. He told Rosa as much, and he prayed with her before trying to leave for the third time.

"Wait," Rosa said. "I thought I recognized you. You're that lawyer who defended the Muslim guy. I knew I'd seen you before."

"Guilty," Alex said. He always blushed a little when people recognized him like he was some type of celebrity. It was happening less and less these days.

"That case was incredible," Rosa said.

Alex hoped Rosa wouldn't want to spend another five minutes talking about the details of it. Everybody had an opinion. There were some who still believed Khalid was guilty.

"Do you think you could take my case?" Rosa asked. "I was thinking about hiring this guy who called me earlier today, but I'd rather have someone like you."

390 || FATAL CONVICTIONS

Alex thanked her for the compliment and reached into his coat pocket for a Madison and Associates business card. Just because Alex had left the firm didn't mean he could no longer share in the profits. He handed the card to Rosa and told her that she should never hire somebody who had the audacity to call her at the hospital.

"The least he could do is show up in person," Alex joked. But his humor was lost on his new friend. Rosa took the card and put on her reading glasses.

"She's the best lawyer in America," Alex said proudly. "Maybe the world. She helped me out in that case we were just talking about."

"Oh yeah, I remember her." Rosa held the card between her thumb and forefinger, staring at it through her glasses. "She was some kind of gymnast or something. But the name doesn't ring a bell."

Alex couldn't resist a small grin as Rosa scrunched her forehead, as if trying to remember, then read the name out loud. He liked the way it rolled off her tongue.

"'Shannon Madison, Attorney at Law.'"

ACKNOWLEDGMENTS

Another book, another page of IOUs. It's getting to be like the national debt.

A big chunk of that debt is owed to Kamal Saleem, a former Islamic terrorist who wrote about his conversion to Christianity in *The Blood of Lambs*. I interviewed him at length and, with his permission, used variations of his experiences and mind-set as the basis for my book's antagonist. Kamal is one of the most intense and committed persons I've ever met. You should read his story and, if you get the chance, hear his testimony.

Joel C. Rosenberg's book *Inside the Revolution* also helped form one of my main characters—a reform-minded Muslim cleric on trial for murder. The imam is patterned after the Islamic moderates portrayed in Joel's book—an eye-opening study of the political and spiritual dynamics in the Middle East.

Research is just the beginning. There are many other "bondholders" whom I'll never be able to repay. They include:

- The hall-of-fame team at Tyndale House Publishers who believe in these stories and make it fun to be an author. Karen Watson, Jeremy Taylor, Stephanie Broene, Ron Beers, and many others have shown me more patience, grace, and encouragement than any author deserves.
- My agent, Lee Hough, whose vision and skill keep me on track. Lee is not just an excellent agent but also a great story doctor and friend.
- Mary Hartman and Michael Garnier, two other friends who review my manuscripts and have way too much fun identifying the inconsistencies and inaccuracies that I manage to sprinkle throughout my drafts. I can't imagine writing a book without their help.

- The folks at Trinity Church, where I serve as teaching pastor. They are a constant source of encouragement about my books and never cease to amaze me with their passion for Christ.
- Rhonda, Rosalyn, and Joshua, the best family on the face of the planet. I might be a lawyer, but you can trust me on that one.

Before I get to the final prop, a word about separating fact from fiction might be in order. When a lawyer/pastor writes a story about a lawyer/pastor, readers probably assume that many aspects of the story track the author's life. That assumption would be incorrect. Other than the occupations, Alex and I have little in common. The Virginia Beach churches where I've had the honor of preaching—Trinity Church and First Baptist, Virginia Beach—are amazing churches with none of the pettiness that Alex faces in the book. Moreover, unlike the book characters, my legal assistants (including Tracy Garcia, who helped on this book) have been top-notch, and the judges in Virginia Beach are some of the best anywhere. The bottom line: I don't pastor a church or practice law the way Alex does, and I certainly don't solicit clients like he does. I'd prefer to keep my law license.

And finally, though it seems trite to put the Savior of the world in an acknowledgments page—how could I leave him out? This book is the story of an advocate who stands up for a client when, from all appearances, the man should be condemned. Come to think of it, that's also the story of my life.

> *But if anyone does sin, we have an advocate who pleads*
> *our case before the Father. He is Jesus Christ, the one who*
> *is truly righteous. He himself is the sacrifice that atones*
> *for our sins—and not only our sins but the sins of all*
> *the world.* 1 JOHN 2:1-2

ALSO BY RANDY SINGER

Fiction

Directed Verdict
Irreparable Harm
Dying Declaration
Self Incrimination
The Judge Who Stole Christmas
The Cross Examination of Oliver Finney
False Witness
By Reason of Insanity
The Justice Game

Nonfiction

Live Your Passion, Tell Your Story, Change Your World
Made to Count
The Cross Examination of Jesus Christ

www.randysinger.net

CP0232